CW01433466

PRETEND PEACE

The Charlemagne Files Collection
Volume 2

Lion Tamer
State of Nature
Vory

K.A. Bachus

Copyright © 2015, 2020, 2021, 2024 K.A. Bachus
All rights reserved

The characters and events portrayed in this book are fictitious. Any similarity to real persons, living or dead, is coincidental and not intended by the author.

No artificial intelligence or machine learning technology was used in the creation of this book or its cover. No part of this work may be used in the creation of machine learning or artificial intelligence technology without the author's express permission.

No part of this book may be reproduced in any form or by any electronic or mechanical means, including information storage and retrieval systems, without permission in writing from the publisher, except by reviewers, who may quote brief passages in a review.

Published in Bangor, Maine, United States of America
Contact the publisher at info@charlemagnefiles.com

Library of Congress Control Number: 2024921724
ISBN: 979-8-9916011-1-5

Visit: https://www.charlemagnefiles.com

Cover by Marigold Faith

CHARLEMAGNE FILE TIMELINES

Volume 1 - The Team
Trinity Icon, early 70s
Cetus Wedge, early 80s
Brevet Wedge, nine months later

Short Story Collection
A Lighter Shade of Night,
mid 60s to early 70s

Volume 2 - The Passion
Lion Tamer, five months later
State of Nature, early 90s
Vory, a year later

Volume 2 - Retirement
Swallow, five weeks later
Quiet Move, late 90s
Goat Rope, 1999.

CONTENTS

LION TAMER

A few months later

PROLOGUE

Buddy faced a dozen of his most senior agents arranged around the conference room table in the SCIF. He had an announcement.

"I just sent The Woman off to the UK on a Charlemagne op that the Brits are hosting."

The reaction was as expected: stunned silence followed by loud sputtering and a few bangs on the conference table. Buddy raised his hand for silence.

"She is, and has been, our senior officer and has earned the assignment."

"She doesn't even have a coin," squealed one man with an unfortunate tendency to squeak.

"Now Squeaky," said Buddy, "that's not true. She has a coin, and she produces it on occasion. That time you paid for everybody's drink when she should have shared the tab because she also didn't have it with her is your fault entirely. It's not her fault you let her get away with it."

"But Bear hates her," said somebody else.

"Bear doesn't hate her, Sturgeon."

"He hates his nickname, and she gave it to him," said another.

"You hate yours, Cod, and that's as it should be. The whole point of our nicknames is to bring us down a peg."

"But Bear might kill her now that he's operational," squeaked Squeaky. "And what about Charlemagne? What if they rape her or something?"

Buddy's round, bulging eyes gave the stare this question deserved.

"You know them better than anybody, Buddy," said Sturgeon. "You were their babysitter for twenty years. You know what they're capable of. It's common knowledge."

"No, it's not common. Nor is it knowledge. I've never known them to be capable of what you're suggesting, and as you say, I am the person in the best position to have such knowledge."

Buddy did not share with them his private concern that she was more likely to get her throat cut.

ONE

My game name for that op was Barbara Kemp. I loved Barbara from the minute I learned her legend. A successful business-woman from New York. That's me. Well, successful government hack from Virginia is more accurate, but close enough. I paid for an upgrade on my government-bought trans-Atlantic ticket just to cele-brate. The bubbly was delightful, and so was dinner, complete with soft music and no turbulence. My neighbors did not bug me, so even though I did not sleep, I was fresh as an alpha mare when I arrived at Heathrow ready to break a few more glass ceilings.

The guy who met me at arrivals stood half a head shorter than me. As usual. He glowered at my left earring.

"Is it far?" I asked the top of his sparsely planted head.

"Not far, Love." He pronounced it *lurve*.

I'm not your *lurve*, I told him silently, nor your love.

"Will you brief me during the drive then?" I asked aloud.

"We'll see."

We'll see you pounded into the nearest ditch, Elmer.

I sensed the beginning of a strained professional relationship between me and this bona fide pain in the ass with the Oxbridge ac-cent.

The luxury of my new position just didn't quit. Shorty here led me to a Jaguar. I settled into the leather passenger seat on the wrong side and watched the February rain in the headlights as we negotiat-ed an endless series of roundabouts.

"Are you going to tell me about it or not?" I asked after an en-thralling fifteen minutes of watching the windshield wipers make their rounds, or should that be straights?

Nigel, as he introduced himself after I demanded the name he was using more than a few times, took his time with an answer to my repeated questions. He used 'um' and 'now then' as parentheses around every phrase, but finally summed it all up with, "We'll have to see if they will accept you."

I pushed an escaping pin back into the hair gathered behind my head, careful not to damage any strands. After all, it represented a lifetime of growth. At thirty-eight, I still had no grey in the bitter dark chocolate color, and it reached to my waist. I kept it pinned up during business hours.

"They asked for me," I said.

"They asked for an American babysitter."

"That would be me."

More ums. Then a "Ye-es, well."

Nigel, I thought, you should meet the guys in my section back in Virginia. You have a lot in common. For one thing, you take up a lot of space—in that seat and on the job. Just like they do. I had to maintain perfection to claw my way to this peak, but you've been here what? Fifteen years? Not running five miles a day and living on carrots and spinach salad all that time I see. I wonder how you would fare against me in a marathon? No, I don't wonder. I'd beat you by hours, not minutes, but it wouldn't make a difference. They'd still pick you over me.

I examined his puffy face under the motorway lights. Small eyes, reddish nose. Diet soda was not his tipple.

"So you don't think they'll accept a woman babysitter," I said, stating the usual.

"Have you met them?"

Of course not. One does not go around seeking casual meetings with teams of specialists. One works with them if that is one's job, and this was now my job. One works with the team assigned and only the team assigned, and again, now assigned to me. If one works very hard and saves countless impossible situations caused by incompetence all around and by a touch of psychopathic madness in the second-rate teams assigned to one, then, after twelve years of 'not the right time,' one can beg and plead and threaten civil rights lawsuits to gain promotion to the best team. The one now assigned to *me*. Then one will have the privilege of sitting in a Jaguar northbound on the A1 with an upper-class Englishman who affects a few working-class phrases but never got his nails dirty and doesn't think one will hack it with Charlemagne.

The name of my new team made me push in another pin self-consciously. I hoped I would hack it. I hoped I'd be given a chance to hack it. No, I decided, I would not be *given* a chance. I would have to take it.

"Do you happen to know anything about them?" he asked, dripping condescension.

"A little." I had read each dot of ink on every scrap in the section file. It amounted to a little.

"Well, it's all changed."

"What's changed?"

"The team. They've all changed."

"How?"

"It's hard to explain to somebody who hasn't met them."

"Try."

I braced myself for the usual lecture, hoping I could glean something useful. Let's see, he'll say, in my umpteen years of invaluable experience, during which time I was equally invaluable to superiors and subordinates alike, not to mention colleagues, oh, and let's not forget the team itself, I have found them to be ...

"In the fifteen-plus years since I agreed to take on the Charlemagne account," he began.

Am I a prophet or what?

"I've had a great deal of experience with them," he continued. "I know how they work, the make-up of their personalities, and so on."

And on and on.

"This is one of the things you'll find that will accrue to you as you gain in experience with teams of this caliber." He would spell it 'calibre,' I suppose.

I peered straight ahead through my lowered eyebrows. That is how high I had rolled my eyes upward. I listened. I endured.

"As I was saying," he said, "one of the things that always struck me about these men—I must stress to you they are men, Barbara—quite traditional and somewhat old-fashioned, I must warn you. These men are closed. By that I mean they show us very little; the rest is carefully compartmentalized. Thus, we see only their killing sides, the human computers that make the plans, predict the outcomes, and kill the target. All a babysitter has to do, should do, is provide intelligence and logistics, not psychoanalysis and not bloody backup firepower like you lot allow your babysitters to do."

He was referring of course to Steve Donovan, now a member of the team he once babysat.

I felt Nigel staring at me.

"Please watch the road." I said it aloud. Sometimes safety is more important than tact.

"Ever been out with a team like that, Barbara?"

"Once or twice."

"Whatever milk toast team or solo you may have met, this time it's different. I doubt you're prepared, *lurve*."

I repressed an urge to pop him one. He was driving after all.

"So what's different this time?" I hoped he would just brief me and not return to Spy Studies 101. *Please, powers of the universe, make it so.*

His tone changed. It changed so much that I paid attention.

"This time," he said and then sighed. "This time, they are a mess. The compartments are gone, and everything is stewed in together. It's a bit uncomfortable, like sitting on a grenade without a pin."

"Can I have a for instance?"

"What a quaint expression. It must be American, I'd say. I must remember it."

I felt my hair loosen at the back of my head but did not allow myself to adjust the pins. Who knows what else may be so quaint that it stops him answering my questions?

He was concentrating. I could tell by the wrinkling on his brow and the way he ran his hand over the top of the steering wheel. It looked painful.

Finally, he said: "For example—excuse me for instance, as you say—between the tasks necessary to lay a trap for the target they keep themselves busy by beating each other to a pulp."

"All? All four?"

"The two older ones, Mack and Louis. The younger ones spend their time as referees. There is a bit of a dust-up every few hours."

"You're telling me there's a fundamental split within Charlemagne?"

"I'm telling you whatever information you may have had on them is obsolete. I suppose, in a way, it is a blessing for you because if they let you stay, you will not be any worse off than an experienced babysitter. At least, where understanding the team is concerned. But, then again, I sincerely hope you can run fast on those long legs, *lurve*, because I will not carry you when they detonate."

I'm not your lurve, mate.

I looked at him in the red glow from the dashboard and ignored the clump of hair falling down my back.

"So abort the operation if it's that bad," I said.

"We cannot. There is too much at stake."

TWO

Hello, Heathcliff, I thought, as I stood on the gravel driveway and gazed upon the edifice before me. There was a moon that night, playing its light over the swaying trees, the spattering rain, and the gothic pile of a house in front of us. The house and trees stood alone in a large expanse of flat fields. But this was not a moor. It was The Fens of East Anglia. The house was Georgian, a rectangle with straight lines and large sash windows symmetrically placed, two rows of three each on either side of a double door placed in the middle with a central window above it on the second floor. An extra wing had been attached on the left, set back from the facade.

The house was imposing to be sure, but also decaying. An overgrown garden surrounded it, covering its walls with tall weeds and vines and providing far too many hiding places. The windows were dark. Plywood covered some of them.

Dormer windows above the second floor suggested attic rooms and small ground-level windows announced a basement. The basement entrance was probably around the back affording an intruder yet another means of ingress. The driveway swept past the front of the house from left to right, turning left after the building and heading toward a decayed stable block surrounded by an overgrown copse. Talk about a hidey-hole heaven.

The house was too large to be easily secured. The team would inhabit only a few of the many rooms, leaving the others open to infiltration. The remote situation could be a plus, though. Any enemies approaching over the flat terrain would be seen and could be easily detected if there wasn't so much vegetation crowding the walls. But inspecting all those rooms every time we went out was going to be a pain in the ass. What was Nigel thinking? Give me a small, neat, isolation bunker with no windows any day or at least its nearest equivalent.

No ghosts of tragic heroines were likely to greet us as we crunched our way to the front door, only four men, heavily armed and, according to Nigel, strangely lunatic.

So much for romance.

We passed two cars as we walked up the drive. Both were pointed toward the road and I was reminded about this very basic security measure. I added Nigel's failure to do the same with the Jaguar to a growing list of reasons I did not trust him. Not that I thought he might be dirty, only incompetent.

The contradictory cars copied everything else in this operation, like the crumbling mansion and the bumbling babysitter. One car was the trademark Charlemagne sleek and shiny armored Mercedes that babysitters worldwide knew to obtain when the team was in town. The other was a heap of indeterminate color and make, shedding rust flakes into the gravel and threatening to disintegrate at the lightest touch.

We approached the door where Nigel commenced the Let-Us-In ritual.

We were greeted, if you can call it that, by Steve Donovan. He had been first my subordinate and then my immediate predecessor as babysitter of Charlemagne. Bad move, I had told the boss when he picked Steve over me. Men so hate it when a woman tells them 'I told you so,' but of course, I said those exact words to Buddy. Steve was inexperienced, unprincipled, and just a bit too violent himself. A babysitter should not have anger issues. Our job was to support and direct the team, not join them in their work.

Still, Steve had the most beautiful pair of liquid brown eyes I've ever seen on a man.

"Hello, Teddy Bear," I said when he opened the door.

He reddened. Steve never seemed to understand the effect he had on women. "Don't call me that," he mumbled between his teeth.

Nigel waited for me to go in.

"After you," I said.

"After you."

"No, no. I insist. You are, after all, my senior."

This had the desired effect. Nigel did not know what to do. He squeezed himself through the half-open door and stood in the hallway searching for a way to introduce me to somebody I already knew.

We stood in a long hall that reached to the back of the house. Twenty feet from the door a wide staircase on the right began its curving ascent to the second floor. A small table stood next to a coat rack against the wall on the left. Two worn oriental rugs lay end to end making a pathway along the side of the staircase.

"What the fuck is Frank thinking?" said my former colleague and failed babysitter Steve Donovan. "What the hell is he doing?"

"The right thing, for a change," I said. "I am the senior person in The Section, Steve. I have been for some time."

I wanted to add: I was senior when you were chosen over me, you bastard, and see where that got us all, you included. But I didn't say it.

"Fuck, Barb, not now. I give you twelve hours' life expectancy."

Nigel stood nodding in a corner with a poker up his butt.

"I wasn't aware that black ops require a penis," I said. Maybe it required being dickish, but the two don't always go together. Besides, I think he'd agree I was perfectly capable of that.

"Don't be crass, Barb," said Steve. "This is the fucking worst of all possible scenarios. We...."

By way of introduction to the worst of all possible scenarios, the Frenchman, whom the files sometimes referred to as Louis, flew backward through the open drawing room door in front of me and to my left, then across the hall, thumping into the wall beside me on my right, breathless but still on his feet. He had been described to me so thoroughly that I knew immediately who he was, but descriptions are like pornography, just never enough when the real thing is required. So I wasn't prepared for the real thing. I reacted strangely. Physically. Not to unduly belabor the analogy, I kinda got a little warm.

At that moment, though, there was not a whole lot physically to recommend the team's chief marksman and gadget expert. Somebody had rearranged his perfect face. There was quite a lot of bruising under his eyes, suggesting the broken nose might be recent. The various regions of his black hair with its sprinkling of silver at the temples followed different travel agendas, and a scruffy beard sprouted unattractively. But the eyes. Black and wild and wickedly sexy. Plus, did I mention he was French?

He shoved himself off the wall and toward the door he had come through. Steve moved fast. He hit Louis squarely in the chest with the heels of both hands, forcing him back up against the wall.

In one of my more boneheaded moves of all time, I covered my weapon. What was I thinking? That everybody was armed to the teeth, check. That emotions were running high, as in outer space high, check. That all by myself I was going to play peacekeeper with my dainty little nine-millimeter, check. It doesn't get more stupid than that last item.

A stream of language flew back and forth through the doorway. Four voices, using French, German, and English. I understood all the words, but little of what they meant. There was an older German voice in the other room. That will be Mack, I thought. He was the legendary leader of the team, a mind reader with flawless—though deadly—judgment. Also, he was purported to be very good with a knife. Funny how we use words like good. A younger voice shouted across the door to Steve in American English. Must be Mack's son, the one The Section had dubbed Charlie. And, of course, Louis was not shy with a lot of French words they don't teach you in school, all of them used in fresh, imaginative ways.

Charlie and Steve kept up a running dialogue aimed at keeping the two older men separate. I stood there, still stupidly keeping my hand on my gun.

The shouting died down eventually, but the emotional testosterone release had charged the atmosphere. It would be unwise to light a match in here, I thought. So Nigel did just that. Imbecile. Even more than I was at the moment. Together we became imbecile squared. What a team.

First, he tried soothing words. Not surprisingly, a general atmosphere of 'shut the fuck up' swallowed that attempt. Then he hit on a new tactic. I acknowledge my part in this. I know my hand had no business being where it was, but really Nigel? Your dick is so small you have to play the big man by getting me fucking killed? I'm still a little emotional about it.

"This is your new American babysitter," he said to no one in particular. "Can you believe they had the nerve to send a bird?"

And I stood there with my hand still on my weapon. But only for about a nanosecond more. In that time, my weapon hit the floor and my body found the wall behind me. Louis had shrugged off Steve like a down quilt on Sunday morning. I can't say I stood against the wall. It was more a case of trying to become part of it because the man twisting my wrist and crushing my ribs was forcing the barrel of his gun down my throat by way of the underside of my chin, making impossible any verbal arguments I might want to make, like please, please, please let me live. With my toes barely touching the floor, we stood nose to broken nose. He had not washed in some time. Louis twisted my wrist a little bit more and a treacherous tear escaped one corner of my eye. The glee in his smile caused more treachery in my body and I shivered. I concluded that I no longer found him magnificent. Fancy that.

Steve picked himself up from the floor saying, "Fuck. Fuck. Fuck." It had always been his favorite word to use in any sentence or as in this case, as a sentence in itself.

A new presence—I was sure it was Mack—said, "Let her go."

"She threatened me. I will shoot her."

Steve's twelve-hour prediction was looking generous.

"Do as you wish."

This was unwelcome.

But it turned out to be open sesame. I was on the floor the next second, trying to hold my ribs together but still alive. As he walked away, Louis kicked me in the kidney saying *Americaine* in a way that sounded like an expletive.

The last to leave the hallway before me was Steve, looking mighty disheveled and disgusted. He caught my eye as I used the wall behind me to force myself to a standing position. I told you so, said his teddy bear eyes.

"Oh, shut up," I said aloud.

I picked up and holstered my weapon, then followed him into the drawing room.

THREE

"A woman is not acceptable," said Mack. I stood there feeling less like a woman and more like a cartoon cat, gangly, speechless, and with bits of hair sticking out all over. The large room we were in also had seen better days. Stained and torn upholstered chairs occupied odd places without arrangement or even consistent purpose. I counted three equally sad, shabby sofas turned in random directions, one facing and another perpendicular to separate fireplaces and a third slumped diagonally on three legs It seemed to have no function other than as an obstacle to movement. Springs poked out in uncomfortable places on all three and most of the stuffed chairs.

Mack looked about the same as the other members of the team. The little bit of grey at his temples was not as noticeable as Louis's because it mixed well with his blond hair. He had not shaved in days. His shirt was a wrinkled mess, but his holster and the SIG Sauer it contained gleamed. Come to think of it, all their weapons were pristine. Mack's tired blue eyes x-rayed my soul, surveying me as I surveyed the room. I had read his file a million times. He read my mind a million and one. It took me years. It took him a mere instant. He never blinked, only regarded me with terrifying intensity.

I croaked out my reply to his statement.

"I'm experienced." True. "I'm competent." We won't mention the incident in the hall just now. "I'm all that's available." Ah, now there's the essential point.

"Then we will do without," said Mack. "Nigel, take her home."

"Touch me and I'll flatten you, Nigel, you twit." Nigel quelled. I stood a little taller, deluding myself that I could handle anything.

"You need me," I told Mack.

An incredulous snort came from the Frenchman leaning against a high mantelpiece a few feet away. He picked up a fireplace poker and drew figures in the cold ash.

It was the briefest of distractions, so I did not notice when Mack produced his knife. He was that fast. Or I was seriously off my game. Or both. Probably.

The knife filled my worldview, so to speak. Or its edge did. That edge was fine satin, but I could see my reflection in the polished base. Mack's eyes were almost even with mine, but I felt like I was looking up.

"Leave," he said.

"No."

"You can do nothing here. This is beyond reason."

"That's where I do my best work. In Crazyville."

The satin edge receded. I saw a wavelet of doubt on his face; I let him see a tsunami of relief on mine. No use trying to hide what he can see anyway. Maybe he appreciated the honesty. He grew a half smile.

"Try," he said.

I turned to Louis, still keeping a third eye on Mack and ignoring the three spectators who had morphed into disinterested toad lumps. Wait. Was that a glimmer of malicious hopefulness in Nigel?

"Get some rest," I told the Frenchman. "You have last watch. I'll wake you when it's your turn."

"I set the watches," said Mack.

"No. I do. You have enough to do." Bravely said, considering I had no idea what he was doing here at all, besides beating up his best friend.

"Get some sleep," I said again to Louis.

He took two steps toward me, raising the poker and pointing it at me, his tongue between his teeth, lips curved in a wicked half smile. I did not flinch. He put the poker tip through the space in my blouse left gaping by buttons that had gone missing during our recent get-acquainted session in the hallway. A reminder, I supposed. He drew a horizontal line in cold ash across the ribs just below my bra.

"I do not take orders from women," he said, his eyes hooded.

"I'm not giving orders," I said, purring. "I'm just reminding you of what's good for you. That's what women are for. Now go lie down."

"Come lie down with me. That is what women are for."

Once again the all-mighty dick must be irresistible to women no matter how squalid its package.

But I digress. I had a job to do.

"I'd love to, Baby," I said, "but you need sleep first." *And a fucking bath.*

I wisely left that last sentiment unspoken.

He gave me plenty of time to get out of the way when he threw the poker at me. He gave me time so I could duck, so I could bow to his superiorness. He slammed the hall door behind him.

I did not crow like I wanted to until after Mack also followed my suggestion to get a few winks at the opposite end of the house. I didn't crow at all, though it was my greatest ever victory because I foolishly thought I'd wait until the others congratulated me.

Still waiting.

"I don't like this at all," said Steve. "He's never pulled his knife just to threaten somebody right off the bat."

"I suppose we'll have to brief her. I suppose they'll let her stay," whined Nigel. He sent a beseeching look to Charlie, hoping for a negative.

Charlie nodded and I thrilled to the delicious taste of victory as that whiny little bastard Nigel swallowed a helping of crow and began to brief me, Charlemagne's new American babysitter, on the operation his government had named SIEGE.

FOUR

E ven though our mutual loathing was pretty plain to all observers, Nigel continued to call me his *lurve* as he unrolled his operation like a London fog. I wondered what he might call an actual lover. Sugarplum? Light of my life? I looked at his pudgy face, his thinning, almost ginger hair, and the few extra pounds he wore about the middle so that you could not see his belt buckle because of the overhang and wondered unkindly whether any woman would want to be called his sugarplum.

We sat at the coldest end of the drawing room, away from the other fireplace with its dying embers and extra degree Fahrenheit and near a second, boarded-up grate. This bit of desolation, if it were possible, made us even colder. Even spiders had refused to build on this depressing bit of real estate. No cobwebs decorated the grimy wooden boards. Despite a good-faith effort, the wood failed to stop tufts of dank air from invading down the chimney in a putrid miasma.

Steve and Charlie took the old leather sofa facing the door. Nigel and I faced them and each other from wingback armchairs. I caught myself pulling stuffing from the arm of my chair. Not a good idea to telegraph nervousness in this crowd. A small table between us held the obligatory perpetual coffee machine. Cozy, but like I said, fucking cold.

SIEGE, it turned out, was an elaborate trap laid for an IRA killer who was so deep his name had to be manufactured by Nigel's section. Cú Chulainn's hallmarks were small, surgical bombs—bomblets really—placed unerringly so they took out only a few bystanders along with the target. The press is part of the game and it seems that while a terrorist's agenda may require a few ritual sacrifices, too many dead innocents can be bad for business in some arenas, like

Ireland. A collateral benefit to such careful sacrifice is that it tends to isolate future targets. Nobody fancies an unguarded stroll down the street with the Prime Minister, for example.

A thoroughly reprehensible character (Cú Chulainn, I mean), he well deserved to be an assassin's target himself, but his cover was so incredibly flawless there seemed no way in.

Until one day, he missed.

"How did he miss?" I asked.

"Target went to the loo at the last moment," said Nigel.

I shrugged. "Things go wrong in a big operation."

Nigel leaned forward in his chair. "We have word his next operation will be even bigger, and Cú Chulainn is determined it will not go wrong."

Steve got up for more coffee. "He has no choice. Miss your target once and your credibility goes to shit. Fail twice and you become a prime entree on this week's most lucrative assassination menu. If he doesn't want to be a fucking bullseye, he can't mess this one up."

"So what's the plan?" I asked.

I thought this was one of those obvious questions, totally in the context of the conversation and all that, so why did they go all tense and start throwing eyeballs at each other?

Charlie, as de facto leader in the absence of Daddy, broke the eyeball ping pong and spoke. "We began by asking what Cú Chulainn would want most."

A target who never needs to pee, I thought. I am pretty sure I did not say it out loud.

"We decided he'd want a target that does not move unexpectedly," said Charlie with a malevolent smile at me, "or a bomb that detonates only when the target is in range."

I suppressed a shudder at the like-father-like-son mind reading. Charlie is a young version of Mack, but more personable, says his file. *Was Mack ever personable?* Charlie wears his blond hair a bit too long for these modern times, and his face is more mobile than his father's, so it is easy to think he might be more socially apt. Maybe. Or it could be just his youth.

"Louis designed a detonator that will work only when the target is close to it," he said. "So we put it out on the market and waited."

"How can a detonator do that?" I asked.

"Voiceprints."

"Brilliant. But that would require a sample and a real-time program, and...."

"Darling," Nigel interrupted, "the next target is most likely to be very prominent. Plenty of recorded samples in the public domain."

"I'm not your darling," I snapped, "nor your *lurve*."

He looked away first. There was an uncomfortable silence as I extended my stare for just a little longer.

"What if the target takes a vow of silence at the wrong moment?" I asked.

"That's Cú Chulainn's problem," said Steve. "And anyway, the target's a politician."

I smiled at the joke, "Why not just use a radio?"

"Range and interference become big problems when security is as good as it is with somebody that prominent. Also, we're talking big city environments, obstacles, competing radio traffic, and unexpected passersby."

"What about the programming?" I asked Charlie.

"We're offering the programmer as part of the package."

"Cú Chulainn will never buy the Frenchman." I said it to myself, mostly.

"No kidding," said Nigel.

"Sarcasm does not become you," I snapped.

"That's why we began shopping for a dangle," said Charlie, sticking to the topic, bless him. Was there a note of caution in his voice? He shook a clump of bright blond hair off his forehead. Definitely being cautious.

"We figured it would be a very long time before Cú Chulainn would deal with an Englishman, so that was out."

"And it had to be somebody credible," said Steve. "Somebody who could have invented it."

"We figured we would let the trail lead to the dangle," said Charlie, "and substitute Steve as the seller once we had a nibble."

Why were they both evading eye contact with me while explaining way too much? What the hell were they up to? *Oh, what have you done boys?*

"So did you find your dangle?" I asked aloud.

That stone fell down a deep well as the three men looked at me.

Nigel spoke. "We found an American lieutenant colonel near here at RAF Alconbury. Avionics engineer and commander of a maintenance squadron." He was very proud of this. Smug, even.

"And you want me to get approval for you to use an American citizen as a dangle," I said. Not so bad, I thought. Easy procedure. The answer probably would be no, but Santa can't stuff everything down that chimney.

"What's his name?"

"Diane Rutherford," said Steve, "and we're already using her."

Nigel gave me a gotcha look, like a woman as sacrifice was somehow new. I had no time for the toad, being preoccupied with the news that she was already in play.

"How committed is she?" I asked.

"Totally," said Charlie.

I find fuffing with my hair a great way to hide stress. Nothing like taming waist-long hair to create a pause and give you time to think. It also annoys the men, something I rather enjoyed doing just then.

I slid the last pin into place and looked up into those light blue eyes of Charlie's.

"There's no hope for her?" I said, forcing the obvious into a question just for the sake of a little hope.

"No."

I took a moment more to stare at him. His answering stare sent a shiver through me. So much for the illusion of affability in junior here. I looked away first.

"We let a few advertisements lead to her and then put some light touches on her home and office," Charlie resumed. "Both are on the air base."

"It wasn't easy, I can tell you," whined Nigel. "Her people sweep her office periodically, so we had to touch the sweepers as well. I could have used some cooperation from your people, but I don't know the resident here and to find out, I'd have to go through my channels, and...."

"And once you did, the whole world would know," I said, nodding.

He glared at me. Security breaches are a sensitive subject in the land of Burgess and Philby, not that we haven't had our fair share of disastrous treachery.

Their touch was just enough to reveal any new contacts. A full day into the op and three days before I arrived, a new man entered the dangle's sphere. He was an Irishman calling himself Keegan Teague. Charlemagne found him interesting and from that time conducted all the surveillance themselves. Nigel's people were very good, but not always sufficiently subtle for an op this delicate.

It took an exhausting and painstaking two days before they saw the first sign of tradecraft in Mr. Teague. He insured himself against a tail on the way to his work the morning before my arrival.

"Is he Cú Chulainn, do you think?" I asked.

Charlie shook his head. "No. He's a cutout."

"Can you verify?"

"We put a very light touch on his car," said Steve. "He has a car phone. Yesterday our effort paid off. We heard one side of a phone call. The phone was secure but the car wasn't, and we heard him tell the unknown other party that Diane was the real deal. He asked for instructions."

Charlie was almost apologetic. But only almost. "We did not expect verification to take so long," he said. "If we try to substitute Steve now, Cú Chulainn will spook. We can't risk it."

"So Rutherford is in to stay," I said. "Does she know?"

The answer was no and that's what we need you for. And oh, by the way, don't tell her too much. We don't want her so nervous that she blows the op, just cooperative enough within the strict bounds of need to know. That is, she doesn't need to know her likely outcome. You could appeal to her patriotism. She is military after all.

But this is a British operation, I pointed out to Nigel. Allies, he replied, cousins even. Then he called on my care and concern for my newly appointed team of killers, as I am so anxious to be an equal in this field of men, yada yada. I am also responsible for the safety of American citizens, I told him. I can't just push one blindly into danger without approval from a higher pay grade and I'm not likely to get that.

"Why can't she just take their money, hand over the device, and leave?" I asked. "Is Cú Chulainn in the habit of killing all his suppliers? How long could he operate with that business plan?"

Nigel rolled his eyes to contemplate the ceiling, but Charlie enlightened me. His taut patience seemed a tad condescending, but the words were clear.

"We want Cú Chulainn, not a cut-out. Because his security is above average, well above average—perfect, you might say—it follows that he must be the only one who knows his target right up until the last possible moment. By using a voiceprint to arm the detonator, a voiceprint that is to be programmed into the device by an expert, we force Cú Chulainn's presence at the sale. When the lieu-tenant colonel hears the voice, she will know who the target is. She will die as soon as the test is shown to work. They cannot afford to do otherwise."

Tut, tut, *lurve*, was Nigel's answer. Just brief her briefly. Then set Steve up with a cover that will let him get in close enough to teach her the program. The team will do all they can for her.

I looked at the two members of the team in front of me. Even if there were a lot they could do, they did not look likely to do it. Both men were exhausted, worried, and pretty much empty of the milk of human kindness. Steve's rumpled coat was open, exposing the Beretta he now wore too easily under his left arm. Long ago, only last year, he had been a compassionate man. Some reports in the file hinted at the same quality in Charlie. There was no sign of it in either of them now. There may have been regret somewhere deep down, but the question was academic. As the trap had been set, there was little they could do about the doomed bait anyway.

Apparently, Nigel had no regrets, or his dislike of me overshad-owed his humanity. I felt him generate a wave of glee at my position navigating a fast course between Scylla and Charybdis. But then, I might have been misled by my distaste for the portly little chauvinist prick.

"I'll have to think about it," I said, as I fixed a pin in my hair.

They did not like my answer. Their expressions told me clearly what my decision could cost me.

FIVE

"I hate to tell you this, Barb," said Steve.

This is the male version of 'no offense but…', which is common among women.

"Then don't," I said.

"Don't what?"

"Don't tell me. I wouldn't want to spoil your day."

He looked annoyed.

"You're not as good as you think you are, you know," he said.

Not having time for deep philosophical discussion, I ignored him and went about my business. Nigel had bugged out on some lame-ass excuse, leaving me with one hundred percent of the babysitter watch responsibility on *his* operation.

The team never allowed a babysitter to have sole watch, and though I had usurped scheduling authority from Mack, babysitter duties did not change, so I got to stay up late with my former colleague, old Teddy Bear. Despite his sobriquet, Steve was not a cuddly man. I never said he was when I nicknamed him. He just looked like he was, with big brown eyes, rather luxurious brown hair, and a melting expression.

I did a physical security check of the doors, of which there were too many, while he with the beautiful eyes gazed at the gadget console monitoring the perimeter sensors Louis set up, lighting up blips and dots in a visual language all its own.

"Why can't Louis brief Rutherford?" I asked when I came back into the room. "Why does it have to be you? I mean, isn't the whole thing his brainchild?"

"He's too well known to the IRA," said Steve. "They will be watching. I'm new, so not as conspicuous."

"Why don't you just brief me, then, and I'll brief her." A little straw grasping was worth a long shot, as the aphorisms say. Sometimes a lateral move in the game can pay off.

Steve looked at me for a long second, then turned back to the sensor console. He sat in a particularly decrepit armchair before the little table that held it. I sat in the chair across from him.

"Louis hasn't told me how yet," he said. "He won't until the last minute."

"Why not?"

"Because as soon as he does, Misha is going to kill him." He took a long pull on a mug of lukewarm coffee, then said, "And I'm going to help him do it."

"Misha? You call him Misha? You really are one of them?" The hard look in his soft eyes gave the necessary confirmation.

"So the Frenchman has done something inexcusable?" I asked.

Steve nodded.

"Well, are you going to tell me?"

"No. I'm not a good witness. I don't live at Vasily's Carpet."

"Where?"

"Vasily's Carpet. Where it happened," he sighed. "I don't live there."

"Where is Vasily's Carpet?" I was not surprised this question got me bupkis. "Is this a town, a village, a...."

"It's a place. Okay?"

He was more than irritated, which, given his new close relationship with 'Misha,' could be bad news for me. But I've never been known to back off when pressing on could merely get me killed.

"What sort of place? A house?"

"Ask Charlie."

Like that was going to be easy.

"Any ideas on how to get Rutherford away safely?" I asked, more as a way to change the subject than to elicit actual information.

He wrinkled his brow and scratched at his beard. It occurred to me that this was the first time he had examined the possibility. I found the thought disturbing. Saving innocent American lives once had been his occupation, too. He started to say something, then stopped.

"What?"

"Nothing." He shook his head.

I pondered the problem. "What if she delays?" I said. "Assuming you guys are right behind Cú Chulainn, you could...." I did not know how to finish this sentence.

Steve gave me a crooked smile. "You're asking for fucking surgery here? If this goes down at Teague's cottage, there won't be time. You might have noticed that the ground around here is flat. It's a former swamp, Barb, and Teague's place is as bare as a baby's ass. There's not even a few flowers to get in the way of the view. It'll be a fucking bullet hurricane in a small space." He handed me his coffee mug.

I stared back at him. I don't fetch coffee. Besides, before he joined Charlemagne, Steve had been my subordinate.

He smiled back at me with the merest hint of venom. He's been taking lessons from that fucking mind reader Mack, I thought. I took the mug. I had to make a new pot. It took some time to fetch and carry from the kitchen half a world away.

"You think it will be there, then?" I asked when I handed him the mug. "Teague's place, I mean."

He nodded. "The device will work on battery power once programmed, but it will need a computer for the programming, and that requires mains power. The cottage is perfect. It's a helluva lot better safehouse than this pile."

He had noticed the things I noticed, which meant the team knew Nigel's arrangements were not optimal. I wondered why they were putting up with it, but then they had a host of their own problems at the moment.

"About the only thing this place has going for it," Steve continued, "is that it's almost big enough to keep those two separated."

"Do you think Teague will be alone?" I asked, driving an idea from my head almost as soon as it was born.

He answered in his own way. "I'll do my best, Barb. We don't know how many there will be, but I'm pretty sure Teague's men won't be all that accommodating."

SIX

"You should cut your hair," said Charlie when he came on watch.

His own blond mop stood out in all directions.

"I bet you say that to all the girls," I said. "I haven't been so flattered since a bald, fat man in a wife-beater t-shirt wolf-whistled me."

His blue eyes stared through me with an expression a trifle too malignant for my taste.

We settled down in the drawing room after checking the perimeter and the sensors once again before sending Steve off to bed.

Charlie took a long sip of a tepid cup of coffee. It is a rule enacted by the universe of operational discomfort that coffee remains just over room temperature during any operation. That is, when there is coffee at all. Hot coffee must be discouraged. It would make us all comfortable and weak. At least, that's my theory. More likely it's a case of overworked coffee machines which must be completely dead before cheapskates in government offices will allow replacements. I've never been on an op with a recently replaced coffee pot but have often wondered what such a nirvana would be like.

Charlie wore the same shirt as earlier but had ditched the coat and tie. His Glock 17 was strapped under his arm. He was rumored to be almost as accurate with a firearm as Louis.

"You're too old for such long hair," he said.

"I was not aware there was a statute of limitations on hair length," I said. Hello pot, I wanted to say. He was young, but no teenager.

"Just trying to help."

"With …?" I raised one eyebrow.

"With Louis."

I had to run through the entire year-long five minutes of my earlier encounter with that particular deranged killer. Was he talking about my mock flirtation at the end?

"Are you talking about the little bit of flirting that helped get him to go upstairs?"

"You know I am."

"No, I don't know. I figured you were smart enough to recognize a bluff."

His blue eyes scanned my mind, even the parts I couldn't read myself. I felt myself blushing and all my attempts to squash it made it predictably worse. I'm sure my head looked like a beet with long hair, which is why I found us a new topic to talk about.

"So what is Vasily's Carpet?" I said, apropos of nothing.

If the topic shift puzzled him, he didn't show it. But he did take his sweet time answering.

"It's a carpet."

"Let me guess. It's a carpet that belonged to Vasily." Let's all join the smart aleck society, shall we? I left this part unsaid. I think it was his ability to be perfectly still that most unnerved me.

Vasily had been the bomb expert of the team for almost twenty years. He was killed eighteen months before this operation, just before Charlie joined the team.

"You think you're witty, but you're not, you know," he said.

I am ever so grateful for all the help I'm getting these days from the Barbara Kemp Improvement Coalition. Especially from those members who think they know what I think. I would have said this out loud, but I understood he was quite the expert with that Glock. The files were very clear on this point. Also, he was far too accurate in the freaky mind reading he must have learned from Dad.

"So Steve said it's a place. How is a carpet a place?" I asked. "I mean, other than for fleas."

"It is the name we have for the place where we live," he said. "Vasily spent much of his youth in various prisons. During an early operation in Beirut, he commissioned a carpet to cover the length of the hallway in one wing of our house. It is otherwise a barren hallway because of our security needs. The rest of the house is monitored, but there we have some privacy, with just a few very secure cipher locks, and no surveillance. Papa and Louis swore at him the whole way out of Lebanon as they lugged the carpet with them, but he would not leave it.

"My father knew Vasily's prison history made him very spartan because he did not decorate his rooms. But after they laid down the carpet, he realized even for Vasily a long hall with a locked door at the end was too stark. The carpet made our home into a Not Prison. So it is a place. It is our Not Prison."

This was way too much information. Was I, like Diane, also not expected to live?

"But Steve does not live there?"

"No, he doesn't. His wife Sally refuses, despite the risks."

"Is it not sufficiently 'Not Prison' for her?"

"No, I don't think so. It is a pleasant enough place. She objects to the other inhabitants." His half smile seemed a trifle sad, I thought.

"You have to be a bit of a lion tamer to share our cage," he continued. "And she is not." He smiled. "You are, though. That was a nice piece of work you did with those two earlier."

I basked in the compliment. "Thanks. Steve seems to think I'm not a good babysitter."

"I did not say you're a good babysitter, only that you did some nice work then. You succeeded with my father and Louis because you are a woman, not because you are especially competent. And maybe you have experience with a whip and a chair," he said with a crooked smile.

Welcome to my circus, I thought. What funny thoughts men get up to. I changed the direction of the conversation by posing the same question I had given Steve. Charlie thought about it and shrugged. He and Steve were becoming two of a kind.

"She is military," he said finally. "I presume she is prepared to give her life for her country." He stretched his arms behind his head and yawned.

"This op is not for her country," I said. "It's for Nigel's."

"Then why are you here?"

I was pretty sure he wasn't asking for an explanation involving the special relationship, so I rolled my eyes and waited.

With a sigh, he said, "Somebody would have to go in early—and all that, as Nigel would say. It would blow the op, but it's that or bye-bye Diane." He flicked his long fingers. I was suppressing a lot of shudders during this conversation, this one being the most challenging.

"Would the team do that?"

He shook his head. "Can't. We would never work again. It will be hard enough without Louis. You need to find another team."

Snowball in hell, and all that.

We settled into a companionable.... well, comfortable—make that careful—silence for a while, at least on my part. Charlie ignored me pointedly, but I was acutely aware of his presence. I checked all the entrances, the windows in all downstairs rooms, the locked door to an extremely creepy cellar, and the upstairs rooms not currently occupied by sleeping specialists. Another staircase—there were three in this house—led to an even creepier attic. I came down from there covered in cobwebs and told myself the feeling of things crawling up my leg was purely psychological.

Back in the drawing room, I sat down in one of the chairs by the fireplace still generating a wisp of heat, and lifted my pant leg to re-assure myself that the crawly feeling was all in my mind. There was, indeed, a not very large spider at my ankle. I brushed it off with a shudder but knew enough not to shriek because I felt Charlie watching me. I could not afford to let him think I was some shrinking female who is afraid of spiders. I'm not. I am a shrieking female who is terrified of the creepy things. It was a close distinction in my mind, between Mack and his knife and the spider on my leg.

I looked up. Charlie was gazing first at me and then pointedly at his empty coffee mug. I wondered if he thought he could intimidate me into waiting on him. He would be wrong. I ignored him.

He snapped his fingers. I examined my nails. I never heard him and had no idea he was next to me until he picked up my hand, put his mug into it, and pointed to the coffee machine ten feet away.

I put the mug on a small table next to the chair and resumed looking at my nails. I have younger brothers. I'm good at this game, but Charlie cheats. He pinched the nerve at the base of my neck, the one my mother always made most effective use of.

"Ow! Cut it out. I'm not your servant."

He pulled me to my feet and grabbed an arm. I defended myself quite adroitly, but he had an even more clever move that landed me on my back and out of air. I rolled as I tried to breathe and tried to crawl out of his way, but he was sitting on top of me, pressing his advantage with his weight and an iron grip on my wrists. I was ready to use my legs to unseat him, but he anticipated the move, stretching out on top of the length of me, with his nearly equal length and stronger legs. He pinned my wrists to either side and grinned at me before he took full advantage in a way my brothers never did.

It was invasive, aggressive, and almost violent, and I knew I could not stop him, was trying to resign myself to it, to the ignominy of falling prey to this kid, when somebody said, "Charlie, cut it out. Your dad will be pissed if he finds out you're not watching the sensors."

Really, Steve? I wanted to shout at him. I'm down here in peril and you're worried about the fucking sensors? I couldn't say it though because Charlie still had his tongue in my mouth. I was tempted to bite down, but there was that Glock. He broke off the kiss in a leisurely way, nuzzled my ear, bit my neck, and said, "An opportunity must be seized, Steve. Do me a favor and watch the sensors for me."

"I'm not sitting here while you rape the babysitter."

"I am not raping her. She consented. She started it."

"Sure she did. Come on, get up. She has to go wake your dad and Louis. Which one should she wake first?"

But Charlie had resumed his ownership of my mouth, pinned both wrists in one hand above my head while the other unzipped my pants and began exploring inside them. I tried to struggle but was completely immobilized.

"I think she should wake your dad first," said Steve. "He will want to be up earlier."

"It's not rape, Steve. Who ever heard of a specialist raping a babysitter? She would not get me a cup of coffee. What use is a babysitter who won't get me a cup of coffee?"

"You know she used to be my boss. I'd prefer she not be damaged."

"Are you going to stop me?" With that, Charlie continued his campaign, sliding two fingers into me.

"I guess I'll go ahead and wake up Misha then, since the babysitter's busy." Steve stood up.

"Fuck, Steve." Charlie rolled off me, picked up his mug, and walked over to the coffee pot. "Louis is okay. It is my father who has gone off the deep end."

This was said with such nonchalance, one would think there was no woman on the floor picking up the pins dislodged from her hair.

"Okay? Louis is okay?" Maybe the incredulity in my voice had something to do with the memory of the dent Louis's gun had made under my chin. The memory did not help to still the shaking of my hands as I buttoned my pants.

"I mean he is his usual self." Charlie looked down at me with a patient look on his face in such a way as to make it clear he was fast losing that commodity and I would be well advised not to accelerate the process.

He held out his hand to help me up. I hesitated with just a smidgen of distrust until I saw him become still, set his jaw, and give me that blue gaze. I took the offered hand. He nearly threw me onto my feet.

"His dossier says things like he is usually joking, jolly even," I said, trying to keep things businesslike.

Charlie took a sip of his coffee. "True. That part of him is gone. As it should be, given what he did. But it is my father who needs more sleep right now."

I was going to have to take his word for it, even though my stomach knotted at the prospect of waking the Frenchman alone and unaided.

"Will you be helping your father kill him after he shows Steve the program?"

"I have not decided yet."

"The jury's still out, then?"

"No. It's in. It is only a matter of sentencing."

"You don't agree he deserves death?"

"I just don't know if it's the best thing for the rest of us, but yes, he does deserve to die. I think that is pretty clear."

Charlie began a physical check of the doors and windows, leaving Steve at the console.

I was still shaking.

"He was probably just intimidating you, Barb," said Steve. "You can be a pain in the ass sometimes. It might help if you were a little bit more afraid of us. There is plenty of reason to be, you know." He looked at me with those deceptive brown eyes and I had difficulty keeping the fear down to just a little bit more.

I wondered about it as I climbed the stairs to the room where Louis was sleeping. I wondered what crime a professional killer could commit that his closest friends would find unforgivable.

SEVEN

I sang as I climbed the staircase. I don't remember the song, just that it gave me a few chances to belt out some notes, all of them happy, because happy is the order of the day—or night—when one is about to wake a specialist during an exhausting and dangerous operation in which his team has lost its fucking collective mind. I stood in a long hallway connecting the two symmetrical wings of the house and stopped at the door to a room where the Frenchman was presumably having sweet dreams. Taking cover at one side of the door, I knocked.

"Hello there!" I sang the greeting in the happiest voice I could muster.

No answer.

I swung the door open, still staying away from the opening.

Continual, creepy nothingness.

I peered inside, then followed my nose cautiously, keeping up a cheerful banter all the time.

The room was large, square, and very dim because its window was one of those that had been boarded up. Early daylight had to force itself through spaces between the boards. A double bed was pushed up against the wall opposite the door. Beside the bed stood a broken dresser. Two large wardrobes occupied either side of the door, leaving it pretty much indefensible. Despite all this dangerously positioned storage space, nobody had seen fit to use it. Bags and gear littered the floor. Clothing was heaped on the bed.

Also heaped on the bed, fully clothed, even wearing a loosened tie, lay Louis. His legs stretched their considerable length toward the door. He had flung his left arm over his brow obscuring his eyes in the uncertain light from the hallway. His right hand lay loosely on the weapon in the shoulder holster on his left side.

I was going to have to approach him. He was making sure of it. I gently wiggled the toe of his left shoe. "Rise and shine, *mon ami*. It's your watch."

No reply. Did his hand just now tense on the gun pulled half-way out of its holster?

"All right, Buster," I said in English. "I know you're awake. I'm not stupid and I'm not coming any closer. Get up."

I turned on my heel and stalked out the door, expecting a bullet in my back the whole way.

Because I survived, I was able to put on a fresh pot of coffee downstairs before he arrived. *Lucky me.* Louis and Charlie exchanged curt nods by way of shift change procedure, and the great ignoring began. We spent the first hour in silence.

Of course, I was the one making coffee. And where the hell was Nigel?

I sat on the three-legged purple sofa near the chair where Louis occupied himself with his gadgets while Steve raided the refrigerator in the kitchen. All the reports had described Louis as fastidious and expensively tailored. What I saw was flatulent and slovenly. Were the reports a lie? Charlie said he was still his real self. Was this his real self?

Maybe I was staring too much in horror, because just then he spoke to me, for the first time acknowledging my presence in the room.

"Do you use that bluff often?"

My mouth opened and closed again without anything at all coming out, let alone anything intelligent.

"I am wondering," he continued in a strange aristocratic French that I had not heard before in real life, "whether that was something you made up in another flash of idiocy, as when you put your hand on your weapon in my presence, or whether you have used it before and somehow survived the experience. Perhaps a witch doctor gave you a talisman to keep such things from blowing up in your face."

He looked at me while he drank his coffee.

I squawked "What ...?" Then remembered the flirting tone I had used earlier to get the job done. It seemed to have these guys so, shall we say, exercised.

"What?" He screeched, mocking me. "What I am asking, Barbara," he said, leaning toward me, "is have you been raped on the job before? How many times?"

I got a D in Pokerface 101 at Spy University, so he saw my dis-comfort.

"So you are willing to risk it again?" he asked. "Maybe it was not so bad, eh?" He cocked his head and looked at me with narrowed eyes. "No," he said slowly. "Something has happened. Here. Now. Turn around."

To refuse would confirm his suspicions. I was a lot more than a little bit afraid now. I had thrown my hair back up under its guard of pins, but without a mirror or comb, it was tufted strangely. There was no help for it. I was more than a little disarranged.

When I faced him again, he said, "I wonder what Misha will say when he sees you. Perhaps he will say you wanted it."

Nothing like a nice hot shot of anger to help one find one's voice.

"Don't be ridiculous," I said. It wasn't as if I could say fuck you, which was my first choice. He might take me up on it. So I sounded like June Cleaver instead.

"I am never ridiculous." His black eyes studied my face. "Rape is a fear then, as it is for most people, even men. But it is not the best way to hurt you, eh? What is the best way, I wonder?"

If I knew the answer to that, I certainly was not about to en-lighten him.

"So tell me what happened at Vasily's Carpet?" I said, by way of deflection.

"Who told you about Vasily's Carpet?"

"Charlie."

"But why you?" His brow wrinkled as if he were genuinely puzzled. "Maybe you remind him of his mother, eh?"

That was a creepier question than he knew. "You're saying I look like her?" Tidbits of gossip are part and parcel of intelligence work.

"No. She was very beautiful."

Your new nose doesn't exactly make you look like Adonis either, Sun-shine. I pushed a pin back into my hair.

He regarded me steadily. "What else did Charlie say? Or … do?" He paused. "He has used your sex to intimidate you, has he not?"

"Another word for it is assault," I said, still seething.

"Any assault is an invasion of the body," said Louis, "but one that involves sex is more terrible because it is more intimate. How intimate was he, exactly?"

I did not want this conversation. No part of it was comfortable or comforting. But he would not leave it alone.

"Did he enter you?" he said.

I took a shuddering breath. "His fingers," I said. And his tongue, I might have added, but it was all of a parcel and no one detail felt less invasive than any other.

"Let me see," Louis speculated, "he immobilized you. You had no way to defend yourself. On the floor, perhaps?"

I stared at him open-mouthed with 'how?' unvoiced.

He smiled. "I know how he fights. After all, I am one of his teachers. His purpose was to intimidate, of course. Charlie does nothing without purpose, like his father. He was setting the parameters of his relationship with a new babysitter. You would do well to heed him."

"You're saying he's dangerous?"

Louis's eyebrows drew up in surprise. "We are all dangerous."

"But is he as dangerous as his father?"

"Oh, no. More dangerous. Much more dangerous."

"What did you do to make Mack so angry?" I said after a moment to deflect the conversation away from me. I needed to breathe again just a little.

It took him a minute to weigh his answer. "I raped his wife."

"Um, his wife is dead." I put my hands in my pockets so he could not see them shaking.

"He married again."

"Yeah, that would do it then. I can see why he's not taking it well."

"He says I betrayed him."

"Wait, she's raped but he's mad because it's about him?"

I got to see the wrinkled forehead again, but it didn't last long.

"I told him it was not about sex! I hated her! It was the best way to hurt her! You are right. It was not about him. I never thought about him."

"Never thought about your best friend and lifelong business partner? Okay. But why did you want to hurt her?"

Something broke or snapped or whatever you call it. Some reserve drained, past his teeth, into the air around my ears. It was a jumble. None of it seemed familiar because none of it came from the files back in The Section. Much of it I could not understand. Though I speak French fluently, his accent was so obscure I had difficulty with it at times, and I had no frame of reference for the things he was telling me.

"She has a problem with sex," he said.

"You said this was not about sex."

"Rape is about power, not sex. Her problem with sex made it the best way to hurt her. Why does nobody see this?"

"Presumably she's okay with sex in her marriage," I said, doubting that a man like Mack would take up celibacy even outside of marriage let alone with a wife.

Louis ignored this, which was probably a good thing. "That Chicago operation—she would not say, so we chose playing cards and Misha picked the ace and Vasily was disappointed. But again, there was our own Chicago op later, for revenge. We came home, and Vasily was dead, and Misha's wife and daughter were dead, and he wanted comfort, he said, and she gave him comfort. Like nobody else wanted comfort? I loved them all, too, of course. How could anyone not? So now they are married and Miss Holy Pureness ..."

A pin made its way out of my hair before I could push it back. I looked at the man with the broken nose sitting before me. "You're right," I said. "It wasn't about Mack."

EIGHT

We spent the rest of our introductory alone time talking, even while we checked doors and windows and as Louis kept one eye on his precious sensors while I made pot after pot of coffee. The only thing we did not talk about was the op itself. There was also no more explanation of what had happened at Vasily's Carpet.

Despite that, I learned more than I could ever include in the file. For example, the original team members, Misha, Louis, and Vasily were distantly related and had grown up in each other's houses. Misha's family had raised Vasily, who gave Misha his name. Until then, he had been simply Michael. I heard about childhood squabbles with each other and with their siblings and the interference of nannies.

"Nannies? You guys had nannies?" I asked.

"Yes. Of course."

Doesn't everybody?

"I caused Misha's nanny to be fired," said Louis. "When I was four years old my older brother ruined my baby sister's christening blanket while playing with a bottle of ink. He blamed Misha. I tried to tell them he was innocent, but Misha's nanny could not speak French, so she decided he was guilty and should not have supper that day. Misha said it took him a long time to forgive me."

"Forgive you? What about your brother?"

"Misha was three. By the time he understood what happened, he and I had become good friends. Friends are easiest to blame and hardest to forgive."

"There is some truth in that," I said.

"When Misha's mother found out what happened, she fired the nanny and hired one who spoke French as well as German. I think Misha was bothered more by the loss of his nanny than by his unjust punishment. He did not like the new one. He connected the unwanted new nanny to my sister's christening and so to me."

During our second security check, we came to a small room off the kitchen where piles of tractor-feed computer paper had been stacked in a corner. These were the transcripts Nigel's people made of the various taps on Diane Rutherford's home, office, and life in general. Louis picked out a loose page and showed it to me.

"What is this?" I asked.

"The colonel's boyfriend wants a family. Look here." He pointed to a line about a third of the way down the page.

"I'm a warrior, Mace," Diane had said. I gathered Mace was the boyfriend. "No babies. No home. No two-car garage. I'm just not made that way. This is all there is for me. Sorry."

"This is all there is for me," Louis said, reading aloud.

I was beginning to like our doomed dangle. That is not a good thing in my business. I caught myself entertaining fantastic schemes, all at the last possible moment, refining the suggestions I had already gleaned and overestimating my heroic capabilities. Diane seemed a worthy object of rescue. I just didn't know how it could be done.

I looked at Louis, wondering.

"So you're a warrior," I said.

"Yes. I am the second son. First inherits, second fights, third son prays. I have a younger brother who is a priest."

"How did you find this particular conversation in all those piles of paper?" I asked. This was not something that would have been flagged by Nigel's bean counters.

"I read every word she says."

"So who is Mace?"

"A U-2 pilot on the base. His name is Mason Leupena. Keegan Teague's attentions have made the relationship difficult."

I did not want to revert to talking business, but the sun was almost up, and it was past time to wake everybody. We ended our house tour in the drawing room where Louis said something that made us both laugh.

Mack's scowl as he came through the door swallowed any weak joy that might have lingered in the room. He glared at Louis, who lifted an eyebrow in a dare. I occupied the excruciatingly uncomfortable space between them. I'm a pretty good fighter for my weight class, which is way outclassed by these guys, as I had discovered only a couple of hours before. I would have to intervene alone, without Steve or Charlie, and I would lose. Mack looked at me, turned, and stalked out of the room.

I followed him into the kitchen because I wanted to talk to him. I made him breakfast because I wanted to placate him. Well, that and

I could not bear the massacre of half a dozen eggs being perpetrated by his hand as I closed the door behind me. What a mess. I wondered why Nigel had not hired help. It would be simple enough to vet people from among his own section's staff and just keep them in the house for the duration. They would have the necessary clearances and the place was certainly big enough. I filed it away as a future suggestion for Nigel, whenever he might decide to show up for work that day.

Now that the household was awake, everybody went about their own business. Louis conducted endless security checks, testing each sensor and tweaking its placement along the perimeter. Charlie stayed in the front room to watch those sensors. Steve spent the morning in the bathroom vomiting, mostly coffee. His ulcer was making him too sick to eat.

That left me alone with Mack. Not only was he up and awake, but his tie was straight, and he had shaved. His collar and cuffs were dirty, though. He carried his SIG in a shoulder holster. It and the holster were spotlessly clean.

"How about an omelette?" I asked. I tried to use an elbow as I took the pan from him. I am a fraction of an inch taller, and my elbows are pretty pointy, but I may as well have tried to move a tree. He glared at me.

"Sit down and I'll make you breakfast."

He sat.

"So how is your wife doing?" I said as kind of an icebreaker. "This has to be a really tough time for her with you away and all." I looked over my shoulder at him sitting there as I whisked the eggs.

"It is not your business."

I noticed he had no timekeeping mannerisms. The table was populated by all kinds of clutter. Most people would at least push a plate away or pick up a saltshaker. The files had mentioned he was economical with movement, but this was on another plane entirely. He was economical because he was prepared to move in any direction, in any situation, at any time, and you knew looking at him, that he would reach that destination way before you. I suppressed a shiver. His blue, blue eyes told me he saw me do that, too.

"On the contrary," I said, admittedly with a bit of a squeak, "it is very much my business, or at least it is my job to keep the team whole and intact during an op. I've heard some disturbing things, disturbing for a woman to hear that is, and I would like to interfere as much as necessary and as little as possible at the same time, to find that sweet spot that would allow you guys to get your job done without any unnecessary, um, ah, unnecessary bloodshed."

Especially my own.

"Was your wife hurt badly?"I chopped up a bell pepper and cubed a bit of cheddar.

I gave him time, but nothing came. Just as I opened my mouth to continue this enthralling conversation, he spoke.

"She was not hurt."

"Physically? That's good," I said. "But, you know, there can be emotional damage in this situation. Has she been able to see a counselor?"

"No."

I turned from the cutting board. "She should see someone. The effects of such an event can be devastating. You must urge her to get help." I used my most sober, serious voice, and matched my face to it as I turned back to the chopped veg.

"She said she was not raped."

"Wait. What?" I spun around to look at him.

The royal blue eyes that normally held no emotion at all were not troubled in any way, but I could see a hint of confusion.

"She said it was only a kiss. She was not raped."

"Then, why?" I swept my arm through the air in a wide arc to encompass 'all this.'

"Louis says he did."

"And you believe the man rather than your wife?"

"She would protect him. And me. I believe him."

"Well, that's a first for the record books. Not only is a woman's word unbelievable when she claims rape, but now it's no good when she denies it?" I let my skepticism show a smidgen.

"Women have many strange reasons to lie," he said, not making my blood boil at all. "There are women who deny their husbands beat them. Their injuries are always caused by something else, often doorknobs and staircases."

"And men never lie?" I asked. "Louis could not be lying for some equally strange reason?"

Like a death wish.

Mack turned inward and was silent for what seemed like an hour, but after a minute said, or rather ordered, "Make the omelet."

After this interesting exchange, I tried a light banter, mostly about cooking, hoping to avoid any other touchy subjects, but he had used up all his stock of semi-polite conversation, probably for the year.

You could say we were charmingly domestic in a country farm-house, with a well-stocked kitchen (okay, credit there to Nigel) and Nebraska cooking. I put plate after plate in front of him and he put away an omelette, hash browns, half a pound of sausage, breakfast biscuits, toast, and jam, thin buttered pancakes rolled in powdered sugar, and some leftover ham simmered in pineapple juice and brown sugar. The man could not cook, but he could eat. He was also a master of the insult. The language he used was incredibly clever, with layers of meaning, all of them hurtful.

He did not insult the food, though. Nor did he thank me for it, but I guess getting through an hour alone in his presence unscathed was thanks enough.

The clean-up was left to me, of course. I did not mind the lack of company as I stood before the sink, dead on my feet. Washing dishes requires little coherent thought, so I must have put my senses on hold.

In the middle of an op.

With Charlemagne.

This bit of choice boneheadedness might have eclipsed my introductory move in the hallway the day before. Either way, my brain was on idle, and I was enjoying the kitchen solitude when I turned from the sink into the chest of Louis. I had not heard him at all.

He lost no time. The pins popped out of my coiled braid and fell tinkling to the floor as he laced his fingers through my loosening hair and pulled my lips to his.

I am no blushing virgin. I work in a field populated by mostly attractive and very fit men, despite the few Nigels out there and I don't often say no. I might add that on occasion it may be my idea to initiate, and they also do not say no. But this kiss, this was new. It was an appetizer, the kind of appetizer that is a meal in itself and anticipates a more satisfying repast in the future. His tongue danced with mine but was absolutely in the lead, owning the territory of my mouth, exploring at will, conquering. It was an intrusion, impudent but not violent, more of a promise and an announcement of what was to come. The man had confessed to raping his best friend's wife. I knew what he was capable of, what he intended, and that I had no defense, not because he had taught that abominable kid how to fight, but because my body would not allow me to say no to such a man.

Hell, I'd have consented to lie across the kitchen table, but he broke off the kiss, looked at me with a slow smile, turned, and walked out the door.

I gathered what I could of my hairpins and my dignity and left the room looking like a scarecrow. A rather titillated scarecrow.

Nigel showed up just as I crossed the hallway. He stared. I tried not to look well kissed. He continued a steady regard and I almost saw him as he once must have been, before he became complacent and convinced of his male superiority.

I brought him up to date on the events of my over-long shift. Well, most of the events. I could see in his eyes that he already knew about that second kiss. Maybe it was the tangled mess of my hair, the look on my face, or his weak imitation of Mack in the mind-reading department. Or, it could be the mysterious male alertness to all things sexual in a woman. Pheromones, maybe, or other subtle cues that all men seem able to read, even gone to seed puddings like Nigel.

"I want to run something by you," he said. "Let's go somewhere we can talk."

My uh-oh radar powered up. We went outside into a grey, cold February day in England. I shivered. My hair hung in clumps; my eyes streamed with fatigue, and I was grasping my rescued hairpins too tightly in my left hand.

"I think we should team up," said Nigel.

"As in?" I asked. Surely not, I thought.

"As in we should work together on a plan I have been considering."

"That's what we're doing, isn't it?" I said with some relief. This did not have the feel of the usual opening line. "You know, the one where you decided to sacrifice a U.S. citizen to rid yourself of an IRA killer? Don't tell me you're only now putting in the considering part."

He scowled. "There's that, yes. But I think it would be good for both of us if we added a small modification."

"What modification?"

"We should keep the detonator. Think about it. If we could count on precision like that, and have it at our disposal, we wouldn't need specialists. At least not as often."

I knew, in my bones, he had something risky, probably deadly, up his sleeve. "The programming?" I said to throw a roadblock in his way.

He gave me an exasperated look. "Our lads are quite up to that sort of thing. Remember Enigma? And I'm sure my government would share it with yours, especially if you helped me obtain the thing."

I quelled my internal laughter ruthlessly. "Why not just buy it? Maybe the Frenchman would sell it to you."

He raised both eyebrows and said nothing.

"That's true," I said. "He would build in some weird ability to inform Charlemagne any time you did use it. How do you propose stealing it without them knowing you took it?"

More important but unspoken, without them killing you. I was beginning to think maybe Nigel was not incompetent; he was off his rocker.

"Have you seen them?" said Nigel. "Did you notice they are not exactly in top form these days?"

I did not point out that his lousy arrangements in this godforsaken broken-down, insecure safehouse were at least part of the problem. But tact and diplomacy are my middle names.

"I know this chap," he continued. "He's ex-SAS. He says he can get a few of his mates to help us. We should meet and put our heads together to come up with a plan. Are you heading to the base?" he asked, raising an eyebrow.

"After I sleep."

"Don't leave it too long. I'll call Stan and arrange a rendezvous when you get back."

I glared at him. I had not slept for twenty-five hours, in part because of his less than dedicated presence on the job, and now he wanted to throw me into some harebrained plot that would take my time, put the team—my team—further at risk, and destroy the mission. And those were best-case scenarios. Another thought flew out of my head before I could grasp it. I was too tired for anything but sweet dreams. Nigel was proposing a lunatic nightmare.

I climbed upstairs, found my way to the room that held my suitcase and threw myself on the bed. My eyes closed on a vision of the satin edge of the worst-case scenario. I was too tired even to shudder.

NINE

Two and a half hours later I found the Frenchman making coffee in the drawing room. We were alone, which I both did and did not want, but hey, it's a job.

"You didn't rape her," I said.

A pause. Then, "My nature is well documented in your files. Also in Nigel's files, in the files of many others."

"But you didn't rape Misha's wife."

The coffee machine hissed and Louis came toward me. He stopped a few feet away.

"Misha took her, you know."

"You said he married her."

"He did. But he took her first. In Chicago. She was the dangle."

There was, no doubt, more to this story. He had to be talking about an op that took place over a decade ago, another Chicago op before the most recent one. There was no dangle in CETUS WEDGE. Plenty of tragedy, but no dangle. I remembered an old op-rep, or operation report, my boss Frank had written. It was pretty bare bones as far as information went, sparing the reader such uninteresting details as who, what, when, where, and why.

"Was she as doomed as Diane?" I asked.

He nodded and looked away at my mention of the lieutenant colonel.

"She must have been younger than Diane," I said, "Frank mentioned a college student in his report."

He wore a stone mask and spoke in op-speak, terse and emotionless. "Twenty," he said. "A virgin. Misha took her." He gazed toward the coffee pot. It had begun to burble.

Hardly a parallel with Diane, aside from the fact that somehow the woman had lived to marry Mack. And there was a connection in Louis's mind.

"Did he rape her?" I asked.

He turned his head abruptly, looked at me, and frowned. "No. Of course not. She consented."

I was having difficulty with this conversation. None of it was in our files, but he seemed to think it was. Though he had mentioned a young woman involved in that op, Frank indicated nothing about her being a dangle.

"You said something about drawing cards," I prompted.

Louis sighed, distracted. The coffee machine began to spit. Soon it might reward us with the magic liquid. He certainly had an unholy fixation on it. He swept his hand through his unruly hair, sighed again, and said, "Vasily wanted her. He had her agreement, or he said he did, to provide what they wanted."

"They?"

"Ill Wind. The terrorists. They planned to bomb a tall building. I don't remember what they needed, another detonator, maybe. It's always a detonator. Technology is difficult to keep up with in this business. Expensive. No, I think that time it was a laser trigger, very expensive. We decided to dress her up as a tart and let them get part of what they needed from her."

"Part of the detonator or rather, trigger?"

"No. It was something they needed to buy the thing. A painting, I think. Part of it. It had parts to it. I think the coffee is ready."

He gave me a pointed look. God forbid an aristocratic male should pour his own coffee. But I needed this conversation to go on. It was pure gold and would make my career. What a coup! Besides, I needed to understand, to know what was going on, or there would be no operation, no career, and no Diane Rutherford.

I grabbed his mug from the coffee table, stepped to the machine, and poured. I did not pour one for me. The last thing I needed right now was to be interrupted by an urgent need to pee. It can interfere with the ability to listen.

"There were parts to the painting, you were saying," I prompted as I handed him the mug. The essential beverage was in that brief magical state of being hot and I was jealous. I knew the pot would be tepid by the time we finished this conversation. I felt very noble in my sacrifice of the ultimate luxury, a hot cup of coffee, in the acquisition of that boon of all boons, more information.

He sipped and nodded. "We gave her one part of the painting. We needed Ill Wind to stay busy trying to make her tell them what she did with the rest. To give us time to get in there."

"Did she tell them?"

He looked up, incredulous. "Of course not. She did not know. We did not tell her."

"And Vasily got her to agree to this?" I was demanding perfect stillness from the muscles in my face. So far, the team's concept of consent did not match mine.

"Yes, he liked her," said Louis. "He wanted her to live. If she gave them the whole painting, they would kill her right away. If they thought she knew where the rest was, they would press her, then kill her when they realized she did not know. Vasily did not want her to die."

What we do for love, I thought. She married Vasily and eventually Mack and was currently living at Vasily's Carpet, the Not Prison.

"So drawing cards?" I prompted again.

He rolled his eyes at my ignorance. "She was a virgin. Even worse. She considered sex, any sex at all, a sin. She had determined to hang onto it until old age, I think. She quaked at the sight of us. Well, not so much at Vasily. Maybe that is why he liked her. It was new to him. An innocent who did not fear him."

"So why was her virginity such a problem?"

Louis stared at me again, giving me too much attention. I gave myself an internal shut-the-fuck-up command because I needed him to stay in the past and keep talking.

"Innocents do not walk up to terrorists and hand them the means to blow up a building full of people," he said. "We gave her a legend to give her access. She was a tart after money, trying to sell them what they wanted. Stupid, venal, easy. Of course, they would check. Hell, Misha checked. And then they would know she was a dangle, and they would kill her before we could get to her. Do you understand?"

I nodded. Appalled.

"We all argued, but not Frank. He was not there. Eventually, Misha relented. He told Vasily to take her, but Vasily would not, so Misha told her to choose one of us. She refused. She had already agreed to the whole thing, but she would not sully herself in that way—or some such crap. We drew cards. Misha had the ace. He told her again, choose. She would not. Vasily was not happy, but I think he did not want to start with her that way. He wanted everything to be not what it was. Not Prison. Not babysitter's daughter. Not raped innocent. Not doomed dangle."

"Frank was not there," I said. "She was a twenty-year-old virgin with religious convictions, and you all played a card game with her to determine who would give her a plausible legend in a deadly op? And she consented?"

I thought my summary was pretty dead on. So did Louis, I think, because he squirmed a little, squinting one eye and letting out an elongated "*Ouiiiii*."

"And she is Frank's daughter? Is that why he didn't write any of this down?"

"No," he said, looking puzzled.

"You said she is a babysitter's daughter."

His eyebrows raised. I had given him information about our files and my boss.

"Not Frank," he said. "Fred. He was retired. I believe he was Frank's boss once, and I told you Frank was not there. He could not write what he did not know."

His lips curled upward in a crooked smile unsupported by the eyes he had fixed on mine. I wasn't sure this information made me safe. He finished his coffee, put the mug down, and stepped in front of me, not in kissing range, but close enough to reach my breast. He circled my left nipple, ever so lightly with one finger.

It's not as if this kind of thing never happened in this job. It did frequently. Normally, I would simply step away. Sometimes, I would slap the man, even if he were a crazy, beefed-up killer. Never did I allow myself to be demeaned like this. For the first time, I didn't feel demeaned. Nothing was normal on this op, and that included my response to this man.

"Your breathing has changed," he said with that slow smile. "You desire me as much as I desire you."

Charlie and Nigel came in then, following the scent of coffee.

TEN

As I drove the beater car to the air base, I spent twenty minutes considering all my options and the various bits of advice Steve and Demon Charlie had given me regarding Rutherford. I generated ideas, checking each one against reality and the odds. Fleeting thoughts of the past few hours came back to me, and I made a few tentative plans. None of these involved getting myself killed in Nigel's crazy scheme. There was something very wrong there. I would have to watch him.

I introduced myself to Lieutenant Colonel Rutherford in a bare room called a SCIF (pronounced skiff). The steel and acoustic countermeasures that encased the room were supposedly impenetrable by all the people in the world with Louis's skills. Having met Louis, I wondered and doubted just a bit.

The colonel had a firm handshake and straightforward gaze. A tall woman with long slim hands, she moved with natural grace and stood ramrod straight. She had green twinkly eyes and spoke with a low, fast voice that was somewhat breathless. Her short hair glowed with a too-even blonde color that I doubted was natural. I liked her and hated her immediately. We sat down at a large conference table in the room.

"Colonel, it is imperative...."

"Please, call me Diane."

I took a deep breath. I prefer my sacrificial lambs anonymous, thank you. I learned this important point as a child when a tiny yellow chick named Fluffy I raised for a 4H project grew into a surplus rooster and Sunday dinner. He was delicious but accompanied by tears.

"Diane, it is imperative you tell no one about this meeting or about the things we are going to discuss."

She nodded. I suppose she could not help the twinkliness of her eyes. Must have played hell with the people she commanded.

I told her just enough. I described Steve and told her he was a Hughes Aircraft technical representative, which was the cover I had managed to get him. *You're welcome, Nigel.* I explained that she should expect contact.

She nodded again, seemingly delighted with it all.

I did not tell her about the disintegrating Frenchman who doted on every word she had spoken in the last three days because of a niggling problem with the definition of consent, the man who would teach Steve what he in turn would relay to her in what I hoped would not be a disastrous game of telephone. I did not tell her about my intricate negotiations with a cold, knife-wielding specialist who had extracted my promise to fully cooperate with the odious Nigel in return for Louis's continued life until the end of the operation. I also neglected to mention my deep reservations about Nigel's ability or even his desire to pull off the op at all, let alone without a lot of unnecessary blood, only partly because I couldn't mention Nigel or the true nature of the op at all.

Our conversation made me even more uneasy. Diane was so … nice. She had an ephemeral quality that made you glad just to be in the same room with her.

"When I say it is important you not mention this to anyone," I insisted, "I include Mr. Teague. I can't say this strongly enough. It's important that you not mention this to him."

This was risky. I was disclosing that her activities, her life even, were closely watched, a breach of security protocol, but I had a feeling she did not take the situation entirely seriously. Maybe it was the twinkly eyes. Her almost playful manner made her someone I would be glad to go clubbing with, but we were not clubbing. We were discussing her possible—probable—death, though she did not know it. I wanted to tell her I was being as serious as a heart attack—her heart attack.

"Keegan?" she said. "Not Keegan! What has he done?"

"Just don't tell him any of this. He is likely to ask you about the device. Act like you are selling it. Let him make the arrangements. Steve will provide some protection for you."

Some. Right. Another breach. Was she getting any idea of the danger she was in? If she did, her perfect features did not say so.

"But I can't believe Keegan would be involved in anything like this," she said, chuckling. "Who'd have thought, huh?" An idea did occur and her brow furrowed. "He's not in any danger, is he?"

I was momentarily speechless. She was not catching on, though she was not stupid. I began a verbal tap dance. Danger for everybody. That sort of thing.

Some of it got through. Maybe. The smile dropped, but I was still pretty sure she was not concerned for herself. This can be dangerous. In an operation like this, self-preservation is assumed to be a dependable motivator. Altruists can be unpredictable. Especially when they know only a fraction of what's going on.

"Do exactly what I tell you," I repeated.

"Anything you say." She gave me a mock salute. "Whatever it takes to get the job done. But I hope Keegan won't get hurt. Have you met him? He's half a head shorter than me, but believe me, he makes up for it."

When Diane had gone and I found myself alone in the SCIF, I called my boss over the secure line. It was still morning in England and five hours earlier on the East Coast, but I caught him at home having his first cuppa. Now that he was the boss, his house was equipped with all the gadgets a spook could want, including a secure phone. Frank is a pudgy, bald, nervous man, differing from Nigel in both competence and physical presence. Neither man looks like he can hold his own in a fight, but I happen to know that Frank can do so with deceptive alacrity.

"What's going on?" he said. "The cousins don't seem to like you."

"Good morning to you, too, boss-man," I wondered which cousin he could be hearing from. "The cousins don't like me because of my genetic handicap. I'm female."

"They're saying you're not a good fit for this op."

I had an inkling 'they' consisted of just one man.

"That would be my cousinly colleague. He disappeared for ten hours last night, so we've not been acquainted long enough for him to know. As it turns out, I am a perfect fit."

I thought about that second kiss.

"So, Chicago," I continued.

"What about Chicago? Everything relevant about that op is in the file. Did you read the file?"

He knew I read the file. It was one of the many ways I annoyed the guys in The Section. I always read the files.

"Not CETUS WEDGE," I said. "Earlier."

After an unnaturally long pause, he said, "So what? Sobieski's dead."

Ahhh. He knows about the dangle.

"His, uh, legacy is not."

I packed a great many things into the last comment. I was telling him there was a problem in the current op, that it involved the team dynamics, that a woman was in the mix, that I knew he kept her out of the earlier file to ensure her safety, that the disaster of CETUS WEDGE was not over because the danger to the team's significant others was still extant.

It took him a while to unpack it all.

"Duly noted," he said. "What else?"

He wanted off this topic, so I outlined SIEGE and the bleak future of Lieutenant Colonel Diane Rutherford.

"I think survival here is more important than success," I said. I did not limit this to Diane's survival, because I was beginning to think her continued existence was the key to the survival of the entire team. Catching one IRA assassin whose targets were as yet hypothetical seemed remote in importance compared to the present reality of Diane Rutherford of the twinkly eyes and the effect her demise would have on a set of ruthless killers who had been in the game too long and had seen too much unnecessary carnage.

Did he get all that, I wondered as Frank took the longest pause yet.

"Agreed," he said finally. "You are the best fit for this job. Check in when you can."

...

The cousins were not going to be happy about the realignment of my priorities.

ELEVEN

One of the perks of my job is the chance to see new things. The old things, like jet lag, no sleep, lousy food, and homicidal associates can wear you down after a while, which is why I accepted Diane's invitation to tour the flightline at RAF Alconbury. Maybe it was a little too public an excursion, but I needed a break. Like the break the toad Nigel took the night before, doing what, I didn't know.

Speaking of toads, we drove past a series of wide concrete bunkers squatting like warty amphibians around a cement pond. Some had their huge doors open, with equipment, generators, and metro vans dotted in among scores of maintenance people dressed in battle dress camouflage uniforms like their commander, my host. I noticed they did not salute her when she stopped to ask a question.

"It's not safe to salute on the flightline," she said when I asked. "Imagine a guy with a wrench in his hand. Does he bean himself or drop it in the airplane? So, this is a no-salute zone. Also, no hats. They can fly off your head straight into an engine."

There were no salutes then, but there were plenty of 'yes ma'ams'—something I had read about in books but never experienced myself. I also belonged to a hierarchical organization, with respectably high rank, above middle management anyway, yet no one ever said yes ma'am to me even figuratively. I get it that in my business the need for creative thinking takes precedence over instant blind obedience, and as a result, we do not encourage outward acknowledgments of rank, but inwardly the hierarchy colors everything, as it does in most organizations.

What I saw on the flightline was more than yes ma'am being said in blind obedience. It was a genuine and general acknowledgment of Diane's authority. I have worked very hard to be as good as or better than every man I have seen in this job. When I make a mistake, though, often the difference between me and the man next to me is that my mistake becomes a monument to the proposition that a woman just cannot hack it in this field.

Diane was clearly hacking it in her field. I resolved in that moment to keep her alive.

We stopped in front of a U-2, called a TR-1 in this part of the world. It reminded me of a video game featuring birds with impossibly long wings flopping up and down. One of these black birds squatted at rest, covered in matte black paint with non-reflective markings, where there were any markings at all. Long red flags attached at various places flapped in the cold English wind. The wings were impossible. They were supported solely by what were called pogos, a single wheel at the end of each wing, designed to fall off once the Dragon Lady became airborne.

Diane's people stayed busy coming and going. Cables and lines of all sorts crisscrossed the tarmac and generators blared. I was impressed.

A metro van pulled up and a spaceman stepped out. Or so it seemed. He was huge and wearing a mustard-colored suit with a space helmet, boots, and gauntlets set into the suit. Tubes snaked from the airplane to ground equipment close by. From the pilot's suit, more tubes were attached to a suitcase he carried with him as he walked a few feet to the airplane. I wondered how they would get this mountain of a man into that small cockpit. It took three people to do it, but they managed without a shoehorn.

We were standing on each side of the truck with the doors open, and I was so fascinated by the scene that I did not notice Diane's silence until a pause in the booming radio chatter gave me a chance to look at her. She stood very still. I was tempted to wave a hand in front of her eyes.

She broke her focus on the cockpit and began to turn away when a radio squawk from the truck announced a problem. Diane walked over to a crew chief wearing a headset plugged into the front of the aircraft. She took the headset from him and had a conversation, presumably, with the spaceman in the cockpit. I watched her face. She was all business; no sign of anything else. The only reason it was remarkable is because of the change from the strange pensive quiet of a few moments before.

Other people, these in civilian clothes, began to swarm, each taking a turn on the same headset. Among them, I recognized my agency's Resident. We did not acknowledge each other.

Once the problem was resolved, the Resident came back to the truck with Diane. They were discussing inertial navigation. The subject not being one of my strong suits, in fact not in my wardrobe at all, I did not join them in the conversation. Also, I figured for the sake of security, the Res and I should not be publicly connected. I'd gone to a lot of trouble keeping his identity from Nigel's hounds.

He smiled at Diane and patted her shoulder before leaving. Then he handed me a piece of paper.

So much for my most laudable security consciousness.

I read the paper in the truck while the airplane taxied by in front of us. Diane was discreet, saying nothing about the odd connection between me and the Resident. I'm not sure I could have answered her anyway.

The single page was a telex from Frank, marked SENSITIVE COMPARTMENTED INFORMATION and stamped FLASH. FLASH. FLASH. BARB, COST IS NOT AN ISSUE IN THE SUCCESS OF SIEGE. FRANK."

I felt the ground shake as the airplane left the runway, but I did not hear it roar, because I had my own roaring going on. Someone had called Frank. I already knew that. Someone told him I was not supporting the operation. I knew who that was now, too.

Now I knew what Nigel had been doing all night. The bastard got hold of my boss. The bastard went behind my back. The bastard.

And, I suspected, he hadn't told Frank the full cost of the American share of SIEGE as I had done just an hour before. I looked at the date time group of the message. Without knowing it, I achieved a reversal of Nigel's dirty work. The sticky part was that his success was in writing. Mine was not.

...

I fumed for an hour while I checked my back, taking the long way home to the safehouse. I drove through The Fens, past huge fields of drained former swampland. It was lovely and flat, mostly cropland with few trees and, it seemed, the only straight roads in Britain. I could see for miles as I checked for tails, but I took no chances. Besides, it allowed me to rehearse what I was going to say to Nigel.

I found him alone in the kitchen, scarfing large portions of the leftover ham.

"You son of a bitch," I said. "What the hell do you think you're doing going to my boss behind my back?"

He spluttered a few upper-class noises, then managed a word or two along the lines of, "Who me?"

"You know very well what you did," I said. "You called my boss."

"No, no I didn't," he insisted. Perhaps the sudden fear in his eyes had something to do with the carving knife I had picked up from the sink. "I only talked to him briefly about that idea I had. Really. That's all."

"Yeah, right. What idea?"

I could see he didn't want to tell me. I carved myself a slice from the ham in front of him. I couldn't help it if the blade just happened to be pointing at his black heart.

"What idea?" I said again.

"Just a small suggestion, the one I told you about early this morning," he said. Nervousness painted his face bright red, and his eyes refused to make contact with mine. They were busy watching the blade.

"Enlighten me again." I vaguely remembered him spouting some ridiculous scheme when all I wanted was sleep.

"What if we had that detonator, *lurve*? What if we could take out anybody we want with a hundred percent reliability? We wouldn't need specialists."

I had to agree I was in a dirty business. He saw my brain work. I can't play poker worth a shit. He began a long string of what-ifs. I managed to insert a question here and there.

"Collateral damage," I said.

He shrugged. "You're always going to have collateral damage."

All well and good unless you are the collaterally damaged.

"Verification."

"We'll verify. Of course, we'll verify, *lurve*."

Of course, you will. Personal vendettas or just plain incompetence never happen in a bureaucracy.

"I'm not your love!" I waved the knife at him.

Allies be damned.

He put up his hands in defense and lost some color, but then sputtered an outline of his plan for accomplishing this utopia. As I listened, I knew I'd never be any kind of love or even like to him. Maybe simmering hate, but that would be best-case.

The man was nuts.

"Anyway," he said, "your boss wants you to cooperate with me on this."

"Did he say that?"

Nigel didn't have much of a poker face, either. More of a sunburned blowfish face.

"He said something to you," he said, "or you wouldn't have come in here swearing at me like a fishwife."

I reflected a moment, hating Nigel in his brief minor triumph. I went over every word of Frank's message. It had burned itself into my memory.

"Did you tell him about Rutherford?" I asked.

"Well, no, I did not. I just told him about your whining in general."

That searing internal blast of aha! along with an accompanying boatload of anger clarified the rest of the message for me. Frank had given me an order concerning the more ordinary costs of SIEGE, a properly verified, diplomatically cleared operation put together by our allies. He was specifically telling me not to join in Nigel's goofy ad hoc bid for glory. And I now had it verbally straight from Frank that Rutherford was my priority.

"Who picked Rutherford?" I asked.

I could see wheels turning behind Nigel's eyes.

"I don't recall," he lied.

So Nigel picked her. "Why?"

There were sputters and eye rolls before he managed "Um. She. Um. I didn't know she was a woman! The list of names just gave initials. She's an electrical engineer, a military commander, for God's sake, how was I to know? Tell me that. She's got the chops to be believable and she's agreeable. She's perfect for God's sake!"

Agreeable like the dangle in Chicago had been agreeable. Instinct told me somehow this little piece of incompetence was part of the puzzle. Instinct, and the rising hysteria in Nigel's voice. He knew it, too.

I smiled. When I raised the knife for another slice of ham, Nigel watched the blade and blanched completely, red face to white, just as the team walked through the kitchen door to see it. Sweet.

I had a fraction of a second to enjoy the spectacle of him running away from me and out the door, spouting nonsense about things to do.

Mack rummaged in the refrigerator while Charlie and Louis arranged themselves at the big farm table. Steve grabbed the last of the ham and headed back to the drawing room to watch the sensors.

I stood by the sink, savoring my momentary illusion of power. Mack closed the refrigerator door, demanded lunch, and even snapped his fingers at me.

I had just vanquished one son of a bitch. I was ready to take on the next.

"What?" I said. "Your arm broken?"

"You say you are competent," he said. "Get me some competent lunch, woman."

He spat the last word. I was already on top of old Smokey, and it was about to blow.

"Get it yourself, maaaan." I stretched out that last word, giving it all the contempt I had in me, which was considerable. I got the cold blue glare that has made the man famous in certain unsavory circles.

"But I am not an award-winning cook," he said slowly.

"Neither am I."

"But you are."

I did not like his growing confidence on the topic of me, a subject I hold dear and very, very private, especially in, again, certain unsavory circles. Even more, I became more than uneasy as he became very still.

"You won first place for your pickles when you were, let me see," he lifted his chin a fraction as if to calculate something, "thirteen years old."

It had been a point of pride back then at the Nebraska State Fair. Now, and here, not so much. But I never turn down an invitation to spar.

"So what do you want pickled for lunch?" I asked. "Your balls?"

He smiled ever so slowly. Never a good sign.

"Why don't you wear the pink chiffon dress you wore to the prom when you were sixteen?" he said. "Will it not fit? Did your date like it, the one who stood no higher than your shoulder? Did he offer to take it off of you? Did he force it off of you? Did he succeed?"

I caught his sideways glance at Louis.

"And tell us about the baby you had at seventeen," he continued. "Was your prom date the father? Why did the baby die? Did he kill your baby? Is that why you prefer the company of violent men?

Are we sufficiently violent for your tastes? So no husband, no baby, no kitchen drudgery, no warm body on a cold night, and no strings to tie you down. Empty. No longer so awkward, but still so empty, and always at risk by your own poor choices."

Geez, these guys knew how to gather intel.

I stalked out the door and stood shaking in the hallway. Crying was not an option, but I was so very tired. An arm came around my shoulders and I looked up at Louis. He was rested for a change. The circles under his eyes had lightened, but were the eyes full of concern, or was I just imagining it?

He led me upstairs to the room he used. I protested. He made me lie down, covered me with a blanket, and said, "I will wake you in three hours."

He was babysitting his babysitter.

He stopped at the door. "You should not enter the cage like a matador, *mon cher*. You must tame Misha not goad him, because you will have no chance against him that way. He will know how best to hurt you."

TWELVE

I fell asleep in an instant and awoke again an instant later. Steve was on top of me, busy with the button on my jeans and relishing the fight I was putting up.

"Fuck, Steve," I said.

"That's the general idea." He nuzzled my neck.

"Get off me, you son of a bitch," I fought furiously against a multi-level black belt martial artist and tried not to think about the odds.

"It's my turn," he said as he covered my mouth with his. My sports bra slipped upward, with my struggle only aiding the effort.

I felt a weight shifting on the bed.

"A little fucking privacy would be nice," said Steve, breaking the kiss. As my t-shirt finished coming off over my head, I looked up into a pair of hard blue eyes and knew I was sunk.

"There is no privacy on this team," said Charlie. He was sitting with his back against the headboard and legs stretched out alongside our battleground.

I continued to fight, found an opening, and bit Steve's arm.

"Ow! Fuck," said Steve. "Don't distract me, Charlie."

"This is not a good idea."

I agreed with Charlie.

"You want a threesome?" said Steve.

For the first time in this op, I wasn't just afraid. I was terrified.

"No, I want her gone. We will all be dead by tomorrow if we cannot behave as a team."

"So let's team up with a threesome."

"My purpose was to convince her to leave," said Charlie. "To show her she has no chance against us. What is your purpose?"

His immediate purpose was to remove my jeans. They were coming down steadily.

"Pure payback," said Steve.

I was in the fight of my life and had no contribution to make to the conversation besides a frenzied effort to keep my pants on. He pinned one hand above my head.

"For what?" said Charlie.

"The nickname, for one thing."

"It would not have stuck if it were not apt. You do look like a teddy bear."

Steve paused to glare at him.

"Okay. You are not a teddy bear. You only look like one," said Charlie, hands raised. "What other reason?"

"She belongs to The Section. They all want to do this, so this is for them. They made my life hell after CETUS WEDGE, so this is to them. Pick one."

"Fuck, Steve. What have you and I been doing the last few days? Certainly not concentrating on coming out of the operation alive. How will my father ever trust you after this?"

There was a pause, then a nip at my neck, next to the one from Charlie, then a sigh, and finally, "Shit." Steve removed his fingers, let go of my hand, and rolled off me. He headed for the door.

Charlie looked down at me with a raised eyebrow and smug expression before following Steve.

I contemplated a career change while putting my clothes back on, sobbing quietly and thinking about flight schedules out of Heathrow. This was the lowest I had ever been, even counting all that had happened in Nebraska, every crazy group of villains I had dealt with on the job, all the dirt and the violence and the pain. This was the worst. I hadn't been fully penetrated, but near enough and now put in mortal dread of it. And I knew it was still not the best way to hurt me, as Louis would say. I was ready to pack and get out before that happened.

Then a spark of anger lit a slow burn in me. I had struggled and fought for so long to do this impossible job and was about to be robbed of it by two testosterone-crazed delinquents with hot and cold reasons for wanting to make me sorry to be a woman. I am not sorry. I'm glad of it and unashamed of what I consider to be my strength, not weakness.

I decided I preferred Steve's hot reasoning. I was indeed a pain in the ass in The Section, but they would nonetheless consider me one of theirs if something happened to me. And they did bully Steve without mercy. It was all within the bounds of human behavior, and I could deal with it.

Charlie's cold calculation was not. There was no room for mercy in it. Circumstances might limit him, but compassion did not. He was indeed more dangerous than his father.

As I curled tightly into a ball, with unending silent tears descending to the pillow, I remembered Diane Rutherford. I was the only person, besides Louis perhaps,—and only perhaps—who wanted her to live. My resolve to stay and struggle solidified even as I allowed myself the luxury of falling asleep while a complete basket case.

I woke when I felt the all too familiar weight of someone sitting on the mattress. I had learned fight was impossible, uncurled myself, and launched into flight. A hand held my t-shirt, stopping me before I could get a foot on the floor. Louis took both my shoulders and turned me to face him. He sat exactly as Charlie had done but with longer legs and held me firmly while he examined my face. I knew my eyes would be puffy and my reaction would be telling. I also could not hide the trepidation in my mind that I was in for another session of intimidation and payback, this time with the most formidable foe of all, precisely because I did not want him as an enemy.

He sighed. "Did Steve succeed?"

Of course he knew, I realized. They all instinctively knew where everybody else was. It meant Mack knew, as well.

"Only as far as Charlie did," I said as if the word 'only' had any use at all in this context.

"Was there a reason?"

"Payback."

He nodded. "A grudge, then. That was also my reason."

"They had an entire fucking conversation while… while…" I felt the tears burning my sore eyes again.

He took a clean handkerchief from his pocket and dabbed my face with it. We were surrounded by filth and squalor and he smelled like the unwashed, unshaven, broken-nosed killer he was, but he had a clean handkerchief in his pocket. Go figure. At least he had it until it came in contact with the mascara streaming down my face. He then required me to recount the entire fucking conversation, in those words, as closely as possible to the original.

"Charlie is right," he said. "You should leave."

I did not mention Diane, the survival of the team—of far lesser importance to me right then—or the survival of my career. "I won't let them destroy me," I said.

He gave me an inimical look and said coolly, "I am one of them. If you stay you likely will be destroyed."

"If I go, I most certainly will be."

"You did not fight my kiss as you did those two. Why?"

How to explain desire? I considered the question before answering, "Your kiss was an offer. Theirs was a taking."

"Sometimes," he said, "a man must risk being mistaken in order to create the offer."

"Oh, we often want men to try. We always want the right to decline."

"I guarantee you will not decline the next time I try." He smacked my thigh, swung his feet to the floor, and said, "Go. Make yourself presentable before you come downstairs. Misha will know what happened anyway, but you should try some concealment if only to save Steve a serious tongue-lashing."

Tongue lashing? If I had my way, he'd be beaten to a pulp.

THIRTEEN

Looking refreshed and presentable, but not feeling it, I entered the drawing room feeling rather chuffed that I was still alive. Everybody was there. Louis sat back in one of the wingback chairs facing the sole source of heat, the fireplace burning a small heap of coal. He was reading the latest transcripts of various taps on everybody's private lives.

Charlie sat in another chair farther back from the fire, glued to the sensor console. It occurred to me that cold was his natural element. I had an uncle who would have said, "That boy ain't right." It was not a comforting thought. Steve lay sprawled along the three-legged sofa, drifting in and out of sleep.

Mack occupied the other wingback chair by the fire, cleaning his weapon. Despite their current difficulties with each other, the group acknowledged Mack and Louis as the senior decision-makers and treated them accordingly. When they weren't busy throwing them against walls to prevent murder, that is.

Nigel was making a new pot of coffee. This explained why everybody ignored me. I was comfortable with that, but I forced myself into a renewed dedication to the job at hand and decided it was time to call a meeting.

I stood before the fire, enjoying the warmth on my backside, and screwed up my courage to address the room. After a few polite starts that went nowhere and interested no one because evidently, I was invisible, I brought out my command voice.

"Listen up! We are going to discuss this op using The Method to see whether we can determine the most helpful hypotheses to use in going forward."

Too many big words. I tried again.

"I'm talking about the various steps we should run the information through, like examining assumptions, quality of information, potential for change, and so on."

"That's analysis," said Nigel. "It's what the women do. We're operatives. We don't have time for that shit."

Charlie raised an eyebrow at his use of the word 'we' and turned up one corner of his lips in a half smile that made me concerned for Nigel's safety. Almost concerned, I should say. I would be fully concerned if I cared more.

Mack looked up from his gun and contemplated my face. It is the best word to describe that searching stare. I had used eyedrops, powder, eye shadow, and mascara creatively, but his blue eyes were too intent. I began to stutter.

"If... f... f w... we can get a firm grasp on what we know about Cú Chulainn we may be able to identify him and take him out before he meets Rutherford. We should start by examining our assumptions. What's the most rock-solid thing we think we know about Cú Chulainn?"

Steve, bless his black heart, broke the ice for me. "His tradecraft is perfect."

Mack tore his searching gaze from his son's studied impassivity and transferred it to Steve, who knew it and whose face immediately told Mack everything he wanted to know.

"Evidence?" I asked.

"We don't know who the fuck he is." Steve had decided to brave it out.

There was a quiet chuckle all around, except Mack, whose eyes were on Louis.

"What else?" I continued.

"He's Irish," said Nigel with a smirk.

"Again, what's our evidence for that?" I felt the cold blue gaze back on me.

"He blows up Englishmen," said Steve.

Nigel bit his lip before saying, "Teague, the cutout, is unquestionably Irish."

"But couldn't Cú Chulainn be a solo specialist working for the IRA?" I said. "Couldn't they just hire him from time to time? It might explain the impossibly deep cover."

"The IRA is not sufficiently funded to hire a specialist of this class," said Louis. "He is in house."

"It is always about money with you!" exploded Mack. He threw down the patch he had been threading onto a cleaning rod. His gun was in pieces; *thank heaven for small mercies*, but the knife was still somewhere on him.

Steve moved in front of Louis and Charlie in front of Mack before the next breath and I was smack dab in the middle. I heard expletives in three languages used with imagination and ingenuity.

"You put your filthy hands on her to betray me, you son of a bitch!"

"You were fucking indecent, the both of you, every morning at breakfast, she with her blushes and you smiling, damn you, smiling! All the time smiling!"

Evidently, smiling was something not generally done at the breakfast table at Vasily's Carpet. I could relate. I grew up on a farm. There was a lot more back and forth about how disgusting they both were. Again, I could relate, until Louis pointed to me.

"She agrees with me," said Louis. "This had nothing to do with you."

That's not exactly what I said, but explanations were superfluous under that blue gaze. "What does it have to do with, Miss Kemp?" Mack asked softly, politely, with his hands in fists and a vein standing out along the side of his scarred neck. "Is it your theory," he spat the word, "that my wife was asking for it? Did she wear her dress too short? Was there too much makeup? Did she provoke his lust?"

"Of course not," I said with some vehemence. I noticed Charlie give Steve a signal with the smallest eye movement and Steve hustled Louis out of the room to do a perimeter check. I was left under the incredibly still stare of four blue eyes, with Nigel the only other person in the room. He was busily making himself as invisible as possible by trying not to breathe.

"You will tell me," said Mack, "what you think this is about."

I had no idea what it was about. I had gone through the looking glass so many times all I had in my brain was the phrase, *off with her head*. So I was left with pulling something out of my ass. Now, it seems perfect and profound. At the time, it was a pathetic evasion that was likely to get me killed in the next instant.

"Listen to his words and his voice," I said. "They tell you why it happened."

He gave a disgusted snort, picked up the pieces of his gun, and told Nigel to meet him in the dining room with the layout of the place we thought would be the venue of Cú Chulainn's demise.

I was left alone with just the young pair of blue eyes vacuuming my mind until it became a void.

"No fists thrown," I said, trying to smile. "Nothing unsheathed or unholstered. That's progress, don't you think?"

Charlie's stillness as he regarded me was freakier than his father's had been. "You are a disruption," he said finally. "If I were in charge, you would be dead now."

There is no snappy comeback for this, nor any assertive rejoinder, nor suitable question even. Groveling for mercy was beneath my dignity; even if I thought it might help, I would not demean myself. I clamped down on my expression like a drill sergeant with a platoon of conscripts, willing myself to show no concern. I tried a slight glare of defiance but could not help the hard swallow my throat demanded from me.

He was satisfied with that, the bastard, and walked away.

FOURTEEN

Keegan was a very dull boy. He hadn't called Diane or come over for two days. We knew he was in town because of the very light touch Nigel had on his car. This put us in boredom mode for a couple of hours that late afternoon and we used it according to our various talents. I organized the refrigerator. Louis taught Steve how to program the device. Mack didn't kill Louis. I didn't kill Nigel. Charlie didn't kill me. All in all, things were working out.

I took a few quiet moments to contemplate Nigel's plan for getting his grubby little hands on the detonator. I came up with questions I should have asked him at the time. Could that even be done, stealing from his own team, without getting himself killed? He said he had another team ready to help him, led by some guy named Stan. Did he intend to set up a different specialist team to attack his own? It made no sense. But so far on this op, that was nothing new. There were too many treacherous intentions mixing with sharp objects for my comfort.

Louis read more transcripts from Life of Diane and grilled me about her charms. I reminded myself this was business; the man meant a promotion for me, nothing more.

"What is this word you use, twinkly?" he said. "What does it mean?"

"Twinkly. Her eyes are twinkly. They twinkle."

"Then why do you not say that? Why not say only 'her eyes twinkle' instead of 'her eyes are twinkly.'"

"Because it is more than an occasional verb," I said. "It is a quality of the eyes that is always there. The eyes don't *do* a twinkle; they *are* twinkly."

"And you are strange."

Evidently, strange was on the menu today. Louis was so delighted not to be dead (yet) he invited me to celebrate with him. Upstairs. Where he had some etchings to show me.

I declined with a sigh several times that afternoon, each episode accompanied by heavy breathing. On my part.

"Forget it," I said finally. "You need a bath."

"We can bathe together." His dark eyes twinkled. Verb-wise.

"What about Diane?"

He wrinkled his forehead. "She is words on a page; you are real." His hands were busy kneading my bottom.

"But strange," I said.

He put his arm around my waist. "Oh yes, very strange. Come. I shall die in a few hours. My last wish is yours to grant."

How many times have I heard that line?

The tub was in the bedroom he had been using. It stood on claw feet by the boarded-up window, was long and deep, and had two faucets specializing in freezing and scalding water. We soaped and scrubbed and had a water fight. There were no towels, but it didn't matter. We dried off naturally on the bed, staying warm by making love like we had been together forever. It was so joyous an act, I had no time to regret the reality around us.

He asked obliquely if I had ever done this before, as he kissed my neck. I was confused at first. I've never been mistaken for a virgin, even when I was one. But he wanted to know if I'd ever had sex with my team members before. I didn't answer right away because by this time he was sucking one nipple and playing with the other and my mind was elsewhere. No, I gasped. Why? He reached my navel, with both hands on my breasts, every caress making me ache for him. *What is this, an essay exam?* I don't find specialists all that attractive as a rule, I told him. I felt each touch of his tongue on all the nerves of my body simultaneously, a deliciously warm electrical charge buzzing everywhere, but especially between my legs. But you find me attractive, he wanted to know as he reached the zone of awesomeness.

I find you incredible.

I might have screamed that last bit.

After a lot more incredible awesomeness, in several positions and all with vigor, we flopped, side by side. I glowed. He snored.

"I told Mack you never meant to steal his wife," I said during a break in the snoring.

"You did what?"

"I told him this morning before I left to meet Diane."

Louis chuckled and looked at me. "No wonder he is so fond of you. Misha would consider the topic to be not your business. What did he say?"

Louis was eager and curious, like a child. I suspected, no I knew, I was in this too deep. But I could not explain, even to myself, what was wrong here, and I had begun to think our collective survival depended on knowing what it was.

"He said something like it might be true in one sense but not every sense and anyway I was as stupid as you, but he shouldn't expect anything more from a spinster like me."

Louis' brow wrinkled. "What did that mean?"

I shrugged. "I asked him that."

Louis patted my thigh. "You are so brave," he said. "Sometimes I think you are not very bright."

"I think the world of you, too, Stud Muffin."

We then discussed a string of American idioms, each one prompted by an explanation of the one before it. After I inadvertently expanded the never-ending list by telling him I was no fuddy-duddy, I steered us back on course. "Do you want to know what he said?"

He nodded.

"He said when you hurt her, you hurt him. Thus, you betrayed him."

"He has said that before," said Louis. "It is not true. He is not her. She is not him. And I did not hurt her. I raped her."

"I did tell him it seemed he was more concerned about some boundary around his property than he was with compassion for her."

And I'm not convinced you raped her, I thought, but I kept my own counsel on that.

"I do not understand," he said.

I spoke carefully. "I think men can behave as if harm to someone they love, especially a woman, is an affront to their manhood rather than a crime against the woman."

"But everyone is upset when a loved one is harmed. It is a good way to intimidate a man. Threaten his women."

"Yes, but especially in cases of the rape of a woman, its aftermath can be more about the man than the traumatized person herself. This is the impression I have from the entire team. Even you."

He looked at me with question marks above his eyebrows.

"I can't believe you would ever rape a woman. Seduce, yes. Rape, no." I said, not sure if I could ever get him to understand, or for that matter, if I fully understood. It made me nervous not knowing the limits of this conversation.

"We are all capable of all things, good and bad," he said. "Rape is rage. It is always rage, against one person, against all people, against powerlessness."

"Powerless against what?"

He was silent.

"You could have just beaten her," I said, "or shot her. Why rape?"

He did not answer for a moment, and I expected a repeat of the 'best way to hurt her' stuff. I was wrong.

He said, "She does not like me."

There are so many reasons, so many aggravating factors, so many mitigating factors, that classifying any given rape is stupid.

"It always boils down to an act of violence," I said. Aloud this time. "Even when the victim submits to it."

"I am a violent man," he said. "Why is everybody so surprised?"

"But rape? It deranges the very core of a person's identity. Other assaults are exterior; rape is interior. It is monstrous and you are not a monster."

He turned his head to look at me. Black hair against a white pillow. His eyes, also nearly black, regarded me.

"I kill to live," he said. "Of course, I am a monster. Again I ask, why are you surprised?" He got up and started looking for his clothes. "And besides, Alex should not have told Misha about it. I blame her for all the trouble."

You are a unique form of bastard, sweetie, and.... I lost that particular train of thought when her name hit whatever brain center filing cabinet it is that stores such things in an intelligence agent. I had known it all along, of course, if I had been paying attention, but the spoken name made the connection real and present.

"Alex?" I might have screeched it. "Not Sobieski's widow?" I had thought it was the history, from one doomed dangle to the latest one with the twinkly eyes, that complicated the current madness. This threw a lot more puzzle pieces into place. My intuition had been spot on.

He nodded. "It was a surprise to everybody. They married last autumn. Vasily and Katya were not yet cold in their graves."

I wondered why a killer who faces sudden death himself at almost every moment could be so bitter about these two deaths. Or were the dead making themselves silently convenient for hiding the living people who bugged him?

"I thought Alex and Misha did not get along," I said.

"They didn't. They don't. They argue. But they are best friends as well as lovers. They are disgusting."

"Louis," I said, "you know she didn't have to tell him. He reads minds."

He looked at me for a long moment.

"He was not reading your mind in the kitchen today, Barbara. I found that information about you. We gather as much as we can on everyone in your section. Did you think you were the only ones who created files?"

"But the dress?"

"A picture in your high school yearbook."

I digested this slowly, suddenly conscious of the stretch marks on my belly, the bullied scars on my psyche. Had he seen them? Should I tell him that the farm girl in that picture and I were not the same person anymore? I waited until I had control of a threatening teardrop before turning my head to look at him.

He gazed at me without judgment.

"But you are correct," he said. "Alex did not have to tell him."

FIFTEEN

I made sure the long upstairs hallway was empty before scooting out and across to the room where I had stowed my suitcase. I was in no condition to exchange how d'ya do's with anybody who might nod in a friendly way to a tall woman topped by a nest of dark hair hanging in snarls and with a rather satisfied look on her face. I carried my clothes and did not bother to close the bathrobe Louis had loaned me for the twenty-foot scurry.

I was within five feet of my destination when a door opened to my left. I jumped like a six-foot bunny. It was Mack. When I saw his face, I prepared to run. Prepared as in releasing all the adrenaline necessary for the flight portion of the human response to an emergency. The fight portion was out of the question. For one thing, I was pretty much naked. Funny how being naked makes you feel especially vulnerable—as if a few yards of cotton or wool or rayon or viscose are the ultimate talisman against a bullet or Mack's knife.

Flight was also not an option. Before my brain could motivate my feet, I was against the wall, pinned by Mack's hand around my throat.

He was furious. Not with jealousy, of course. I can feel a man's interest as palpably as a soft blanket on a thorn bush. Mack genuinely couldn't stand the sight of me. He said some things I could not answer because it takes breath to operate the vocal cords and my breath was absent for the moment. His questions all boiled down to a confused "Why?"

He loosened his grip just enough for me to croak an answer.

"He needed comfort," I said.

We both became aware at the same instant that Charlie had come up the stairs and stood to my left, Mack's right, staring.

"What are you looking at?" said Mack.

"A scene I remember in Vasily's Carpet," said Charlie, "the morning after we came back from Chicago last year. But it was Louis who had Alex by the throat. He said what you said. And when he let her speak, that was how she answered."

Mack glared at him but let me go suddenly and pushed past his son, leaving us to stare at each other in the empty hall.

Charlie's face was expressionless.

I already knew his opinion and let go of another involuntary hard swallow. It registered with him and he let me squeeze past him.

...

"This is not a good idea," I insisted. "If we meet Diane in public and Cú Chulainn gets wind of us, he will fly!"

Steve put on his patient look. "Let me explain this again, Barb. We don't know how soon Teague will ask for the demo. If he wants it tomorrow morning, we're sunk unless we do this tonight. I have to brief the colonel. So I must be introduced."

"I've described you to her," I said. I picked up my comb again. My hair was still a giant tangle. We sat on a sofa in the drawing room. Charlie sat across from us in a decrepit leather wingback chair that leaned on a crooked leg. Despite the squalor around him, he looked like he belonged to the world of leather chairs and fine cigars. Louis fiddled with his gadgets in the transcript room across the hall. Nigel and Mack were doing the perimeter rounds, checking the sensors.

It had begun as a peaceful evening. I should have had plenty of time to untangle my hair, but Nigel's people picked up a phone call and rushed the transcript to us. Keegan had asked Diane out to dinner.

"Will your description of me suffice when I approach her at two in the morning?" said Steve.

"Okay, but I still don't see why I have to go," I said. "I could blow the whole thing. It's dangerous." I winced as I pulled at a knot. As that resolved under my comb, the one in my stomach grew. I did not want to get in a car with Steve.

He and Charlie exchanged a private comment by rolling their eyes.

"It's dangerous to the op," I insisted. "I don't mean to me personally!" I could see they did not understand. "Look, Steve, Cú Chulainn himself is going to be there, and if he's as good as you say he is, he'll know I'm not your type. He may even know me from an earlier op. I've been around for a dozen years in this business. It's too risky."

There was a serious silence.

"What makes you think Cú Chulainn will be there?" asked Charlie.

"He'll want to check out the colonel himself. If he's that good, I mean. If I were Cú Chulainn, that's what I would do."

They both blew air through their teeth.

"Well, let's thank our luck you are not Cú Chulainn, then," said Charlie.

...

I received no oohs or ahs as I came downstairs to the men waiting in the hall. Nobody said a word about my flawless jade-green dress or the way my thick chocolate hair swung freely about my waist. Instead, I heard, "Come on, damn it," and, "Where the hell is she?"

They stood at the foot of the stairs fidgeting with their ties or staring at the front door, hands in pockets. Louis had shaved. He wore a clean suit and looked like the man of my dreams, tall, handsome and tall. He smiled at me. Mack glared at me, evidently relishing his role as the man of my nightmares. Everybody, even Nigel, bless him, looked presentable, though only Steve and I would be seen in public.

As we filed out the door, Nigel mumbled into my ear, "New competitive edge, is it? Offering them, or at least the Frenchman, something other babysitters can't?"

I looked him in his bloodshot eyes. "Why? Were you wishing you could offer the same?"

It was an offhand remark, meant as an insult, as it would be to many of the men in my business, but Nigel's reaction surprised me. I hoped I had hidden my surprise better than he masked his blush. Well, well, well, my dear enemy, I thought. Now I have you by the balls. One word, one hint from me, and fifteen years of service are over in the space of a sigh. They won't be likely to go near you, except maybe to cut your throat.

I found myself reluctantly admiring my rival. To spend fifteen years near these guys, especially Mack the mind reader, while giving no hint of his secret took considerable professional skill. I suddenly had newfound respect for Nigel but stashed my ultimate weapon in a safe but accessible place in my memory, in case I might someday need to use it.

If our new shared understanding altered my attitude toward Nigel, it seemed like it did the same for his attitude toward me, or at least his behavior. He respectfully opened the car door for me. Steve and I were taking Nigel's Jaguar. The others would follow, Mack and Charlie in the Mercedes, Louis and Nigel in the heap.

As he started the car, Steve began our evening together with a lecture. He is one of those drivers who cannot maintain a steady acceleration. Or maybe his topic made him start and stop without reason until I was glad my stomach was empty because it was threatening to spew like a volcano. Unlike his driving, Steve's words came smoothly, punctuated by rhetorical question marks. Did I know how disgusting it was to see me and Louis smiling at each other? Like a couple of teenagers at a school dance? And anyway, didn't I realize the man was made of stone? Or, was I some kind of masochist? Huh? Did I know he's a rapist? Or doesn't that cut any wood with a feminist unless the victim is also a feminist? Wives and mothers don't count?

"That's rich coming from you," I said. "As I recall, none of that mattered to you a few hours ago. Also, he's paying for it, more than he would in a court of law and maybe soon he'll pay a lot more than that." I did not mention my reservations about the truth of the accusation. Even Louis was still maintaining his guilt, though I had challenged him on it several times. I think it was the hesitation in his answers, among other things, that made me continue to question it.

"Not enough," said Steve. "He's not paying enough. You haven't met her. It's like destroying innocence itself, which does not apply to you. And none of us, least of all Misha, appreciates you giving Louis a conjugal visit."

"That's especially rich coming from all you guys, Steve, considering that for all practical purposes, Mack raped her in the first place."

He slammed on the brakes and skidded to a stop on the side of the road.

"What the fuck are you talking about? What rape? She was Sobieski's wife in the first place. In the second place, you don't know shit about them."

"I know more than you think, Steve. I actually read the files, remember that about me?"

And pillow talk is the richest source of nutrition in espionage, but I left this little bit out. I was already rueing the fact that I brought it up at all. Information like this loses its value when it is spread too thin.

"Tell me," he said when he made the pillow talk connection.

I hesitated. "It's not pillow talk," I said. "He told me during one of our watches together. You can probably get it just by asking."

He grabbed my throat so fast, it took my breath away, and so hard, there was no way to suck in some more. He released a little pressure but kept his hold and said again, "Tell me."

I knew he was capable of violence, but it had now become his go-to reaction in all scenarios. I set aside my impulse to horde the information he wanted and told him, between gasps, about the card game some fourteen years before.

Charlie walked past the headlights to my side of the car. Steve reached to operate the electric window. "What?" he said.

"It looks like there is a problem," said Charlie. "I'll be happy to help you kill her anytime, though I know you're quite capable."

"Yeah, thanks," said Steve. "Not this time."

He let go and I massaged my throat.

I was tempted to bring up my misgivings, about doomed dangles, about questions of consent and rape versus seduction, among other things, but Steve had become an alien creature. As a fellow babysitter he might have been able to view the issue in a practical way, but he was no longer a babysitter, and I had the bruises to prove it. As for making some kind of human connection, that was foreclosed by the subject. He was the most male individual I had ever met and had shown me too much of his intentions towards me. I would get further by explaining Cinderella to a Martian.

...

I had to duck through the low medieval doorway at the Cock and Bull, or whatever the hell they call it, in Godmanchester. The ceiling was not comfortable either, with low-hanging beams that threatened my dignity every time my forehead connected with one. I tried to stay within the troughs between them, but that sometimes made me move sideways like a spider crab. I don't remember a time when I wasn't the tallest girl in the family or the class or the room. I'm used to being conspicuous. Diane and I were bound to be remembered in that room that night, and I worried about it. Cú Chulainn would be there for sure, whether Steve and Charlie thought so or not.

I thought I'd give it one more try to warn Steve. If I failed, hey, I would have done my job. So I tried to catch his eye as we made our way to the bar, but something or someone else was way ahead of me. The alarm on his face said it all. He was in some trouble of his own.

SIXTEEN

"**D**an!"

Steve turned white. I thought he was going to faint. An enormous figure moved across the room toward us, ducking ceiling beams, with a wide grin and outstretched arms.

Steve stood frozen. I prepared to catch him on his way to the floor.

"Whaddayadooinhere?" The sound echoed off the walls and the booming voice continued, "Haven't seen you since pilot training!"

The giant grabbed Steve's hand and threatened to pump his arm off at the shoulder. Then came a back slap and "Whaddayadrinkin?"

Steve fell back on his training and did the only thing he could. He went on the offensive, returning the backslap, getting loud, and sticking to his legend.

"Mace! Great to see you! Small world! I'm over here working for Hughes. What are you doing these days?"

There followed a loud exchange in which one was flying the TR-1, the designation of the U-2 in Europe, and loving it, and the other was Steve's total fiction. I wondered, was he loving it?

This was a surprise, something people in my field do not like, and it was monumental. The situation deepened my already gloomy prognostication about the evening. Mace was a recent boyfriend of Diane's. For some reason, he didn't count as being of interest in Nigel's professional opinion. But the man's presence now, which would have been expected if there had been just the lightest touch on his activity, was threatening the entire op. *Oh, Nigel.*

A woman I had not yet noticed joined Mace, putting an immediate and rather depressing damper on the boisterous reminiscing. Mace began introductions.

"Fiona!"

I don't think Mace could speak without an exclamation point.

"Fiona, look who's here! An old buddy of mine from pilot training...."

"Steve Donovan," Steve interrupted, his voice low and smooth as whipped butter. He took her hand, bowed over it, and kissed the back of it. Hokey, but brilliant.

The maneuver held her attention, giving Mace time to mask his shock. His performance also was flawless. "Steve and I go way back," he said without a hiccup.

Within five minutes I knew Diane was a fool to give this guy up. It wasn't just his enormity, though being tall is always a desirable manly trait in my book. It was his hearty goodwill. His black eyes sparkled with friendship. His wide Polynesian face smiled easily. He had a quick wit and a firm handshake, making you feel like he was on your side. It almost made me forget Louis.

If Diane made a mistake in letting him go, Mace wasn't doing any better in his choice of a replacement. I took an instant dislike to Fiona and found myself judging her mousy brown hair, sensible shoes, and nondescript dress printed with one of those little flower patterns. I suppose she was pretty in a way, but I see no beauty in domestic doormats. Why Mace would trade the stately Diane for this ostensibly fertile stick figure was beyond me. The worst thing about her was she was not stupid, as I would have expected from household breeding stock. I watched her observe the room sharply. I wondered if the homely manner was a put-on designed to capture one large American pilot. She seemed to have succeeded. He was very attentive.

Diane and Keegan showed up and we went through the introductions a second time with everybody acting surprised to see everybody else. I searched the room for Cú Chulainn. Who could it be? The bar was filling quickly. It was hard to tell because just as I had predicted, Diane and I drew more than the usual stares. I figured Cú Chulainn would not openly stare and contemplated the few men who did not seem to notice us, but none of them seemed likely; too old, too young, too out of shape.

We did the ladies-to-the-ladies room routine, all together now, the three of us, leaving the men to discuss airplanes. Or, I should say, leaving Teague to listen while Steve and Mace discussed airplanes. I don't think Steve noticed I had left or even remembered why he was there. He seemed to think he had come to talk about the TR-1 because that was all he did that night.

Diane and I engaged in a sign language and lip-reading conversation while Fiona was in a stall.

"Him?" said Diane silently.

I nodded.

"When?"

"Tonight."

She nodded.

There was still an evening to get through. A night of fun and frolics before Steve and Diane got to work. Diane had fun. I got the frolics.

When Mace headed down the hallway leading to the toilets, I excused myself again, acting a little tipsy to cover the second trip, and waved Diane back into her seat.

It helped that the hallway was narrow. I had no trouble getting close.

"Hi." I gave him my most knowing (and knowable) smile and swung my hair about my shoulders. I looked up at him. Way up. The man made me feel like a pixie sprite.

"Hi."

Evidently a man of few words, he acted like he wanted to get past me. I did not let him.

"You're a friend of Diane's aren't you?" I said, putting my hand on his arm. "She told me about you. We should have coffee sometime. What about tomorrow?"

"Why?"

"Well, I'm new here and need to meet people. You'd be a good start since we have a friend in common."

"What about your friend Steve?" He lifted his chin toward the pub lounge and stressed the name.

"Oh, him? He's a blind date. I'm not sure we're hitting it off." I gave him a smile that I hoped explained what I meant by hitting it off.

Mace looked down on me with a serious scrutiny that made me glad he flew an airplane armed with a camera. He'd be scary with missiles. He considered for a long time before saying, "My guess is you're some kind of spook and this is official, so yeah, I'll meet you tomorrow or any time you like. Coffee's not necessary. But if I'm wrong and you're just some stranger who wants to talk about me and Diane, I'll pass."

"Fair enough." I said. "Meet me at the SCIF at seven."

"O-seven? Just to be clear," he said.

"Yes. O-seven."

SEVENTEEN

The radio in Nigel's Jaguar stopped working, bringing us down to just two cars. Steve and Louis holed up in the Mercedes to go over the program again, so I was shunted to the heap with the others, parked in a copse near a little village called Abbot's Ripton, a straight radio shot from the base. From the moment they arrived at her apartment at eleven o'clock, we heard every breath Diane and Teague took. They did a lot of breathing.

I was groggy and punch-drunk from fatigue. The few hours of sleep I managed to steal that day were long worn off. I guess that's why I did it. That and the moans and other little noises coming from the radio made me uncomfortable, sitting as I was next to Mack in the back seat behind Nigel and Charlie in front. Maybe it was an unconscious attempt not to listen.

Mack leaned up against the door, huffing or snarling every time I moved, sighing, scowling, and growling at me. I don't like people who do not like me. I don't know why, but it is automatic, and I return that dislike immediately. I suppose it's because I have no patience with people who don't have the good sense to recognize all of my fine qualities. Mack was certainly in that category of person. It was a pity, because he had such a reputation for being a good judge of character, though he was also known to like only very few people.

I knew I was not destined to be one of those people, so I took it as a kind of special license. We sat there in the car with a good two hours of soft-porn listening yet to go, and I felt like I'd been shut into a nail-studded coffin, nails pointing in. When Mack started the snarling nonsense, I decided to give him something to snarl about. I leaned on the other door and stretched out my legs, crowding his. He kicked me. I kicked him back, but softly, kind of deniably, so as not to infuriate him—I knew better than that—but only to irritate. It bothered him when I moved, so I moved a lot. And I flicked my hair around as much as possible. This really sent him up.

Nigel turned around and looked at us in the dark. We were still and silent. He turned back.

I stretched noisily and shook my head again and then remembered where I was and who this guy was next to me. No, Louis is the hothead, I told myself. The reports are unanimous. This one is cold as ice. You cannot goad him, you can only pay him to kill, and even then, you need incontrovertible proof. He had been quite still for some time, with no hissing, so I flicked my hair again, defying my good sense.

Mack grabbed a handful of hair at the back of my head and yanked me down into the seat.

At that moment, Louis knocked on the window and Charlie started the car. Mack let go of my hair and I sat up in a hurry. Teague left Diane's apartment. Steve had an appointment with her at the SCIF immediately. I took the driver's seat in the heap and drove him there while the others went back to the safehouse in the Mercedes. Nigel drove the Jag in mechanically imposed radio silence.

I mulled over whether there would be consequences to my pointing a chair and whip at Mack when Steve came out of the SCIF and took the wheel for the ride home. He started in on me right away. First, he ragged me once again about the whole Louis thing, calling it unprofessional and out of bounds. What are the bounds of professionalism in the killing game, I wondered out loud. Raping your babysitter over a nickname? Is there a code of ethics? Thou wilt not consensually sleep with a specialist, only help him in a firefight? Did Steve have that written on a stone tablet somewhere? Steve had an answer. He always had an answer. Whatever caused failure, he said. Whatever impeded them or threatened them. He looked at me with those melty brown eyes empty of any warm thing, like a glass-eyed teddy bear. Thou shalt not endanger us, was the core of his philosophy.

"Look, Steve," I said finally, keeping my voice as steady as I could. "I've had all I can stand of double standards. I work within the parameters of my personality, just like you and everybody else. You make allowances for the oddities of every male you come into professional contact with, but somehow, I'm supposed to be made of molded plastic like a Barbie doll, both body and soul, no word, no gesture, no thought out of place. It's time you gave me the same breaks you would give a man not made of marble. Quit trying to prove through me that a woman can't do this job. It's not true."

"Of course, a woman can do this job, Barb," he said. "That's not the question. The question is, should she?"

"I think I've contributed. The team is still intact."

"True." He was silent for a moment. "Only just. But you create as many problems as you solve. Maybe the question is not whether another woman should but whether you should."

I smarted at that comment too much to trust myself with an answer.

"You know, Barb, your personality is in the way here. It's not just me and Charlie. Mack can't stand you. That's not healthy, or didn't you know that?"

I grunted and he kept on.

"You are up to your neck in the disintegration of a lifetime relationship. You're more deeply mired in it than you have any right to be. You have been here less than two days, and already you're acting without any real understanding, least of all of what those two are capable of doing to you. Charlie and I are minor league in comparison. Alex knew more, understood more when she met them years ago and she wound up badly hurt, more than even I realized if what you say is true. I'm wondering what's going to happen to you?"

"You're such a comfort, Steve."

We pulled up to the house in silence.

...

I slipped into the safehouse as unobtrusively as I could, staying as still as a flag on the moon with every step, hoping like hell Mack had forgotten about me.

No such luck.

EIGHTEEN

It began when I tried to tell Nigel I needed sleep, asking him as a colleague if he would cover me for the span of forty winks. We were all in the kitchen under bright ceiling lights that made my eyes stream. Nigel stood on my right. I sensed rather than saw Mack step behind me and to my left.

I guess my hair swung when I turned. I guess it hit Mack. I guess he caught it. I saw the light reflected in his knife, my throat held stiff by the grip he had on my hair, and I was sure this was the big It. The next moment, I wished it had been.

Without a sound but for the noise of sheering in my head, a sound from my private nightmares, his knife glided through my hair without effort. That was how sharp he kept it. One swipe, from crown to nape, leaving a four-inch-wide swath no more than an inch long. A curtain of once waist-long hair fell around my feet.

Nobody moved for a long time, or maybe time just halted for a while. I don't know. I was busy crying, silently. Steve, Charlie, and Nigel stood looking at me and Mack, risking only an occasional surreptitious glance at Louis.

My silent tears dropped into the hair on the floor.

"S... sie..." Mack pointed the knife at me, but only to point.

I watched his face redden. He was not threatening me. He wasn't even talking to me. He was talking to Louis.

"*Sie. Ist. Ein. Engel,*" said Louis. The reference to a past event became more clear in his next sarcastic sentence. "You wanted her for yourself. This is a betrayal of me!"

Louis folded his arms and stood defiant, matching fury for fury.

"That is not ..." Before leaving the room, Mack cleared the counter, creating a cascade of pans, dishes, cutlery, and assorted leftovers to the floor in a succession of smashing booms. A jar of coffee broke and scattered its contents to mingle with my late hair.

I lowered my head, letting the tears fall into the mess at my feet. They came faster, and a gasp, not quite a sob, escaped me. A finger under my chin gently lifted my face.

"Come," said Louis. "You need sleep." He took my arm and led me past the three men still standing dumbfounded in the kitchen.

I remember Nigel stepping aside, but the rest was a blur until Louis tucked the covers around me and kissed my forehead.

"In the morning, I will cut your hair properly," he said. "It will look beautiful. You will see."

"No. You can't." Impossibility had become a very real part of my life, "You will be dead. Diane will program the device for Cú Chulainn and then he will kill her, and you will kill him, and Mack will kill you."

He put a finger to my lips. "Go to sleep."

I touched the back of my head. Louis pulled my hand away and I fell asleep.

I had a nightmare that my hair had been cut.

Morning came three hours later. Louis did a tolerable job with the scissors and I tried to look appreciative.

I could feel he was uncomfortable. He worked in an awkward silence. His introductory belligerence that first night was preferable to this, so I thought I'd loosen up the conversation, or more accurately, lack of conversation. Besides, it would stop the snip-snip reverberating through my head.

"So what happened when you kissed her?" I asked a violent man wielding a sharp implement near the nape of my neck.

"I do not want to discuss it," he said. "It is between Misha and me."

"But it began as something between Alex and you."

"I told you …"

"I know, I know. It was about power. You hated her. You were angry. No doubt."

"Yes. It began that way."

"How did it end?"

He faced me, jaw tight, scissors pointed at my nose.

"You are angry with me right now," I said quietly. "Will you rape me, too?"

"Certainly not." He spat the words.

"So how did the kiss end?"

He was getting a little savage with those scissors, but so far only my hair seemed to be suffering.

A great mass of chocolate brown hair fell into my lap before he spoke. "I relented," he said. "Then she relented. Then she said no."

"And you stopped."

I waited.

"Yes. I began angry. I wanted to have my chance with her," he said after a long pause and the removal of a long piece of another swath of my hair. "Everybody has tried, even Charlie. I was never able to. I wanted to see...."

I waited some time, filing away this factoid concerning Charlie, then prompted, "And?"

"She liked the kiss. I could tell. But she said no."

Another long silence before he decided how to tell me what the fuck this was all about.

"Misha knew immediately. Within an hour. She could not hide the fact of the kiss or that she liked it. Most people are transparent to Misha. Alex's mind is completely naked before him and she feels guilt about everything. If she takes the last biscuit she considers herself selfish. We were about to climb into the jet to come here. He saw her guilt, she dropped her eyes, stammered, and trembled."

Louis ran his fingers through his hair and began work on another section of my head, this one around an ear.

"Alex is terrified of Misha," he said. "She has always been so. She loves him, yes, but he frightens her. He frightens most people. They think I am too jolly to be very dangerous, but I am the hasty one, not Misha. She knows he would not hurt her. She knows it here." He pointed to my head, then to his gut. "But here, when he looked at her, she turned to melting snow."

"You told him you raped her to protect her?"

"Yes. No." He yanked away a cut section of my hair savagely. "We did not have time for explanations. There is no room for any complication that does not belong to the operation. We were leaving. We always know we may not live. I did not want him to leave angry with her." Then in a softer voice, "Or for her to wait for him fearing his return."

Until then it was about great sex. At that moment, I fell in love.

"So you told him it was rape so that he would be mad at you and forgive her before he got on the airplane," I said.

"Yes. Even when there is nothing to forgive, such things can take time and assurance, and we did not have those. She did not have them. The kiss was my fault. I could give her this much at least. Also, I was angry with him for being so damned lucky to have her. It was a good way to hurt him. I thought I would explain privately to him when we got here. But he went mad. You saw him. Michael and Steve have kept me alive and now Misha is the unreliable one. It seems maybe it was too good a way to hurt him."

"He knows how lucky he is," I said. "You reminded him how easily such luck is lost. You have to tell him the truth, all of it. Somehow. I might be able to help you wordsmith it, but it will be up to you to say it."

"I do not think the smithing of words will be possible in the time he will allow me to speak," said Louis.

Charlie came in, cutting down the time I could glory in the sad triumph of being right, and I rushed to finish getting dressed. I wore black, like Nigel and the team, but I like to think my turtleneck and clean pair of jeans fit me better. Before I found my jacket, Charlie held me by my shoulders and searched my face.

"How are you?" he said.

Annoyed, was what I wanted to say, and more than a little nervous when you hold me that way.

"Fine," I answered not forgetting what he would have done to this particular disrupting influence.

"You are going to help Louis get away today, right?" He was in earnest. I could see it in those ice-blue eyes. So now he welcomed my disruption? I did not voice this. I did not want to remind him of what he previously thought should be done about me.

I looked at Louis. He stood next to a tall dresser, with one arm on the top, the other in his pants pocket. He seemed to doubt the younger man. "Michael," he said, "what makes you think I want to get away?"

Charlie let me go and faced him. "You've got a chance. I am giving you a chance. You can go solo; her government will help you."

I wasn't so sure about that last part, but I nodded anyway.

Louis played with some coins on top of the dresser.

"I would not last two weeks solo, Michael. I have no judgment. It is your father who has kept us alive until now."

"Give him time to cool down."

"He will not cool down. He will not forgive me."

Charlie bit his lip.

"Alex forgave you," he said. "Papa will, too."

"Alex is a saint," Louis sneered. He picked up two coins and laid them flat again.

"Give him a chance, please, Louis," said Charlie, then in a whisper, "for me?"

Louis studied the coins, glanced at Charlie, sighed, and nodded. "What is your plan?"

As plans go, it was pretty straightforward. I was to move the Jaguar to a spot near the back of the house, hide it in the brush, and wait for Louis there. Charlie made sure I understood it thoroughly and threatened me pretty convincingly if I didn't do as I was told.

After he left the room, I broached again the subject that had occurred to me while I watched Louis's depressed fingering of the coins. He stood with both hands in his pockets now, leaning on that dresser, watching his toe draw circles on the carpet before him.

"You must talk to him," I said.

"He will not listen to me." It seemed more than depression; it was despair.

"He will listen to me," I said, sounding more confident than I felt.

"Barbara, I need to talk to you," Nigel shouted from down the hallway.

Louis caught my arm before I reached the door.

"I am changing Michael's plan," he whispered. "Leave the car and the keys and get away. You must not be near when Misha catches me."

NINETEEN

Nigel hauled me outside through the front door the moment I came downstairs. He led me around the side of the house and through the brush into the stable block. We stepped over rotting planks and dusty loose bricks into a roofless room filled with rotting harnesses. A taller version of Nigel stood there, a bit more fit and with a lesser thickening in the middle suggesting he was only ever so slightly off his game, which was remarkable considering the amount of grey creeping up from his temples. He wore jeans and a sweatshirt and a relaxed upper-class manner that only the British can master.

"This is Stan," said Nigel. "He's SAS."

"Ex-SAS," corrected Stan. "I'm retired. Now I run a school library." Stan's dark eyes conveyed a wry look that matched his half-smile.

"Stan's going to help us get that detonator," said Nigel. "He's got the experience we need, what with being SAS."

"Ex, Nigel," said Stan. "I told you I never saw combat. The timing wasn't right in my career. Too much peace, don't you know? The IRA is pretty formidable, but I was never posted ..."

Before Stan could finish his resume I asked him, "What do you know about Nigel's plan?"

"I know he hopes to steal a gadget from some guys who want to sell it to the IRA."

I looked at Nigel. "You told him about this op?"

"He's cleared. He is SAS."

"Was!" Stan and I said it simultaneously.

"Well, I trust him," said Nigel with an infatuated look in his eyes that told me he was besotted. Stan blushed.

"Nigel," I said slowly and clearly, "if I gave a retired special forces *general* compartmented information, I'd be shipped off to a listening post in an igloo on the Bering Strait. What the fuck do you think you're doing? We're in an op! We're live! But now who knows for how long?"

Nigel began sputtering.

"No, you listen Nigel. Whatever your government may think about this breach, mine expects me to report it, and both governments are fucking sieves so when it gets back to you know who, there is no corner of the world where we can be posted that will be out of range. Have you noticed my haircut, Nigel?"

Stan shuffled and said something along the lines of, um, very... interesting.

But I was in mid-rant and not to be deterred. "You were there when I got this haircut, Nigel, just a few hours ago. Have you forgotten how that knife went through all that thick hair like soft butter? Have you forgotten the look on his face?"

Nigel stood stupefied, but Stan picked it up right away. "Are you saying Nigel's in danger?"

"Yes," I told Stan. "And the guy he wants to steal the device from is the one who gave me the haircut."

"Not from them," said Nigel, "from the IRA."

"Because the IRA is also a bunch of really nice guys?" I looked at Stan and could see he was worried. He looked at Nigel full of concern. It turned to outright alarm as Nigel outlined his plan, born out of too many suspense movies.

"What I thought was I will leave the assembly point early," he told Stan, "meet up with you at the team's car. Then you and I and any others from your old firm who will join us—patriotic duty and all that—will pile into the car and drive it at top speed into this bow window at the front of the cottage. Surprise them, you see, with a big bang and all that. Then everybody jumps out of the car and sprays everything that moves in the cottage with automatic weapons fire, killing anybody who happens to be in our way. We grab the device and escape into the Jaguar. She," here he pointed at me, "will have moved it to the back of the house, unbeknownst to the IRA or Charlemagne, you see."

We babysitters like to pretend we are not bloodthirsty.

I very nearly burst out laughing when I heard this. Stan stood blinking slowly and rubbed his chin.

"Nige," he said, "we need to talk about this. I keep telling you the career doesn't matter. They're going to screw you over and nothing you can do will stop it. I want you alive, Nige. Forget the damned job!"

"They?" I asked. "Who's they?"

"His governors," said Stan. He gave me a measuring look and decided I looked trustworthy. "They know."

"So the lousy safehouse, the security breaches ..." And, unspoken, my doomed dangle.

"Stress," said Stan. "And sabotage. They wouldn't let him have a decent safehouse and told him it was the only one in the area, take it or leave it. He's for it, and he knows it. Look at him."

Nigel could have been mistaken for a statue if he hadn't been shaking so much.

"Yeah, well," I told Stan, "the words 'for it' will have a lot more meaning if this gets back to the team. Being a danger to them is unhealthy."

Stan raised his forearms, palms up, "Any suggestions?"

I bit my lip. "I have a meeting in twenty minutes. Give me a phone number where I can reach you in an hour. Take him with you." I pointed my chin at Nigel.

"You can't," said Nigel. "You can't just leave. I can't just leave. Not today."

"We'll both be here for the op. Go get some coffee or tea or whatever it is you Brits drink to stop the heebie-jeebies."

At that moment, a cask of whiskey would not have been enough for me.

Taking me aside, Stan sheepishly assured me he could talk Nigel out of it. He had his work cut out for him if he was going to keep his partner alive.

TWENTY

H ere was the plan.
No, I take that back. Here were the plans. I knew four of them and suspected two more, for a total of six. That may be all there were, but I was still not completely sure of my plan.

The official plan, the one briefed by Nigel and Mack before lunch, was this:

Teague wanted the programming and demonstration to take place at his house at three o'clock that afternoon. He needed the remaining daylight to make use of the security advantage long, clear fenland vistas around the cottage gave him.

We gave Rutherford a story to tell him of the many precautions she had taken for her protection, but it was a lie, designed to look like a lie. We wanted him to think she was on her own, unattached to any trap.

While I was having my nap and nightmare in the wee hours, Louis had gone out to Teague's house and put his own touch in place. The device he set was undetectable until activated and would not be turned on until just before the actual demonstration. There was always a chance Teague might do a last-minute sweep. I thought the team's more sophisticated tap should have been there all along. I was sure we had missed something vital.

Teague lived in a charming, old thatched cottage set in a tract of open fields outlined by hedgerows and dotted with isolated stands of brush and low trees. These were good enough to hide in but getting to them across the fields meant total exposure.

A hundred yards from the house, an octagonal World War II pillbox stood obscured by bushes in an overgrown hedgerow. It was approachable, if one stayed low, through a ditch from a road a quarter mile behind. It measured eight feet in diameter and boasted an excellent, though screened, view of the approaches to the house.

We would watch and listen from there until Cú Chulainn's arrival, at which time the team would move in. Nigel and I would then position the team's car on an access road leading onto the nearby dual carriageway and wait for them there. He had a cleanup crew standing by, he assured me. Once Charlemagne was gone, we would proceed to the house in Nigel's Jaguar for the mopping up.

"We have intelligence of six IRA operatives in the area," Nigel told us. "Three are confirmed, and three are strongly suspected probabilities. They arrived yesterday. One of those confirmed is a sniper."

"So seven with Teague, eight with Cú Chulainn," said Charlie.

"Unless Cú Chulainn is one of the six," said Steve.

There followed an internal discussion about the sniper, mainly between father and son.

Something niggled at me when I heard this ordinary conversation. It wasn't the odds. Bad odds were part of the business. It was the assumption that Cú Chulainn would be a threat, a fighting threat. I suppose it arose from the fact that the late explosives expert of the team, Vasily Sobieski, had also been a martial artist capable of killing a man bare-handed. But on the teams I had encountered, the explosives expert was usually the softest member. I began to re-examine all my assumptions.

Nigel ended the briefing with special instructions: if possible, incapacitate but do not kill Cú Chulainn. We understand this is not likely, but in any event, please try to leave at least one of his people alive. Thank you. Payment terms and procedures standard.

Charlie's plan: while Nigel moved Charlemagne's car, I was to move the Jaguar to a twisting road on the side of the house and in sight of its back door, hide it behind a screen of trees that line the road, wait for Louis to join me there and then drive like hell to the base.

Louis's plan: I was not, under any circumstances, to wait for him. I suspected he did not intend to survive.

Mack's plan: I had no way of knowing what his plan was, but I deduced that he intended to shoot Louis immediately after killing Cú Chulainn. Mack would forgo using the knife this time, I thought, in the interests of efficiency and perhaps a lifetime of friendship, not to mention the real probability Louis knew perfectly well how to defend against a knife attack, even Mack's.

Steve's plan: this is another conjecture, but an educated one. Steve would make sure Louis didn't run out the back door.

My plan: I would wait in the Jaguar for Louis. I would drive him myself as Charlie had instructed, and I had already begun to arrange the transportation needed to get him out of the country. I had a few other contingencies in play as well.

Teague's plan: I figured he would shoot Diane the moment Cú Chulainn was satisfied with the device. I noticed none of the plans, including my own, made any provision for the possibility that he might shoot her before this. I began revision number one thousand and one to my plan.

As it turned out, what happened was none of the above.

TWENTY-ONE

We had been in that pillbox for two and a half hours, after positioning ourselves well ahead of any of Cú Chulainn's pickets, when Diane blew the whole operation.

I was spending plenty of time feeling exposed. My neck stretched upward like a chicken's gullet under an axe. Back in the days when I had hair, I would have worn it up anyway, but in a breezy World War II pillbox surrounded by specialists, I missed it desperately. No, that's not true. I was indeed surrounded by specialists and my hair was not there to protect me, that much was true, but the only one who bothered me was the one with the knife. I had felt that blade once. Well, my hair felt it. I did not want my throat to feel it too. I swallowed a lot, telegraphing a giant tell as to what I was thinking.

It was drizzling outside and damp inside. A thin slurry of mud covered the concrete floor. We had been standing the entire time. Everybody— except Mack, of course—shivered visibly at least once. I shivered a lot more than that, and not always from the cold and damp. Another tell.

Louis turned on the transmitter he had placed in Keegan's cottage. It was neither too early nor too late, so reception was perfect. Diane arrived a little before three and may have meant her conversation for Keegan alone, but she had a large and varied audience a hundred yards away and according to our intelligence, an even larger contingent inside the house.

"I had an old house like this before I took command of the squadron and moved on base," she said. "It had mice. In the kitchen. Hordes of them."

"What did you do about them?" said Teague. You could hear the distraction and boredom in his voice. He was watching for Cú Chulainn.

"I set traps for them." She paused. "I caught six of them one day. I would trap one and the bait would be gone. I figured dead mice don't eat cheese, so I reset it each time with fresh bait. I wondered if the mice had a black lottery going on down in the hole somewhere, drawing straws to see who would go next so the rest could eat."

"What the hell is she on about?" It was Nigel who said it, but we were all thinking it.

"She's warning him," I said. For the best of motives, I might have added. Now she would have the opportunity to watch her Dr. Jekyll become Mr. Hyde.

It did not take Keegan long to swallow his special potion. He began to sound alert, opening with some pointed questions for which, of course, she had no answers. We listened in silent tension.

"Let go!" Diane's voice rang with panic.

"She's blown it. I'll kill her," said Nigel.

He got the look he deserved from all of us.

I realized Mack was looking at me without love and affection. He was irritated that I existed, and no doubt figured rightly I had a plan to thwart him in his desire to kill Louis. This was my moment to put my plan into action. He looked ready to shoot me on the spot anyway, so I carried out one of my more outrageous contingency plans by stepping right up to him. I hoped his reaction would be hampered by the HK he had slung on his shoulder, making the plan a tad on the happy side of plausible. I put my arms around his neck and kissed him. On the mouth. I tried to make it sensuous and alluring but there are just some occasions in a woman's life when that's out of reach, like when she's kissing an unwilling half-crazed specialist with the adrenaline rising in his blood, so I kept it brief.

"That's what he did," I said, stepping back. "That's all he did. She said no, and he stopped." Sometimes a visual aid is more powerful than a lot of words. I sincerely hoped so.

Nigel gaped. Steve and Charlie exchanged a glance.

I figured I'd leave it up to Louis to explain all that stuff about Alex's fear of him being mixed with fear for him if and when he got home, assuming my gambit worked, and Louis lived.

Mack looked at Louis behind me.

"You were right as usual," said Louis in an exasperated voice. "I was angry with you. It was the best way to hurt you, but not to betray you. I am sorry."

Mack swung the HK off his shoulder. I closed my eyes and did not see him hand it to Charlie. When there was no firing, I opened my eyes and Mack was right there before me. In the next instant, his arms encircled me like a vise, and he kissed me, thoroughly, with plenty of tongue and a hand on my bottom. I must confess I was not unwilling by the end of that kiss and he knew it.

He broke it off, stepped back, and looked at Louis, now only a step or two behind me. "So, we are even," said Mack. "Come. Let us go." He took the HK from Charlie and led the way out.

"No!" said Nigel. "You can't! Cú Chulainn isn't there yet. Stop! Come back!"

I kept a steady watch through binoculars as the team made its way crouching along the hedgerow to a small copse behind the cottage. There was still no sign of a car that might contain our quarry.

Nigel sputtered and complained, then ran out of the pillbox, absconding quickly while mumbling about the Mercedes. He waived the key he thought he had as evidence of his intention.

The Mercedes pulled up to the front of the cottage just after he left. My private army got out. Stan skulked to the corner of the house and began firing an M-16 I had managed to pick up from the Resident. Mace got out of the driver's side, strolled to the front door, pounded on it with both fists and forearms and screamed, "Diane, get your ass out here!"

The door opened with a shudder; she ran out and Mace threw her on the ground, covering her with his body as gravel spurted like a fountain all around them. He rolled them both against the wall directly under the sniper, who redirected his fire toward Stan.

I put down the binoculars and ran to the Jaguar, for which I did have the key. I followed Charlie's plan anyway, thinking even if Louis was out of the woods, it would be good to have transportation close by that house. Besides, if Louis was still in danger, I did not want to risk Louis's life and my own by disobeying Charlie.

After the op, I listened to the tape of what happened in the cottage. Diane kept to her script and did not compound her initial mistake. She programmed the device under considerable duress but without a word about me, Steve, or the Resident. When the pounding on the door began, Teague swore and must have loosened his hold just enough for her to break free to make an exit under cover of the noise coming from two directions, followed in two seconds by even more noise as the team entered.

TWENTY-TWO

It would be easier to count the things that went right in the plan, or I should say gaggle of plans, which turned into a cluster fuck.

Change of Plan Number Infinity: my hiding place for the Jaguar was already occupied by a white Ford. I had to drive on and look for another spot, which I found around a bend in the road further up. I scrambled back along a ditch crouching low and hid myself in the hedgerow at the rendezvous point where I was to meet Louis if things did not go well for him.

I was in a good position to see him coming from the house, which is why I could see a figure slipping along another ditch not far from the Ford. The figure came closer, heading for the other car. This was not Louis. This was a short female. I watched her from my hiding place. My reassessment of assumptions had told me who she was. She was at the pub that night. I remembered her sharp perusal of the bar. Now I had confirmation. She carried the cigar box I knew contained the detonator with its battery.

Fiona climbed out of the ditch and ran for the Ford. Of course, I had been ready to fire but was not quick enough. I collected myself and ran onto the road firing at the white car as it bore down on me. To tell the truth, I fired at the wrong side. It was a British car after all. I did manage to blow out the windshield in a spectacular shower of glass. The car swerved a bit, not to miss me, but because Cú Chulainn was thrown off balance. She righted herself quickly and hit the gas.

I ran after her like that was going to do any good and reached the Jaguar in time to see the Ford negotiate a curve at top speed almost half a mile away by road. The route over the fields, cutting the curves, was shorter. So I took it. Actually, there was no route over the fields. I made one.

What I gained in directness of travel I partly lost in speed. I made one, well a few, doughnuts in the mud, but all in all I made good progress in getting behind my quarry. I was only a quarter mile back when I reached the road. The Jaguar's superior twelve cylinders took over from there.

I spun out on a sharp left curve and put that incredible machine back on the road by way of a ditch. What a car! But now I was almost half a mile behind again.

Cú Chulainn's Ford was no match for the Jaguar. I behaved myself on the curves now and gained on her again. I was just about to close the final gap when the road ended in a T-intersection. Cú Chulainn turned left. It was not a bad turn, considering her speed, but though she was fast, the truck coming from the right was faster. It climbed up the back of the Ford as if it were a ramp truck. But it wasn't of course, and it flattened with a pop. I was relieved to see the truck driver scramble out just before the explosion that could not have come solely from the gas in the Ford's tank.

I noticed a tire was rubbing the Jag's fender as I sped back to Planned Hiding Place Number One where I heard a few pops of a dying gun battle and a final boom from what had to be a sniper rifle. Then, silence.

Sinking despair. Rising panic.

I screeched back onto the road and raced to the team rendezvous. Nobody there. I punched it the few hundred yards back to the driveway of the cottage, screeched through the turn, and pulled up beside the Mercedes where Mace and Stan had left it. Nigel stood a few feet ahead, arms folded, a large welt on his left temple. The team was moving toward him from Teague's house. Something was wrong. One of them was being half carried, half dragged toward us.

"Where is the ambulance?" demanded Mack.

The fool shrugged.

Mack shoved him when he was close enough but could not wipe the insolent glare from Nigel's eyes.

"You blew it," said Nigel.

There were more demands for an agreed-upon ambulance. Nigel stonewalled. Mack and Charlie checked the Mercedes for alarms. This was an exercise in futility, given Stan and Mace's recent use of it, but good habits save lives. Louis supported Steve, who clutched a bloody spot on his abdomen.

"Why must you be such a bullet magnet?" said Louis.

"Why do I have to go in first all the time?" Steve said, gasping.

They laid him across the backseat. Louis rummaged in the trunk.

"Did you leave one alive?" Nigel demanded of Mack, ignoring the fury on his face. "Did you do that at least? Did you get any leads?"

"We know who is Cú Chulainn. If you will not provide an ambulance, at least give us a doctor to travel with us. We will send him back when ours can take over."

"If you know who he is, then go after him for bloody Christ's sake!" Nigel's enraged fleshy face wobbled like red jelly.

I was watching the utter self-destruction of a former professional, and it was not pretty. The contrast with Mack's cool rationality was sobering.

"Some other time," Mack said as he turned away.

Louis shouted at me from the car. He was stooping in the open back door, holding Steve's shoulders.

"Hold his legs!"

I did as directed. Steve began to vomit, the spasms intensifying his pain to increasingly unbearable levels. Charlie took over Louis's position at the head so Louis could measure a dose of morphine he had taken from a satchel in the trunk. The fact that Steve was being given morphine while still operational meant it was serious.

Louis shoved the needle into an arm, and the retching eased, then stopped. Steve relaxed, but I kept one hand on an ankle while I reached for the car phone on the console.

I caught Mack's eye as he leaned in the front door and reached for a separate radio mike.

"Where's your airplane?" I asked.

He told me. I told him to move it to the air base at Alconbury and started dialing from the carphone while he barked into the radio.

The Resident answered my call himself. I don't think I blew his identity, as if that were even important at the moment because everybody was talking at once and nobody had time to pay attention except for the nearly unconscious Steve. Nigel still sulked by the Jaguar obstructing the team's progress, but not making any progress of his own, so he was equally oblivious to my calling our resident on a clear line.

Anyway, I was prepared to blow the Res's identity and smash a host of flash instructions just to keep the self-destructing basket case busy while I got the team out of there.

"An escort will meet you at the Alconbury gate," I told Mack. "They'll lead you to the flightline and a flight surgeon will meet you there."

Mack pointed his chin at the short round babysitter, clucking and moaning with tears in his eyes as he ran a hand over the Jaguar's roof and bonnet.

"What if he closes the airways?" said Mack.

"I'll take care of him. You go. Now."

It did not occur to me that Mack might not trust me, so I was mystified at first by his transient hesitation. Then I remembered all the events of the past two days that had been squeezed out of my mind under the pressure of havoc. I had only one goal at this moment: to protect my team. It took Mack a second to assure himself about my intention and then force himself to take an order from a woman.

Charlie sat in the muck that covered the back seat, Steve's head in his lap. Mack and Louis climbed into the front. They were gone before Nigel looked up from his inspection of the Jaguar.

"What the hell…?" he said as they sped away. "Where…?"

I shrugged. "Maybe they went after Cú Chulainn."

"Can you believe it?" Nigel was addressing a point somewhere to the left of my right ear. I turned quickly, but no one was there. He continued his address to an imaginary listener.

"They never failed before. For anybody. And when the day comes, they fail for me. Never missed a shot, and when they miss, it's got to be me. Fifteen years of fucking flawless precision, shattered when I need their top performance the most. Unbelievable. Un-fucking-believable."

He went on for a long time, in pretty much the same words, liberally punctuated by words like 'me' and 'fucking'.

I interrupted on the third iteration.

"Nigel, do you have a cleanup crew standing by? Don't you think it's time we went into the house?"

"What in all hell happened to my car?"

I wasn't sure he was entirely there anymore. You would have thought the car was his vital appendage. It took precedence over Charlemagne. He never even tried to call his people to order an intercept or even to monitor them. There was a car phone in the Jag, which was now emitting a high-pitched whistle, but he did not look at it even once as he and I moved the car up to a position in front of the house that would not interfere with the cleanup crew. Nigel had taken success very well, but he was disintegrating under failure.

"How do we reach your cleanup crew, Nigel?"

"What did you do? Enter a fucking rally? What in hell am I supposed to tell my boss?"

"The cleanup crew, Nigel," I insisted as I stopped in front of the silent little house.

I dreaded everything, going in alone, going in with Nigel the Nut, going in with the clean-up crew, going in without them. Were Mace and even Diane alive? Louis's expression had given no hint. His concern was centered on Steve. Was that a good sign or a bad sign? The house's eerie stillness was not encouraging.

"There's a car wash in Huntingdon," said Nigel. "That will help."

I rubbed my eyes and pinched the bridge of my nose. It helped keep me from decking him. Screaming at him was still a possibility.

TWENTY-THREE

We approached the silent house and found four people. Three sat on the gravel driveway against the wall under a busted bow window. Teague's hands were behind his back. Stan stood over him pointing the M-16 at his chest. Mace and Diane completed the tableau, her head on the big man's chest. She appeared to be asleep. It was not yet four o'clock, but dusk came early in February. It was cold and drizzling and they were outside.

"They told us not to go in there," said Stan.

"So who the fuck is the target?" Nigel asked Diane.

She shook herself awake. "Target?"

"The voice. Whose voiceprint was it?"

She looked puzzled. I noticed, even in the gloom, that one eye was badly bruised and swollen almost shut.

"I... don't know," she said. "It was somebody British. With an accent, I mean."

Teague dropped his head and swung it from side to side. He had been about to kill her for her knowledge of the target.

Mace looked at me. "I didn't know," he said, "about Fiona, I mean."

"Not your fault. Thanks for doing what I asked."

I turned to Nigel. "We are going in there now," I ordered. "If the phone in there is working, I will call your crew for you. What is their number?"

"I know of another car wash in St. Ives if the Huntingdon one isn't working." He turned his head and looked at me for the first time. "It freezes up sometimes, you see."

"Yeah, sure. I see. Listen, Nigel, what do you say we ask your cleanup crew to give it a wash when they get here? Give me the number and I'll call them."

"Cleanup crew?"

"The one standing by. What's the number?"

He fumbled for his wallet.

"No, Nigel, it's in your head. Look for the number in your head."

He wrinkled his forehead and spewed out numbers. I wrote them down as they came, every one of them, praying one set would be the magic one.

"On second thought, Nigel, I'll go by myself. You help Stan guard the prisoner."

Stan took his arm while still covering Teague. I had to admit he knew what he was doing.

Nigel continued to sputter and resist Stan's life-saving restraint.

"Knock it off, Nigel," I said. "You owe this guy your life. Exercise some discretion for fuck's sake." To Stan, I said, "Our agreement holds. Whatever you have to do to muzzle him, do it. I heard nothing, never met you, have no idea what you were doing here. Thanks for helping my guy Mace save the colonel. I don't owe you, because we're even." I looked at Nigel. "Your career, such as it is, is still intact, Nigel. My silence is bought and paid for, but Stan is right. It's only a matter of time before your hierarchs find a way to jettison you in the most painful way possible. Don't give them the satisfaction. Settle down and have a nice life."

I went in through the front door.

I found the number for Nigel's cleanup crew on the fourth try down the list, using the phone at a quaint table seat in the very tiny, very English cottage's entry hall. As I hung up on the last call, I stood in silence, staring at three closed doors, a staircase, and one open door. The open door was the way outside next to me. I was tempted.

I had left it open so I could monitor Nigel as he muttered to Stan.

Professionally speaking, maybe I should have looked inside before calling for cleanup. I might have been in a better position to specify what we needed. But I took it for granted that Nigel had thought of everything back when he was still thinking and had planned accordingly. Whatever else he had been driven to become, he began as a top-rated intelligence officer and babysitter. I had to believe that when allowed to, he would do his job. His boss wouldn't know anything about cleanup crews.

Also, I had an overwhelming urge to procrastinate. Can't think why.

With the crew on the way and Nigel busy muttering about the car, I finally screwed up the discipline to open door number one. It was the kitchen. Very charming. Nothing amiss. Door number two turned out to be the dining room, all in perfect order.

I chided myself for my cowardice as I put my hand on the last door handle. Please don't make me climb the stairs, I thought. I was sure that amount of creepy would be too much. I took a deep breath.

It's a very good thing I held my breath initially. Had I walked in breathing, I would have tossed the breakfast I had not eaten. Of course, there was blood everywhere. I've seen lots of scenes, many of them worse, but this one had tied itself to me. It was a serpent coiling tightly around my ankles and I could not dance enough to shake it off, but I did jump involuntarily. Again, I was glad I had skipped breakfast.

The small lounge was stuffed with easy chairs, a two-seater sofa, rug, overturned coffee table, television, and three bodies with AKs still in their hands. The usual. The fireplace had been walled in and now sported a two-burner gas heater. Flowers and songbirds papered the wall. A dead man lay in front of the gas heater. He showed signs, or rather wounds, that suggested he'd not gone down fighting. He went down talking. It was amazing how much blood a human body holds.

I climbed the stairs because I had to. At the top was a little room over the front door that the British call a box room. It had been used as a sniper perch. Empty shells littered the floor. A rifle with a decent scope on it still ticked as its heat cooled. A movement on my left made my head jerk around again. I moved a chair to investigate. The man was still alive, but barely, and obviously in considerable pain. He seemed to be dying, but that did not mean he could not be dangerous. I was not ready to let him take me with him. Another body lay, quite dead, behind the sniper rifle.

"There is an ambulance outside," I said to the man still living as I checked him for weapons. "I'll have them give you something for the pain."

"Don't count on it, lass," he said.

"Just tell them what they want to know," I said, "and tell them quick."

His face set in defiance.

"Look," I said, "we already know who she is, or was. Don't suffer for nothing. Just tell them."

I worried as he closed his eyes that he would not live to say anything. I did not want to be debriefed. Between Teague and this guy, the facts could easily be established without my information. My involvement would only raise questions, primarily about me.

The cleanup crew had arrived and were lifting the bloodless corpse from behind the rifle.

"That's not Mack's mark," said a voice behind me.

I jumped even as I recognized the accent of my raving colleague and looked at him carefully. His face had become thoughtful. Sane? To be determined.

"Who else uses a knife?" I wondered.

"None of the others that we know, but Mack didn't do that."

"Why?"

He shrugged.

"It looks like his mark." I tried not to make it sound like a challenge. "It looks just like the examples in the file."

He stared at me a moment. "I know. But the ones I've seen were not in any file. And this is not like them. The one in the lounge is his, though, and two watchers on the approach and in the brush out back."

"What's different with this one?"

He shrugged again.

"Then yours is a theory," I said.

"No. Worse. An intuition."

He looked at me through bleary eyes that swam in the fatigue and despair that filled the sockets. Behind those eyes, Nigel had returned to reality. I still did not like him, but it was good to have him back.

...

Louis later briefed me regarding the action in the house. Mack was running point as usual. He had taken out two watchers in the brush on the approach to the house and was about to enter the cottage to look for the sniper when chaos and gunfire boomed from the front of the building. A woman ran out the back door toward a small copse to the left. They could not see if she carried anything because of the angle at which she ran. There was automatic rifle fire to the right front, and the boom of an unsuppressed sniper rifle at the front center, evidently upstairs or in an attic, but nothing was coming their way.

Mack led the way in through the kitchen door, directed Charlie and Steve upstairs to take care of the sniper, and proceeded through the lounge and out a side window to take out the automatic rifle outside. Louis covered him in this effort, killing two. Charlie and Steve came downstairs into a fierce battle with Keegan and two others firing at Louis. One of their rounds hit Steve. He, Charlie, and Louis managed to kill one and take Teague and one other as prisoners. Mack returned and conducted an interview with the other man to gain the identity of Cú Chulainn and then dispatched him.

They left Teague alive per Nigel's request, taking him outside to the corner of the house where a man continued to fire an M-16 into the air. He stopped firing when he saw the knife blade before his face. Louis took the rifle but returned it when Mack ordered that the prisoner be turned over to this man.

Stan had handcuffs with him. *Is this something you learn in SAS school?* He secured Teague's hands behind his back and led him to the front of the house. The team went back inside briefly to make it safe. One was alive upstairs, but not for long. Charlie disarmed him and rendered the sniper's rifle unusable, not that the dying man would ever have been capable of getting to it.

The reason I had this last bit of information is because of the discussion Louis related between father and son when Charlie came back downstairs. Mack was sharp with his criticism of leaving a man within reach of a weapon, no matter how wounded, no matter how short a time, especially when, given the layout of the place, the man would inevitably be at his back. Charlie took the rebuke like a stone, Louis told me.

By then Steve's injury was asserting itself and Louis had to half carry him outside.

The entire action had taken a little under four minutes.

TWENTY-FOUR

I had plenty of reasons to resign. Pick one.

    The thrill was gone.
    I reached the finish line but lost the race.
    Personal problems.
    To spend more time with my family.
    A reassessment of my life.
    Identity crisis.
    My health.
    I couldn't hack it.

That last one is no more true than any of the others but the men in my section would have picked it and they would be wrong.

I resigned because I had fallen in love with a killer and there were two things I could not bear: the thought of seeing another example of his work and zipping him into a body bag like the bags I had seen zipped in that English cottage.

There were contributing factors. I was more of a pariah than Steve had ever been, even though no one knew about my part in Cú Chulainn's death. The Section seemed mad at me for coming back alive.

The guy in the box room lived just long enough to tell Nigel who Fiona was. After persuasion, Teague corroborated the fact, so I was off the hook there.

Speaking of Steve, he deserves credit as one of the biggest contributors to my decision. The pain in those Teddy Bear eyes as he came out of the house and the muck he lay in with his head on Charlie's lap made me realize I could be on the same road Steve followed. I got the hell off it. So what if the only way off was in a ditch?

I re-defected to my old friends in the FBI and took a job in Miami, not too junior, but not as far up as I would have been had I stayed.

It was kind of nice to be Millie Aldrich again, all the time, and at home all the time.

I suppose.

I had two months to wait before starting the job and after setting up my new apartment near the beach, spent the rest of the delay back at my parents' farm in Nebraska.

My family put on a big picnic for the Fourth of July. They set up tables and chairs in the meadow that bordered the house where I grew up. Dad officiated the barbecue. My brothers and brothers-in-law cooked steaks for the adults and hot dogs for my nieces, nephews, thieving dogs, and the piglet one of those nephews was raising for 4H. Mom and my four sisters provided baked beans, coleslaw, three kinds of potato salad, six fruit salads, and apple, blueberry, and cherry pies.

I did nothing and enjoyed it thoroughly, sitting in a lawn chair drinking gin and tonic, disturbed only by an occasional badminton cock the wind blew my way. I was otherwise left alone to meditate upon the view.

The house and meadow are set at the top of a rise in the rolling Nebraska prairie. From my lawn chair, I could see for some distance along the winding dirt road leading to the farm and the house. I wondered vaguely who could be coming this way as I saw a glint of metal in a small dust cloud rolling toward us. The vision grew into a distinct shape and color. I stopped drinking when I thought the color was black and the shape a Mercedes. I stood up when, at a half mile, it turned a final bend and made me suspect I had been drinking too much.

"Now who could that be?" Ma stood at my elbow, genuinely curious.

I tried to hide my alarm. Not here, I thought, as if the road would lead anywhere else. *No. No. Don't come here.*

But they did.

And Ma was right there to greet them when they got out of the car. So was Dad. So was I, nervously. The four men wore lightweight suits which would never be light enough in that July sun. Charlie took off his tie almost immediately, but not his coat. Steve loosened his tie and also kept his coat on. He was pale, thinner than he had been five months before, but fit. Sunglasses hid Mack's royal blue eyes. I was glad. I did not want him to frighten my mother.

"You know each other from work?" said Ma. "How splendid! I don't think we've ever met anybody Millie works with."

I stumbled over introductions and my parents led the way back to the meadow. They were jolly beyond belief at the prospect of introducing a whole set of Millie's friends—all of them men!—to the family.

We ate. I watched Charlemagne watch each other's back as I navigated the conversation through torturous topics in which their answers were every bit as vague as my family's questions were pointed. They were in business, they said. What kind? In Europe. My brighter nephews caught on to this right away. They were themselves quite experienced at evading pointed questions from the family. Louis answered a few of my nephews' questions with a silent stare and they went off to play softball. *Bright boys.*

I worried about two teenaged nieces. Between them, they had glued four wistful eyes onto Charlie. Steve sat on a tree swing watching his back as Charlie leaned against the tree, beer in hand, a girl on either side, and a smile on his face. I remembered my lost wrestling bout with him, his words about my being a disruption, and the bloodless sniper. I found an excuse to call the girls over and direct them toward my aunt Jo who didn't need any help with the chili, but I pretended she did. When I turned back to my seat, Charlie was watching me, and the smile was gone.

My once lonely lawn chair became part of a crowd. Mack sat on my left, Louis on my right. Ma sat down next to Mack and tried to start a conversation. He was polite enough, I suppose. I was still fretting over my nieces and so found myself caught off guard when Louis made a loud announcement in French. He asked the assemblage if anybody spoke French. Blank smiles all around.

"*Bon,*" he said to me. "I know this is very rude, but I want some privacy. You have quit your job."

I nodded and asked how things were with him, politely not mentioning that I was pleasantly surprised he was still alive.

"*Bien,*" he said. An all-purpose word with a meaning that ranges from fantastic to good enough.

Now that he had dragged my attention to him, I had to discipline myself not to drink in every detail. I knew Mack would be watching and nothing would escape him. I forced my gaze away from Louis's black eyes from time to time in an effort, probably obvious, to hide the hammering my heart was doing in my chest.

"Nigel paid us finally," said Louis.

"Did he?"

Louis nodded and sipped his beer. "He refused at first, you know."

"I heard."

"Even before they identified Cú Chulainn, Nigel said he would not pay for an accidental death."

"Oh."

"Then they found a bullet in what remained of the body. Did you know Cú Chulainn had bled out, or so they think?" He arched an eyebrow at me.

"Oh?" I did not dare look him in the eye.

"We argued the bullet meant it was not an accident. Payable. Nigel sputtered about it not matching any of our weapons, but he paid in the end, just before he retired."

I sipped the last of my gin and tonic and contemplated the ice cubes in my glass.

"What I am wondering," said Louis, "is whether you are coming home to claim your share."

I watched Steve swinging slowly, relaxed, but I knew better.

"I'm flattered," I said, "but I can't."

He said nothing, but there was no smile. I still could not look at him directly, so I studied the ice in my glass as it melted.

Mack stirred. "Excuse me," he said to my mother to break off their one-sided non-conversation. Then to Louis, in French: "Barbara does not understand you."

Louis frowned at him.

"She thinks you are asking her to join the team."

Freaky mind reader.

Louis looked at me, puzzled. I found the courage to look at him and he chuckled.

"*Vraiment?*" he said. "Did you think…?"

I managed only the beginning w sound in well yes when he laughed in earnest.

"You a specialist?" he said. "You are barely competent as a babysitter!"

Even Mack allowed himself a short chuckle.

Thoroughly confused, I began to cry into my melting ice cubes when Louis stopped laughing, leaned over, and took my hand.

"No," he said, "not with us, with me. I am asking you to come home with me. Home to Vasily's Carpet. I ask poorly because I have never...."

I was more confounded than ever.

"What about Diane?" I asked.

"She married her pilot." He wrinkled his brow and shrugged. "And she is not my type. You described her very well. She is quite beautiful, and it was good for us that you saved her life, but...." He gave me the smile that always makes me wonder what he's up to. "She is no lion tamer."

I didn't go with him right away. We stayed for pie.

I did ask the usual pertinent questions. Do you love me? He said he didn't know but he had never asked a woman to marry him before so that might be an indication, and also something about not being able to stop thinking about me and talking about me. Misha nodded wearily at the latter statement. I wondered if he was to be in on all our most romantic moments.

Eventually, my mother moved to the other side of Louis to force more non-conversation with him. Misha apologized for cutting my hair. Sort of. What I mean is, he said he was sorry he lost his temper but not sorry he cut my hair because he likes it better short.

I will never get used to him.

"I was to take out the sniper," he said in German. He did not check if anyone spoke German, because he knew no one did, damn him, the freak. But he continued, "I was diverted by someone firing an automatic rifle, an M-16, an American weapon. Someone we did not know. I was about to take him out. He was an older man with dark hair, not entirely fit, but more than competent with the rifle. He never heard me." He paused. "At the last moment, when my knife was poised, I realized he was firing into the air and drawing fire from the tangos."

"He had strict instructions not to endanger the team," I said.

He waited. I was going to have to confess.

"He was covering for the guy rescuing the dangle."

"You should have told me," said Misha pausing again. "Michael and Steve had to take out the sniper. A few weeks later, in April, I met this man I had almost killed. He is Nigel's lover. Nigel has retired at his insistence. We offered to meet with his superiors to do what we did for Steve to keep him from being dismissed, but Stan said it would not work. He is right of course, and Nigel would be difficult to work with now."

"Because he's gay?" I asked.

"Because he is no longer a good babysitter." He bored holes into me even through his sunglasses. "Good babysitters do not make private plans during our operations."

I will never know if he was referring to my rescue of the dangle or if he knew about Nigel's half-baked plan to steal the detonator. It was probably both and included my silence about the stupid plot and his egregious security breach. Misha's statement was both specific and ambiguous at the same time, a hallmark of his unique species of threats. One may be in doubt as to the complete meaning of what he says, but never about his intent in saying it. I shivered visibly.

"*Bon*, as Louis would say," he said with a half-smile, acknowledging my capitulation. "Make your goodbyes. We leave now."

...

As I dodge the daily snarls that animate life at Vasily's Carpet, I find I do have a first-class talent as a lion tamer, primarily because I have developed a profound awareness of their claws.

EPILOGUE

Buddy faced his second tribunal in less than two years. Gizmo and Bruno sat on either side of the chairman. Again.

The chairman, a political appointee, looked at the folder before him, striped with red tape and emblazoned with the word WEDGE. He seemed to have a recollection that he had seen it before, but this particular department of the organization was so incomprehensible to him, he had no mental framework upon which to hang the memory. He looked at the file knowing he did not want to open it. He was certain he would not like this hearing and he would leave it with no clearer understanding of what the hell these men were talking about than he had after the last time.

He thought about lunch instead.

Bruno opened the proceedings. "Buddy, we're here to discuss the fact that you've had a second babysitter join Charlemagne."

Charlemagne, mused the chairman, was the first Holy Roman Emperor, though he wasn't a Roman and probably not holy. Sort of like these guys, a loose collection of is and is not.

"Not *joined* the team, Bruno," said Buddy. "She married one of them. She didn't become operational. Except as a wife, I suppose."

The chairman wondered briefly if Charlemagne was somehow involved in childcare, but then reflected on the specialized jargon used by all departments in this organization and wisely kept his mouth shut.

"That's even worse," said Gizmo. "Pillow talk can lay everything bare." He frowned at his unfortunate phrasing.

The chairman was deciding which wine he wanted with lunch.

Buddy swiveled his froggy eyes at the ceiling before replying. "Gizmo, she was a senior babysitter. *The* senior babysitter. We have alerted her former team there is a possibility of a breach, but not a probability. Her team before that one was wiped out thanks to the bonehead who replaced her as their babysitter. I might add I had nothing to do with that selection. Her teams prior to them have all either disbanded or been blown to smithereens in various parts of the globe. It's not a long-lived profession."

"I don't think you can crow about your ability to select babysitters, Bud," said Bruno. "You've lost two in eighteen months to the same team."

The chairman was now certain they were not talking about childcare.

"I'll admit I made a mistake on the first one, but Millie was the right choice for this op. She saved everybody's ass out there. Even the cousins are pleased."

The chairman frowned. It sounded like they were referring to families again.

"Everybody's ass except the tangos," Buddy clarified.

Dancing families? The chairman contemplated a refreshing, crisp white wine to counter the morning's tedium.

"That explains why the cousins are happy," said Gizmo. "But you don't think it was a mistake to assign a woman to such a team? They have a reputation for being pretty brutal."

"No, Gizmo, I don't. I don't think a man would have been able to save the situation. From what I understand, brutal is an understatement in this case."

"So bottom line, you're saying the possibility of a breach is remote?"

"I'm saying exactly that," said Buddy. "She was a first-class agent and besides, she defected to the FBI before she accepted Charlemagne, so she's already been thoroughly debriefed."

Finally, something the chairman understood. He spent most of his days repairing the damage done by daily internecine battles waged by these subordinates. He and his FBI counterpart often joked the Soviets enjoyed more respect in their hallways than members of the sister services. The word 'defected' was a telling use of their peculiar language. The chairman's spirits briefly improved before being brought back down again by Bruno's next observation.

"Accepted them, Buddy? She didn't marry all of them, did she?"

"She married the Frenchman. But the dynamics of the team are such that she may as well have married all."

"Really?" The three members of the panel said it simultaneously. The chairman understood this point with no trouble at all.

"Minds out of the gutter, gentlemen," said Buddy. "I mean that except for what you're thinking about, she now lives in a cage with all of them and must deal accordingly. I have no doubt she will do so admirably."

The chairman took his dignity into his hands and ventured a brief question. "Did you say she is, or was, now with the FBI?"

"Yes, sir."

"Then why are we here?"

The others stared at him. These were the five most profound words they had ever heard him say.

"You are correct, Sir," said Gizmo. "It is the FBI's problem."

The chairman adjourned the panel with no conclusions for an indefinite period because the proper agency to address the issue was the FBI.

This was the second time the chairman understood things perfectly. He was becoming quite adept in this strange world.

The End

STATE OF NATURE
The early 1990s

ONE

He belched before he spoke. He introduced every new paragraph with a frog call from deep within his ponderous belly. Mara did not mind it. She was used to better manners in worse men, but this one's habits did not bother her. He was good company and competent guidance and that was all that mattered in the field.

She turned at every belch because it sounded like a throat clearing, a summons to attend. Her manners were impeccable and ingrained and nearly cost her the operation. If she had not turned back quickly, she would have missed what she was looking for, what they had spent six weeks holed up in a deserted room over a derelict store to look for.

"You know, Mara," said Seal through a mouthful of redolent pastrami (with mustard and sauerkraut, my girl, don't forget), "I wonder about you sometimes. I like looking at you, but I like wondering, too."

Mara concentrated on her job, peering past the greasy smear Seal had left on the binocular lens during his watch, and past the decade of dirt on the window before her. She watched the news vendor at the corner below make change for a customer. "Yes," she said aloud, to show that she was listening.

"I mean, take the name for instance." Seal took a long pull on a straw in a can of cola, fully leaded—none of that diet shit for me, girl. He followed it with a particularly satisfying belch.

Mara stopped herself from turning and concentrated again on the vendor. Her arms were tired. She did not encourage Seal to continue.

Seal swept the thin, graying hair back from his forehead with podgy fingers, leaving a suggestion of mustard on his right temple.

"That name of yours is famous, girl. Did you know that?"

Mara's rudeness in not answering did not affect him. He continued.

"Yup. Sobieski's a famous name in the biz. Not strictly our business, you understand, but a branch of it. No, not CI and I still don't know why you're in this lousy division. Somebody told me you volunteered, but that's absurd. You'd have to be nuts, and you ain't nuts. Must've been an enemy of yours who told me that, girl. You got any enemies, honey?"

Mara did not move.

"Whew, you're a cold one, anyway. Never wrong and never warm, and that reminds me." Seal shifted on the old sofa that was the only furniture in the room. He crumpled the bag his pastrami had come in and threw it onto a growing pile in the corner.

"What was I saying? Oh, yeah. Sobieski. He was a legend when I came to the biz. 'Course, I got tapped for Counter Intelligence right away, but one of my buddies from training went upstairs and sometimes I saw him in the cafeteria. That was a long time ago, and he'd tell me stories about all the great killers there is in the world. I liked hearing his stories 'cause all I'd ever done at that time was run background checks on Ma 'n Pa Apple Pie and their kin. This Sobieski guy was a mean one, though, what they called an ace, a solo specialist. Those are terms you should learn, girl, especially as your name's Sobieski. So your granddaddy Sobieski, oh, I know he ain't no relation, but he'd have to be your granddaddy if he was because he was dead before you were even thought of. Now there's a thought."

Seal's voice trailed off. He must be falling asleep. *Rejoice.* Mara held her binoculars with one arm, let the other drop, and stretched to give it a rest.

But he resumed. "He had a boy, you know. I know that because my buddy felt sorry for me, cooped up in CI all those years, and so he took me to a place called a sovereign house. Know what that is?" Seal did not wait for an answer. "It's a place where people can meet without shooting each other. Hard to explain, but there are rules in the black world and my friend by that time knew his way around pretty good. He took me to one of these here places—it was in New York City—and he said to me 'Seal, we've hit pay dirt. They're here.'

"I didn't know what the hell he was talking about, but I followed his eyes to a table over on the west side of the room, and let me tell you, girl, in those places, it's important which side of the room you sit on. You may need to know that someday, and I've just told you. Somebody'll probably train you in that event, but if they forget, you just remember old Seal told you it's fucking important. You can have all the rules you want about shooting people over a drink, but they ain't worth nothing if you put deadly enemies at the same table with guns and intentions."

There was no sign of a letup in Seal's monologue. Mara rested the other arm.

"Anyhow, at this here table on the west side of the place were these three guys. They were at their best in those days; ain't heard much about 'em since, but then I ain't been in a position to hear much about nothing. The tallest one had black hair; they called him the Frenchman. The shortest one, now this is where your famous name comes in, honey, he had those deep-set Slavic eyes, and my friend says to me 'That's Sobieski.' Well, I give him a surprised look and he explains. 'Son of,' he says. The third guy was the one that made me shudder, though. He was like a blond piece of sculpture, perfect and still, and my friend tells me they call him Mack in the biz, so to speak, because he cuts throats for a living, silent and sure, and he's sort of in charge of the team, for that's what they were—still are, for all I know, though I doubt they're still alive, but they could be for sure. The name was Charlemagne, the team name, that is. That's a name that was only whispered back then. They were the best, got the best prices, because they never, ever failed."

Mara picked up a radio from the windowsill with her rested arm.

"That's him," she said into it, "headed east on Fourth."

"We got him?" Seal heaved himself from the sofa and took the binoculars from her. He did not see her nod as he watched his street crew round up vendor and customer, quietly, as in a pantomime. "How do you know?"

"He is the only one whose paper was handed to him. Every day. All the other customers picked up their own."

Mara's voice matched her hair, blonde and smooth like a slow river flowing over round stones. Seal loved to look at her and listen to her and he took in his fill now, regretting the end of the operation. He was sure she would be moved up. Had to be. She sure didn't belong in CI.

"I was telling you about Charlemagne," he said, noting the change in her eyes, a change that would be imperceptible to a less experienced man. "I was telling you because it's funny. You've got a

name like Sobieski and it's a big name in the biz, in the biz of the upstairs folks, that is, and I'm sure you're destined for better things,
honey. But if I had to say who you bring to mind, it ain't Sobieski,
though I suppose there's a touch of the Slav about those green eyes
of yours. Nope. The guy you bring to my mind is Mack. You're like
him—toxic and exquisite, and I'm gonna miss ya."

"I'm not going anywhere, Seal."

He sighed. "I just hope I taught you a few things to take with
you."

"We're a team, old man." Mara put the binoculars in their case
and slung the strap over her shoulder. Her ponytail gleamed in the
fading afternoon light as she opened the stairwell door opposite the
window. "Hurry up or we'll lose gloating privileges."

Seal sighed again before following his pupil to the interrogation.

TWO

The afternoon desert heat kept the laundry room empty. Hot water washes and tumble drying only improved the place.

The heat insured privacy. In cooler parts of the day, Mara could walk more comfortably back and forth to wash her clothes, past the apartment complex pool, past the picnic area, into the laundry, and back again to her apartment, but that required hellos and smiles and polite answers to rude inquiries. How these Californians liked to pry!

Mara wore shorts and sandals and a loose blue t-shirt with the inscription *'It's a CInch'* that only Seal and her classmates in training would understand. More training than Seal ever imagined alerted her now, well before the event happened. She armed herself with a cup of bleach.

"Hi." He smiled beautifully, a shining, merry smile, like Louis's, but without the underlying malice.

"Hi." Mara kept her grip on the measuring cup.

"I am Sergei Pavlenko."

"Yes, I know." She waited and studied him for the clues that were not present in photos she had seen. His straight, light brown hair was unruly, or else ruffled by the stiff, hot desert wind. No, that was surely a cowlick in back. She remembered her father's struggle against a mop just like it and smiled.

Sergei Pavlenko smiled back.

"What do you want?" Mara recovered the mistake, barking the question and holding the bleach further in front of her.

He stepped forward. She raised her arm and he stopped.

"I need your help."

The washing machine behind her began a noisy spin cycle. This was not a subject to be shouted, but she did not want him to come any closer. She raised her voice, hoping no one else would hear her.

"No deals, Pavlenko, I got them; iron tight. If they were yours, I'm sorry, but that's the game."

He raised a Slavic eyebrow and smiled again. "They were not mine, but congratulations anyway. You have a knack." He looked around the room. "Is there someplace we can go—to talk? You can get your weapon if you do not trust me. I understand. I will wait for you here. See, you have plenty of room to leave safely. Get your weapon and come back for me. I won't follow you to your apartment. I will wait here. Go. Go."

He set a plastic chair against the far gallery of dryers and sat down on it, well away from the entrance. Sweat beaded on his forehead, but he did not move to wipe it away.

Mara did as he suggested and was well armed with her Glock and a plan for a rendezvous when she returned for her laundry.

...

She had picked someplace trendy, but not too crowded. The decor, old-world California-style, provided some privacy, with deep booths and staggered floor levels. The plastic stained glass poured colored lights over oak tables pretending to be antiques.

For the benefit of their waitress, Mara and Sergei feigned a casual conversation while she kept her Glock pointed at him through the handbag in her lap and he kept his hands above the table. They sat in the smoking section, because, he said, he smoked, and indeed he did. A careful upbringing and many hours of Seal's company had prepared her for nuisances. She waved away the smoke.

"I see you are right-handed," he told her in Russian. "Unlike your father."

Mara replied in the same language while the waitress lingered in the area, filling coffee mugs in front of them, then water glasses, though they had not asked for water.

"What do you know of my father? He is long dead—of no concern to you."

Pavlenko did not answer immediately. The waitress hovered, expecting an order. He shook his head, and she found some other errand in the kitchen. He continued in Russian.

"I know much. About him; about his, um, associates. I was trained by the man who arranged your father's death."

"I did not see you there that day." Mara did not hide her contempt.

The waitress came back like a pesky fly. Mara forced herself to lighten her grip on the trigger.

Sergei put out his cigarette, blowing the last of it over her head as he leaned back in his seat. He waved away the pesky fly and the waitress left, pretending to have something else to do.

"Your father was my special study," he said. "I wrote my training thesis on him. It was very good. I was destined for a brilliant career." He grinned at her. "Then the wall came down."

"A great tragedy."

"A shocking bore. During the Cold War, you knew what side you were on. Your friends and enemies were distinct. Now they are muddled. Everybody's thinking is muddled. Mine is itself a dark cloud."

"You have my sympathy." There was, of course, no sympathy in her voice.

He stared into Mara's steady green eyes. Her arm did not move, but he had no doubt it would take her no more than a twitch to pull the trigger under the table. "Your whole supply of sympathy?" he asked.

"Every molecule."

"Then I am rich indeed." He looked away, looked down, then up, mastering the rancid taste of business that rose in his throat as he spoke to this exquisite young woman.

"I am sorry about your father," he said, trying to look as though he meant it.

Mara was not buying it. She said nothing.

Back again, the waitress would not go away this time, so they perused their menus. Mara held hers with one hand. Sergei began a monologue in fast, quiet Russian as his eyes scanned the lunch list.

"I need your help. I promised myself I would not begin with that. Let me try again. I am having some difficulty staying alive. I cannot tell you why because I do not trust you, though I come to you as the only hope of trust that I can have. I once was sworn to kill your father and his associates and now that the world has turned inside out, they are the only ones I know. That is, I know them. I studied them and did my best to defeat them. But all I once knew is dissolving. Somehow, I cannot conceive of Charlemagne dissolving, can you?"

"You did your best."

"I said I was sorry."

"That brings him back to life then. He was not armed that day."

"He was not?" Doubt. He chewed his lower lip. "He did not abandon his beliefs? He did not embrace some other philosophy, did he?"

"No." Mara paused. Pavlenko deserved nothing, no explanation, but she noticed a hunted look, man as quarry, and recognized it. "My father liked to escape the game sometimes," she explained. "He pretended he lived a different life."

"Yes. Yes. He would. It explains his women. They were as removed from the game as possible, every time. I was young and did not understand the dossier then. Yes. That explains it." Sergei looked up sharply. "Until he married your mother, of course."

The waitress cleared her throat. They ordered to make the woman happy and headed off her first personal question by pretending not to understand it.

"Why are Americans so prying?" he asked when she had gone. "You have studied them. Tell me."

"I am an American."

"You know what I mean. You are as much an outsider as I am. But you know more. I can get your Polish citizenship back for you, you know. Your father never gave it up. Or I could do that a week ago. Now, I don't know. Tell me why Americans pry."

"It is an open society," she said. "Privacy is unknown; secrecy not trusted. People discuss the most intimate aspects of their lives in everyday conversations."

"Shocking."

"No. Just tawdry. But it is impolite to show boredom. One must be interested."

"A legacy of capitalism, no doubt."

The waitress set his soup before him, saving Mara a useless conversation.

"Are you going to eat that salad?" he said. "May I relieve you of it?" He reached across and dragged the plate toward him without waiting for her answer. "Why did you order Italian dressing? I like French. No, no, I insist on helping you in this way. You can keep your finger on the trigger, do you see, inconspicuously. I like chicken, too. I am glad you ordered it."

Mara watched him eat. His nails were grimy, arms dirty. She noticed odd patches he had missed in shaving. A long scrape ran under his shirt from his left ear. He fought to keep his eyes open.

Mara smiled.

The smile arrested him, mid-chew. Mara was no longer a mere beauty. She became cute, adorable, surely incapable of firing the loaded weapon in her bag. There was no charm like this in his world, in their world. Where did she get it? He soaked himself in it, knowing better. But hope is hope.

His thoughts were transparent to Mara. How many times had her father and the others come home—shot to pieces it seemed, filthy, tired, disgusted—and looked at her that way? She was no threat; therefore, he was no threat. When the chicken came, she let go of the trigger and picked up the fork with her right hand.

"How long do you have?" she asked him.

"To eat?" he asked. "Or to live?"

THREE

Michael played Chopin. Mara hated to interrupt him, but she must finish the interview, and if successful, fly back to the States within the day. Seal did not know she was gone.

She crossed the parquet floor of the small ballroom, walking toward Michael's back.

"Mara! What are you doing at home?" He spoke German and did not turn around, finishing the Nocturne before standing to meet her. He held her by the shoulders, kissed her cheek, said all the platitudes, and waited, smiling.

"You are as incredible as your father," she said, "with eyes in the back of your head. I was very quiet."

"You were, but not quiet enough. And he is our father, ...Sister." He did not let go of her shoulders.

"When—how—did you find out?"

"Yesterday. Your mother told me—us. Papa is in a state. Your timing is awkward."

"It has never been anything else, but I must see him. Now. Was it a surprise to you?"

He shook his head. "Not for me. I have suspected for years now." He led her to the mirrored south wall, where the parquet floor seemed to repeat itself forever. They stood side by side.

"Look at us," Michael said.

They were separated by fifteen centimeters, ten years, and gender. Was her blonde hair a trifle darker? Her eyes were green, not blue, but light eyes are light eyes seen two meters from a mirror. They had the same training. His had been more intense, and more practiced. He was a musical genius, she reflected, while she was merely competent, without talent in that area. She marveled at the lottery that is inheritance.

"Papa, on the other hand, was stunned," he said. "Which is amazing. He observes so much and never saw this. Look. We are so obvious. Even with different mothers. You look more like me than Nadia did." He turned toward the staircase on their left. "I will take you upstairs and announce you before I go riding."

She followed him across the polished floor, making no sound. There was an echo, though, when she said, "You will need to be there. This is operational."

Michael laughed and the echo laughed, too. "He has found out that you are his natural daughter, his long-lost Nadia come back to life, God bless her sainted soul, and you think you are going to discuss operations?" He laughed again, put his arm around her shoulder, and squeezed affectionately. "You will be lucky to leave home to go shopping. Maybe next year."

"Here is Mara, Papa," Michael said as he dragged her through the vaulted door of the office. "I told her she might go shopping next year."

Misha stood behind his desk, his sleeves rolled to the elbow, leaning over a map. Behind him, the walls were covered with more maps, some political, some geographic, a few on cork boards with colored push pins, others behind lighted plexiglass marked by grease pencil. He looked up. The gray hair at the edges only dulled the otherwise brilliant blond hair at his temples. There were more lines in his face than in Michael's, and a long scar down his neck, an operational token. Mara remembered the day he had come home with that.

Misha shook his head. "I will find her a suitable husband before then."

Was Misha joking? Did Misha joke? Could she think of an instance? Everybody feared this man. She never did. Hated, resented, respected, in varying amounts at different times, but never feared. He would not cut her throat, she knew, but marry her off to some weak-chinned European aristocrat? Here was true danger. Her tightrope frayed. To be disobedient would reflect badly on the beloved Vasily. To obey meant what? A life of tepid luxury as opposed to...? Standing for hours in a squalid room with Seal? She shuddered before she could catch it and noticed him smile at it. Joking and smiling, both in one day, a red-letter day.

"I am not joking," he said.

Misha was always one to put people at ease.

"Oh dear," she replied.

"Do not think you will get around me with that smile."

"Of course not."

"I assume you have come to your senses and walked away from that silly job."

"Then you are slipping."

He took the bait but spat out the hook. "I will allow you…"

"Allow me!"

"Yes. I will allow you this one operation because you are foolishly trying to help someone else. It is not likely to last long. Your role is to be purely supportive. You will do as I tell you, stay out of danger, and give your resignation to the Americans at the end of it."

"I agree to none of this."

"Is it that seedy boss of yours? Is he in trouble again?"

Again? Mara shook herself. "You are not listening to me, Sir. I do not agree."

"I am not interested in your agreement."

Mara heard her voice rise and strove to bring it under control. "You are my stepfather now that my mother married you," she said through clenched teeth, "but you are not and have never been my father, no matter what the genetics may be. I am an American citizen and Vasily Sobieski's daughter. I will use my name and my talent to benefit my country."

"Is this rehearsed?" Misha sat down in a comfortable leather chair, indicated a plain wooden one across the desk. "Sit."

Mara felt grateful for the five-foot expanse of mahogany between them.

"Mara, I consider a woman who kills an abomination. Especially if it is for her country."

He used his patient tone, the one reserved for women, children, and idiots. Mara suspected that, to him, she fit all three. His tone was triple smooth, his best attempt at putting a person at ease. It failed, of course. It was impossible to be easy in Misha's presence.

"That is nonsense and I do not kill," she said. "I am in counterintelligence, a quiet branch of it. Very routine."

He raised his eyebrow in an eloquent Oh, yeah? An expression that he would never be so low as to say. "Who is this friend for whom you risk my displeasure and perhaps my life, if it is not Seal?"

He knows Seal. Of course, he knows Seal. Probably has a copy of his personnel file. Probably knows what Seal had for dinner yesterday. No doubt he can smell the pastrami on my clothes. *I traveled six thousand miles to give him this intelligence.* She said, "It is not a friend. It is an enemy."

Misha sat forward, his forearms on the desk before him, and waited.

"I do not know why I believe him," she said, "or even if I believe him enough to bother you with this. He is Sergei Pavlenko."

"He came to you? For what?"

"I don't think it is a trap."

"I did not say it was."

"But you thought it."

"You are improving," Misha said through an almost smile. "Tell me why it is not a trap."

"Because he was too weary to be faking his fear."

FOUR

Everything was wrong. Every single thing. Every alarm, every signal, every safeguard had been tripped. The doorknob was bloody. Mara held her gun hidden by her side and worked the key left-handed. She slipped the door open slightly, waiting, more open, more waiting. Yes, Papa, you brought up a good daughter. A daughter who knows how to use her gun, knows she will use it, knows she will regret using it. A daughter who will live or die free, not locked up safely at home, nor gunned down on a final night at the opera, like little Nadia. That's what you wanted, Papa, to be normal. Normal—more or less.

She felt the trigger rest, the round chambered, the hammer cocked. There was no sound inside her apartment. Noisy children were coming down the stairs around the corner. They could come through only one way. They would pass her door. She slipped inside her living room. No one, no sound. She pushed the door closed behind her and locked it softly, left-handed. No point in being ambushed from behind. The children passed the door, their laughter fading as they headed for the pool. Mara saw bright flashes of pink and green through the edges of the blinds as they passed the kitchen window to her left. Blots and dabs of brown, and clots of viscous red made a trail on the carpet to her bedroom.

Mara checked the hall closet on her way. She did not care to be shot in the back, or taken from behind, or… Did Misha really cut people's throats? This she had heard from other sources before Seal mentioned it. Such details were not discussed at home. Her training had included many things, very effective things, in the martial arts and the use of weapons, many weapons, but not that, though she knew the theory. Misha had a knife, sure. Presumably... How much could heredity account for anyway? Was there an appreciable difference between growing up the daughter and granddaughter of two world-famous political assassins and discovering she was the biological daughter of the deadliest?

Her bedroom was empty but rumpled. She had not left it this way. In the bathroom to her left, something choked and gurgled. She pushed with her left hand and pointed with her right. The door swung open slowly, stuck on a bloody towel. Swirled smears of blood pointed toward the far end of the little room, where the bleeder sat crumpled between the toilet and the wall.

"You are very, very good, Masha. I did not hear you or I would have fired."

"I'm glad you didn't. My neighbors hear everything. Are you finished here, Sergei Nickolaevich? Shall I help you to bed?" Mara did not put down her gun, because Sergei still covered his loosely as it lay on the floor beside him.

"Your Russian is very pretty," he said. "But that should not surprise. Your mother's father was Feodor Dolnikov, wasn't he? The older Sobieski's babysitter? I wonder what he felt when your mother married his specialist's son. Did you learn your Russian from that grandfather? Dolnikov was a respected enemy. Even enemies must find it disgraceful to be too close to the trigger." He paused to gasp. "I killed two last night. The others ran. How did you know my patronymic?"

"Take your hand off your gun, Sergei, and I will help you into bed. Stop leering that way. You are in no condition. Who did this?" She pulled his damp shirt away from the skin.

"I want to discuss philosophy. Start with death. Does one who kills begin to die?"

"We begin to die at birth, Sergei Nickolaevich. Who did this?" She probed the round wound in his belly. Fresh blood, mostly clotted, almost black.

"My friends, of course. And my enemy comes to save me. Did you see him? Mack, I mean. The Americans named him Mack, because of his knife. I am quite well acquainted with the culture, you see. I have seen Mack's mark. This is nothing compared... blood everywhere. You call him Misha. Am I correct? I read files, too. Did you get my patronymic from the Americans? Or from Mack?"

"You have no fever. Stop acting delirious."

"I am not acting. Delirious or otherwise. I am ... I need a word."

"Overwrought," she said in English.

"Good word. In pain is better. There must be an even better one in Russian. I am not emotionless like Mack. I cannot kill and then sip cognac with a bloody hand."

Did Misha do that? *Would he?* It seemed to be part of the enemy's folklore. Mara dabbed the wound with a gauze pad soaked with alcohol.

"Owww! Oh! That is terrible. Stop!"

"He hates his wounds being dressed as much as you do."

"Does he?" Sergei lifted his head off the pillow and watched her, frowning. "Does he vomit? It was not the bullet that made me use the toilet."

Mara considered. "I have seen him sick, certainly, but I did not know the reason."

"He says nothing under interrogation," said Sergei. Their eyes met briefly. "Or so I have heard. Nor did your father."

Mara cut a ten-inch length of cloth surgical tape with scissors. "And Louis?"

"The Frenchman? He screams obscenities."

Yes, of course.

"The young one sings. Songs, I mean. It is very irritating."

"So you have heard."

Sergei said nothing.

Mara helped him sit up. She bound his abdomen with an elastic bandage over the gauze.

"The American reminds me of your father sometimes. He is very fast. Your father could beat a man to death in minutes. I lost several agents just on the rumors of it."

"You have met Steve and Michael? I must have been in school. I do not remember being told of it."

Sergei did not reply immediately. "We had them once. Briefly."

They were silent for what seemed a long time. Mara took his pulse for something to do. His knuckles were calloused. New scrapes had done little damage. He was about Michael's age, say somewhere in his early thirties, well built, and in top condition for a man with a bullet in him. He had lost some blood and was continuing to lose it, though slowly, she decided. He was not turning yellow. There was time.

"Will they be there too, do you suppose?" he asked. "Yes, of course," he answered himself.

The weary, hopeless look took possession of his face again, and while she considered that he likely deserved it, Mara found herself perhaps not so far as the point of pity, but at least up to the edge of regret.

"Get some sleep now. I must make the arrangements."

"Masha?"

"Yes?"

But he was already asleep.

FIVE

Seal sat alone in his apartment at the end of a lowboy lounger sofa long decayed. He pointed a remote control at a widescreen television in the corner: channel change, volume up, volume down, channel change. He had been through forty channels a dozen times this evening. The night was young.

"Shit," he said aloud when the phone rang. He had found an episode of *Lucy* that he did not remember seeing. Was that possible? The phone rang again. Should he tape it? His finger hovered over the VCR record button. No point. He would get only half of it. The phone rang again. Anyway, should he erase the tape in the machine? Was there a tape in the machine?

He drained his beer, reached for the phone on the table next to him, picked it up because it insisted, and breathed a beery "Yeah?" into the mouthpiece.

...

He drank coffee while he shaved, spilled some on his t-shirt, changed, spilled again, said "what the fuck," half a dozen times, and left the shirt on until the coffee ran out, then changed again. He anointed himself with splashes from the fancy black bottle of men's cologne his sister sent him for Christmas. He splashed the mirror, too, and grinned at the dripping streaks as he brushed his teeth. Yeah. It had to be intelligence related. Probably something going on with the people in the upstairs division, where Mara belonged without a doubt, famous name and all. He was needed for a briefing maybe. She wanted him for a reference probably. He stuffed some less decrepit specimens of underwear and a few cleanish shirts into a carryall and danced to the door, a jerky but joyful movement that shook the remote control off the little table.

No contest, he decided. Old Lucy could never compete with the prospect of spending a few days with a girl like Mara.

He checked his back frequently. Joy and confidence grew as he crossed the parking lot and entered the labyrinth of sidewalks that led to Mara's apartment. He was Bond, James Bond. He had not felt like this since training. How long ago was that? That was way back, before dirty and gut-wrenching even, which was before tedious and mind-numbing. He knocked on her door.

Shave and a haircut, two bits.

She opened right away. She wore yellow rubber gloves and held a sponge.

"What are you doing?" he asked as he closed and locked the door behind him. He pretended for one more minute that this was not business. His nose told him it was, but he ignored it. What was that smell? Besides the disinfectant?

"I'm cleaning up the blood stains," she said. She knelt and sponged the carpet. There was a bucket of soapy water next to her. Wet spots made a trail to the hallway. "I have to pay a cleaning fee if I leave stains on the carpet."

She finished with that stain and stood up.

"So what's going on?" he asked.

She took off the gloves and checked her nails. "Come into the kitchen."

He followed her and carried the bucket for her. She turned on the radio while he poured the bloody, soapy water down the kitchen sink.

"You went to some fancy East Coast school, didn't you?" he asked her, trying to avoid the inevitable revelation, whatever it was. "Ivy league wasn't it?"

She smiled and he melted, as usual.

Mara took a cotton towel out of a drawer and dried the bucket. "I need you to get us both a few days off, Seal. I thought I could do this by myself, but there has been a glitch. Can you come with me?"

"Where?"

"I suppose you have a need to know, but first tell me if you can get us leave."

"Yes, I can."

"And will you?"

"Of course. Now tell me."

"Later. First, we need a car."

"Mine's parked outside."

"Not that one. How much is a used car? One that will get us, say, as far as Seattle?"

"Are we going to Seattle?" He wanted to shake her. He did not appreciate being handled, though he knew he would continue to do everything she said, like an insect in a web bouncing to the spider's step.

"Maybe," she answered. "How much is a car? A fast car."

"I can probably get one for seven or eight grand, but...."

She took a bag of flour from a cabinet and rummaged through it, bringing out a baggie stuffed with money. It reminded him of something. God, don't let this be a drug thing.

She counted out ten thousand dollars, in hundreds. "Make sure it has a radio," she said.

Had to be drugs.

She opened the silverware drawer, lifted the tray, and took out two plastic cards. "You probably shouldn't use your own name."

"I can go get my...."

"No. Not your official game name, either, Seal. Here. I made this for you. Be Stan Bremmer for now."

He looked at the plastic cards in his hand. One was a California driver's license. Where did she get the picture? The other was a credit card.

"The credit card is no good, though." Her voice came through his confusion. "I didn't have time to match numbers, so don't use it."

He was scared. He didn't shake or anything stupid like that. He just didn't move. Like that time back then.

"Go, Seal. Buy us a car."

Did Ivy League beauties do drugs? Wasn't there a political movement, what were they, libertarians, that wanted drugs to be legal? Were they fancy eggheads? God, why didn't he pay attention to this shit? He looked hard at Mara, trying to see past the beauty, the physical perfection, to the soul. Could he find that, when he didn't even know where his own was?

...

He bought a Camaro. It was green, mostly, with a few rust spots that it didn't get in the desert. It still had Florida plates. That, and the engine, a 350, were the deciding factors in his choice, along with the AM-FM cassette player.

The heat put moisture under his arms, but the bright flowers on his shirt didn't show it. A strand of hair came loose from its anchoring mousse at the top of his head and exposed a glistening piece of sweating scalp. Desert dry heat my ass, he thought. Heat is heat.

Progression normal, he decided, threading his steps through the sidewalk maze. *From Bond to gut-wrenching, next step dirty.*

Shave and a haircut, two bits.

Mara opened the door, and he almost forgot how afraid he was. She wore jeans and running shoes and a plain tee shirt in pale green, like her eyes. She had pulled back her hair as usual and tied it with a large bow that matched the t-shirt. Her shirt was not tucked in, he knew, because it had to cover the Glock 19 she wore in an inside holster. She always packed. He never did. That stuff was for subordinates who did the actual nabbing of the bad guys.

"Take your shirt off," she said, "and put this on." She was holding a shoulder rig. "I'll help you adjust it. That shirt is perfect, it'll go over it just fine."

"What is this?" he asked, as she fiddled with the buckles. "It looks like a Makarov."

"Sorry, I didn't tell you to bring yours."

"I dunno if I could even find mine, honey. What am I supposed to be doing with a Makarov?"

"You'll need one. It's his, but I'm not going to let him hold it just now."

"Him?"

"Yes. Come and help me get him to the car. I think it's dark enough outside."

She led him to the bedroom at the back of the apartment. When she turned on the light, he could see a rumpled pile, roughly human, on the bed.

"My god, that's Pavlenko," he said when the pile moved.

"Americans are so astute," said the voice from the pile.

"Help me get him up, Seal."

Mara and Pavlenko babbled away in Russian as Seal helped him walk to the door. They were silent outside, getting into the car quickly, Pavlenko lying on the back seat, Mara sitting in front.

As Seal started the car and turned on the lights, he was so overjoyed that Columbian cartels were not his particular problem this night, that he forgot to worry about the possibility of treason.

SIX

W hen the elevator hit the top number, Seal put the plastic card Mara had given him into the slot. The elevator went higher. To the moon, Alice. Seal rocked back and forth, toes and heels, caught himself holding his hands behind his back. "Whatever you do," Mara had said, "Keep your hands where they can be seen." Of course, he knew that; didn't need reminding from some close-mouthed, secretive, maddeningly cool little slip of a girl.

The hotel elevator brought him to a tiled anteroom. The mir-rored wall before him had no apparent doors or even buttons. He smoothed the hair over his right ear and wondered what to do. There was a buzzing sound. He pondered it. There it was again. Of course! He pushed on the glass in front of him. It swung inward on silent hinges. He stepped through into another anteroom, or maybe it was a continuation of the first one, with the same tile, and the glass wall, not mirrored on this side, behind him. In front of him stood a man with an AK-47 pointed at him.

"Where's Mara?" the man demanded. He made his point with the gun, holding it casually with one arm and swinging it at Seal's favorite flowered shirt. He was youngish, Seal decided, thirties, ear-ly? With brown hair and over-large brown eyes and over-long eye-lashes. Mara's boyfriend? Did Mara have a boyfriend? If she did, this one would probably be a contender. Seal felt regret, not jealousy. There had been a time when he would have been a contender, too.

He babbled his name.

The man was not listening. "I know who the fuck you are," he said. "Weapon?" He rested the barrel against Seal's sternum.

Seal moved to retrieve the Makarov from under his shirt. The barrel pressed harder.

"Just point to it," said the man.

The formalities complete, Seal was shown into a sumptuous reception room in the penthouse suite of O'Malley's Casino in Reno. He was led down two wide marble steps, across a white Berber carpet, and through double doors into a dining room. Here, quiet luxury gave way to activity and the familiar (to Seal) mess of an intelligence operation. Three computers lined the buffet. A printer buzzed on a trolley. An ugly African-American man wearing a shoulder holster and suspenders stood over it, reading the words as they spurted from the inkjet. The large table was strewn with documents and little Styrofoam coffee cups, some on their sides with brown rings around the inside bottoms. The table could seat twelve. It was meant for better things.

Only three men sat there, at the other end, a world away from Seal, their shirt sleeves rolled up, their ties loosened. They all wore guns in shoulder holsters. Seal recognized a Glock. Was that a SIG? His eyes stopped on this one, on the blue, blue irises that halted his gaze mid-sweep. He sensed, rather than saw, the third man, with dark somewhat wavy hair and dark eyes, to the left. This one, though, the one looking through him, old blue eyes here, was familiar. He remembered.

"Let us dispense with introductions since we know each other," said Mack. "Where is Mara?"

Seal swallowed. His jaw worked, but no sound came out. He knew he looked like Ralph Kramden in front of the boss. Did this guy know *The Honeymooners*? What a stupid question to be asking himself now.

He worked at it a little more. The dark-haired man tapped the table in front of him with a pencil. "She's at a motel," Seal managed. "Not too far. She said she had to change. The guy threw up on her. Just like a Russian, he had to have pickled herring, he said, and vodka. Well, we couldn't get no herring, so we got oysters. And Mara wouldn't let him have no vodka, on account of his condition, so she picked up a bottle of table wine, she said. But when she got back to the car, it turns out it was Boone's Farm Apple. I don't blame the guy for being sick. Mara just don't know these things; I try to teach her."

"Which motel?"

"I don't know. I can take you there. We need help getting him up here. He's pretty bad. He needs a doctor, too. He's got a bullet somewhere in here." Seal waved the flat of his hand vaguely around his abdomen, never taking his eyes off the man with the SIG.

Mack looked at the man by the printer. "Jay, can you bring us a doctor?"

The man tilted his heavy head forward, affirmative. "Listen, may I advise?" He waited. There was no objection. "I'd like to bring a babysitter, too. Things are becoming awkward for me. I will have to get back to Chicago." He ripped a string of pages off the tractor feed, waved them, pointed at them as if they might be read, as though the damp ink on them could float over the table for better communication.

"What babysitter?"

"Frank Cardova."

"He is on the East Coast."

"I took the liberty of having him come with me to Reno when you called. Something is up. I think we'll need him. I know it has been a long time since you worked with him, but there is a sea change here, and he is an experienced mariner."

...

Mara wore a white and navy nautical outfit, with a little white pleated skirt, blouse trimmed in navy, and little blue low-heeled pumps. Her hair was French braided, with a large navy-blue bow at the end. She did not belong in the dirty little motel room. Her perfume mixed with, and was overcome by, the stench of vomit and blood. It was this vision of a perfect rose on a battlefield that first mesmerized Seal and the two men who had come with him, Charlie, the younger blond man with the Glock, and Steve, the brown-eyed man he'd first met.

Something moved on the bed, breaking the spell. Pavlenko tried to sit up straighter against the headboard, his shirt front stiff with vomited blood and oysters and Boone's Farm. He wanted to stand, maybe, to face these two. Seal was aware they were enemies, but he was not prepared for the hopeless fear in Pavlenko's eyes as Charlie and Steve stepped toward him. The Russian tried to shield himself, feebly, at first.

Seal could see there was no defense, against the blows, against the sickening sound of them, against the conflict between being glad it wasn't him and wishing it would stop before he, too, threw up. He looked at Mara for relief, for an oasis, for a return to sanity. He could comfort her, protect her, lessen the ugliness for her by turning her pretty head aside. He was not needed. She was as emotionless as ever, as unimpressed by the hand-to-hand killing of a man as by the passing of a secret document.

Seal was sure he was going to throw up.

Pavlenko fell at Mara's feet. Steve raised his foot for another of those blows not seen, a species of kick Seal knew happened only by its effect on the body of the man on the floor. You never actually saw those kicks coming, did you? Mara placed a dainty, well-manicured hand on Steve's forearm and it stopped. Seal kept his dinner. Pavlenko caught his breath and spit out three teeth. Mara picked up the bloody teeth, and put them in her handkerchief, while Charlie and Steve carried him to the car.

On the way back to O'Mally's, Seal stopped the shaking in his hands by squeezing the wheel.

Mara sat next to him, saying nothing except, "Michael, stop it."

"I am not doing anything," came Charlie's voice from the back seat. "And my game name is Charlie. And this is Steve."

"Oh." She paused. "Should I have a game name? Stop hurting him; I can hear the changes in his breathing; you will kill him."

"Your father never used one. His name was an advantage, but not to you, Mara. Papa will send you straight home, no matter how cute you look. It does not matter if I kill this insect."

"Yes, it does. I have given my word to help him. Stop it."

SEVEN

John Fairfax put his right hand in his pocket while he walked through the parking lot of O'Malley's Resort and Casino. His left hand carried his call bag, with the instruments.

"Doctor Fairfax," said the short, fat man named Frank who walked beside him, "have you ever been out before?"

"No."

"May I suggest that you always keep your hands in the open, where they can be seen?"

That was the sum of their conversation. The FBI agent, Jay Turner, said nothing after the initial introduction. He put a forefinger in front of his large, ugly face and then pointed to the car whispering, "Not secure."

John had just finished a busy shift on call, with two appendectomies and a knife wound to the kidney. He did not relish earning the past year's worth of standby stipends from the FBI on this particular night. The pay would triple, though, since he was being called out, and that was good for all those outstanding student loans. And you never knew, the case might be interesting. Still, he had seen enough ordinary gunshot wounds not to count on it, though the secrecy added some interest. Both these men, the ugly one and the older, hairless fat man seemed serious about their business.

The penthouse apartment they took him to was like any other, except for all the guns, and the man, his patient, bleeding on the Berber, and the beautiful girl in a blue and white sailor dress trying to help the bleeding man up while she argued in the most enchanting French. She argued with a tall, dark-haired man who had just kicked John's patient in the ribs. John heard the crack as he walked into the room. He stood on a marble step between the FBI man, Jay, and the bald one, Frank, and watched.

The patient crawled to a spot in front of someone obviously in charge, also in his shirtsleeves and wearing a gun in a shoulder apparatus that looked uncomfortable. This man was about John's height, blond and blue-eyed like him, too, but much older, though not as old as his father. Late forties, maybe.

"Jay Turner has only English," said the man. He had a heavy, German accent. This was shaping up like a war flick. "Do you speak English, Sergei Nickolaevich?"

The patient did not answer but swayed on his hands and knees, which was as far as he had gotten toward a standing position.

"He speaks English." The girl answered for him. She did not have an accent, but why did she seem foreign?

The patient made it to his knees, looking at the blond man in front of him briefly, before he fell forward again and caught his fall with his hands. John stepped forward off the step. Frank held him back.

"What do you have for us?" the blond man asked the patient.

"When… we… get… there."

"Where?"

"Allow me to guess," interrupted Jay Turner. "To San Antonio. Am I correct?"

The patient nodded and wheezed.

"The whole world is going to San Antonio," explained the FBI man. "Every spook known to man or computer is there or is headed there. We have been instructed to let them all in and search any coming out. All documents are to be sealed and sent forward."

"If I may interrupt," said Frank. "Am I correct that this is Sergei Pavlenko? It's hard to tell."

A fat man in a loud shirt nodded at Frank.

"Just before Jay here contacted me," said Frank, "I was given a commission against Pavlenko." He looked at the pitiful lump on the floor. Everybody looked at it.

"Why?" asked the blond man.

Frank shrugged. "I was not privy to that information, Mack. I am authorized to offer twenty million." He took his eyes off Pavlenko and looked at the man he called Mack.

"Are you offering me the commission?"

Frank hesitated. "It's been so long and there is no verification this time. It has been getting bad lately, but this is the worst. I think it was assumed that we would use People's Fist for this one."

Mack's eyebrows rose, amazed. "People's Fist? They are Eastern."

"Yes," said Frank. "Like I said, things are, shall we say, different. If you want the commission, you can have it, for the full amount. The man is unarmed."

"Is this all your people want? Just the body?"

"And any documents he has on him. They should be sealed and sent directly up the chain."

"No questioning?"

"No. And no sign of torture. I might have to deduct for the teeth."

"Hah! You said full amount!" This came from the tall rib-kicker. The accent was French.

Mack held up one hand for silence. The patient, the Russian, whom they called Pavlenko, still swayed on his knees, supported by his hands, panting and wheezing like an injured dog. Mack looked down at him. "It is an enormous sum for one corpse. What is this document they want so badly, Sergei Nickolaevich?"

The Russian did not answer right away. The room became completely silent when he finally spoke, and even then it was difficult to hear him. Several words were lost in his noisy efforts to breathe. "I... with... Semianov... died."

"You were with Semianov when he died?" asked Mack.

A painful nod, then, "I... three others."

"You and three others. Where are they?"

"Dead."

The Frenchman took his gun out of its holster and pointed it at the patient. "Let him join them, I say. Then we can collect Frank's commission and go home."

No one moved. Mack looked at each man in the room in turn, as if taking a poll. His gaze swept over John on its way to Jay Turner. Then he looked at the girl for what seemed a long time.

Finally, she said simply, "I gave my word that I would help him."

EIGHT

"Is this the doctor?"

The man gazed at him with an unpleasant, cold, and invasive examination of the soul, probing and measuring John with pinpoint accuracy. Acutely uncomfortable, John swallowed hard.

Jay nodded.

They laid the patient on a large mahogany table in the dining room, or what would be the dining room if it were not full of computers and empty coffee cups. The patient's belt scratched the finish as they slid him into position, more or less centered at the far end.

John opened his bag and looked for a place to lay out his instruments. Someone moved a printer, and the girl trundled the trolley it had been on to his side. She laid a clean tea towel on top. He set out his instruments, still in their wrappers, freshly autoclaved. She helped him put on his surgical gloves. He turned toward the patient, whose shirt was already cut off. Across the table, the Frenchman, the one who had been ready to shoot the man, had taken his call bag and begun the IV. He was already hanging a bag of fluids, even though John gave no order. No, the Frenchman told him, there were no drugs, nor anesthetic. Proceed, he said.

John was sure he had something in his bag. He was already sterile and was about to ask them to look again when a brown-eyed man in his thirties, the one they were calling Steve, opened a wicked-looking street knife with his thumb, roughly cut off a length of Pavlenko's belt and shoved it in the patient's mouth for a gag. He did not put away the knife, but let it hang there in the air, pointed in John's direction. The dying man bit down hard and closed his eyes.

"Proceed," repeated the Frenchman.

Steve pushed past John to the other end of the table to hold the patient's legs. John gave him a sharp jab with his elbow as he passed.

He decided he disliked Steve. He did not like the violence in his eyes and his manner and he despised the way the man looked at this girl. John already considered her his own, by the way she anticipated his every order. Steve could take a hike.

"Are you a nurse?" he asked her.

"No." She smiled a half-smile, melancholy. "I grew up doing this. I always helped the doctor when they came home."

"That is true. Masha sewed me up after the last time we met you, Sergei Nickolaevich." This came from the younger blond man who now positioned himself at the patient's head. "You remember Tbilisi, don't you? My leg was broken, and you made me stand on it. The doctor was not sure he would save it, but with Masha's help...." He jabbed a fist into the patient's broken ribs.

"Mara's help will be of no use to Sergei now," said the Frenchman, who held down the IV arm and the far hip. "This doctor is too young to finish secondary school."

His remark seemed directed at the round man who had brought him here.

John paused, the scalpel ready over the wound, while Mara swabbed again. Steve and the blond one—Mara called him Charlie—held the patient's legs and shoulders. Jay Turner took the near arm.

"I don't have time to list my awards," said John, "but I became a fully qualified forensic surgeon before age thirty, board-certified, and I graduated summa cum laude from the best medical school in the country."

"A typical American braggart," said the Frenchman.

John looked into the dark brown, almost black, eyes of the older man across the table from him and involuntarily shuddered. "I am trying to put the patient at ease," he said through clenched teeth.

Ha ha ha! All around the table. Even the girl smiled. Steve's laugh was the loudest. John already knew what he thought of that one. The patient began to sweat.

John worked quickly, did the minimum. Enough to stop the bleeding, repair the diaphragm, disinfect, and suture. The Frenchman came up with antibiotics from somewhere and administered them, again, before John could order it. The last straw, though, came as John pulled the final suture tight. From nowhere, the Frenchman drew out a bottle of morphine, measured, and gave the dose. The patient relaxed. Charlie pulled the leather gag from between his bleeding gums.

John faced the Frenchman across the table, scissors still in his hand. "Are you a doctor?" he demanded. He did not wait for any reply. "This is my patient. I order the meds. You said there was nothing here for pain. You are a liar." He pointed with the scissors to give his accusation emphasis.

John remembered the Frenchman vaulting over the table so fast he could only know of it by memory as he lay on the floor on the other side. Breath was also history; there was none in his body. He felt himself lifted off the floor, saw the fist headed for his eye, felt the impact, fist then wall. Pain registered. He thought only, oh god, please not my hands.

He heard a foreign voice, Mack's voice, and for a moment he saw himself on his hands and knees on a white Berber carpet; no, that was the patient. He was on his back against a wall, under a chair, everything looking pink, and his face was wet.

The voice said, "Do not kill the doctor, Louis," softly, indifferently, as in, I'll have my fish sautéed, not broiled.

Another voice, American with a soft Southern accent: "Just break his hands." This one was venomous, not indifferent. Had to be Steve. John rallied briefly, managed a breath, raised an arm to fend off the chair, and was lifted again against the wall, with one arm twisted and great pressure on his throat.

He looked into the dark eyes of a man of violence. The twisted arm turned again and he winced, saw amusement in those eyes. He tried to look defiant, another twist, an involuntary gasp, and the Frenchman smiled.

"You are summa cum laude from the College of Fools, Doctor, if you insult a man you cannot fight."

With great effort, he stayed standing when he was let go. The wall helped. It gave support. The girl helped. She was watching, giving him incentive to not crumple in front of her. Steve helped the most. His grin hit the other eye, the one not swollen, with triumph. John stood by force of will.

He had three great comforts. First, his hands were undamaged. Second, the girl did not gush over him, but only handed him a handkerchief. He thought at first it was to wipe the blood from the cut over his eye, but there was something in it. He opened it without shaking much and found three bloody teeth. It puzzled him at first; he had not lost any teeth; then he remembered. She had a bowl of disinfectant ready. He cleaned the teeth and put them back in the patient's mouth. There was some wire in his bag; he made a makeshift brace and while he fitted it, Mack provided the third comfort.

"So you think he will live," said Mack, not asking, just reading his mind. "When will you allow him to speak to us?"

It could only have been sweeter if the Frenchman himself had said, 'You are the doctor here.'

"Oh, by morning. Certainly, by morning."

NINE

In the absence of any guidance, in the universal lack of deference to him as a surgeon and the presence of actual hostility from Steve and the Frenchman, John stayed in the dining room with his patient. It seemed the safest thing to do. The girl stayed, too. John admitted to himself, privately, that this was his real reason for staying.

When everyone else left the room, she cleaned the cut over his eye. She said, "Please be careful around Louis, Doctor. He can be dangerous with strangers. He is much more volatile here than he is at home."

"What's your name?"

"Mara."

"Mara. You speak beautiful French. Are you related to Louis? You said 'at home.'"

She chuckled, and shook her head, amused. "My father was the explosives expert for the team."

"Was? Team?"

"He died ten years ago. This man killed him." She pointed to the patient with her chin as she cut a length of gauze to dress the superbly sutured wound.

John waited, confused.

"He relayed the order," she explained, "which carries a degree of responsibility. Don't you think? I am not talking about collective guilt, you understand. Sergei was directly in the decision-making chain, not merely attached to it. One can deny responsibility all the way to the trigger, can't one? And finish with the absurdity that the gun alone did the killing."

"Then Mack is not your father?"

The half-smile vanished. "He is my stepfather," she said.

"Step?"

"He is married to my mother."

"Oh. And so Charlie is ..."

"My stepbrother." She clipped the words.

He wanted to ask about Steve, but as if summoned by the thought, the man walked in, shaved and dressed in a suit and tie. He took the chair next to John and sat there smirking at his swollen eye.

"Mara, why don't you get some rest now," said John. "Thank you for your help. You're quite an expert."

The quiet little smile, the one her eyes did not join in on, came back and she shook her head. She sat down in a chair on the other side of the table. The blood on her white dress had turned brown and much of her hair escaped the braid at the back, hanging down in fine gold wisps around her face. Her eyes streamed from lack of sleep, leaving a smudge of mascara on one cheek.

"Mara's not going anywhere tonight, or she will lose her project," said Steve.

"He'll be all right," John told her.

"No, he won't," said Steve.

"I will watch him," said John.

"You'll watch him die," said Steve, laughing as he continued, "You don't think you could stop me, do you? Or any of the others? How about Louis? Fend him off with a fucking scissors, or better yet, fling insults at him. Deadly."

Steve finished his laugh and spoke to Mara. "You should go home, Mara. It isn't just a matter of a few bumps and scrapes. Other things happen to us. You saw Louis. In twenty-four hours, it will take all three of us to pull him off the doctor here, and by that time, I won't want to. Not that I'm all that motivated now."

"I have never known you to be such a bully, Steve," said Mara. She yawned. "What makes you hate the doctor so much?"

"He's arrogant."

"So are you," said Mara.

Charlie came through the door, also dressed to go out. Behind him was the man in the loud shirt. This was a different loud shirt. This one was clean.

"I thought Frank was going with you," said Mara. "Why are you taking both babysitters?" She narrowed her eyes at Charlie. "You are going to look for women, aren't you?"

"Louis is looking for women," said Charlie. "Frank will stay with him. We'll keep Seal with us. Jane Jared is in the hotel. We're hoping to run into her."

"Of course, you hope so. You think you are God's benefit to women, don't you?"

The man in the flowered shirt cleared his throat. "Uh, Mara, you mean God's gift to women."

"Thank you, Seal." She smiled and turned back to Charlie. "Jane Jared is not good for you, Michael Joachim. You like her too much."

"My game name is Charlie, for the hundredth time, and this is business. You just go on protecting your KGB bastard and let me get on with my job."

John had almost two seconds alone with her when they left, enough time to turn in her direction and open his mouth before Mack came into the room carrying two large Styrofoam cups. John closed his mouth.

Mara nodded where she sat. Her mascara poured freely down her cheek as she fought to keep her eyes open.

"Go," Mack said to her. "Get some sleep."

She looked at him doubtfully, worried.

"I will not touch him," said Mack. After a pause: "If they return, I will not let them touch him." Another pause: "I give my word."

John thought this would be a good time to go, too. The patient was stable, and Mara was gone and maybe he might find her in another room.

"You stay here tonight, Doctor."

The weight of one hand pushed him back into the chair. One hand backed up by excessive physical conditioning, John decided. He noticed the corded muscles on a scarred forearm. The knuckles were also scarred and calloused. The man took the next chair, turned it to face him and the door behind him, and sat down, within an arm's reach. He pushed one of the Styrofoam cups along the table toward John. "Coffee," he said. He took a sip from the other one.

The coffee was black and vile, but John drank it gratefully while he studied Mack.

Mack, of course, studied him back, with blue eyes in a faintly scarred face. Another scar, long and nasty, ran from the man's right ear to below the shirt collar. He wore his hair longer than his son did, and at the temples, the blond color had turned a more transparent gray. He wore a white shirt with the sleeves rolled up, no tie, top button open. Thick leather straps ran vertically down from his shoulders on either side. From one of these hung what John considered to be an enormous gun in a holster, from the other, a couple of long leather pouches.

John addressed the gun at first, forced himself to look into the blue eyes, then back to the gun. It seemed safer. "You are not an American," he said to the gun.

"No. I am Austrian."

"But Mara is American."

"Her mother is. Her father was Polish."

John forced himself to confront the eyes. "Charlie's English is very good."

"My wife, Mara's mother, taught him. He is very good at languages. I am not. I speak only a few."

John wondered. "I speak French," he said finally. "My mother is French Canadian."

"Yes. I know. You are from Baltimore, Maryland. Your family is wealthy, Catholic, and long established there. You have quarreled with your father and are paying for your medical training on your own. Jay gave me your file. I read it."

John did not know how to answer this.

"I suppose it is some distinction in this country to have two languages," said Mack. "Since many Americans cannot even manage one. I have difficulty, sometimes, deciphering the series of grunts and gestures that some pretend is English."

This was not exactly what John considered polite conversation. He concentrated on his coffee. After five minutes of silence and a few more gulps of caffeine, he felt better and tried again, out of curiosity.

"What kind of gun is that?"

"It is a SIG-Sauer P226. I have had modifications made." Mack took it out of the holster, pulled back the slide, and pointed to something he called a compensator. "It helps to control recoil," he explained.

"Have you ever actually used it?"

Mack stared at him.

"So, all that stuff Frank said about twenty million for this guy's body is true? Are you a hitman or something?"

"Hitman?"

"Assassin. Killer. That kind of thing." Why the hell was he asking this? What answer was he looking for?

"Yes. Assassin is close."

"No kidding? And you work for Uncle Sam?"

"When he pays us."

"And Mara?"

"What about Mara?"

"She is an American."

"Mara only thinks she is American," said Mack. "She grew up in Europe and has no concept of how life is lived in this country. We thought her boss, Seal, would help in his peasant way, but he treats her like a fine crystal goblet, standing back to admire but doing nothing about the contents. I do not know what to do about her. I should send her home in the morning."

"Yes, you should." It was the patient who spoke.

John jumped up, grabbed for a pulse, and checked the eyes.

"Send her home. It occurs to me thith ith a trap," Pavlenko lisped through his wire brace.

"Such things usually are," said Mack. "But how should I send her? Shall I have her bound and gagged? Lock her in a dungeon? I cannot risk open defiance from her. In this family it is deadly, I have learned. Or perhaps that is your plan?"

"I swear to you I had nothing to do with it." The patient showed signs of distress. "Slavin was my boss. He told me to work with Jared. I thought we were going to trap you. I was not informed, and I protested when your wife was killed, and your little girl. I am so sorry. I was reprimanded. It is in my personnel file." He lifted himself on his left elbow to look at Mack.

John pushed him back down. Mack stood, walked to the buffet, and opened a drawer. Pavlenko continued to talk.

"Semianov told us, me, to give it to our enemies. The others tried and were killed. They were sold. There is no honor anywhere. You are the only honorable enemy left."

"What is it he told you to give me?" Mack took a metal box from the drawer.

"The file. The complete file. All of it." The patient was sweating. The pupils had dilated. "The list of all his work in this country. He ran the illegals and the agents of influence."

"Yes, I know. And why did he want his enemy to have it?" Mack handed the box to John.

"So that someone would appreciate the completeness of our victory."

"I have always known about your victory here, and I do not much care."

"Mara cares. I don't want her to be hurt. You must protect her."

Mack looked at the ceiling. John looked in the box. It held some disposable syringes and a row of morphine bottles. He took one of each and drew up a dose.

"All the roads open to me are perilous, Sergei Nickolaevich," said Mack. "If I send her home, she will defy me. Now that she has rescued you, she is in the game on a new level. People will think she is operational, and she will become a target. If she responds as she has been trained, she becomes a killer. Which do you recommend?"

John prepped Pavlenko's arm. Mack held up one hand. Wait.

"It does not have to go on," Pavlenko said finally.

"In my world—in the state of nature—it does. She is a third-generation Sobieski who has had two years, seven months of freedom. She is not twenty-two. Do you want to tell her she can leave the dungeon only if she kills? Do you want to show her the difference now that you have crossed that threshold?"

"I am truly sorry," the patient wheezed. "I did not understand. I had not yet crossed it when I asked for her help."

"You are sorry." It was a dead statement.

Mack nodded and John administered the dose. Pavlenko drifted back into unconsciousness.

John asked Mack one more thing before the others came in.

"You will court her whatever I say," was Mack's answer. "As long as you do not touch her, I will not stop you. Neither will I protect you."

TEN

Seal attacked the trolley when Jay wheeled it into the dining room. He took a bread roll off the top before Jay brought it to a stop. He had it buttered before Jay sat down at the table next to Frank. He had never been so hungry. He was glad to see this dawn and the breakfast that came with it.

"Is that blood on the table?" asked Jay.

"Where?"

"In front of you, where the crumbs are falling."

Seal shrugged.

Jay looked around the room. "Why is there blood on the wall?"

"Oh, that's the doctor's." Seal spewed breadcrumbs over a wide area.

The doctor came into the room. Jay studied his shiner and the gash above it, noticed the man's seedy condition. Jay had not slept that night either, but he had been able to shave. These three were not shaved. The doctor was a mess, like the dining room, spattered with dried blood. Like Seal, he demolished a bread roll before collapsing into a chair at the head of the table.

"I leave you for a few hours thinking all is well," Jay said to Frank. "The team is in the capable hands of not one but two babysitters, and you guys let them beat up my doctor."

"What's a babysitter?" asked John.

"We are," said Frank. "We keep order, arrange logistics, try to avert disaster, that sort of thing."

"For the FBI?"

"No, no. We're not FBI. Jay is FBI, anti-terror. He's been the team's de facto babysitter for the past few years because of some strained relations, but we're the trained babysitters, though Seal hasn't worked in the field lately. Pavlenko's a babysitter, too, for the Other Side, or what used to be the Other Side."

"Not anymore," said Jay. "He has graduated."

Frank handed out Styrofoam cups. "I suppose if you define a specialist in terms of how many people want to kill him versus how many he has killed, then Pavlenko qualifies now."

"He is fully qualified," said Jay. He lifted an ornate china pot from the trolley. "I told them I wanted coffee. These look like teapots. Wait, it is coffee. Anybody?" Everybody. He poured. "Pavlenko killed two last night in California—probably the two who put that bullet in him. The message came into the Reno office this morning. I happened to be there to see it. Where is Charlemagne, by the way? Charlie met me at the elevator."

"Charlemagne?" asked John.

"The team. It's the name of the team," explained Frank. He turned back to Jay. "They're showering and changing. They had what they called a semi-workout on the covered terrace. They must've thought we were all asleep." He waived vaguely at Seal and the doctor to define all. "We hid behind the double screen by the piano. Even Pavlenko joined us when he could sit up. I'd have had popcorn for everybody, but the crunching would give us away. As it was, Pavlenko's gasping nearly tubed us a couple of times."

"Mack knew we were there, Frank," said Seal.

"Of course he did. He knows everything. He allowed it. Don't ask me why." He blew on his coffee.

"So a specialist kills people but a babysitter doesn't? Am I right?" asked John, trying to understand. "And because Pavlenko killed somebody, he's now the one and no longer the other? Is that what Mack meant about crossing the threshold?"

"Mack?" Frank looked at the doctor, puzzled. "Let me piece this together for you. Yes, a specialist is capable of killing if it's necessary. And we don't normally employ them unless we think it's going to be necessary. A babysitter doesn't and mustn't do any actual killing but don't think that we deny responsibility."

"Yes, I understand that. Mara explained it."

"Mara?" Frank's normally bulging round eyes seemed ready to pop out of his head. "You've been discussing the game with Mack and Mara? They spoke to you about it? I want every word."

"Don't start that, Frank," said Jay. "I stuck my neck out to get you here. The rule is NO MORE FILES."

"I know. I know. After thirty years in the game, it's hard to break the habit. This morning's workout was incredible. I've never been this close."

"What was incredible?"

"The girl. The girl can fight, can't she?" Frank looked at Seal, who nodded. "She decked the Frenchman,"

"She what?"

"Laid him out, well, doubled him up, I should say. She kicked him in the groin. They were sparring."

Seal and John nodded. Witnesses.

Jay's heavy jaw fell open.

Frank continued, "She apologized and worried over him and when he could talk again he said don't worry about it but don't think you're so great until you can do that to Steve. The doc here translated for us. His French is not as rusty as mine. We were writing all this on paper so they wouldn't hear us whisper. I have it here somewhere."

"I'd burn it if I were you," said Jay. "Then what happened?"

"So then the Frenchman took over guard duty from Mack and they traded sparring partners until eventually it was Steve against Mara. She did very well at first but complained he was holding back, so Charlie told him to stop holding back. Well, Steve hit her square in the solar plexus with what they called a thrust-kick and she flew across the terrace and landed against the wall. I had to sit on the doctor here to stop him from getting himself—and maybe us—killed. Seal clamped both hands over his mouth. You have us to thank that he's even alive. He's done nothing but get himself in trouble since he got here."

"If Pavlenko's up walking around, I'd say he's done a little more than that," said Jay. "Who blacked his eye?"

"The Frenchman."

"Starting early, is he?"

"He's in a fine state," Frank replied.

"But it's Steve who's gonna kill your doctor, " said Seal.

ELEVEN

Mara smiled at the groggy, unshaven group at the table. She wore tight blue jeans and a plain brown T-shirt. The shirt was tucked in and the stock of her Glock 19 protruded from an inside holster on the front waistband of her jeans. She rummaged through the buffet and began setting out plates, forks, knives, cups, saucers, and finally, damask napkins. She wiped the blood and breadcrumbs off the table and set ten places.

Charlie stood in the doorway while the babysitters scrambled to get out of Mara's way. Sergei Pavlenko stood behind him, in borrowed clothes: a clean, red polo shirt and chino trousers.

Charlie waited for Mara to place the last fork, then said, "Now go change your clothes, Mara."

"You're not the boss of me, Michael Joachim," she said in a little girl's voice. She began to transfer serving dishes from the trolley to the table.

The babysitters and the doctor edged away. Charlie took a long time to reply.

"Yes, I am the boss of you, Mara. You have no status here. We are on an operation and my word is the same as Papa's. The same, Mara. Go change."

Seal sucked in his cheeks. After seven months he knew how best to get her to cooperate. This was not it. Mara's face showed surprise at first, then doubt, rebellion, and then it turned pale when Mack came in through the double doors, looking very distinguished, Seal would say, in a three-piece suit like something out of a rich people's catalogue. He had shaved and was alert enough, though, like the rest of them, he had not slept that night. He brushed past the Russian and Charlie and stopped in front of Mara. There were no words. Mara blushed, then walked quickly out of the room. When she came back, she was wearing a skirt and blouse, in a pink knit, that covered the Glock and matched the ribbon around her ponytail.

She took the seat at the opposite end of the table from Mack and played hostess like she was born to it, with the doc to her left and Steve on her right, glaring at each other across the table. Charlie sat on his father's right, Louie at Mack's left. Sergei and Seal took seats between the doctor and Charlie, and across from them sat Jay and Frank.

Jay started talking first before a piece of toast was buttered.

"I cannot get your jet into San Antonio," he told Mack. "I am under surveillance myself. There is a lawyer from the justice department on my tail and she's been given my best special agent as an assistant."

"I know," said Steve. "We saw Roger last night. Is this lawyer's name Judy something or other?"

"Simons," said Jay. "That's the one. Disconcertingly serious and sensible. Worst nightmare. I can see you have met her."

"I told Roger we were here to discuss a proposal from Frank," said Steve. He looked at Mack. "I left out the details."

"You were too busy fending off the lawyer," said Charlie. He put his knife and fork down, sat back in his chair, and smirked down the table at Steve.

"That was one of the longest hours of my life," said Steve. "I thought you'd never finish with that girl. I still say she's dirty, Charlie. Why don't we ask the Russian?" He looked at Sergei. "Jane Jared. Is she in the game?"

"Who? Eben Jared's daughter?" Pavlenko winced as he sat up straighter. "Her mother is."

"That is not possible," said Jay. "We cleared her many years ago."

"She runs a cell of illegals. One of them is the man in your organization who cleared her."

"Who?" demanded Jay.

Pavlenko shrugged. "I don't know. It is on Semianov's list. I did not have access." He put a forkful of scrambled eggs in his mouth.

"But the girl," insisted Steve. "Is she dirty?"

"She's not, Steve, she..." Charlie was interrupted by his sister.

"Jane Jared?" Mara asked. "I told you when you danced with her at my graduation that she's in the game, Charlie."

"No, she's not, Mara. She is only misguided. A true believer who thinks she will save the world. She told me how she nearly had you expelled over that party of yours. She regrets being so overzealous."

"She's in the game," insisted Mara. "She knows all the tradecraft and practiced it flawlessly in school."

"She is the daughter of a specialist, for heaven's sake. What do you expect?"

Sergei used a piece of bread to clean his plate. He was still chewing when he spoke. "I think Masha is correct."

"Verify it, Pavlenko." There was heat in Charlie's words.

"I cannot. I did not have access. I can only tell you two things. First, you know that I was trained by Eben Jared. But I am not a specialist."

"Was," muttered Steve.

Sergei paused and nodded. "Was. I was not a specialist, but at the time I entered the directorate, we had lost so many babysitters, that it was decided we should be trained just as well as the specialists. It was thought that babysitters were dying because they could not defend themselves."

"No thought ever given to ordinary incompetence?" Frank rolled his round eyes to the ceiling.

Sergei shrugged. "My section commissioned Jared to train me and another man. During our training, one time, I made a mistake."

"Only once?" Steve asked with one eyebrow raised.

"Only once." Sergei glowered at him. "I do not recall what I did, but I remember what Jared said to me. He said, 'I know a little girl who can do that better than you.' This was about twelve years ago. Jane Jared is how old now, twenty-two?"

Mara nodded.

Charlie said: "So she was trained to defend herself. That does not mean she is operational."

"What is the second thing?" asked Mack.

Sergei winced. He shifted sideways, then sat straight against the back of his seat. He pulled at the bandage around his abdomen and ribs.

"Go lie down," the doctor told him.

Sergei waved him off impatiently.

"You are in pain," insisted the doctor.

"But not from the wound," whispered Sergei. He pushed his chair away from the table. The doctor was the only person in the room who did not recognize a defensive posture.

When Sergei spoke, finally, his words came at a steady, measured pace, while his eyes swept the room, pausing, in turn, to study Steve Donovan, the Frenchman, Mack, and Charlie, in turn, continuously.

"Last year," he said, "I attended a special course at Moscow University with the other man who trained with me under Jared. We learned the language of the new politics. When we finished, we received our assignments."

He took a deep breath, then plunged. "I was assigned to Mara. She had recently graduated from her college. My orders were to watch her until she became operational and then attempt to recruit her. If she declined, I was to kill her immediately."

Mara's right hand rested gently on Steve's shoulder. He stayed in place and so did the other three specialists. Sergei still held the edge of the table, prepared to use it as a springboard, only waiting for the first sign to figure out which way he should run.

TWELVE

"That's pretty stupid. You must have some real idiots in charge over there." It was Seal who broke the silence and relieved the tension all at once. He was still eating. The words came through a mouthful of sausage.

"Yes." Sergei sighed.

"Stupid?" demanded John. "You mean evil!"

Seal's fork paused a few inches from his face. He frowned. "No. Stupid. Evil in relation to what? Pavlenko was a babysitter. It was goofy to expect him to kill like that. Impossible. I know."

"I don't understand."

"What he means, Doctor," said Frank, "Is that such a killing requires a specialist. A babysitter doesn't have the right psychology. Pavlenko's superiors should have known that."

"They did not," said Sergei. "Seal is correct. They were idiots. My new boss has never met a specialist."

"I still don't understand," muttered John. He looked up in surprise when Frank spoke again. He did not expect an explanation from these people.

"When you practiced your cut and sew techniques on our Russian buddy here last night, what were you thinking, Doctor?"

John squinted with one good eye. "Thinking? I don't think; I just do. I concentrate."

"You blot out, however briefly, the fact that this is a human being under your knife. It is a clinical skill, Doctor. Take away the Hippocratic prohibition against killing, add some physical training, and you could be a specialist. A babysitter, generally, could not, at least not just like that, especially with the commission being a beautiful young woman."

Mara blushed.

John was dumbfounded. He looked at Mack. "Does this mean that you could?"

"Could what?"

"Kill a young woman?"

"That was not Sergei's order."

"It was."

"No. The order was to kill an operational enemy specialist. Any specialist can do that."

"Then you're saying you'll kill anybody for money?" John's tone became belligerent. He could not scrub it clean. He waited while Mack eyed him thoughtfully.

"I said nothing of the kind," Mack replied. "Tell me, Doctor. Do you remove any organ for money?"

"Of course not. It has to be diseased. I run tests."

Mack inclined his head and raised an eyebrow. Point. He focused again on the squirming Sergei and cleared his throat.

"You were telling us about the course you attended with Maximovich."

Sergei stared at him a minute, then shook himself and shrugged. "Yes. I attended with Maximovich. We both behaved ourselves long enough to graduate. Volodya and I celebrated with vodka. We had a long conversation that night."

"And you discussed your assignments?" asked Frank.

"We are never so unprofessional," insisted Sergei. "No. But we did talk about the question of which has more influence, heredity or environment?"

There was a long pause.

"That's it?" asked Charlie. "That's your second point?"

"I did not bring up the topic," said Sergei. "Volodya did."

"So?"

"So he also mentioned you in his argument, as an example of the power of heredity."

"It is natural for a babysitter to use a well-known specialist in his examples," said Frank.

"We had been shown a film of you that day, before receiving our certificates," said Sergei.

"What film?" asked Charlie.

"A new film, only a few days old, of a graduation ball in the United States. The film featured you, with still frames and closeups, dancing with a partner who was deliberately obscured. Her face was not shown."

Charlie did not answer.

"She had soft brown hair, in tight curls."

"Use the method, Charlie," said Mara. "Think."

"Be quiet, Mara."

"I will not be quiet. I will give you more to think about." She watched him roll his eyes at the ceiling. "I was awake last night when you and Steve came in. I listened, there, at the door." She pointed behind her. "I heard all of Steve's jokes about the ugly lawyer, and I am sure they were very funny, you all laughed so hard." She looked at Steve. "Did she really unbuckle your belt?"

Steve reddened. Mara did not wait for an answer. She spoke to her brother. "I know you think I am naive, but I have learned some things, and I can use the method as well as you can, and you know it. If Steve said that you opened the door to an adjoining room, a bedroom, and came out of it with Jane Jared, that means that you were first in it, and with the door closed. I know what that means." She wagged a finger at Charlie.

The expressions around the table were mixed wonder and amusement. Jay Turner did his best not to choke on the coffee he had just inhaled. Seal's mouth gaped open. Only John smiled openly at her, clearly delighted.

Charlie suppressed a smile. "What does it mean, Mara?"

She opened her mouth to answer but closed it again on a warning look from Mack. "I do not know much," she said more humbly. "Stop laughing at me; I know you are." She kicked Steve.

"Ow!"

"I do not know much," she repeated. "But I know about women and after two years at school, I know Jane Jared. An ugly woman with no self-respect may run after Steve, but Jane Jared is very beautiful. She runs after no one. And she would not descend into bed," Mara paused, doubtful, and looked at Seal.

"Ah, I think it's 'hop' you want." He wiped at a smear of jelly on his shirt.

"Hop. She would not hop into bed with you without a purpose."

There was a low-level explosion in the room, coffee spewed, forks and knives hopping off the table as it was pounded, Frank's bald head shining crimson, and Louis's outright guffaw.

Spanish had been Seal's expertise, so he didn't catch Charlie's next words in German, but he knew a threat when he heard one. This one was lost in the noise. He looked across at Frank. Not lost entirely. Frank always had been a sponge. Seal was sorry, though, that nobody said 'you're right' to Mara, because, of course, she was, and what a waste that such a mind, essentially a male mind, though parts were feminine enough, should be packaged so deliciously, making people think it was a truffle, treat it like a truffle, when it was pure protein, prime beef grade-A, with language being the only problem. Her English was perfect, American, with absolutely no cultural content whatsoever.

Mara incorporated the oddest combination of traits he had ever met in a person, and he suspected he was one of only a few people in the world who saw her as a person with traits as opposed to the other way around. He would have gone on thinking, but he felt Mack's blue eyes on him and when he glanced up, he saw that instinct had told him right. Mack's gaze was one of those that make you glad when it ends, and he hasn't shot you. Seal was glad accordingly.

Jay started talking again. He had one of the most pleasant listening voices ever made, deep and confident. You could crawl inside it and feel safe. The topic was enemies here and bad guys there, but everything was all right because Jay's voice was in charge. Seal felt himself nodding. There was a thud on the table. He forced his eyes open.

"What was that?" somebody asked.

"The doctor is asleep on his toast," somebody else replied.

Seal looked and it was true. The doctor's blond head was nestled on a plate of toast. There was butter on his nose. He snored through it. The meeting went on and on and on.

THIRTEEN

John Fairfax woke when the meeting was over because it was over. He could sleep on a gurney stuffed in a corner of the ER, on a desk at the nurses' station or a dining room table in a hotel penthouse, but he could not sleep without noise. Silence requires a comfortable bed.

He picked his head up off the plate, moved his stiff neck slowly, and thought he heard it creak. The room was silent. The people were gone; the computers, even the printer, had disappeared. The remains of breakfast were there, plates, cups, forks, knives, spoons, butter bowls, bread plates, crusts of rolls and toast and hash browned potatoes, spilled coffee in fine china saucers, overturned Styrofoam cups with more coffee, spilled and cold and forming map projections in sodden furniture wax on the table.

Gone? Mara, gone? She had to be gone. No woman he knew would allow such a mess to remain this long—he checked his watch—until afternoon. Gone, and in trouble? His addled impulse was to save her. He dashed into the hall and heard voices to his right. He followed the noise down the hallway, and heard a stereo or maybe a radio, playing Chopin. He came into the apartment living room, where last night he had watched the Frenchman break the patient's ribs.

And there she was, still in her pink knit outfit, playing a card game with three men at a small, square, table. Her back was to him. He lurked in the hallway, not feeling presentable. Pavlenko faced Mara on the other side of the table, playing as her partner, pale except where the bruising made him purple. The two babysitters sat at the other two sides of the little table. Frank nodded at him.

With Mara safe, the next great urgency presented itself. He tried the doorknobs along the hall.

"What do you need, Doctor?" Frank interrupted the game to help him.

"A toilet." Bad. He fought with the next doorknob and pushed his shoulder into the door.

Frank pulled him away. "I wouldn't do that, Doctor. Mack's asleep in there. Or was. Please stop trying to get yourself killed." He pointed down the hallway, past the kitchen. "Third door on the right. It's open. And did you know you have a piece of toast stuck to your face?"

The bathroom held the same odd recipe of six-parts luxury to four-parts squalor. The room was large, tiled in white, with every-thing in it: a toilet, bidet, and marble shower, which dripped, and on the white tiled floor wet towels, t-shirts, a tie with regimental stripes —who wore that?— and pantyhose.

Toothbrushes, new ones in packages, various used ones, tubes of toothpaste, opened and not, disposable razors, and a large jar of aspirin littered the sink. John settled for four from the jar, though his headache demanded more. He sucked up water with his hand; there were no glasses. He brushed his teeth washed his face and decided he would shave when he got home.

There was precious little time between now and then to at least get her phone number. He ran into the hall and into Mack. It was like dashing himself against a wall.

"I am sorry," Mack said after he pushed John away. "Did Frank tell you that you must come with us to San Antonio?"

John wondered about telepathy. The news was good, at first, until he forced himself to remember where he was. He shook his head. No. He wanted to court her from the comfort of a normal life, even long distance, occasionally flying to—where did she live?— someplace, any place, away from Steve Donovan.

"We can take care of Pavlenko," said Mack.

Pavlenko? The patient. That's right, there is a patient. Take care of? As in?

"But Frank has told his section that we accepted the commission on him," Mack explained. "We will drive to San Antonio in what Jay Turner calls a recreational vehicle in order to hide him. If we let you go home now, I am afraid they will have it out of you in five minutes that he is alive and with us."

"I assure you, sir, that I won't tell a soul." John's voice trailed off under the steady strength of Mack's gaze. Telepathy came to his mind again, a peculiar kind of communication without words. "You don't mean they'd torture me, do you? My own government, or whatever they are? You're not serious? You are serious."

Mack pointed at one of the red-brown stains on John's sleeve. Pavlenko's? His own? Who knows. "This is not television, Doctor. You cannot turn it off."

The credits rolled to the sound of a piano. "Isn't that Litolff?" John asked as Mack moved past him. "What a brilliant recording!"

"That is not a recording. It is Charlie—on the piano, by the terrace."

John stood in the hallway, listening. This was not just good; it was genius. Genius wears a gun. Genius makes love to a woman his sister swears will kill him. Genius stands for hours on a broken leg. Genius beats up a man who once tortured him. A misplaced application of genius, buried by circumstance. Crowds will never hear this. Critics will never acclaim it. The man will die young by all indications. He will die never having been known or heard beyond this hallway and whatever little world these people crawl to when they're not doing... this.

Because 'this' is all there is outside of... John searched for a word to define what he considered himself to be in and this to be outside of, a word that would encompass law, art, road signs, and hospitals. Civilization. The uncomfortable suit of dress-up clothes that everybody wants to change. Make it new. Go back to something older. Change its fabric, its history, its weight, its style. Rip it apart and start over. Start over and this is what you get: cool slaughter, of geniuses and young women and of the sensibility that there is anything to be preserved in such people, not the least of which is the limit on their ferocities. He looked at his hands. What about a talented surgeon? Ditto diddly. That's what about. He'd be another blond cadaver. He hoped he wouldn't. He hoped he'd come home from San Antonio, he'd get the girl, live happily ever after, and tell his grandchildren about the adventure. His one adventure. He didn't want any more.

Litolff became Liszt. The mood depressed itself, synchronized with his own. A telepathic family for sure. He heard the bathroom door open, turned, and looked down the hall. Mack walked toward him, and in that walk, accompanied by the Second Hungarian Rhapsody, John knew more about the man than poor fat Frank had learned in decades.

"Are you all right, Doctor?"

John nodded. Mack went back into the bedroom to sleep again.

John found an uncomfortable ladder-back chair in the living room, moved it near the card table, and sat down to watch the game.

"There!" Mara threw a card down. "I have trumped over you!" she said to Frank.

"Ah, just trumped, or trumped it. You trumped the card, Mara," said Seal.

"Oh. I thought perhaps it was related to triumph."

Seal shrugged. "It's my trick, anyway." He put an ace of trump, in this case diamonds, on top of her ten.

She was incensed. "But I have not turned any tricks. I will lose the melds."

Seal gathered the cards toward himself. "Pulled tricks, honey, pulled. Prostitutes turn tricks. In Pinochle, we pull them. And it's meld. Just one for all the points, and anyway your partner has pulled a trick, so your meld is safe."

Sergei held up four cards to show her, though he was not at all confident of their meaning. They smiled at each other, in mutual triumph.

Mara frowned again. "Prostitutes play cards? Oh, hello, John. Frank and Seal are teaching us a card game. Do you want to play?"

Seal again: "No, he can't play. He would need a partner."

"We could wake Steve."

John shook his head. "No. No. I'll watch."

"It's your turn," Frank reminded her. After she put down a card he said, "So, Mara, do you mind if I ask, who is Udo Bitlerburg?"

"No." She went on looking at her cards, grinning and full of mischief. "You may ask."

It was Sergei who said finally. "So who is he?"

"The Baron von Bitlerburg? A completely odious man who must be forty at least, with no chin, moist hands, and a laugh like a donkey's bray. I danced with him once at a ball and Mi... Charlie has never let me hear the end of it." She threw down a queen, her last card.

Sergei said, "Charlie threatened to make sure you marry him."

John sat forward in his seat.

"The case is shut." She looked at Seal, brow furled.

"Closed. Case closed."

"Yes. It is." Then to Sergei: "Are you going to deal?"

He shuffled the cards and dealt. Mara picked up her cards one by one and arranged them thoughtfully. She looked up in response to the silence. Nobody else had picked up their cards. They all stared at her, waiting.

She sighed and put her cards down. "Babysitters are so nosy. You are like three little old busybodies. Four. You, too, John. I am not going to marry the Baron. Charlie was teasing, one of his nasty teases, but just a tease. When I finished that dance with Udo, he left me there. Right there on the ballroom floor." She swept over the table with a graceful gesture, making a ballroom floor out of it. "He marched then to Misha and did not ask, no, he demanded my hand."

It was Frank who managed to close his mouth long enough to ask, "What did Misha, uh, Mack, say?"

"I have not been told the exact words," she said. "But I understand that they were colorful and had to do with the Baron's ancestry, which in places is doubtful. But I think that Misha just wanted to squish him."

"Squish him?"

"Yes. Some say the Baron has Nazi sympathies. Misha despises Nazis."

"Worse than communists?"

"The same. He considers them the same."

"Squish him? How?" John asked.

Mara placed a manicured thumb on the table and rubbed. "Squish is a very descriptive word, don't you think?"

"But how?"

"He hoped the Baron would challenge him to a duel."

"A duel? With what? Pistols at dawn?"

"Sabers, of course."

"And Mack would win," said Frank. "Of course."

"Of course. But the Baron's friends were there, and they managed to clamp their hands over his mouth and drag him out. Later, he apologized to Misha. Case closed."

"*He* apologized?" Frank murmured.

But Mara picked up her cards again and gave the cold green stare that Seal translated, by mouthing it silently, as "case closed." Frank looked at his cards and began sorting them.

They played another hand of pinochle. Mara was an expert now, telling everybody what cards they held, winning decisively. Sergei supported her, grinning. He did not look right to John.

Drugged, no doubt, with God knows what out of the Frenchman's stash.

The Frenchman breezed through the room once or twice, carrying a pouch of tools or a canvas bag that clanked. One of these times, after he left through the door to the elevator, Frank asked Mara, "How is Mildred, by the way? I have not heard from her in a long time."

"Mildred?" asked Seal.

"Louis's wife."

"Louis? Married?"

"To a former babysitter." This came from Sergei. Frank looked at him sharply.

"Mildred died last year," said Mara.

"I am sorry." Both American babysitters murmured.

"We were, too, in a way, but as these things go, it was peaceful. She died of cancer. It was more of a release for her. We are not accustomed to death from natural causes."

As if to remind John of the alternative, Steve Donovan entered the room from the hallway. At the same time, Charlie came in from the terrace. John noticed that everybody was well dressed, white cotton shirts and silk ties, summer-weight wool suits, gray for Charlie, a light brown for Steve. Steve's brown hair was combed. Frank's little bit of hair was also combed, a fresco around a dome. Even Seal wore a clean shirt, wrinkled and loud, but clean. It made John feel seedy, unkempt, unshaven. He was beginning to smell a bit. He knew the purple eye did not flatter his face.

Steve walked up behind him and jerked the chair out from under him. He was quickly on his feet again with his fist ready and heading for Steve's left brown eye, but his arm stopped well behind him. Momentum made him reel and upset the card table.

The patient, who was holding his arm, said, "Doctor, come and change my bandage."

John said not now, but the Russian had a firm grip. John tried bringing his left arm over to break free, but this, too, was held—by Charlie.

"I can lend you a change of clothes," said Charlie.

What with flailing about and reeling across the carpet, the fact that he needed some cleaning up was pretty obvious, but John could not give Steve-the-jerk such an easy victory. He used his wits and settled down. He spoke reasonably. "In a minute. It's okay. I'm not a fool."

They released him slowly. Steve grinned and stepped closer.

John prepared to launch.

"How do you tell the difference," said Sergei, stepping between them, "between a brave man and a fool?"

Mack, Louis, and Jay Turner came into the room, adding to the circle standing around them.

"How *do* you tell the difference between a brave man and a fool?" said Jay.

Sergei stepped up to Mara, gathered her in his arms, and kissed her, for what seemed centuries. It must have been awkward, with one side of his mouth swollen and a wire holding his teeth in place.

Awkward or not, it sent John straight into the general fray, which eventually resolved itself into two piles: the specialist team, all of them: Mack, Louis, and Charlie, holding Steve; the babysitters, including Jay, holding the doctor.

Sergei held up one finger didactically. "The answer? The man who survives is a brave man. Come, Doctor, I need medical attention."

Mara's smile reminded John of the Mona Lisa.

FOURTEEN

Sergei pulled John down the hallway. Charlie followed them into a bedroom and locked the door behind them.

The room was meant to be splendid but was littered with assorted trunks, boxes, and canvas bags, some of them spilling their contents on the floor, one or two on the huge bed itself, which was rumpled but intact, with the pillows still covered by a chartreuse spread. Clothing had escaped most of the duffels, and crumpled or folded, was strewn everywhere, under, around, and next to black-painted equipment, flashlights, radios, ropes, and boxes of cartridges. Charlie handed John an olive-green bag filled with gauze, tape, and antibiotic creams. Sergei lay on the bed, pulling his shirt up and over the abdominal dressing, showing only an inch or two of the elastic bandaging that encased his ribs.

There was nothing wrong with the abdominal dressing, and anyway, John was not a nurse.

"Change the dressing, Doctor," said Charlie.

"You are a great challenge to babysitters, Doctor," said the patient. "I wonder if you will outlive me. You were busy making yourself into a fool, soon to be a dead fool."

"You kissed her." It was the only thing John could squeeze between his teeth as he removed a perfectly good dressing.

"Yes. It was painful but delicious."

Charlie rummaged in a suitcase.

"I will tell you a secret, though," said the Russian. "It was not brave or foolish. I knew they would pull him off me. Your reaction, I did not worry about, but Donovan's? I knew they would not let him kill me. When the time comes, there will be a decision. It is more likely to be Charlie here. Am I correct?"

Charlie held out another polo shirt like the one Sergei wore. This one was green. "Perhaps," he said.

"Perhaps?" John touched a betadine wipe to the edge of the wound. "Just like that?" He wiped the incision. It looked healthy. He admired the sutures, small, neat, and tight. A-plus work.

"He killed my mother and sister," said Charlie. "I have a claim."

"I did not! I did not know! I told your father last night. Slavin lied to me. I was part of the operation. I take responsibility for Sobieski, but I did not know they were targets. I could not. Ekaterina, your mother, was my cousin. My bosses knew that. They said nothing to me. When it happened, I protested and was reprimanded. It is in my personnel file. I can show you. We are cousins. I do not kill women and children."

"Cousins, Pavlenko?" Charlie reached into another suitcase with a cool, controlled movement that reminded John of some of Mara's manners, precise, simple, and emotionless. Considering the topic, he wondered at it.

The patient pushed John's hand away where he had been swabbing distractedly.

"My father changed the name during the first purge, for survival, to a name from my mother's family. They were Ukrainian."

"Is survival all there is, Sergei Nickolaevich?" asked Charlie.

"You tell me, Mikhail Mikhailovich."

They stared at each other.

"The shirt should fit you, Doctor," Charlie said finally. "But trousers may be a problem; you're a little shorter than me. Steve's may fit you, though." He opened another green canvas bag.

John could not bear the thought and it registered on his face.

"Doctor, forget Mara," said the patient. "She is not for you. Too much cholesterol. She will clog your arteries, give you heart attacks." Pavlenko laughed and wheezed. He paused and became serious. "She is not for Steve Donovan, either if that will make you less of a danger to yourself."

John looked up sharply. "Why is that?"

"In addition to being as American and bourgeois as you are, he is also divorced. It will not do. He knows this."

"Then why?"

Charlie answered. "He despises your presumption, John. Sergei is right. Forget it. Steve is not an ordinary rival."

"Also, Doctor," said Sergei, "you must, very quickly, learn specialist psychology. I did not save your life just now because I think anything of you, grateful as I am for your work. It was my babysitter instinct. When the violence begins, anyone in the way, anyone who does not know what he is doing, is at risk. You may think right now everybody is only sitting around, but this is deceptive. The specialists are becoming more open to attack, and therefore more edgy. They are preparing to die and preparing to kill. The more you play with Donovan, the worse he becomes, harder to control, more difficult to predict."

"Play?" John concentrated on finding the beginning of a gauze roll. "Mara's an American and I'm not bourgeois."

"You are bourgeois. All Americans are bourgeois, even the rich ones, especially the rich ones because they are Puritans at heart. Mara only thinks she is an American. Her mother, Alex, left the country at age twenty. All she has is the language. Mara does not even have that. Listen to her taking lessons from Seal."

"How do you know about Steve's divorce?" Charlie asked Sergei.

Sergei shrugged.

"Do you know where they are?"

"The ex-wife and the boy? Yes. It was in the file. One of my subordinates found it while I was away. He was promoted and it was put in the file. I know everything about all of you, though I must admit I was not prepared for the Litolff. I knew you here," he pointed to his head, then to his heart, "not here."

"What file?" said Charlie. There was the same simple control again, making his voice flat.

John shivered involuntarily.

"I destroyed it," said Pavlenko. He motioned to John privately with his fingers, hurry up.

"Tell me about the file Sergei Nickolaevich."

The patient began to perspire. John tried to concentrate on folding the gauze.

"It had everything in it, even from your grandfather's day. Felix never destroyed anything, you know? But I did. I burned it."

"When?"

John laid the gauze on the wound.

"When?"

"In February."

"Next big question. Answer it well, Pavlenko. Well and completely. Why?"

John could not find the beginning edge of the surgical tape. Damn it. His patient's nervousness was affecting him.

"I went home for a visit. I destroyed it."

"Why, Pavlenko? You want me to ask you another way?"

"No. No. I went home to check the file. I needed to verify a theory of mine. I saw the new notation about Donovan's family and it bothered me, raised the ghosts of ten years ago, so I destroyed it."

"The whole file? For the one notation? Come on Pavlenko." Charlie threw down the pair of blue jeans he had been holding and took a step toward them.

John put the tape on crookedly.

Pavlenko held both hands up, just as Charlie grabbed his shirt at the front collar. The bandage dangled.

"It had been copied!" Pavlenko whispered hoarsely.

Charlie let go. The man fell back on the bed. John tore off another strip of tape.

"My alarms were tripped, all of them. I could tell it had been tampered with, and I have a chemical that will tell me when a document is photocopied. I destroyed the whole thing in the incinerator downstairs. Then I went to see Semianov. He was dying in a hospital in Siberia. He said he had been waiting for me. He said he copied it for insurance, to make Charlemagne want the file. It is with his list of illegals."

"Then this is a trap." Again, simple, flat, control.

"Among other things. But there is no choice."

"We can move the woman and boy."

"But she is difficult," said Pavlenko. "She is a typical bourgeois American for whom the world is a benign place, one who is offended by storms and earthquakes and thinks the president is at fault. The fuss she made the last time you moved them is what drew my subordinate's attention. Every time you move her you only renew interest. Better to get the file and destroy it."

Charlie stood silent for a long time. Long enough for John to place three more crooked strips of tape.

"You did not tell my father about this file."

"No. I did not have to tell him. He knew, somehow."

"What else is in it?"

"I did not have to tell him that, either. Everything in his file that describes him is accurate, you know. He understands without words. Amazing."

"What else?" Charlie held him by the shirt again.

"Let me explain that I am not stupid, and I know how atrocity begins. I did not put everything I learned in that file. My subordinate put that in about Donovan's family. I would have forbidden it if I were there."

"Damn it, Pavlenko." Charlie threw him back on the bed.

The Russian used this latest release to put some distance between himself and Charlie. He scrambled to the end of the bed, pulling his shirt down over the new dressing.

"I am getting to it. Give me time to explain!"

"What's in the file about Mara? Now, Pavlenko. Now!"

Pavlenko stared, stunned. "You are very much like your father."

John put the gauze back in the bag.

"The file is standard," said Pavlenko. "It has not much more than in Frank's file. Much of what's in it came from Frank's file. His office is riddled with moles, though he has been more careful since the tragedy. I have, too. I do not include everything I know, like...."

"Like?"

"That you are Mara's biological brother. You have different mothers, but the same father. I know this but did not put it in the file."

John stood, scissors in one hand, tape in the other. The patient rose to his feet, back against the wall, trapped. Charlie advanced.

"If it is not in the file, Sergei Nickolaevich, why are you so worried about it?" Charlie took another step closer.

"It is not in the file. I found it here." Sergei pointed to his head. "I am no fool, but I am also not a genius. You are only the second one I have met."

"And the other?"

The Russian shrugged. "Is in my directorate."

"And the file?"

"Contains the verification."

"What the hell are you talking about?" John dropped scissors and tape and stepped forward. "What difference does it make if she's step or biological or from Mars or Pluto? And what verification? Of what?"

Both men looked at him, puzzled. "It makes no difference to us," said Charlie, finally. "But to many of our enemies, genetics are everything. They are obsessed with heredity, race, and eugenics. They will think it is important to us, also. They will think it makes her more critical to us as if that were possible. The daughter and sister of living specialists is an irresistible temptation. We would risk everything."

"You are risking everything," said Sergei.

John looked at Charlie and pointed to his patient. "Your enemies already sent him to kill her. Why is this different? And, by the way, have any of you heard that the Cold War is over? It's been in the news."

"It is not over," said Charlie. "It is only on pause."

"This is merely a rearrangement of terms and alliances," agreed Sergei.

"And the order given to Sergei was casual," said Charlie. "A kind of one-off designed to prevent a future problem, should she become remarkable. But as my father's daughter, and as my sister, she becomes remarkable immediately. She inherits all our enemies as well." He turned to Pavlenko. "What is your verification, Sergei Nickolaevich?"

"First, I will tell you how I thought of it. May I sit down? Shall we all sit down? Will you let me finish without hitting me?"

FIFTEEN

Charlie guaranteed nothing, except that he could make John shudder with a glance. Sergei took the cold stillness as an affirmative and sat in a wingback chair before a low coffee table. John sat beside him in a matching chair. Charlie took a desk chair and put it on the other side of the table, facing them. Sergei winced and wheezed, shifting in his seat. He would have been more comfortable lying on the bed, but then, comfort was a relative thing in a room with Charlie.

"I told you I was assigned to watch her," said Sergei. "I have also watched you, during the period when we had you in Tbilisi and at other times. Within a month of my surveillance of Mara, I was struck by her resemblance to you. It is not only in looks. Such things are difficult to tell. Vasily Sobieski was Ukrainian and Polish; Alexandra Dolnikova is American, but her parents were Russians. Mara should be one hundred percent Slav, but she is not, just as you are not, despite your Russian mother."

The corners of Charlie's mouth turned down. Sergei winced and hurried to continue.

"This is something that I know and that I realized soon after my assignment began, but it was on the level of a hunch or an intuition that is useless without verification. It is worse than useless if it causes an intelligence officer to read things into a situation that are not there.

"So when I first noticed her coolness, the still walk—a movement, really, not a walk, with no discernible effort expended—that could change from barely perceptible to a blur of speed during the time it takes to blink the eye, I told myself, of course, she would resemble you. No doubt you trained her."

He waited.

"I taught her to shoot," said Charlie. "Louis and I did. Vasily and Steve taught her to fight. That's where the speed comes from."

"Even more reason why it should not remind me of you. No. There is another quality in the way she moves and the way she speaks. Your father has it, too, I notice now, but I have not watched him as much."

"Yes," said John. "I've seen it, too."

Charlie stared at him and he clamped his jaw shut.

"I pushed the idea away for three weeks," said Sergei. "Then, I could not help myself. I reviewed everything I could remember in the file, and that is considerable. I have memorized most of it. Two events in the year before Mara's birth may be significant. About seven and a half months before her birthdate, we know that Charlemagne assassinated a mole in St. Louis. Their jet stopped in Chicago before leaving the country. The next week, Sobieski married Alex Dolnikova in Capri. We have that. We have Mara's date of birth from her American passport. We do not have her birth weight, which should be low after only seven and a half months."

"And the other event?" asked Charlie sharply.

Sergei inhaled deeply. "Six weeks before the assassination in St. Louis, Charlemagne stopped a terrorist team called Ill Wind in the act of trying to blow up the Sears Tower in Chicago. Have they told you this?"

Charlie gave only his still stare.

"Frank Cardova's reports were usually very detailed, quite excellent. All his reports were excellent."

"Don't flatter him to his face that way, or he will rob me of my chance to kill you, Sergei."

"I am touched by your concern." Sergei placed his hand over his heart.

"Frank's report contained much juicy detail," he continued, "including the fact that Alex played a role in the operation, but nothing about what that role was, other than that she was hurt in some way, largely unimportant, though not to her, I am sure. What is conspicuous is what is missing, like her name and a description of what she wore that night. Frank does not miss much, and he did not miss this, either, and commented on not being able to discover it. This means he was not there for much of the time during the hours preceding the operation and had no say in the use and possible abuse of a bystander."

"I don't want to hear your babysitter backbiting, Pavlenko. Get to the verification. Is it in Frank's report? If so, his office has it, too, and if it's as riddled as you say...."

"No. It is not in his report. It is in something only we have, and only by accident. We have a torn, yellow copy of a copy of an old Bulgarian interrogation report, a tedious, very detailed report. We have it only because the subject is Sobieski. I do not think anyone except me ever read it, at least not through and through. I read it long ago when I was still young and enthusiastic, but I still have some of it, here." He pointed to his head. "This is what I went back to Moscow to check, to verify, and that is how I knew about Semianov's copy."

"Get to it." Just like that. Flat, expressionless. Charlie stood when he said it, stepped behind his chair, one hand on the chair, one in a pocket. Even the movement seemed motionless, a mere rumor, he was so still when it ended.

"Sobieski was twenty-two when the Bulgarians had him. One of the tortures they used, while it would not castrate him, could certainly sterilize. Probably did."

"That's it?"

"He said nothing, by the way, for all their efforts."

"Probably sterilize?"

"Well, add to that the record of offspring—you must know they were a wild bunch in their younger days, The Frenchman left half a dozen bastards around the world that he does not know about."

"And my father?"

"He was more selective. There are two possibilities, but the women were well-connected and had other men to claim paternity."

"But Vasily?"

"None. He married almost ten years after that interrogation. Six weeks before the marriage, a confused muddle of an operation involving the bride. Interesting."

"Why didn't you tell my father about this?"

"How? How do I begin? Do I say, 'Mara is your daughter and I can verify it?' Does he know it already, or would I be the first to tell him? Do I want to be the first to tell him? I did the prudent thing. I shut up. Always the wisest policy when the wrong word will kill you."

Charlie smiled slightly. "He found out only a few days ago."

"How did he react? Did he kill the messenger?"

Charlie shook his head. "Alex told him. He was the last to know. Mara was always important; she could not help but be, but now? It is his little Nadia restored, though Mara is nothing like her. Nadia was untouched by life. There was no blemish allowed near her. I thought even toadstools would march away at the sound of her footsteps in a forest. Nothing rotten could withstand her approach."

He sat again, looking downward and into the past. "Nadia was like my mother. Mara is more like me and my father. I do not mean to say she kills. She does not. I mean that she lives more completely on earth and less in heaven. My mother never accepted what my father does. She did not disagree with it or dispute about it; she ignored it. It did not exist for her. Nadia was the same."

Charlie stood a second time, both hands in his pockets, head tilted. John wondered at the stillness with which the man mastered his emotion

"When I was seventeen," he continued. "I took them both, and Mara, too, to the television room. A news program showed pictures from Thailand, where a bus full of people had been held hostage by terrorists. They showed the bus burning and the rescued people and their families, crying. I said, 'See Mama, Papa rescued these people, he and Vasily and Louis, and they will be home in two hours. Louis has been badly burned. We must be ready to help them.' My mother smiled at me. 'Nonsense,' she said. 'Listen to the television. The Thai government arranged the rescue. What imagination you have!'"

The patient shifted in his chair glancing warily from John to Charlie. John held his breath. The air, the words felt... dangerous.

"Only Mara was there with me when they came in," said Charlie. "My mother told friends that Louis had pneumonia. Mara helped to dress Louis's burned legs. Every few hours she would wet down the dressing. She held his hand while he cried. She was seven."

They could hear Pavlenko's wheeze in the silence. Then Charlie said, "The other genius in your directorate, is it Maximovich?"

Sergei squirmed but did not answer. Charlie turned and left the room.

"The Frenchman's magic box is there on the chest, Doctor." Sergei stumbled to the bed and fell onto it, letting his head rest on the first aid kit. "Quickly, please."

"You need to start doing without the drugs now. I can get you some aspirin."

Pavlenko's answer was in Russian. John understood the meaning without knowing the words.

"Listen, Doctor, I am in pain," Sergei said in English. "I want to sleep. I must sleep. Any addiction you give me will last only until I am shot in a few days."

"How can you talk like that?"

"I know it is wishful thinking. But I fear Mack's knife; I fear it more than a bullet. He used the knife on my specialist, you know, the one who killed Sobieski. I saw the photos."

"Surely, you don't think...."

"I don't think Charlie would tell such things to a living man. Which calls into question your status, Doctor." His voice trailed off as John injected the blessed poison.

SIXTEEN

Seal heard "Oomph," as he opened the bedroom door. Frank was right again.

It started with Charlie and Mara arguing in the dining room. Mack played referee. They used lingo Seal didn't know, but Frank soaked it up. You could see the man was in intelligence heaven, learning bits and pieces that he could never write down and so what use was it, anyway? Jay was still downstairs in the RV, and the Russian was awake and lounging around against the wall with his hands in his pockets. While the battle raged, Donovan slipped off down the hall and the Frenchman followed him. Frank looked at Seal and tilted his head toward the hallway. 'Doctor,' he mouthed silently.

Protect the doctor. The doctor still slept in the room where Pavlenko and Charlie had stowed him earlier. The man could sleep, for sure. Must be part of doctor training. Seal's first glimpse into the gloomy room confirmed the "Oomph." Doc was up against the wall, held there by Donovan, whose fist forced another "Oomph" out of him. The Frenchman stood by like another buzzard waiting for dinner. The two buzzards turned when Seal walked into the room. He stood ten feet from them. Donovan turned back to the doctor, who was still trying to breathe. "Go away," he said over his shoulder.

"No."

There was a pause. "Listen, Seal, this is none of your business." Donovan still did not turn around.

Seal sweated, wiped his forehead with the back of his hand, sweated some more. "I ain't leaving. Mack approved me staying on as a babysitter. Frank told me to talk to the doctor. I'm here to talk to the doctor. That's my story and I'm stickin' to it."

What a stupid time to try to be funny. Seal had this lame theory about a good laugh being just the thing to defuse a touchy situation.

The Frenchman frowned at him. Donovan punched the doc in the gut again.

Jokes are no good with people who don't know the whole language.

"Steve." That's all the Frenchman said, just "Steve," and he let go and the doctor slumped to the floor, a little bit blue. The two specialists walked out of the room then, leaving Seal to his private triumph, because that's what it was, simple, spectacular, victory. He could look Frank in the eye, not as an equal, maybe, but not as a loser babysitter, either. The doc was safe, and it was because of him. For now. He was safe for now.

Seal helped him stand up. He brought him over to a chair and put him in it. The doc's color came back, kind of blotchy in places, but he wasn't blue anymore and you could hear him breathing now.

"I... don't understand. Why...?"

"Just breathe, Doc. We'll talk in a minute." Seal sat in the chair across from him. "You okay, Doc?"

The doctor nodded. "Why? It's not like I'm getting anywhere with her, is it? I can't get close to her, haven't spoken with her all day long. What the hell is Donovan's problem?"

"Ah. In identifying the problem, Doc, I mean in defining, in general, whose it is, you might want to own up to it, seeing as how it's you gettin' beat up all the time. Just a suggestion."

The doctor stared at him. Seal noticed that the doc's eyes were almost as blue as Mack's, and almost as hard as Charlie's. But these eyes didn't make him shake.

"I don't get it," said the doctor. "How is it my problem? I have nothing against him. He's the aggressor."

Seal chuckled. "That's okay then. You didn't do nothing to deserve it, so that means Steve didn't really hit you, so you guys are in conflict resolution or something except that Steve's not totally resolved. That's all."

"But I didn't. I did not provoke this, even if you take Mara into account."

"I don't think Mara has that much to do with it. Maybe at first, but not now, and you don't have to provoke it for it to be real, do you Doc? That last punch sounded pretty real to me. The hate that goes with it was, too, and it don't matter what your intentions are. Steve hates you and that's that."

"Why? It's not rational!"

"Of course not. These guys are more and more not rational as the hours go by, Doc. You're like a sliver stuck under their fingernail. Everything about you is right and good and safe and confident, and none of that applies to them and they hate you for it. You're a foreign body. They're like white whadda yacallits, corpuscles. You bother them."

The doctor wrinkled his brow.

"You ain't afraid, Doc. You ain't and you should be. To them, that means you're stupid or you're privileged or you're dirty and have somethin' up your sleeve. You oughtta shake a little like I do. They don't usually bother babysitters. We're beneath their notice."

"Why should I be afraid? And why on earth would I give Donovan the satisfaction of showing it?"

Seal left his mouth open for a minute before he could answer this doozy. "Somebody's going to die in the next couple days, Doc. This ain't the evening news. It ain't gonna cut to a slick deodorant commercial and come out smelling nice."

"Mack used the TV metaphor, too."

"'Cause it applies. Lots of people who watch TV—and I'm a great channel surfer, don't get me wrong—they think everything's gonna be all right in the end. You do, Doc. You came in here with no experience, watched a man get beat up, sewed him up, got hit yourself a couple times, listened to the commissioning of a murder, and didn't even have the sense to tremble when a guy with a gun let you know he didn't have no use for you at all. You think you're gonna live through it, maybe because you're such a great surgeon. But truth is, even great surgeons die young. The world ain't nice and these guys ain't nice and the people hunting them ain't even nicer. Death stinks, and it's permanent. We're all scared shitless, and you walk around worrying about gettin' close to a girl. You're out of sync."

John's brow wrinkled as he leaned forward. "What can I do? Let's say I own the problem; what the hell is the solution?"

Seal shrugged. He rubbed his nose with a fat, crooked forefinger. "I don't think there's anything you can do. Now climb down there, Doc. I know the look an' I ain't taking it from you. You roll your eyes like you're my better, by money, looks, and education, and I risked my neck just now to save yours, so get off it. That's one thing about Mara. She is superior to me in a lot of ways, but she never, ever let on. Always acted like I was the boss, respected me, even when she was doing what the hell she pleased."

"I thought you were her boss."

"As far as that's possible, on paper, with Mara. That's another subject. Right now, we babysitters are getting tired of worrying about you. Trouble is, there ain't a lot you can do about other people's hate, once it starts. Some hate you because you're like them, others hate you 'cause you're different. Once the hate starts, though, you can change a hundred-eighty and it won't stop. Any change you try to make is hated, too. And that's if change is possible, which in your case I don't think it is. It just ain't in your nature to act like your world shouldn't spill over into everybody else's.

"So you could try avoiding Steve, but that's gonna get real hard when we all move into that RV. Quarters is tight, as they say. You could defend yourself so that it's a draw and then you guys just bare your teeth at each other. I don't see you getting good enough to beat Donovan in five years, though, let alone in five minutes, which it's gonna have to be. Seal rubbed a knuckle on the side of his nose, thinking. "How about gettin' yourself an ally?"

"An ally?"

"Yeah. Somebody who could fight Donovan to a draw, and better yet, who wouldn't have to. Somebody he respects, to be kind of on your side."

John shook his head. "Mack said he wouldn't protect me."

"I don't know nothing about that, Doc."

"What about Charlie?"

Seal shook his head, rubbed his nose again, and scratched behind an ear. "Charlie's got his hands full with Mara. Not a good one to approach. And somehow, I don't see you seeking help from Mara, either, am I right?"

John nodded.

"That leaves the Frenchman."

John pointed to his eye.

"Doc, that's perfect. It gives you an opening. I mean, it'd be tough to walk up to him and say 'How 'bout helping me stay alive?' Thanks to that shiner, all you have to do is apologize. He'll figure it out and he'll have to be on your side, more or less."

John gripped the arms of the chair. "Apologize for what? He hit me!"

"For calling him a liar."

"He is a liar."

"No, he ain't." Seal tried one of those looks full of meaning but the doctor was not translating.

"He lied to me!"

"No, he didn't." Seal did not hide his exasperation. "It was a joke, a game. Don't you see that? Didn't all those college classes teach you anything?"

"A joke! He said there were no drugs for pain!"

"He didn't expect you to believe it, Doc. Didn't you see it in his eyes? You know a lot about bodies, but you don't know nothin' about people. People are more than bodies. The Frenchman said there ain't any drugs because he meant he wanted the Russian to suffer, but people don't like saying that kind of thing out loud. He said it with his eyes, and you just listened to the words."

"Oh." Pause. "Tell me what to do." He held out his hands, a supplicant.

"Draw him aside and tell him you're sorry you said that. You were wrong. That's all. He'll know what you're getting at. He might call the snarling dog off you."

John stood up and turned toward the door.

"Wait," said Seal, also standing. "You can't go to him looking pitiful. You need to clean up. Charlie said he left some clean clothes out for you." He looked around the room. "Here they are." He picked up a small pile of clothes from the bed, the green polo shirt on top, and handed it to the doctor. "There's a shower in there." He pointed to a small en-suite bathroom. "There's a razor in there, too. You'd better shave 'cause we're all going downstairs tonight."

"Why?"

"It's decided that we'll explain your being here as Mara's boyfriend. So you two have to go downstairs and act like a number. Charlie and Steve will go with us. I'll be your babysitter. We'll probably meet the Jared dame and the lawyer and her FBI toad. We hope so. Our job is to keep them busy while Mack, Louis, and Frank sneak the Russian into the RV."

John shifted his weight from foot to foot. "Seal," he said doubtfully.

"Yeah, Doc?"

"Why is the FBI on both sides of this? I thought—when Jay came for me, I understood—I was working for the FBI. Who, exactly, is who around here?"

Seal held up both hands. "Don't ask me. I'm just an old counter-intelligence officer turned babysitter. I only know I belong on Mara's side. Jay Turner wants that list Pavlenko says he's got. He wants it bad. So do a lot of people, including this lawyer we'll see downstairs. Frank wants information and he wants to prevent a disaster, God help him. Pavlenko wants to stay alive. Mara wants to be in charge. I don't know what the rest are up to, but I don't think they give a shit about the list. They'd like to kill Pavlenko, I know. There's some bad blood there for sure. They're concerned about Mara, big time, and as far as that goes, I guess I'm an ally of sorts. What about you, Doc?"

"Do you think Mara's in danger?"

"You bet. This game ain't Trivial Pursuit. Word is, wear body armor if you got any. Get washed, Doc. We got twenty minutes."

SEVENTEEN

"Where's that fuckwad doctor?" asked Steve.

"Talking to Louis," said Charlie.

Seal stood with the others in the anteroom before the elevator, all of them looking washed and pressed though fatigue created circles around their eyes. Steve's exhaustion took the form of a restless irritability. Seal yawned. Charlie was as still as ever, Mack more so. Jay had his hands in his pockets, his lips pursed in a silent whistle. Pavlenko came through the double doors dressed in a black sweatsuit. Frank toddled in after him. Finally, Louis and the doctor joined the crowd in the small room. Footsteps were loud on the tile floor. Louis mumbled something to Steve. They all waited for Mara.

She sure could do an entrance. Seal tore his eyes off her long enough to look around quickly. Mack's eyes were concentrated on the skirt. Yes, Seal admitted silently, it was pretty short. Real short. There were only about four inches of shiny purple fabric beneath the glittery soft sweater that hung below the hips and covered the gun. The rest was leg, all the way to the high heels. He glanced around again. Mara cleared her throat, and finally, a few eyes moved to her face. She had her hair up and twisted in the back. Her earrings must have been zircons. They dangled a little and sparkled like her sweater when she moved.

Seal could see that Mack disapproved, deeply, but nobody else did. Jay let his heavy jaw stay open. The rest managed to disguise their delight, though they still concentrated on those magnificent legs.

"Sir, this is appropriate dress for an American woman of my age." She said it firmly but without defiance.

"What sort of American woman?" said Mack.

Louis smiled. "Americans are not concerned with such distinctions. The woman I had last night was quite indistinguishable from a party of wealthy banker's wives in the piano lounge."

Mack frowned at him. "Are you saying American harlots look like respectable women, or that respectable American women look like harlots?"

Louis grinned. "You are turning red, Misha. I am saying that, in this culture, Mara looks respectable, not otherwise. The presence of Charlie, Steve, and the doctor will prevent any unwanted signals, and I think the outfit is perfect. Anything less would make her look out of place. Besides, it is simple charity to give the watchers something decent to look at. Their eyes will be glued to her, and we will have no trouble getting our KGB friend into the vehicle without being seen. Stop wanting to shoot everybody for enjoying what you never failed to enjoy in the past."

Mack looked doubtful, glanced again at Louis, glared at the doctor who was enjoying himself too obviously, and sighed. "You had better go," he said to Charlie.

Mara's smile broke out in full force in the elevator until Charlie turned it off with a warning scowl. He turned back to face the door and Mara stuck her tongue out at him. "I saw that," he said, though he could not possibly have.

The evening began in the piano bar where they found Jane, Roger, and Judy, ordered scotch all around (to keep it simple, said Charlie), and sat looking at the silent piano. Seal gagged on the scotch and wished for a beer. Charlie yielded to pressure and played the Litolff Scherzo at the doctor's request. Mara watched Jane carefully. Seal watched them all.

There was no doubt the Jared woman was beautiful. But while Mara's beauty was something you had to be careful not to break, Jane's was the kind that would break you. She was tall, even taller than Charlie and all of it leg. She also wore her skirt short, so that in a leg-to-leg competition, Seal reluctantly named her the winner over Mara. There could be no contest in the rest of their beauty, though, because they were too different to be compared to each other. They were exquisite examples of their types; any choice would be in the chooser. Jane's voluminous brown hair could not be tamed by a

French twist like Mara's. Her honey-colored skin was flawless; her long, perfect nose balanced a long, perfect face in which her eyes, as brown and large as Steve's, held no hint of softness.

This woman was only for the adventurous type. Seal suppressed a shudder, acknowledging to himself he was never all that adventurous.

The lawyer was something else again. She was not ugly. Under good management, she could probably hold her own in the company of any woman on a rung just below Jane and Mara. The problem was, there was no management at all. Judy Simons had her hair done at the Bad Haircut Emporium. Clothes by Show The Lumps. Makeup under the direction of Blotch and Disfigure. Worst of all was the way this specimen clung to Steve Donovan like plastic wrap.

Wasn't he the funniest, the handsomest person? She simpered until the giggles ran up and down Seal's spine like fingernails on a blackboard.

Not man, 'person' was the word she used when she talked about Steve. In five minutes of giggling inanity, Seal decided the woman had no concept of the masculine and was not even aware that this was the quality that attracted her. While Steve was good looking, maybe, he wasn't the best looking of the bunch. That had to go to Charlie. But Steve was the most thoroughly, instinctively male 'person' Seal had ever met. Yep. He carried a lot of his personality in his gonads. He was funny, too, quick witted, slow speaking, with just a hint of his native Texas drawl. Sometimes his humor was cruel. It was always aggressive.

A crowd formed around the piano. Roger and Seal exchanged concerned glances. Charlie finished the Scherzo and accepted the applause with a solemn, stiff bow. Roger ushered them all out, with Charlie none too pleased, until Seal showed him the bottle of single malt he had procured, and they went upstairs to Roger's room to drink it.

Roger had your basic single room with a connecting door to Judy's basic single room. They managed to get two chairs out of Judy's room before she yanked Steve through the connecting door, saying "It's our turn," and locked it behind them. This left the rest of them to find a place in Roger's room for the important business of drinking Charlie's scotch together and watching each other for mistakes.

They gathered at the far end of the room from the entrance door. To the right of that door was the connection to the other room. From there to the chair where Jane sat, a hotel dresser stretched along the right-hand wall, holding Roger's suitcase, an ice bucket, assorted hotel pamphlets, an ashtray, and a television.

Jane and Charlie held court in chairs between the dresser and the far wall. Nearest to them stood a small, round table, leaned on by Roger who sat in the chair beside it. Seal sat at the other side of the table. The bed was centered on the left wall of the room. Here, Mara leaned against the headboard and stretched her lovely legs before her, demurely crossed at the ankle. John sat on the bed next to her, close to the edge.

The match began and the trouble started right away.

"How long have you known Mara?" Jane asked the doctor.

"Not long," John said simply. He was as cool as anybody could want. No sweat.

"What happened to your eye, Doctor?"

"Please, call me John." He paused, sizing her up, as one Frigidaire to another. "I ran into a fist." He smiled as if the joke were original.

"Over a girl?" There was a dimple in Jane's smile, more mischievous than endearing.

"What else is there to fight about?"

Old MacArthur's speech ran through Seal's mind. Duty. Honor. Country.

The conversation, if it could be called that, kept going this way for a few minutes.

Seal and Roger watched the exchange between Jane and the doctor like spectators at a tennis match. It was a civilized game until it became a doubles tourney with Mara's first volley.

"You've known Charlie a long time, haven't you Jane?"

"We met ten years ago if that's what you mean."

"That was when he saved your life, wasn't it?"

Charlie gave Mara a pretty obvious shut-up signal.

She ignored it. "Wasn't it Charlie who shot some guy trying to kill you? What was he called? The Barracuda, wasn't it? Charlie nailed him and saved your life, as I recall."

The shut-up signal became insistent. Nope, thought Seal as he watched the Jared girl's big brown eyes, sorry Mara. Jared has no remorse. Nothing will soften that resolve. You're right. She's here to kill him.

"Since you weren't there, Mara, you must be an avid reader," said Jane.

Ah. There's a reaction from Charlie. At least he has to acknowledge that she's in the game. She knows about files, and she knows about research. Point, Mara.

"I remember little of it, myself," continued the Jared woman, "except an unfortunately vivid recollection of your father cutting a man's throat."

Ace.

Charlie changed the signal. Seal did not understand it, though it seemed to be directed at him. No, not at him, past him. The doctor. Of course. The doctor gathered Mara in his arms and dutifully kissed her.

Your father... your father.... It might have been a fruitful reflection, but it was driven out of Seal's head by Steve and Judy's entrance. The doctor sat up at the edge of the bed. Mara smoothed herself and sat next to him. Steve pushed Seal out of his chair and sat in it, within arm's reach of John. Seal made the air conditioner at the window groan under his weight. Roger gave his chair to Judy, who moved it closer to Steve and took his left hand. Roger sat on the dresser next to the TV. Single malt made the rounds again and everybody had a fill-up.

This was appalling and Seal found himself thinking about how sane and unambiguous a James Bond movie was, with all the women beautiful and understanding. Not ridiculous and demanding like this lawyer. Bond's women weren't carved out of tombstone granite like Jared, nor were they dangerously intelligent like Mara. Oh, for the good old days of espionage. At least then, you knew who your enemies were. They were the ones who fed you to the sharks. This was Seal's second glass of scotch and he wasn't used to it. He caught himself seeing sharks.

The lawyer was babbling something about fancy Eastern schools only letting in quota blacks, which earned her daggers from Jared and made her backpedal frantically to correct the mistake, because Jane was black, an obvious thing that was easy to overlook and made Seal almost feel sorry for the lawyer. When you saw Jane for the first time you might say to yourself "Wow, what a stunner!" or "I don't wanna mess with that iceberg," but never, "By golly, she's black."

One more discomfort endured. How many more to go?

Judy let go of Steve's hand and reached over him to squeeze the doctor's knee. "You really shouldn't turn so many shades of red over a little kissy face, John. We're all adults here, except maybe for Mara. But then, in her case, it's experience over age that matters most."

Seal sucked in his lips, tried to suck them right down his throat. The woman's got a death wish, he thought. The shut-up signal was flying through the room, ignored. Would Mara understand the lawyer? Was her English good enough for this? There was a lot of vocabulary she was missing, Seal knew, and he hoped there was still a big gap in the sexual insult domain. He watched her, same as everybody else.

She was so still. Her face became a perfect, pleasant blank. She smiled a little.

Oh God, she got it.

"I'm trying to remember," she said sweetly, "the term for some-one with plenty of age, but no experience. Old maid, isn't it?" She cocked her head at Seal and raised an eyebrow.

He kept his lips sucked into his cheek and tried his own version of Shut Up.

Mara ignored his signal, too. "Typical of an important broad like yourself, though, Judy. With no tits and no man."

"You bitch," was Judy's frank reply. "It's only fair to warn you that I'm armed." She reached under her blouse and pulled out an enormous .357 revolver with a six-inch barrel, thus explaining and eliminating one lump. She began waving the thing around.

Charlie, Jane, Steve, Roger, and Seal all had their hands on their weapons but did not draw them yet because, so far, the lawyer couldn't get her finger in the trigger guard. Mara was perfectly still and did not reach for her Glock. She waited.

To Judy she said, "I see you have your very own," she looked at Seal, who was not about to help even if he knew the direction her words were going, "... dick. So why do you want to pull on Steve's?"

The finger found the trigger and the barrel swiveled toward Mara with the sound of a female snarl, but the hammer was never cocked because in the next moment, the revolver flew across the room and the lawyer landed on the floor with a whoosh of expelled air and a thud. The chair she vacated fell against the window and tipped over. It, too, made a thud, the last sound made until she caught her wind and began to shriek, "I'll sue you, Bitch!" between wet sobs. By now everybody was standing; only Mara was smiling, and Seal noticed the doctor shudder right along with him. At Charlie's direction, Doc and Steve helped the bleeding woman to her room. The physical damage was not excessive: a fat lip, a loose tooth, and a bloody nose, but the shrieking did not let up. Words could not express how sorry they were for Roger as they left him, so they didn't use any. Seal shook his hand with a sympathetic look. Condolences. Jane refused an escort to her room, and anyway, they didn't know where that was, and she wasn't about to tell them. She left them by the stairs.

They rode the elevator up to the penthouse in excruciating silence.

EIGHTEEN

M ara lost a high-heeled shoe in the elevator room as she fought Charlie on their way to the dining room. The other shoe came off when she tripped over the two steps into the sunken living room. Charlie had her firmly by the arm, though, so she did not fall on her face.

"That hurts. Stop twisting!" She did her best, her very best, to sound defiant. Tears will ruin my makeup, she told herself, but she could not stop the flood. It did hurt, the way he held her arm. It was also embarrassing to be dragged through the living room and hallway with stocking feet and running mascara.

She discarded defiance in the dining room and replaced it with fear. She had thought she did, but really, she did not know this man. Yes, she had grown up with the body. She recognized the blond, blue-eyed physical shell she played duets with on Christmas mornings. But the man who held her against the wall was not Michael; he was somebody named Charlie, somebody nasty and hard and incredibly angry with her.

Mara grew up surrounded by violent men but never saw this much violence in the eyes of any of them. She was an expert shot and an expert fighter and she was utterly helpless against the fury that held her. He was stronger. He was more determined.

She was afraid.

She allowed the fear to register on her face because she had no choice. She could not disguise it.

He spoke in a low voice, in German, through his teeth. "You will kill us all if you do not learn obedience. When I give you a signal, you are to obey instantly. Less than that is death. Before I let you kill us, I will tie you up without mercy and glue your nose in a corner for the duration of your time here. This is not a threat. Is my first point clear to you?"

She nodded. Her chin hit the top of his hand.

His eyes still burned holes through her.

"Point two," he said. "You will apologize to Steve for referring to him in that disrespectful way. Again, clear?"

Another nod.

"Finally, you will stop provoking the men here. Don't try to look ignorant. You are deliberately provoking them, especially Steve, by the way you speak and the things you wear. No more short skirts; no more gutter language."

She was genuinely confused. "Gutter?"

"Words like broad, dick, and tit are improper."

"They are the words Seal uses."

"Seal is a peasant, for the love of God!"

"He has been very good to me."

"That does not change his class nor require you to change yours. When you speak that way, especially as a woman, you lower yourself. You make yourself an object of pursuit. You become available. Not only the words you use, but the subjects they describe are improper for you to address. You are not a man. You cannot be a man. When you speak that way you do not erase this fact, you emphasize it. I want your word that there will be no more short skirts and no more inappropriate language."

She hung her head. Her tears fell on his hand. She remembered the language used by Louis's beloved wife and quashed her doubts so they would not be visible to Michael. He would only call Millie a peasant, too.

"Tears will not stop me. I will have your word, or you will suffer."

She looked up at him, exasperated and shielding a rebellion. "I can't! I don't understand you. First, I am told I cannot wear jeans. Now, I am told no skirts. All of my skirts are short. What am I to wear? Mama never covered the English words for some things. I have only Seal's words. How do I know what is appropriate? Am I limited to dinner table topics? The weather and general health? Should I blush when men say things, or won't that make them even more uncomfortable?"

His grip loosened, then he let go, and she realized she'd been standing on her toes. His jaw worked, but he said nothing. He still breathed like a maddened bull. "You will obey me," he said finally.

He was dropping the subject, the uncomfortable, excruciating subject. Mara felt new tears—of joy. "Oh yes, yes. I give you my word. And I will apologize to Steve. I promise."

She promised but was not ready to fulfill it in the very next instant when Michael yanked the door open and stomped out of the room. Steve had been sitting by the door, discouraging intruders. He slipped into the room as Michael left it and closed the door quietly behind him.

Ready or not, she had to make the effort. "I… I'm… I apologize for being… for saying…" The tears would not stop.

He wiped a few drops from her cheek, gently. She could see the kiss coming. She was still standing with her back against the corner wall where Michael had put her. There was no graceful exit.

Sergei's kiss had been momentary, and the swelling on his face made him gentle. John had been acutely aware of both Steve and Charlie when he kissed her in Judy's room. His was a longer kiss than Sergei's, and more insistent, but by necessity, chaste.

Steve was under no restraint.

He engulfed her. Her eyes were wide open; he looked at her briefly and forced her mouth open with his tongue. She put her hands on his shoulders to push him away. One of his hands—he must have twenty—went under her sweater and up her back. It slipped under her bra strap and around to the front, where it cupped her breast while his tongue drove deeper into her mouth. She stopped pushing at his shoulders and tried removing that hand. Another of his twenty hands was behind her, lifting her skirt and driving between her legs. Her body began to respond. It was an utterly new sensation to her, an importunate warmth that made her press against him almost involuntarily. He knew it immediately and pressed himself into her as his hand found the top elastic of her panties.

She was terrified, even before the door opened. When it opened, she thought of new reasons for terror, each one more logically deadly than the last. She understood a lot now. She wanted to run and tell Michael that she would give her word to anything he said. She prayed to God that this was not Michael at the door. She wondered why the intruder did not affect Steve. Surely he knew the door was open. He knew it and was beyond caring.

The door opener cleared his throat.

Steve disengaged the kiss. He rested his cheek against hers. His hands stopped moving, but they did not leave the premises. He sighed lightly.

"What, Frank?"

Frank cleared his throat again. "I thought you might need to know, Mack is looking for you."

Steve let her go. He looked at her before he turned around. In one glance, he told her he was determined and expected to succeed.

He put his hand on Frank's shoulder on his way out. "You're a pal, Frank. A real pal."

"Just doing my job, Steve," Frank said quietly.

Mara stood looking stupidly at Frank. Her skirt was hiked up around her waist. She smoothed it down, turning crimson. She could feel the tears beginning again. Frank had interviewed her once when he recruited her into the game. That was the only time before now that she had met him. Her confusion was total. He was male and he was a stranger and she feared him. Yet, Misha trusted him, somewhat. Thank God it was not Misha who found Steve kissing her like that.

"Can I help you in any way, Miss Sobieski?"

He didn't move. That was good. That helped. She had time to edge away from the wall, to prepare a defense, which she worked on until she realized the absurdity. Frank was not Steve. He was no match for her.

"Do you know...?" She squeaked. She brought it under control but could not stop her legs from trembling. "Do you know where Louis is?"

"He's on the terrace. Would you like me to take you to him?" He held out his arm to her like a dinner partner.

It was the return of civilization, a reinstatement of safety that stopped the earth quaking under her feet. She rested her hand lightly on his arm and let him lead her to the terrace.

Louis leaned on the wall, looking at the neon lights below, his dark head silhouetted by the light from a three-quarter moon above. He turned and left the drink he had in his hand on the wall when he heard Mara running toward him so that his arms were free to embrace her as she buried her face in his chest, sobbing.

NINETEEN

She wailed into Louis's shoulder as he held her. He offered a handkerchief when she surfaced for air. She cried again into the handkerchief.

When the flood subsided, Louis said, "Your big brother has been nasty to you, I suspect."

She nodded.

"And worse than that," said Louis. "He was right, was he not?"

Through the new round of sobs came a few chopped words, "But... I... proved... Jane's... dirty."

"You are crying over a victory?"

She became calmer now. She blew her nose on the handkerchief, making it a dainty act.

"Why the tears, my little precious one?" Louis held her shoulders and stood back a step to look at her. "What else happened?"

"I don't know. I am confused. This morning I had never been kissed by a man, and now I have been kissed by three and I don't know what to do. You are an expert in these things, Louis. What should I do?"

"I know about Sergei's demonstration," he said, "and I am sure the doctor kissed you while you were downstairs infuriating your brother. Who is the third?"

She hung her head. "I am frightened."

He pursed his lips and nodded. "In one day, you have been kissed by Love, by Infatuation, and by Desire and have discovered that Desire is dangerous."

"Will he... do you think he would rape me?"

"Ah. There is a misapplied word. Steve will not deliberately hurt you to cause you pain. He will overwhelm you and convince himself that you are willing. The word for it was once seduction. Equally damaging at times, but not the same. He will certainly seduce you if you allow it."

"But Misha would kill him. He must know that."

"He does. But Michael is the one who would kill him, *Cheri*. Misha and I had a lifetime of friendship behind us when we had our trouble. Steve and Michael have only ten years. It will not be enough."

Louis took his glass off the wall and refilled it at the little bar near the piano room window. He filled another glass and handed it to Mara. She sipped it and rubbed one ankle with the other foot, trying to work out how best to phrase her question.

"Louis?"

"Yes, *Cheri*."

"The trouble you and Misha had, did it have to do with my mother?"

"Yes."

There are limits to some questions. She was dying to know all of it, every detail, and yet she hated the thought of knowing any of it. In Mara's universe, Louis did no wrong. Her mother on the other hand....

"Why is Steve like this? He never was before."

"You were not fully grown up before. Understand, he is a warrior." Louis leaned on the terrace wall and looked out on the lighted streets below them. "He wants to make you his prize, to conquer you, to collect you the way he collected his new Beretta, to cosset you and keep you, the way he modified the Beretta and cleans it and oils it. You are to be had for your beauty. It is quite simple. If sex were not strongly interesting, we would soon be extinct. If Steve did not behave as a warrior, he would not be on the team."

Mara studied him as he drank. The ice clinked when he put the glass down. The shadows played with his face so that she could not be sure of his expression. He was grim; she could feel it. She tried to imagine him behaving the way Steve had done. Yes, of course. She had always seen the resemblance between these two and wondered what it was. Now she saw it clearly.

"What should my mother have done?"

She meant to say, "What should I do?" She did not often speak her thoughts, and this was the one person to whom she always spoke freely, but would he answer it?

He smiled at her, but not in a jolly way. It was an ironic, regretful smile. "She should have chosen me," he said. "She had three chances to choose me. She trusted luck the first time, and I lost, but I wonder if you would have been so beautiful if it were I and not Misha who drew the ace of diamonds." He touched her cheek as he said this. "She married Vasily. This, also, did not pose a problem to me. But when she chose Misha...." He dropped his arm to his side, drew in a deep breath, and let it out again, slowly. Then he turned away from her, back to the lights of the city.

"That does not help you, I know. Steve is not for you. You cannot choose him. He wants your beauty. Though you grew up near him, though he trained you himself, he knows nothing else about you. The doctor, now, sees you more clearly. He knows that you have a personality and that it is not the same insipid assembly line American girl personality he is accustomed to. He is attracted, but he knows nothing about your training, your strengths, or your weaknesses."

Mara slipped her hand under his arm and leaned with him over the city. "You're saying that Sergei loves me?"

"He does."

"But he never looks at me."

"He carefully never looks at you. He knows Misha will read him at a glance. But all his care is for nothing. Misha knows it already. That is why Sergei is still alive. We know that it is danger to you that made him act, not this list."

"How do you know?"

Louis turned and smiled at her in the moonlight. "Sergei is non-ideological, in many ways like Steve. Ask Steve what he thinks of a socialist, capitalist, or fascist, and he will tell you how to kill one. Sergei is the same. He is loyal to his friends and his job and will do it superbly well without ever thinking or caring about the philosophy that underlies it. Now he is betraying not his country, which does not suffer much by the release of Semianov's outdated list, nor his defunct ideology, but his best friend, Maximovich. It is an enormous betrayal for a man like Sergei. His reason must be compelling. You are the most compelling thing in his life."

"He is trying not to betray him. He is trying not to mention Maximovich," Mara said.

"He is not succeeding. I suspect his friend Volodya is the danger."

"Should I choose Sergei?"

"I did not say that. We may yet have to kill him. And even if we do not, Maximovich will not be the only one seeking vengeance."

She searched the lines of streetlights for something to say, quickly, before this line of thought could go on.

"What should I do about Steve?"

"You must be firm with him. Always say no. Never waiver from sentiment or fear. Give him no hope. Never be alone with him. Never be intimate in any way."

"I cannot be friends?"

"No. Business only."

They stood silent, facing each other, for nearly a full minute. Mara sensed a rising urgency in the noises and voices inside, but she did not want to break the spell. There was so much that Louis could explain. She only needed the questions and the time to ask them.

"Jane said she saw my father cut a man's throat," she told him finally.

"Your father?"

"Those were her words. She meant Misha."

"A great victory indeed, little one. Michael cannot deny what she is now. If she knows that, she can only have learned it from Maximovich. But why does it bother you? I sense there is more to it than the obvious discomfort of having Misha as an ancestor. *Blut ist ein ganz besonderer Saft, n'est-ce pas?*"

"Quite so, Mephistopheles."

"You cannot believe Misha could do such a thing, eh?"

"He is so wise and impeccable."

"So, how could he be so unclean?" said Louis. "Soon you will see us all at our filthiest."

"I have seen it," she insisted. "I have cleaned your wounds, washed you, shaved you, and disinfected you. I know it is not pleasant. I am prepared."

"These are physical things. You have not seen the other damage. How can the cold, wise, impeccable Misha perform such a hot crime? The same way we all do. We deny the humanity of the victim and a little of our own dies with him. Should you fear becoming like him? Yes."

"How did you know? Why should I fear it?"

"I know because you would not be here if you were not testing it. You want to know what's inside you. I admire you for not taking the safe road, the squeaky-clean American way to mediocrity and self-delusion, but I am afraid you will not like what you find, my dear."

"What will I find, Louis?" She looked down at her feet. There were holes in the toes of her stockings.

"That, as a killer, you are even worse than Misha, because you are better than he is, not more skilled, but more good. The greatest abomination is killing for goodness' sake. When I kill, I am always evil, careful to be so, a regular Mephistopheles indeed. I am hot with hate and fear, while Misha is cool with plans and procedures. That is why he is in charge, and why Michael is next in charge, and you must obey him, my dear, but that is beside our point for now. You, too, would be a cool killer, one who does the job for some good, but unlike Misha, you are, so far, unaware of the evil. Killing may be justice and it may be necessary, but it is never, ever good, and no matter how good the end, murder is an evil means."

"I do not intend to kill."

"Circumstances will force it, this trip."

"Should I go home? Have I made a mess of things? Have I endangered everyone?"

"Which one first? Yes, you should go home, but we cannot get you there safely. No, you have done what was necessary, and have done well. Yes, you have endangered us all, but not because you had any control over it."

"I wish we could just forget about the stupid list."

"There is also the file."

"And the file."

"There are larger considerations."

"Such as?"

"Jay Turner fears for his precious constitution."

"That does not concern you, Louis. You are not an American."

"True. I am much more concerned with preserving my skin. But Misha dislikes large death tolls if they can be avoided. It is the goodness in him again, and Jay is convinced he must have the list to avert disaster."

Mara sighed and looked at her feet again.

Louis looked at them, too.

"You know that you should not be barefoot in these stockings," he said. "Look. You have big holes in them. Such things can be worn more than once, Mara, if you take care of them."

She chuckled. "You old rogue. You are so cheap."

"Frank called me cheap, too. Last night. He insisted that I tip the woman. You would think that a thousand dollars is sufficient without a tip."

"A thousand dollars! How does she earn it? I am intrigued. What...?"

"Enough education. Come, we must prepare for the drive to San Antonio."

TWENTY

People don't build houses, do coronary bypasses or find deadly lists of irrelevant Soviet agents without first holding meetings. Mack convened one as soon as the RV door closed behind John, who was the last person to squeeze in.

"Are you in yet?" Mara asked from somewhere in the crowd.

"Not a question a man likes to hear," said Steve.

Surreptitious chuckles all around, suppressed by a glower from Charlie.

John stood squashed between Steve, who was all elbows, and a small refrigerator that held a computer.

They chose the twenty-seven-foot Jamboree, Seal told him before they climbed inside because there were so many of these on the road.

"But," John protested, "this model was never designed to hold ten people."

"All the better," was Seal's reply. "It'll be completely unexpected. And anyway, Jay won't be with us. He'll head for Chicago to try to draw off the lawyer. There will be only nine most of the time."

Nine people in a twenty-seven-foot camper. John did the math. He had seen an ugly mottled green car hitched to the back before he squeezed inside. He wondered if he could ride in that.

"That's for gas," Seal told him. "We put an extra tank in it so we don't have to get the RV wedged into a seedy gas station."

John lingered outside as long as he could. Pavlenko had been squirreled away earlier with Jay Turner to babysit him. The others came on board carrying bags and cases. All of these clanked. The specialists wore black. They wore it unobtrusively: old black denim, black t-shirts, black boots. Mack and Steve wore a top layer of plaid flannel to relieve the uniform look and cover their guns. Mara had already gone in before John got there; he didn't get to see her.

Once inside, he still couldn't see her. He was in the main cabin, no more than two meters from her, but everybody was in the way.

The RV had been modified. On the right, the cabin over the cab was stuffed with what looked like radios, a series of navigation gadgets, and other metal boxes with lighted displays of blinking numbers and dangling phone cords. Beneath the comm bank hung a heavy black curtain that separated the cab from the main cabin. Behind Steve, who stood to his right, the window had also been covered with a black curtain. There were no seats on this side of the cabin, but John could make out Frank's back against the wall as he sat on a footlocker shoved under the little window.

There was a booth of sorts on the other side of the space, with bench seats and a small table attached to the wall under another black-clad window. Mack sat in the corner, and next to him, Charlie. Across from them sat Louis with Mara. John caught a glimpse of her hand on the table. Above the window was a shelf holding a row of television screens showing closed-circuit views of the parking lot around them.

What remained of the galley was to John's left. The small refrigerator served as a computer stand. Across a narrow aisle, the stove had been removed and replaced with another large, black box, all lights and knobs, topped with a tape apparatus of big and little reels, two each, that turned intermittently by themselves, two at a time, with no apparent human control. Sergei Pavlenko was attached to this machine by a cord running to the headphones he wore. He leaned over the sink, facing the center of the room. To Sergei's left, John caught sight of a restaurant-style coffee maker, and on it, three full, steaming pots. He hoped the cabinet above it held supplies, food being the chief commodity on his mind at the moment.

Seal had wedged himself in the aisle between the sink and the refrigerator to John's left. He smelled suspiciously and unappetizingly of sauerkraut.

The meeting droned on like any other John had ever attended. Speakers spoke at length about things he did not want to understand, like weapons and enemies. He would have fallen over from fatigue, tension, and scotch, but Steve's many elbows caught him every time he nodded.

Jay Turner spoke about the route and the GPS and how that worked. Then came the typical interminable questions, all of which would have been better addressed one-on-one. Nobody asked what the hell GPS meant, which was the one thing John wanted to know but would never dare bring up in this venue, partly because he sensed Steve was just as impatient with the questioners as he was. There would be better opportunities to irritate the man, preferably someplace where there was room to run.

Mack spoke next, packing vital information into every short, accented sentence, forcing John to listen. Most of it did not apply to him, like the admonition not to wear weapons openly in the cab or the restrictions on cleaning your weapon: permitted, because this is not the airplane, but always point to the rear of the vehicle so there is no risk of shooting the driver or the explosives stored above the driver.

John did not miss any of these and other essential points. There would be two watches, one under Mack's direction, the other under Charlie's. The watch up front would drive, monitor the radios, maintain the coffee pot, and take the car to get fuel halfway through the shift. At the end of each four-hour shift, the front watch would go into the back where there were bunks. If your watch was in the back, you could go up front outside your watch time only with permission of the other watch leader. If your watch was in front, you were not permitted to go back until the shift ended. Fighting was prohibited. Why was Mack looking at him? Mack would personally enforce this. John looked at Steve sideways and smiled.

Were there any questions? No. Mack did not inspire questions. The perfect chairman.

He named the watches: Steve and Mara, with Seal as babysitter, on Charlie's watch. The rest were on Mack's. Charlie's watch was up front first. Jay would drive them to the intersection of I-80 and US 95, then he would leave for Chicago, hoping to lure away the lawyer and her FBI helper. Jane Jared, they assumed, would continue to San Antonio by van. She had told Charlie she was attending a political rally there. She had mentioned a van. They had no idea which van, but they had a good touch on Roger's car and were monitoring it with primary and backup tapes.

If Jay's plan worked, and if he succeeded in luring away the lawyer, and if they were able to touch Jared's vehicle, they would devote the machine to her. Otherwise, if they had to monitor both, they would have to split the channels and keep a close eye on the tapes. Assuming they could touch Jared at all, reminded the Frenchman. Assuming so, agreed Mack.

Getting to the back of the RV at the end of the meeting posed another challenge. Jay started the vehicle and was already driving them out of the lot. Seal and Frank did a dance in the middle of the cabin, trying to get past each other without being crushed. Frank, the smaller of the two, had the worse time of it. He pushed John ahead of him through the galley and into the back. John had only enough time to see Pavlenko hand the headphones to Mara.

His pause to look at her backed up traffic in the galley behind him. She wore a black t-shirt, a shoulder holster holding her Glock, black denim pants, black boots, and a large black bow in her hair. Her hair had been severely swept back and pasted to her head with mousse, the length behind taken up in a tight braid and wound into a knot. The bow was attached to the knot. It was a large, black joke, a militantly feminine defiance of that male environment. As John stared at her, Charlie's arm reached out, took the bow, and tossed it into the sink. It landed on a spent coffee filter.

Shoved from behind, John moved through the narrow corridor to the back room. The doors had been removed from the shower on the left and the toilet on the right. A blanket was nailed over the toilet door, the lone concession to Mara. The shower held equipment. John noticed body armor vests stacked on boxes painted in camouflage patterns.

There was no door to the back room. Four cots, of a military sort, were suspended from the walls, two on each side. These were narrow constructions of pipe and olive-green canvas. There were no blankets. Footlockers and bags in olive drab and black ripstop nylon had been piled against the back wall. More of these were stuffed under the lower bunks. John sat on the lower left-hand bunk. Frank nudged his shoulder.

"Come on, Doc," he said. "You're young and in shape. You jump up to the top and let me have this one."

There was nothing to climb. The cots were bolted to the wall, with canvas straps running from their outside edges, fore and aft, also bolted to the wall a few feet above. John vaulted himself into the upper left-hand cot. The ceiling was too low to sit up. He peered over the edge. Frank did not quite fit in his cot. Pavlenko pushed himself up into the cot opposite John. Mack was still up front. The Frenchman opened one of the foot lockers and took out a rifle, then a gun cleaning kit, and swore softly as he rummaged and produced a wad of round cotton cleaning patches. He sat beneath the patient, unloaded the rifle, and began dismantling it.

"Louis," said Sergei.

"Right here," he replied, in French.

"Did you ask him?" Also in French.

"Yes."

"Well?"

"He will consider your request in his decision."

There was a pause.

"What does that mean?"

Louis laughed. He took a cleaning rod and a patch, dipped the patch in solvent, and rammed it through the barrel with a brass rod. "You know better than to tell your fears to your enemy, Sergei Nickolaevich."

"I thought that since he is an honorable man …"

"You presume too much on honor."

"It is all I have."

Another pause.

Sergei spoke again: "In the end, there is only honor."

"You want my opinion? I am an old killer. In the end, there is only death."

"You are barely fifty."

"How many specialists do you know as old as me?"

"Mack."

"He is younger."

"All right then, as an ancient specialist, tell me why there is no honor."

"Because all choices are evil, even the honorable ones. A truly honorable man knows this, and so I suppose you can say that Misha is honorable in this respect. But you ask the wrong man, Sergei. I am only an old specialist. Misha is the philosopher, especially since he won Alex; she is the true expert on deep things and has made him into a thinking man. I like good food, good wine, and beautiful, willing women. I cannot make love to an idea."

"And song," said Frank. "Don't forget song. Wine, women, and song."

Louis looked up from the rifle and grinned. He polished it absently with a chamois. "No. Charlie is the one for song. But I like a good joke. Philosophy is not funny. Tell me then, what is the most useless thing on a woman?"

"I don't know. What?"

"A babysitter."

"Very funny."

"I think so."

"If all choices are evil, Louis," said Sergei. "How does an honorable man determine his course?"

Louis considered this as he applied the oil. "I believe what Misha does.... You understand that I must speak of him as your hypothetical honorable man because I am not one. In my case, choices are always simple. I choose Lafitte over house wine, chateaubriand over hamburger, a pretty woman over an ugly one. I prefer to kill my enemy before he has the opportunity to kill me. I carefully collect any money anybody offers me to do what I would be doing anyway, which is killing my enemies. I am a simple man and cannot be used as a model in this discussion."

He pointed the cleaning rod upward, didactically, as though presenting an academic lecture. John fought to stay awake and listen. Frank snored.

"This is how Misha uses his honor," Louis instructed. "He determines his general position on any moral point before he is confronted with a specific case. He measures possibilities against a standard. Thus, he is at least consistent, if not always right. Only once was he overcome by emotion and it nearly killed us all. But in the end, he righted himself, and the problem was solved."

"After Ekaterina and Nadia were killed," said Sergei, "I determined never again to participate in the killing of innocents."

"Very noble." Louis reassembled the rifle and reached into the locker for another.

"Is it?"

"Yes. And you would see it as such if the woman you are trying to save were as blameless as little Nadia and if the man you are trying to save her from were not your excellent and lifelong friend. You are plagued by knowing everyone involved and nobody is fitting into your standards as they should. You can comfort yourself with the consolation of preventing death, which is always a good thing to do, but it is not quite true, is it? You have already killed two. Fortunately, you did not know them, so you are not haunted by the grief of their families."

They listened for a while to Frank's snores. Then Louis spoke more frankly. "There will be more deaths before we find the list, you know. If Mara is not one of those killed, what will be the acceptable toll to your honor? If she lives and Vladimir does not, how will honor help you? Be grateful to Misha for shortening your troubles, with whatever method he chooses."

"You are not helping me."

"I am your enemy Sergei Nickolaevich. I miss Vasily. I wish he were up on that other bunk, not this irritating doctor. I wish he were planning the charges that would get us safely into that warehouse. None of us can do it without blowing us all out of the solar system. You must not think I have any desire to help you."

"I can set the charges."

"What?" Louis stopped dismantling the new rifle and looked up at the bunk above him.

"I can set charges. Sobieski was my hero. I tried to copy everything he did, except killing. I had to be as much like him as I could to catch him."

Louis poked the barrel into the canvas over his head. "Shut up." He continued the job he was doing and made himself busy brushing the firing pin.

"A few years ago," Louis said finally, "Misha and I almost killed each other over Mara's mother, Alex. Details are not important, but Steve and Charlie kept us alive."

He looked up at John who peered down at him from the opposite high bunk, as unobtrusively as he could make himself.

"I will tell you Steve did not pull his punches with me as he does with you, Doctor."

He picked up the chamois and began polishing.

"Misha and I were babies together," he continued, "and there we were, fighting over a woman. After such a painful education, I learned, finally, that a wife is the completion of the self. It is possible to give up yourself for a friend, of course, but what true friend would require it? Misha forgave me. Alex learned to stay out of my way. If Volodya is a true friend, you will have no evil choice. If he is not, you have my permission, with glee, to shoot him."

Louis placed the reassembled rifles in the foot locker. He shoved the cleaning kit under his cot, where the bottle of oil tipped over and rolled around the room, leaking a drop at a time, adding to the odors.

John was hungry; he had not eaten since that long-ago breakfast. The scotch he'd sipped in Roger's room did not sit well on an empty stomach. Frank snored already. John stared at the ceiling, debating with himself the definitions of blameless and wife. The priest said, "Repeat after me," and John held up his gloved hands and said, "With these hands, I thee heal." Mara said something in Russian and John told himself he was dreaming.

TWENTY-ONE

I t was a bad dream and waking was no better. John woke in the air on his way to the floor. Steve had him by the collar of Charlie's green polo shirt. John found his feet, stood, and prepared a reply— remarkably fast, he thought, through the grogginess. Why is the bastard smiling? And why doesn't he defend himself? These thoughts came swiftly, but John's fist would be faster. Another thought intruded. Something about Mack personally enforcing....

His fist never reached Steve's face, because he was spinning for some reason and then facing Mack, then hit with what was surely a battering ram. The familiar empty gasp for air resumed and he wondered if his spleen had ruptured. He flew down the aisle into Mara, who stepped aside at just the right time, and he fell at her feet. She helped him up, though he couldn't use the help, needed to breathe first, but somehow, he made it down the narrow aisle on his feet. He landed on his knees at the galley sink and fought the urge to hold his throbbing abdomen. He wished to God Mara was not watching.

"You're riding with me, Doc. Come on." Frank pulled the green shirt's collar further out of shape.

John stumbled to his feet to follow it, still not seeing clearly. Vision and breathing did not clear until he sat in the passenger seat of the cab and Frank turned the key, then shifted into gear.

"You heard the brief, my beamish boy," said Frank. "Rule One. No alterc... no pugil... no fights. Mack will enforce it. You look a little ragged. Are you okay? You're okay. Mack knows how to break things and how not to. I don't think we're at breaking point just yet. It's coming though. You need to cool that temper of yours. Get that chip off your shoulder before these guys knock your head off with it. Take it, it's good advice. Love, Frank." Frank made a smacking sound.

John carefully palpated his torso, looking for signs of rupture. Satisfied that everything was intact, he looked outside at the blackest night on the darkest road he'd ever seen.

"Where the hell are we?"

"We're on US 95 headed south to Las Vegas. We'll cross the Dam and pick up 93 to Phoenix, where we'll get on I-10 and stay there all the way to San Antonio. One thousand seven hundred miles of pure, bare-ass desert, except for the last few miles to San Antone. Thirty-two hours, not counting fuel stops, because we're extra heavy, which puts us at roughly six watches each before it's over, in which to get along with an increasingly wired team of killers in a small space, with a woman on board to add thrills and chills. God, I love it. Yes, indeedy speedy. There," he pointed to a black box on the console. "That's the GPS. Learn how to use it. I'm going to make you drive next, if Mack approves, to keep you out of trouble."

The box glowed green and amber. A series of numbers changed continually on a lighted display.

"What's a GPS?"

Frank whistled. "Global Positioning System. We use a satellite to tell our position. The numbers are latitude and longitude. As we head south, watch the lat numbers change, seconds and minutes. Jay gave us some primary and backup fuel stops roughly four hours apart. Punch this button," he pressed a switch on the left of the box, "for the next stop. The button on the right gives you a backup if that stop's not clear. Jay did his homework, the darling lad."

"Where is Jay?"

"He left us back on I-80, hoping to take her ladyship, the lawyer esquirette, with him, but no luck. She and Roger are about a half mile behind us. I imagine we'll see Jay later, from time to time."

"You said fuel stops. What about food and a toilet? That little marine toilet won't last more than a few more hours with all this coffee."

"Speaking of coffee," said Frank. "How about a cuppa?" He opened his bulgy eyes so that the whites glowed green in the dashboard lights.

Mack sat in a folding chair by the coffee pot, wearing the headset. John poured carefully, careful not to spill, careful not to get too close. The tape machine started and stopped. Louis and Sergei played chess at the table. "Check," said Sergei. Louis glowered at him.

"About food," he reminded Frank when he handed him a cup.

"I don't know why you'd want any now," said Frank. "Don't think any of us will clean it up when you upchuck after getting hit in the gut. But if you insist, you can buy some during a fuel stop—if you get to go out on one. Otherwise, there are some high-energy bars in the coffee cabinet. Don't eat too many, though. The team will need them before they go out."

John wondered how to volunteer for a fuel stop. They would use the car for that, he knew. Maybe he could go with Mara. No. Wrong shift. "I don't have any money on me, Frank. How do I get paid for this?"

This. Now there was a whole host of questions. What, exactly, was this?

"Ah. Now there's a good question." Frank paused. "You see, my friend, money is always a good question, and this time partic... espe... certainly so. I have drawn the first half of the money offered for Pavlenko's hide to make it look good. But I am not a fool, no not me. I have the money sequestered and will return it when all this is over. Uncle Sam will forgive all manner of treason, but don't you even pretend to misappropriate a dime of his mullah or you will groom a golf course in some min-security federal hospitality cell for a very long time. I am not planning to retire that way. The team is funding this operation themselves. It costs plenty, but then, they have plenty, and evidently, they also have plenty of incentive this time. As for your salary, if Jay survives, and you survive, both ifs being questionable, maybe he can get the FBI to pay you. Maybe."

Great. John sipped his coffee.

"Another thing," resumed Frank. "If things do not go well, which is likely, but you have the misfortune to live, then when we are in court, please don't say you came along because you were chasing a pretty girl. It will not go over well. It will not go over at all. You say, my beamish, besotted boy, that you were threatened with death if you did not cooperate. It sounds good; it is the truth; and it will get you off."

"I haven't been threatened."

"Not aloud. It is assumed you can put two and two together. Always thought thinking was a requisite skill for medical school."

The coffee was good on a sore, empty stomach. The sky lightened a little on the left.

"What precisely, Frank," he said between sips, "am I cooperating in? I know about chasing girls, even though I've never been so damned unsuccessful before. When I get close, which is rare enough, I don't usually have the breath to speak to her. But the chase I understand. The rest, I don't."

Frank did not answer at first. He weighed his words, taking a long curve in the road with a leisurely swing of the wheel. Finally, he said, "Think of it in terms of what happens to Semianov's list. You know about the list, right?"

"A bunch of spies or something."

"Not just spies, my friend. Agents of influence. Deep cover illegals who influence different sectors of the country for purposes of disruption. Pavlenko says the list contains upwards of two hundred names. Of course, they are pernicious, but unlike your garden, home-grown variety of American critics, these have been cultivated, nurtured, and harvested by a foreign power, now defunct. Think about it. They will be highly placed, usually in government or communications, and a few in powerful industries. And none will resemble the so-called commies old Joe McCarthy tried to finger. I wouldn't be surprised if he was on that list.

Frank paused for an emotional gulp of his coffee. "Anyway, you have this list that everybody would like to see. I know I would. I know there are some in my chain, or I would not have been given the commission on Pavlenko. Twenty million is an enormous, desperate, number for one dead body."

He pointed down the road, as a visual aid to each point he wanted to make. "The options for this list, then, are these: it can fall into the hands of the listees. They will destroy it and carry on being disruptive. It can be captured by some wacky interest group and be published. God forbid."

"Why? Isn't that the best result?"

Frank sighed. "Look at all the factions in this country, Doc. Do you know anything about the right wing? No? Let me tell you it goes all the way around 'til it's back to being the left. On the way, you've got people convinced there's a worldwide conspiracy to occupy this country with Russkies and hippies. Won't they love the list?"

He warmed to his subject as his voice rose in pitch.

"Then there are the ones who think the white supremacists are the real people of God and to hell with the Jews. Then how about the black Muslim nationalists, eh? And all these people are armed. And so are the great big mass in the middle that doesn't know what the hell any of those isms are—except it's a plot against sacred capital-ism—but knows damn well what a Russian spy is, by God." Frank struck the wheel with hand holding his cup and sloshed the last drops onto the dash.

"The cry will go up," he said with suitable drama. 'They're com-ing for our guns!' First anarchy, then tyranny, after lots and lots of blood. God help the group that isn't armed. It's called genocide. Let's not forget the larcenous and the criminals. The Skinheads, Crips, Bloods, and the various Mafias are all armed with more than hand-guns, my friend. Just think about the impact of a civil war on a coun-try where the lottery is the only way a schmuck can get rich. Talk about a jackpot!"

"Who do you think will win in the end?"

"Hell, Doctor. I don't even know what side I'll be on, let alone what the end will be."

"So why are we trying to stop them from destroying the list? We should help them do it." John's cup was empty. He stared into the bottom of it, regretting its end.

Frank was patient. "If there is another copy, it can surface again. That's one danger. And the people we're talking about have already made a mess of one major power; they can repeat themselves here. That's the other danger. Jay has a better plan."

"Which is?"

"He will use the list to clean things up a bit. If another copy shows up, it will be old news. The country will yawn. Who cares? It's history. Last week is an ancient time in this country."

"How will Jay do that?"

"He'll Hoover it. Not the British version as in vacuum, but the American, as in J. Edgar. He'll arrange for some quiet resignations, a few retirements, maybe a career change or two, out of power, out of action, a few may go to jail. He thinks it will work."

"But you don't."

"If anybody can do it, Jay can. But I don't think anybody can do it. I think we'll be torn apart eventually. If Jay can save a few inno-cent lives in this case, I'll do what I can to help him. As for the guilty, I believe traitors should be shot. That's one of the things I don't like about Jay's plan, but then, he may have some plans along that line that I don't know about. Here's our stop."

John looked at the GPS. The numbers blinked at him. The sun was up now, already hot, in a flawless sky vaulted over brown rock-rubble hills. They pulled off the road at a public picnic table. There was shelter of a sort from a clump of mesquite and a trash can tilted on a stick, inviting use.

A hand reached through the black curtain and twisted John's shirt collar. A voice said, "*Kommen Sie.*" John obeyed without knowing the language, hating his shirt collar and its willingness to be used to order him about. Mack put a set of car keys in his hand as he pushed him out the door and back toward the green car.

"You drive."

TWENTY-TWO

"Turn left," said Mack.

John had signaled right. "Jay's map says to use the station on the right."

"They are going left."

"Who are going left?"

Mack pointed at a blue car ahead of them that John had not noticed, though he'd followed it up the exit ramp.

He shuddered at Mack's patience. The man's stillness did not reassure him. It was not kindly or understanding. Rather, it expressed without words how little John and his mistakes mattered. He thought about the big gun—called a sig-something wasn't it?—concealed under Mack's plaid flannel shirt. Who the hell cares what kind it is? The emergency room taught him that big guns make big holes in people. For the first time, he felt the menace. Until now, it was an intellectual curiosity, something that affected other people. Yes, he could die, but of course, he wouldn't. He was the hero of his own story; how could he die? Painfully. The ER had taught him that, too.

At the gas station, Mack worked the pump and kept watch in a complete circle, like a blue-eyed owl. Roger, the FBI man, poured gas into the blue Ford at the next pump. He fumbled, dropped the gas cap, and had to crawl under the car in his white shirt and maroon tie to retrieve it. He watched the blue-eyed man in the flannel shirt. He acknowledged John's friendly wave with a minimal nod but did not smile.

They were a happy party of four as they lined up to pay for the gas. John picked up a package of little donuts. Mack made him put it back.

"It will make you sick."

John tried to take a small bag of barbecue chips.

"It will make me sick," said Mack.

Judy made trouble, not in a conventional way, but simply by being her own loud, odious, and insensitive self. She stood behind Mack at the checkout, tugging at his sleeve while she smiled and insulted. She mentioned Mack's resemblance to Charlie and then talked about Mara. John heard the word 'bitch' all the way back at the door, where he and Roger watched each other and the cars.

"Get him the fuck outta here," said Roger through his teeth. He hardly moved his lips. The sound was lower than the last shelf of little donuts.

"What do I look like? Rambo?" John answered the same way.

"Aren't you a babysitter?"

"I'm a doctor. I don't even own a gun."

"No shit?"

Mack and Judy came toward them. Mack held her arm; she was strangely silent. He hit John in the chest with a fifty-dollar bill and said, "Pay this," then led the woman out the door and around a corner of the building.

Roger and John looked at each other and paid for their gas. John bought a package of little donuts. It made him sick almost immediately.

...

Louis wore the earphones and gave them a thumbs-up as they climbed into the RV. The tapes turned, top and bottom. Frank pointed John to the driver's seat. He was to drive—with Mack as his passenger.

The place swam in coffee, but he could not think about it. The little donuts played hockey in his stomach and John suppressed an urge to bring them up, though they were insisting. The drive was smooth and straight, from vanishing point to vanishing point, with occasional traffic ahead, a blue Ford following, rocks and scrubby bushes on either side. Mack watched his face.

"Frank," said Mack, "bring the doctor some coffee."

Frank's hairy arm pushed through the curtain with a Styrofoam cup at the end of it. John forced some down and to his surprise, the donuts were tamed.

"I like this desert," said Mack. "I can see a long way."

John searched for conversational topics. He rejected golf, sailing, investments, girls, parties, colleges. Any discussion of the weather would be over in one word, hot. Politics and religion—*dear God, big guns make big holes in people.*

"When do you think we'll be finished?" he said. It was the best he could do.

"Why?"

Because I need to stay awake and conversation is a means to that end and maybe after you have that list, I can get close enough to ask her for a phone number.

"I have a meeting tomorrow," is what he said aloud.

"You will not be there. What meeting?" In his way, Mack was making conversation.

"The Medical Ethics Committee."

"And what are medical ethics? What large questions do you discuss in this meeting?"

John shrugged. "The usual. Things like a doctor's responsibilities to the patient and his family? That sort of thing."

"And what are your responsibilities?"

John glanced at Mack as he scanned the horizon. There were lines at the sides of his eyes, deep circles underneath. His day-old beard formed a shadow over his cheeks and chin. Everybody had this shadow. No one had shaved. Mack's beard was blond and thick, like his hair, with scattered strands of gray that disappeared in some lights. He raised an eyebrow, waiting for an answer.

"I follow the Hippocratic oath," said John. "Above all, I must do no harm. I don't have a problem with the obvious cases."

"Do no harm? What were you planning to do with your fist this morning?"

John resisted an urge to whine about Steve's wake-up methods. He said nothing.

"And what about cases that are not obvious?" said Mack. "Tell me what is not obvious."

"Cases," John began slowly, "like a bypass on a bedridden eighty-six-year old because the hospital needs to boost profits or scraping a fungus infection from the sinuses of a terminal three-year-old cancer patient. The question is, how much abuse should you inflict on a body in an effort to save it?"

Mack did not speak for five minutes, at least. John gave up on the conversation and kept himself awake with what remained of his coffee. He suppressed the growing need to relieve himself and looked at the numbers as they danced incomprehensibly on the GPS. When he glanced up, he noticed Mack watching him.

John was surprised when Mack spoke again.

"No files, Frank."

A voice came from behind the curtain. "I know, Mack. I know."

"The only way to stop Frank from listening is to kill him. It is too late for that now. I should have shot him years ago. I will tell you a story. No files, Frank."

"Yes, sir. No files."

John waited.

"It vass," Mack stretched as he began, so that his accent became heavier than usual, and the words hissed. He yawned. "It was more than twenty years ago, I think, that Frank asked us to stop a terrorist team in Chicago. They planned to blow up a large building, killing hundreds, perhaps thousands. They met an obstacle, which delayed them and delayed us in killing them. We found a girl who could clear their obstacle, and so help us to kill them, and I decided to use her. She would die, of course, but the alternative was hundreds dead and a very loud explosion."

He scanned the horizon continuously. "Coffee, Frank, though I am soaked in it. And for the doctor."

John did not know where he would put it, but coffee had become a primary joy in his life, and he accepted it.

"Did you use the girl?" he asked when he heard Frank settle on the folding chair behind the curtain.

"Yes, of course." Mack sipped his coffee. "The girl was younger than Mara is now, about twenty years. She was unremarkable, typical, and ordinary American bourgeois, not as beautiful as Mara, but pretty enough, I suppose. She had too much brown hair that would not stay put, and she was small, insignificant. We hated each other from the first moment. She thought she knew all about good and evil and I was the next thing to Lucifer. She agreed to help us without understanding what that meant. Her goodness grated on me, or else I would not have thought more than a moment about killing her to save so many, but I knew that my dislike could affect my judgment. So I thought about it."

Mack paused long enough for John to contemplate prompting him with word *and?* He restrained himself.

"It was the right thing to do," Mack said finally.

Did the words suffer from too much emphasis? Like he needed to convince himself?

"Vasily's judgment also was affected by this girl," he continued. "He loved bourgeois American girls and this one smiled at him, giggled at his jokes, ran to him in her troubles. It was disgusting. He pleaded with me for her to have a chance, any chance. I pointed out that to give her a chance would probably result in her torture, and after all, a chance is only a chance.

"'No matter,' said Vasily. 'A chance is still a chance, and torture does not matter.'"

Mack's voice softened in both tone and volume. John glanced at him as he stared down their endless road into his past—into his friend's past.

"Now understand, Doctor," he said, "Vasily was an expert on torture. He blew up communist party meetings with his uncles in Poland when he was fifteen and had been interrogated already when Louis and I took him from a prison in Gdansk at eighteen. After that, there were many more times. Even his mother died under interrogation.

"Vasily was an expert; he wanted the girl, and he was my friend. I could not refuse him."

Breathless and appalled, John had to ask, "What happened?"

"I devised a plan that required her to give the terrorists only part of what they needed. They would ask her for the rest. We dressed her as a harlot, to give her a legend and to ease the interrogation. If they were busy and unimpressed by her, we thought, they might not hurt her sexually. But..."

What must have been a painful memory made the man wince. John dared not insist he spit it out. Instead, he kept his eyes on the road and sipped his cooling coffee until Mack continued.

"She was a virgin and I do not know anyone who does not check these things, even inadvertently when looking for weapons. She was also completely naive. She cried whenever I came near her. We could not send her to interrogation that way, so Louis suggested she should not be a virgin. I agreed, but Vasily would not take the responsibility. He could not hurt her, he said."

Mack sighed. "So, I told her to choose one of us. We knew she preferred Vasily, but she would not choose. She would not participate in any way in such an evil as sex. Imagine it. I am surrounded by so much goodness and nobility, that it falls to me to essentially rape the girl. It was all very civilized. The girl survived. Both me and the interrogation."

"So you are saying we should do whatever is medically necessary?" John said after another long pause.

Mack drained his cup, crushed it, and threw it through the black curtain. "I am saying nothing. I am a killer, not a healer. I do not know what is 'medically necessary.' Also, I have not finished the story. Louis! Frank is not taking notes?"

"No notes. I will shoot him if I see paper."

"*Vielen Dank!*"

John forced the last drop of his coffee down his throat. He threw the cup behind him without crushing it, and really, really needed to pee.

"You do not know what it is like during an operation, Doctor, during my kind of operation. There is a great calm. Even the weapons you fire make their noise as if they are a long way off. Time becomes very slow, because in the next moment, for you anyway, time may end, and it is certainly ending for those around you, those you are shooting, those shooting next to you. It is no different with a knife, or with killing by hand. All your senses are concentrated on killing before you are killed. During the operation in Chicago, one of the tangos…"

"Tangos?"

"Terrorists. One of them took this girl and like the coward he was, used her to shield himself from me. I kicked her out of the way, breaking her ribs. Do you follow this? She has been raped, tortured, and now beaten, but she is alive because Vasily wants her. He has pleaded for her."

It was an emotional narrative, spoken without drama, a post-operative report without reference to the soul within the sutured body. In the next breath, it became even more matter-of-fact.

"The enemy disarmed me. He was a good fighter. We fought with knives, toe to toe, rolling on the floor. He was much bigger than me, at least a hundred twenty kilos. In a fight like that, skill does not matter. Strength always wins. Using all my strength, I could not keep his knife from my throat. I held his wrist, with the point only a centimeter from my carotid. I had my knife in the other hand, but there was no room to maneuver; he was on top of me."

Again, his voice dropped.

"Then this insignificant, silly, bourgeois American girl found my gun on the floor, picked it up by the barrel, and hit a one hundred twenty kilo killer on the head with it. Tap. Like this." He tapped the dashboard in front of him. "Nothing. Less than useless. Except that for a fraction of time, and in slowed time that is a very long time you understand, he loosened his grip on my other hand. I was able to turn my knife and pull, disemboweling him.

"Louis and Vasily had not been completely successful, and I was needed to catch another man who had the means to destroy the building. I caught him."

John waited.

"I thought I would save hundreds by letting one die," said Mack, "when that one saved me, and by doing so, also those hundreds. And only because Vasily pleaded for her."

"So you would never again make a decision like that, to sacrifice one for many?"

"What? Don't be stupid. Of course, I would. It was the right decision. First comes the objective and the life of my team. Everything else is insignificant. Always."

John's exasperation came through in his voice. "Then what is your point?"

"Typical American. You must have everything spelled out for you. The point is that no agonized decision will do away with pain and death. These are inevitable. The question is, is there someone who will plead for you?"

Was Mack asking him? John stared back at him until the RV began to drift.

"The girl who saved your life," John said, "you said she hated you."

"Yes. She did. Almost to the day she agreed to marry me."

TWENTY-THREE

Seal thought the damn rules could be lifted just this once. He thought it while he watched the other shift raid the fridge and grab themselves each a cold one. He licked his lips. Mara handed him a cup of coffee. He glared at Charlie when he burned the roof of his mouth, glared until Charlie turned around, that is, being smart enough to douse the challenge before Charlie saw it.

There would be entertainment this shift change, Louis's treat, an audio performance featuring Roger and Judy in star roles as themselves. Louis changed the reels, gave Seal the headphones to monitor current taping, and cued up the old tape for playback. People scrambled for seats.

The doctor missed his chance because he was too busy complaining. He started on the smell, then some nonsense about hygiene, and finally the heat, and what about…? Steve popped Louis's beer open under the doctor's nose. The doc shook his beer and spewed it over Steve. Mack was at his elbow, so Steve did not liquefy the good doc but settled for flipping him the bird. Busy with their private feud, they were both late when Mara came in and sat in the booth seat with her back to the sink. Pavlenko scooted in next to her. The doctor was quick enough to sit across the table, and Steve sat next to him, across from Pavlenko.

Charlie opened a folding chair and sat next to Steve. Mack shoved Frank out of another chair and set it up near the door so he could watch the sensor screens. All outside sensors were on, both camera and infrared. The Frenchman watched, too, from a standing position near the comm bank. Frank huddled on the locker in the back corner. He may be huddled, thought Seal, but he sure is happy. Frank had a big shit-eating grin on his face. *He has scored some major intel.*

Seal stood behind the sink, where he had a great view of every-body, including Sergei Pavlenko's hand as it reached for Mara's. She pulled hers away. He reached again and she let him hold on. The two testosterone-enriched competitors across from them could not see through the table, but Seal noticed that Mack was in direct line of sight on Pavlenko's right. Pavlenko was a brave man.

The Frenchman gave the signal, Seal pressed the button, and the show began.

"This is what we heard after you met Roger and his lawyer at the fuel stop," Louis told Mack.

The first voice was Roger's. "Jeez Louise, Judy, you gotta stop."

"That man is dangerous, Roger. You should arrest him. Quick, before they get away."

"They aren't getting away. They are none of our business. The office said that since Frank Cardova is with them, we're out of it. We're supposed to follow Turner."

"You follow my orders."

"Jeez Louise."

"These men are up to something."

"Whatever they're up to, we don't want to know about it, Judy. Listen. This stuff is called WEDGE, okay? It's a compartmentalized caveat. I saw it on the boss's desk. It's got stripes and bars and whis tles all over the folder. We're not cleared for it. It's classified beyond Mars, and we got no rockets."

"Then how do you know this is WEDGE? What does WEDGE stand for, anyway?"

"I've heard rumors, bar talk. Shit. I've got a wife and three kids and another one due in December and I want to go back to bank robbery. It's safer. I don't know why I moved to counter-terror. I wanted a smart boss for a change, I guess, and Turner's the smartest there is, but he winds up under investigation himself, and now I have to drive us to San Antonio, while you do your best to get us killed. Killed, Judy. Dead, as in doornail, ding-dong dead.

"We're supposed to follow Turner, a nice easy assignment. He practically invites us to ride with him, but no, you get yourself pu... no that doesn't work... dick whipped by Steve what's-his-name, and I know in my bones he is a killer. He's got the eye, the bearing, and I've heard some rumors, like I said. So we follow him and come up on another character I think I've heard about, and you go and make a scene with him."

"I resent this, Roger. That man took me behind the station and threatened me with a knife. I could have been killed, or worse. It's a good thing I'm wearing a gun."

The RV erupted in laughter.

In the background, Roger's voice on the tape came through, "Jeez Louise. Jeez Louise. A knife. Jeez Louise, it is the one. Judy, that one will cut your throat before you get your hand to your holster. He can cross a twenty-foot space and kill with a knife before most people—even the best—can draw their guns. Let's go back and see if we can pick up Turner's trail."

"No way. These guys are up to something, and I want to know what it is. Something is going on in San Antonio, and we have a sworn duty to uphold the law. Besides, Steve could never kill anybody. He's so gentle and sweet."

The Frenchman doubled over in laughter.

"You've seen a lot more of him than I have, Jude, that's for sure," said Roger. "How many scars does he have? What gun does he carry?"

"Hmm?" She paused. "Oh, it's nice and big."

Seal had never laughed so hard. Mack laughed, a very rare sight. Frank fell off the locker. Charlie punched Steve in the arm. Steve's face turned a deep magenta. Mara covered her face with both hands as she laughed. Steve snuck in a punch to Doc's ribs during the ruckus. The doctor laughed anyway.

The Frenchman and Frank had just picked themselves up off the floor when Judy said, "Roger, you don't think they know we're following them?"

Behind the laughing din, the tape player squawked, "Jeez Louise."

In a high, squeaky voice, Steve said, "Help me, help me. I'm stupid and I can't get up."

Frank fell off the locker again, crawled to the refrigerator, and sat with his back to the side of it while he opened another beer.

At Louis's signal, Seal stopped the machine. Frank was told to break out another round for his watch. He was handing them over pretty freely and Seal almost succeeded in taking one until he felt Charlie's eyes on him, like fucking laser beams burning right through from front to back, the son of a bitch, and he put his hand up to his head and smoothed back his hair over the top, pretending it was what he had his arm out for all along. Charlie didn't let go his surveillance on Seal until Frank threw the can at the doctor. Steve caught it, shook it, and sprayed it over the doc.

As usual, the doctor was losing when Louis called for quiet. "Fun is over," he said. "We return to the game." He nodded at Seal.

The tape turned again, and Roger and Judy talked about Jane.

"Funny," said Judy, "she's just like Charlie. They're made for each other. Anybody warm-blooded would lose skin if they touched them. Like licking an icicle in zero degrees. Isn't it strange how she's so beautiful and Jay Turner's so ugly, yet they're both black?"

"What the hell's strange about that?" said Roger. "It's only strange if you don't see them as people."

"I've won some important affirmative action cases. Of course, I see African-Americans as people."

Roger did not answer.

Seal squashed an urge to say 'Jeez Louise' aloud.

"She's going to San Antonio, you know," said Judy. "She told me she's driving out in a van. I saw her back at the exit off I-80."

"You didn't tell me that."

"I waved, but she ignored me. I figured it was because she wasn't with Charlie. Then I forgot about it."

"What was she driving?"

"It was a green van, but the guy she was with was the one driving."

"What kind of van? What guy?"

"I don't know! A big van. I never saw the guy before. White guy. Long hair, kind of dirty blond. He had a mustache and one of those all the way across eyebrows. Who do you think he was?"

Seal stopped the tape, and Louis brought out a manila file folder with an eight-by-ten glossy taped inside. He opened it and displayed a picture of a man with sand-colored hair, a mustache, and prominent eyebrows.

"We want to watch for a large, green van," he said. "We have all seen Jane Jared. This is Vladimir Dimitrovich Maximovich, her babysitter."

"If you see them," Mack said to Charlie and Steve, "do not hesitate. Take them out."

Charlie nodded and studied the coffee in his Styrofoam cup. Pavlenko drained his beer.

TWENTY-FOUR

The party broke up. Seal adjusted his headphones. Louis dragged out a footlocker full of rifles, submachine guns, and gun cleaning supplies. Charlie told Steve to drive and Mara to ride in the cab as passenger. You could read the disappointment on the doctor's face, but before he could escape to a bunk, Charlie said, "Sit down, John. Then, "Get some sleep, Louis. The doctor volunteers to stay up this shift. I'll clean the weapons."

Louis reached for the ceiling and steadied himself as the RV accelerated onto the highway. He looked at Charlie, who was already laying a cleaning kit out on the table. "Hesitation kills," he told him.

"I know," said Charlie. "I will not hesitate. Get some sleep."

It was just the three of them, Seal on the machine, Charlie cleaning guns, and the doctor trying to figure out what to do with himself. They could hear Steve and Mara talking quietly in the cab.

The doctor poured himself a cup of coffee. "What are they saying?" He mumbled the question to Seal, throwing his head over his shoulder in the direction of the cab.

Seal shrugged. "No Deutsch here, Doc. I did French and Spanish."

The doctor sat back down at the table, across from Charlie, who rammed a cleaning rod through a barrel. John picked up a full magazine, studied it, and put it down. He looked at one of the submachine guns in front of him and reached a hand toward it.

"Don't touch it," said Charlie, without looking up.

John put both hands under the table. He cleared his throat. "What sort of a gun is this one?" He pointed with his chin.

Seal marveled at how stupid a smart man could be. Of course, the man was tired, but somebody should tell him about starting conversations with working specialists during an op. Working specialists with loaded weapons. Every magazine on the table was full; most of the guns held full magazines. The one next to Charlie had a round chambered. Seal saw him chamber it. He should tell the doctor to shut up. He should, but he wasn't about to.

To Seal's surprise, Charlie answered John's question. "That is an H&K MP5 SD3 submachine gun." His voice was almost conversational. Almost.

"Oh." The doctor nodded as if that meant something to him. "What kind of bullets does it use?"

"Nine-millimeter."

"Oh. How big is that?"

Charlie stared at him. He couldn't believe it, either. He put the cleaning rod and barrel down, picked up a stray magazine, and took out a round. He handed it to the doctor. "That big," he said.

"The front is empty."

"We use hollow point."

John turned it over in his hand. "I've heard that word in the ER. It makes big holes in people. How many of these can that gun shoot in a minute?"

"Why do you want to know?"

John shrugged. Charlie reassembled the now clean weapon.

"What about that big one in front of you?" The doc was at it again. He pointed at a beautiful sniper rifle stretched across the table in front of Charlie. Seal shook his head.

Charlie stopped again and stared at the doc. "It's mine."

"What kind is it?"

"It was custom-made for me. In Ferlach."

"Is that a scope on top? Can it shoot pretty far?"

"Yes. It's a stainless steel, thirty-two power, all-weather scope. The range is adequate."

Master of understatement.

"How far does it shoot?"

"Why do you want to know?"

"Why are you so secretive?"

There was a long pause. Seal pinched himself to stop a guffaw.

"How long have you worked for the FBI, John?" asked Charlie. He reloaded the now clean MP5.

"I don't work for them. I'm on a retainer. For emergencies."

"How many other emergencies have you been called to?"

"None."

"How much training did they give you before they put you on standby?"

"Training? I'm a board-certified surgeon."

"How much intelligence training?"

"Oh. That. I've seen all the James Bond movies." John grinned.

In Seal's experience so far, Charlie had no appreciable sense of humor. Like his father, he was more stable than the wild and woolly Frenchman or Steve Donovan, but he was also less likely to smile at anything.

Charlie casually put down the MP5, muzzle pointed at John. "I saw three of those movies," he said. "Do you notice that all of the women are beautiful, cooperative, and benign, all at the same time? If you find one of those here, tell me. Also, Bond's bruises, if he gets any, heal right away. Did you know your eye is the color of French mustard?"

Unspoken, but unmistakable: Do you want the other eye to match it? No? Then shut up.

Maybe it was because he was on Charlie's watch, so he saw a lot of the man, but Seal had become increasingly careful around him, more so than with any of the others, even Mack. Charlie was more than just a chip off the old block. The father observed people. Charlie measured them. Mack threatened; Charlie targeted. The older man was in the game; the son was in the business, and his business was no fuss, no muss, killing. The amazing thing was that the Jared woman had managed to move this one. After her, he was not likely to be moved again.

Immunized forever against intruders, thought Seal.

"Seal," said Charlie.

Seal jumped.

"There are packages of new rope under the body armor in the shower, and there's a box of hooks in the corner on the right. Get those. Bring them here."

Seal noticed it was becoming easier to squeeze between the refrigerator and the sink. The thought made him hungry.

"Do you know how to tie knots?" Charlie asked the doctor, waylaying him in front of the toilet before he could go to the back and lie down.

John nodded.

"I want knots like this." Charlie took a rope end, looped and knotted it through the eye of a hook, and handed it to him. "Untie it and let me see you do it again. Good. Do sixteen of those. Then run every rope through your fingers, the entire length, and look for flaws or frays."

"They're brand new."

"It doesn't matter. Look at every inch. Disasters start with stupid things, like weak ropes."

"What do you use all this rope for?"

"Getting from high places to low places quickly and vice versa."

"Are you going to do that in San Antonio?"

"Maybe. We may have to go in through the roof."

"But you don't know?"

Charlie studied him. "Pavlenko has not yet told us everything."

"Why not?"

"He wants to stay alive a little longer."

John turned the hook over in his hand, scowling. "Is this some kind of plastic?" he asked.

"It's titanium. Now shut up and work on top of the table, where I can see your hands."

The doctor worked quietly, almost as if he understood the threat.

Roger and Judy said little in Seal's ear, only an occasional "Jeez Louise" that made the tape roll. It was like any other mind-numbing stake-out except for the discomfort of Charlie's presence. These were fast shifts, only four hours instead of twelve or sixteen, and this one was nearly half over. Seal thought Steve was pulling over for the midway fuel stop.

But then Steve called out through the black curtain. "I see a green van."

TWENTY-FIVE

I was at the top of my class, of all my classes, John thought as he ran the rope between his fingers. That was not somebody else; I was the one who graduated summa cum laude. These are thugs, killers, spooks, experts in pain and mayhem. They are no better than a street gang. They are frightening only because they are a little smarter—in their field. A lot smarter. They are summa cum laude killers.

The summa cum laude killers were looking at the computer on the refrigerator. They punched in their position from the GPS, and the screen gave them a three-dimensional topographical map of the area. Arizona? Did it say Arizona? When did they pass Las Vegas? Hoover Dam? What did you see on your drive across the country, John? *Guns, fists, rope, and coffee.*

The map showed another side road on the left, about a quarter of a mile down the highway, parallel to the road where Steve saw the green van. How far down was the van? Charlie wanted to know. Half a kilometer, Steve told him. Mara drove. John touched the rope as he pulled it through his hands. He had good fingers; he felt every irregularity. He was a surgeon.

It did not occur to him that the green van meant anything more than a confused account of a beautiful woman he had met briefly and some Russian guy he had never met and did not particularly want to meet.

On the side road, Mara turned the RV around so that it faced back toward the highway and then cut the engine. She turned on all the infrared sensors and cameras. The screens over John's head lit up. He sat with the rope still in his hand.

Steve came out of the back room with a black nylon bag. It was full of new packages of camouflaged clothing, boots, pants, shirts, and T-shirts, in khaki, tan, and sage green, in muted, blended shades, like the desert outside. Charlie brought body armor out of the shower cubicle.

"Shit, not the full armor, Charlie," said Steve. "It's fucking a hundred and twenty out there."

It was approaching the same inside.

"Okay. Soft body armor and no t-shirts. Hurry up."

John sat with his mouth open, rope in his hand, as the two men stripped to their underwear.

"John, get off your ass and help Mara," said Steve.

John dropped the rope and stood next to Mara. She climbed onto a folding chair and pulled wires and gadgets from behind the radios above the cab. She handed them down as she found them. When John had a handful, she got down from the chair and took them away from him, one by one. She put an earpiece in Steve's left ear as he buttoned a pair of camouflaged trousers. A small, stiff wire with a thickened end extended over his chin. She bent it so that it rested under his lower lip, ran the wire leading from there down and over the Velcro shoulder of his body armor, and attached it to a small oblong box. This she clipped to a web belt he had just buckled around his waist. She took another wire and box from John and did the same for Charlie.

Mara gave Seal a wire and box, equipped herself with one, and finally set another up for John while he watched, dumbfounded, as Charlie and Steve completed their outfits with long-sleeved desert-cammie shirts and carryall vests made of sage green mesh. Into pockets and loops in the mesh went binoculars, knives, and an assortment of full magazines from the table and from their shoulder holsters, now discarded. Their handguns went into holsters on the web belts. They put on camouflaged hats with soft brims and covered their faces, ears, necks, and hands with tubes of black, brown, and green face paint. Steve picked up an MP5, checked the magazine, and chambered a round. Charlie picked up another MP5 and the long rifle with the scope. He handed the MP5 to Mara.

"Shoot him if he moves wrong," he told her. Still pointing to John, he said, "You can help her watch the screens." To Seal, "Don't wake anybody until I tell you."

Seal nodded. Everybody turned on their gadgets. Mara turned John's on for him, all the while keeping the muzzle of the submachine gun pointed at him.

John watched the screen as the two men moved up a slope and onto the top of a ridge. They stopped about a thousand feet away and blended in, disappearing when they didn't move.

"What are they doing?" John asked Mara.

She put a finger to her lips.

"But what's going on?"

"Shut the fuck up, John." It was Steve's voice coming straight into his left ear.

"We have a rendezvous, here," came Charlie's voice. "Green van, white van. There's Maximovich. There's Jared. There are one, two, three...I make it seven others. They're transferring equipment. Looks like....Shit... since when do Russians spring for MP5's? John, go get Pavlenko. Don't wake my father."

The words were flattened by the radio. John did not realize his name had been spoken until Mara nudged him.

When Pavlenko was properly wired, Charlie briefed him on the view. "What the hell kind of team is this, Sergei?"

"Describe them."

"Two about Steve's height, dark hair. Tattoos. Three are taller. One is huge. The seventh appears to be the driver."

"The huge one, is he heavily tattooed?"

"Yes."

"Sounds like Drakhiz. But I thought he was released from service two years ago. Who is he working for?"

"What the hell kind of team is it?" Charlie insisted.

Sergei hesitated. He looked at Mara and swallowed hard. "It is an extraction team."

There was a pause. "Seal, wake the others."

"They're already here," said Seal.

TWENTY-SIX

Mara stood in her underwear, donned soft body armor and shifted it upward while Seal adjusted the Velcro at the shoulder.

Misha and Louis were only slightly ahead of her. They wore camouflaged trousers. Frank frantically tried to untangle a pair of wires.

Sergei untied a knot in the wires, then sat at the table with his forehead in his hand. John sat across from him, his mouth open, trying to watch Mara without looking at her. Her jog-bra and panties covered more than any bikini she might wear to a swimming pool, and he was a doctor for heaven's sake.

She did not have time to think any more about it.

They created a plan while Misha and Louis dressed and conducted the conversation over the radio speaker wedged above the cab.

Misha said, "It is your call."

"I want to hit them now." Michael's voice held some urgency.

"There is a risk. Odds are four to nine."

There was a pause. Then Michael: *Numquam periclum sine periclo vincitur.* I want to use Mara. That makes it four and a half to nine."

Hah!

Misha looked at her and pointed to the bag of desert clothing. Start changing. It took him a little longer to say "Yes," out loud.

Mara dropped her indignation at her brother's jibe along with her jeans and rummaged through the bag for a shirt and pants. Seal brought her soft body armor from the shower.

There was one more message from Michael.

"We will use Wounded Wing. Mara will be *Vögelein.*

Louis was dressed and ready. He dug a Škorpion machine pistol out of the weapons locker.

Mara reviewed Wounded Wing procedures. She reviewed the sequence, the hand signals, and the movements. It would be on a downward slope, on the other side of the ridge. She ran her memory back to the basement under Vasily's Carpet and went over once again the instructions that echoed in the workout room during all those cold mornings.

After her father's death, Mara had trained in earnest, never missing a session until she went to college. At first, they were reluctant to teach her all of it, but the little she knew had already saved her life, twice. They reasoned that it could not hurt her to know the weapons and techniques. Steve brought her to black belt. Michael sharpened her shooting. Misha taught her to think, Louis, to react. She was present when they developed and practiced new tactics. She knew the hand language, the radio codes, the operational disciplines.

Louis chambered a round in the Škorpion, folded back the stock, and put it on the table in front of her.

Seal hooked the radio onto the web belt around her waist. Mara stuffed another twenty-round magazine for the Škorpion into a pouch in the belt.

She reviewed signals again, unconsciously moving her fingers and hands. Misha caught her eye. Stop. Not in front of the babysitters. It was a private language.

John began to babble something. He was protesting, by the whiny sound of it, and it threatened to break her concentration, but it didn't succeed. She thought, briefly, that Misha was pushing him back into the booth by the table to make him quiet, but that wasn't it. John's hand had come too near the Škorpion. Misha was being careful.

Louis untied her hair and piled it on top of her head under a soft-brimmed hat. Lose the hat on the way down. She nodded.

They tied Pavlenko to the sink before they left.

Seal gave her what he called positive encouragement. "Don't fuck up," he said.

...

The discussions were over. The endless philosophical debates ended under a desert sun on a blazing afternoon somewhere in Arizona. Mara moved up the ridge with Misha and Louis on either side of her.

When is it proper to kill? Under what circumstances? What is the morality of defending oneself? When does defense end and become, instead, aggression?

Was there a debating point about hitting a team of six killer kidnappers before they could hit you? The only discussable question was, How? By offering a target they would be tempted to take rather than kill outright. That could be only Mara. Misha had said yes. His lifetime of regrets and reservations had no place on an operation. There were no more philosophical questions. How do we hit them quickly, within range, and without getting hit ourselves? How do we avoid leaving a secondary target behind us?

At the top of the ridge, Michael moved Misha to the far right, then Louis next to him. Mara was to take the center, with Steve to her left and Michael on the far left. Michael pointed out their positions behind boulders on the other side of the ridge, and they moved into them silently.

Mara waited at the top with Michael. He had pointed his rifle at a spot two hundred meters down the slope. Here was where he expected the enemy to set up their covering fire. Maximovich and his team were still transferring equipment from the green van to the white one. There was a driver in the white van. In the passenger window of the green van, Mara saw a slender arm, Jane's arm.

When the others were in place, Michael pointed to the spot where he wanted her to land. He gave her the signal, Go.

Mara crept over the top of the ridge and down the other side. She used brush and rocks for cover until she was about fifteen meters from her desired position. She saw Steve crouching behind a boulder on her left, Louis was farther to the right. She was too far left, but there was no way to correct it, and anyhow, she was ready. Now.

Her foot dislodged a medium-sized rock and sent it rolling down the hill, a shower of pebbles and wannabe boulders following like groupies in its wake. She left the MP5 in the rubble and slid down with the stones, left leg straight, taking the abrasions on the right hip and shoulder, but keeping the Škorpion tucked up in the small of her back with her right hand. The hat was harder. It wanted to stay with her. She tossed her head and scraped the hat off on a dead piece of twisted brush as she passed it. Her blonde hair flew around her head.

She stopped sliding less than a meter to the left of where Michael had pointed. Not bad. She rubbed her left ankle, looked worriedly at the vans, and then scanned up over her shoulder to the top of the ridge. As she swept her eyes back around to the road below, she gave a desperate, despairing look to the MP5 lying out of reach above her.

I should get an Oscar.

She could see Steve out of the corner of her eye and sensed Louis and Misha on her right. She watched the extraction team put their hasty plan into action. They leapfrogged up the slope, four and two, covering as they ran, crouching, careful not to hit her. She gazed up at the ridge as if looking for help from there.

Michael fired an MP5 from the top, first from the right, then from the left, acting like four people everywhere at once, giving the impression that her defenders were pinned down. When the enemy fighters came within effective range of the top, two of them blasted the ridge, while the other four crawled toward Mara.

Michael was right. The fighters providing cover had crouched behind boulders two hundred meters down. Only their eyes and muzzles showed over the tops. Not much, but enough for Michael.

She waited. The four coming up the hill did not fire. They moved quickly on all fours. A big man with tattoos looked up at her and grinned.

"*Sofort,*" said Michael's voice in her ear.

She rolled off the Škorpion, brought it up, and pulled. The big man reeled with the impact on his body armor and began to teeter backward. She adjusted for height, and he toppled as his head jerked back from the impact. She felt a shower of something wet. Blood, but not from the one she killed. It came from one closer whose head disintegrated under Steve's fire. There was noise all around her: the silenced MP5s, loud enough at ten meters despite the earplugs she wore and the crack-boom of Michael's rifle, the impacts and the death rattles and inert masses sliding through loose gravel. First one, then the other covering sniper fell silent. Another of Michael's precise rounds traveled at almost a thousand meters per second into the gas tank of the white van, exploding it on impact. The green van's armored tank did not explode, though Michael hit it repeatedly even when it was more than a thousand meters away on its way out.

"*Zurück!*" said Michael, and they turned and ran up the ridge and over the top.

They covered their backs one at a time while Michael spoke to the RV.

"John, start the truck. Frank, status."

"Normal." Frank's voice was calm.

"I want to see John climb into the cab, Frank. Move him."

Louis and Misha checked the blind side, then piled in through the door behind Michael, Steve, and Mara.

The engine was running, but John stood at the curtain to see her come in.

"Go, damn it! Frank, move him!"

Frank turned the doctor around roughly and shoved him back into the driver's seat.

Steve pulled a bottle of water from the refrigerator. The sleeves of his shirt were soaked to the hems and the wetness hugged his biceps. The soaking on his left hand ran pink with mingled blood and sweat. He drank most of the bottle and poured the rest over his face.

Misha cut the ropes that bound Sergei and, with Louis, carried him to the table where they laid his torso backward across it lengthwise, legs stretched toward the door, feet scrabbling among crushed coffee cups. This was the true panic, the lost look, that exceeded even his first sight of Steve and Charlie in the motel room. Mara turned away and saw Michael come out of the back room with a long, black device with a switch, a dial, and two metal ends.

She turned to the coffee pot, found her hair pins and rubber band, and busied herself with these, hands shaking because, oh God, she did not want to watch.

TWENTY-SEVEN

The knot in John's stomach was more than a hunger pain; it was a visceral twisting of his universe. The smell came in ahead of the team.

"What's that smell?" John asked.

"Cordite." Frank said it quietly, almost in his ear.

The team was not quiet. For the past fifteen minutes they had been eerily silent up there on that ridge, but now they were all noise, all movement, loud, violent, invading. Mara, too. And there was blood on her arm. John looked carefully but saw no source. It was not her blood. Steve was spattered with it and again, no source.

He had no time to observe more. He could feel Charlie's eyes on him and Charlie's impatience and Charlie's authority, even before Charlie said a word. Frank did not have to push so hard; he was already on his way back to the cab.

John drove toward the highway, then took the on-ramp and headed for Phoenix. The glaring sun hurt his eyes, made them water and squint and he did not see any green van, ahead or behind or to the side, or in the air, for that matter. Frank rode as his passenger and could look for it himself if it was so damned important.

"What language is that?" asked John. He was trying to concentrate on the sounds behind them.

"Russian."

"Do you understand it? What are they saying?"

"Steve is telling Pavlenko that Drakhiz is no more. They got all six of the extraction team and the driver."

"Got?"

Frank nodded, held up his hand, and listened. He spoke again. "Jared and her babysitter got away. Steve's Russian has improved since he worked for me."

"He worked for you?"

"He was a babysitter. Once."

Seal came through the curtain. His smell announced him. Where was he getting the food to spill on that shirt?

"You don't fit here," said Frank.

Seal made himself fit, between the seats and the GPS console. He laid the curtain over his back, bulging the shape, but keeping it closed. He steadied himself by pushing up the ceiling.

"I gotta be here, Frank. I can't be there. They got an iron, Frank. I can't watch. The girl took my earphones for me. Bless her."

"Then go in the back."

"It's dark back there. I'm afraid of the dark."

John heard a muffled cry, a scream between tightly sealed lips. "What are they doing?"

Frank stared straight ahead. "They're learning The Rest of the Story."

"That's bad Frank," said Seal. "This is no time for jokes, Buddy. My sense of humor said 'so long' and I wanna follow it. Where's your pity?"

"It died with my career ten years ago when that fucking Russian joker in there decimated my team. Shut up." Frank held up a hand.

Pavlenko was speaking rapidly. They heard short questions, longer explanations. Occasionally, he might pause, then he would gasp, then speak again, rapidly.

"Seems our friend Volodya ..." said Frank. "Oh my."

"What?" It came from John and Seal at the same time.

"Volodya is a loose round, working for his old bosses only nominally. He's in—to the blood—with one of the biggies in the Russian mafia, one of the thieves under the code. He wants—they want—Semianov's list. A destabilized America is candy, too rich a plum to pass up. Think of the opportunities, the territories to be gained. Volodya asked Sergei for the list."

There was another strangled cry.

"Sergei would not tell him because...."

A long gasp.

"Because of the file that is with the list. He could not trust Volodya. Volodya would...." Frank shook his head. The talking behind them resumed.

"Volodya knows Mara is the key," translated Frank. "The teams are for her. To make Sergei give up the list."

Steve spoke. Frank translated. "Give him the god-dammed list."

A gasp and more Russian from Pavlenko.

"No," said Frank. "Volodya resented Sergei's victory. He is the better intelligence officer, but it was Sergei who beat Sobieski. Give

Maximovich the file and he will hunt her forever. If he catches her...."

The last Russian words were lost in a full scream.

John swerved, then centered the RV in its lane. His heart pounded.

"Does this happen often?" he asked Frank.

Seal answered, "Too often."

"More than zero is too often," said Frank.

"Because it's evil?" said John.

Seal furled his forehead. "Because it's useless. There are easier ways. But they're not as satisfying."

Frank continued to translate as more Russian words came through the curtain like spurting blood. "What else is in the file?" "Nothing." "What else?" "Nothing." "What else?" "Oh God." A pause. "The location... and... layout of... Vasily's Carpet."

Seal and Frank looked at each other. "Holy shit!"

Frank held up his hand. "He got it from a servant. No! He infiltrated a servant."

"Brilliant!" said Seal. "The man's a genius. Too bad he's about to die."

Frank held up his hand again. "The asshole wrote it down!"

John did not think he could listen to any more of these strangled screams. There was no more talking after this one.

"He's dry," said Frank.

"What is Vasily's Carpet?" asked John.

"Their den, their lair, the place where they like to think they're safe, where they lock up their women and other valuables. Blown. By one bright Russian with an overactive pen. The disaster is enormous. This is worse than ten years ago."

A hand reached through the curtain and jerked Seal backward by the shirt collar. Steve's head poked through. "Pull over," he told John.

John pulled into a scenic stop overlooking a valley of rocks. There were several other cars there, and people with cameras. There was no green van.

"Seal's driving," Steve told Frank. "Get on the phone and grease things. We left all our brass back there."

He looked at John and said, "You come with me."

TWENTY-EIGHT

John followed Steve, groping in the gloom between the bunks, and sensed a body in the lower right-hand bunk. It groaned and moved.

Steve handed him a flashlight.

"He's not beaten up this time," said John.

"That was revenge. This is business. Ask him which one he prefers."

The patient seemed untouched, except for the eyes. They were older. They did not belong in the face of a man in his thirties. John moved his clothing aside and came across the marks, most of them burns, in places that made him shudder.

"This is grotesque," he said.

"No shit," said Steve.

"I mean the whole thing. Everything. The fear, the hunger, the filth, the violence."

"So do I."

John dabbed at a burn with some useless ointment, trying to decide if it would need a dressing. It was an electrical burn. Most of the damage would be under the surface.

"She saved my life," said the patient. He grabbed John's arm. "The Frenchman pulled my head back by the hair, stretching my neck. Mack put his knife here." He pointed at his esophagus. "She put her hand on his hand. He stopped. I am alive. When it began, I knew I would die. When they put the iron there," he pointed to his crotch, "I wanted to die. I had to say it all before death. But, I am alive. Donovan never said anything when we did it to him. But we were enemies, and I did not hold it there that long!"

"You held it twice as long, you son of a bitch." Steve slipped a small bottle into John's hand as he said this.

It was morphine. John drew up the dose.

"God bless you, Doctor," Pavlenko said when he saw the needle. "It was not something she should see."

He drifted off so rapidly that John had a sudden fear that this was some silent form of murder, but he checked the vitals, and all was well. The patient rested.

John stood and faced Steve. "I can take her out of here, out of this."

"I wish you could."

"I have the money, the connections."

Steve frowned and shook his head slowly. "You don't have the intelligence—and I don't mean you're stupid."

...

If John thought their one sane exchange meant a change for the future, he was wrong. Steve pulled him off his bunk as usual four hours later. On this occasion, though, John woke quickly. On his way to the floor, he found time to pull his knee up, pushing it into Steve's kidney. Steve grunted, picked him up, and threw him backward toward the door. John landed at Mack's feet. Louis stood behind Mack, his hand holding the supporting strap of the top left bunk.

Louis chuckled.

"He kicked me in the back," said Steve. "But it didn't hurt."

"You saw him," said John to Mack. "Hit him. He was fighting and fair is fair."

Louis laughed out loud. "Do you remember, Misha, when you were given that new football? How I wanted it! You were only eight and you hit me so hard when I took it."

"I was seven. You were eight, and you fought dirty."

"And all the nannies screamed '*Lieber Gott*, they will kill each other!'"

"And Frau Giesel tried to box your ear. You bit her hand."

"You did that, Misha. I was wrongly accused. But then your father came to stop it. His solution was perfect."

Misha nodded. "We never fought again."

"Until Alex."

"Until Alex." Mack looked down at John on the floor. "I wish I could tie them together for a day, leg to leg, arm to arm." To Steve, who looked more than a little foolish, he said, "Go, sleep."

Louis dragged the doctor to his feet and led him forward.

John grumbled about the injustice until he met Mara in the galley and pulled her close to him. He was feeling irresistible.

"No more, John," she said.

"How can I have more when I haven't had any?" He tried again.

"I said no!" She pulled away and gave a questioning look to Louis. "Like that?" she asked.

Louis nodded.

"Do you think it will work?"

He shrugged.

John watched her walk to the back, heard the words "No more, Steve," and took a step to follow her, but Louis pulled him through the galley and sat him down at the table.

The patient was awake and sitting across from him, looking no more uncomfortable than the rest of them. He wore the headphones attached to the tape machine.

"Hey!" John said to Louis. "How come you trust him and not me?"

"We know him. We know him well. We do not know you at all."

Frank drove, with Mack as passenger. The chess set was out, and John played chess with Sergei. On the fourth move, Sergei leaned over the board and said, "I have taken your queen and my next move is mate."

John launched himself over the table, aiming for the man's throat. Sergei was weakened by his bruises and burns, so the match was almost even, with Sergei slowly winning.

Mack came out of the cab and helped Louis pull them apart.

"I'm okay. I'll stop." John puffed the words and shook himself.

"So much for your Hippocratic oath," said Mack.

John could still feel shame. It was an emotion among many others that crowded in a thronging queue. He slumped into the seat across from Sergei. "I'm sorry," he told him. "I thought you were saying something else."

Sergei's yellow, blue, and green face began a slow smile, partly hidden under the brown stubble, that told John he had not made a mistake.

John clenched his fist. "I'm just so tired," he said. "And I'm so fucking hungry!"

"So eat," said Louis.

"Eat what? There's no food!"

"Who told you that?"

"Who told me that?" John tried to remember. "Frank told me."

Louis laughed.

Frank's voice came from behind the curtain. "Uh, I meant to tell you the truth later, Doc. It slipped my mind. Sorry."

Louis opened the cabinet beside the refrigerator, a cabinet John only now noticed. He took out a flattened black plastic pouch and threw it at John. It was labeled, "Meal, ready to eat."

John was ready. He ate.

Mack poured two cups of coffee at the sink. "For a minute, I thought you were becoming one of us, Doctor. But a true spook verifies everything he is told. He also knows the entire contents of his environment. That is how I knew Jay had good information about you being a brilliant surgeon. No one can fake such a complete lack of training."

"If I'm so harmless, why was I under guard when you went over the ridge back there?"

Mack smiled a rare smile. "If success comes from brilliance, disaster comes from idiocy. Even geniuses have their moments of supreme stupidity. Do they not, Sergei?"

The Russian dropped his eyes.

"You have had more than a few such moments here, Doctor. Please do not be offended if I lock you out of my operating room. I did not say you are harmless. You lack only training and enemies. Everything else is there. But overall, you are what we call dead weight."

...

You would think that dead weight would be allowed to sleep, John thought, as he crawled into the passenger seat of the cab. He was told to stay up through the next shift. Steve was driving.

"Do you think this is their way of tying us together?" he asked Steve when they were back on the highway.

"Get us some coffee."

"I don't think I can drink anymore. The toilet's full again."

"Then get *me* some coffee, asshole."

"I didn't realize we were so close to El Paso," John said when he came back with the coffee. "Frank said you're from Texas. Is that right?"

No answer.

John stared at the blackness outside, the rush of the tarmac under the RV's headlights, the flash of a reflective mile marker.

He tried again. "And Seal is from Texas, too," he said. "And you were both babysitters. I thought Seal was in counterintelligence. That's what he told me, but Frank said he's a babysitter."

"He is in CI, but he was trained as a babysitter."

John tasted relief at the sound of Steve's voice. Keep him awake, Louis had said, or I will add more color to your face. *Whatever happened to simple requests?*

"So why did he leave?"

"He was forced out. There's an unwritten rule in the babysitter business. Killers are dirty; they contaminate. Babysitters hide their consciences behind the fact that they don't pull the trigger. Some even get the idea that their only job is to protect innocents. They take it all too literally, and if you kill on an operation, they give you a hard time."

"And Seal killed?"

"No. I mean, yes, he has killed. He was a SEAL in Southeast Asia."

"The Navy commandos? Seal was a commando?"

"Yeah. He's put on some weight."

"Some!"

Steve drained his cup, held it out to John.

John brought back more coffee.

"Seal didn't kill as a babysitter," Steve resumed. "That was the problem. He took all that shit seriously. He didn't pull the trigger when he should have, and he lost his team."

"Lost them?"

"Dead. Seven men dead, the mission a failure, sixteen hostages killed. It should not have been the end of his career, but he never got over it. Frank told me about it after my first op—in Chicago—because I did pull the trigger. A tango was about to shoot Charlie. I already knew all about what a crock of shit an official order can be, so I didn't have any problem making my decision. But they made my life hell in The Section after that."

"You became a specialist then?"

"No." He took a long sip of coffee.

John found himself thinking, reminded himself thinking could be dangerous. "What, exactly, would you say makes a specialist, Steve?"

Steve sipped his coffee again, adjusted his shoulders, and shifted his hands on the wheel. He glanced at John as he did this, sizing up the questioner with the question.

"First," he said finally, "is skill. Corollaries to that are work, training, experience, and above all, judgment. There are no substitutes." He paused as they passed a car ahead of them. "Second, of course, a specialist has to be able to pull a trigger, or whatever. Able in the sense of having the will, not just the skill."

"Does it ever bother you? Do you have nightmares about people you've killed?"

"Shit, no. My nightmare is getting shot in the face before I can shoot back. It doesn't bother me to kill the reptiles we go up against."

"Mack said something about enemies making a specialist."

"Yeah. I guess that's the third ingredient. It takes all our energy to stay one step ahead of them, and it takes money, information, and guns."

"How do you get enemies like that?"

John watched Steve as he asked this question. He saw the momentary expression of pain as Steve closed his eyes and set his jaw forward. He did not answer right away. When he did, he spoke with a quiet, tired voice.

"You know, John, I could kill you easily. It wouldn't take much to do it, and it wouldn't take much to make me do it. Say you whispered in Mara's ear, or touched her cheek, in front of me, with nobody else around to stop me, and say I was tired and strung out on adrenaline and under constant operational pressure at the time, like I am now. Then I'd probably kill you without thinking about it much, but it would be a fucking mistake, you might say—you, especially, might say—an atrocity, unjustified for any reason. Say you had powerful friends and family who might want justice. Those are the worst enemies, the ones who have a good reason for revenge and the means to carry it out."

"Mara can't have any of those."

"She has all of ours, the kind that wants us dead for good reason and the bastards that don't need a reason. She's a tool, a way to get at us, a way to get us. Now that she's operational, she'll gather her own set, the first ones being the two-bit slugs in every corner of the world who want to make a name for themselves by killing a specialist named Sobieski.

"Right now, that name is a more potent poison than the genetic link to Misha, in every sense, because it's as Vasily's daughter that she is most important to us. He was dead before I joined the team, but I'm always hearing, 'Mara's stubborn, just like Vasily,' or 'Mara fights like Vasily,' or 'Doesn't Mara smile like Vasily?'"

"Isn't that the guy Pavelenko said he helped kill?" John searched his waning memory of the past few hours.

Steve nodded. "It was his life ambition to parole Mara from Vasily's Carpet. We managed to send her to a girl's college for two years, got her that job on the fringes of the game, and arranged for Seal to babysit. Now she's operational." Steve shrugged.

"You mean she has killed somebody? On the ridge back there?"

Steve did not answer him.

"And do you have enemies like that, Steve? Just because you shot one guy in Chicago?"

"No." He glanced at John. "I flew F-15s for the Air Force before I was a babysitter. Do you remember the airliner shot down over the Bering Sea twelve years ago?"

"Yes. Was that you?"

Steve nodded. "It wouldn't be so bad if somebody who lost his family on that airplane came after just me. I could call it justice and almost mean it. But there are half a dozen contracts out on my ex-wife and my son. My ex is an airhead, John. She doesn't know what an F-15 looks like, even after years of looking at the fucking model I kept on my desk. My son was born during the court-martial. If I die tomorrow, the contracts stay in force. So did Sobieski's, by the way, but by the time Mara went to college, most of them had been forgotten."

"But Mack?"

"There, you're catching on," said Steve. "Misha could walk up to his worst enemies right now and offer his body to science and they'd still want Alex. They'd cut her throat over his grave, just to say, 'So there.' Misha's not a good parent for Mara to have publicly. And his enemies don't forget. We're talking centuries here, as I understand it."

"Why do you call it Vasily's Carpet?"

Steve shifted in his seat, impatient. "Sobieski bought a rug in Beirut and put it in the hallway, to make it seem less like a prison. He hated prison. But at least it was safe. Now it's not." He turned on the turn signal. "There's a rest stop up here. Punch up the stop and turn on the sensors. I have to go."

"Hurry up," said Louis from behind the curtain. "We are next."

They pulled into the RV side of the rest stop. The taillights of a car disappeared up the ramp onto the highway. Otherwise, there was no traffic, not even a semi. It was about two in the morning.

John and Steve headed for the men's room on the right. They walked over the Lone Star embedded in the pavement and entered the building from the truck side. Steve checked the parking lot on the other side. There were no cars there.

John could smell it as soon as he came around the stone wall and faced the wall of sinks. He knew the smell now. Cordite. Steve knew it, too, and slammed him against the wall on their left, slammed himself against the opposite wall, and drew his Beretta. They rounded the corner cautiously. There were three stalls. The first was empty. The second was open; the door creaked slightly. Something sticky oozed toward the floor drain. John knew this smell, too.

Steve checked the third stall, empty, and came back to the second. He pushed the door open wide. Roger sat on the commode, in a suit and tie, with a neat hole in his forehead. John tried not to step in the blood as he took the wrist. He looked at Steve. "He's dead," he said.

"Shit, John, I'm fucking glad you went to medical school so you could give me that dipshit diagnosis. How about we get the fuck outta here."

TWENTY-NINE

Seal tried clearing his throat, then waving, then shouting. Finally, he jumped up and down. This cost him because he had to go as bad as the rest of them, but it was the only way. When at last they turned toward him, he pointed to the tape.

Charlie told him to turn on the external speaker.

"But why didn't Roger tell me this?" said Judy over the wire.

"I told you he said he'll meet us in San Antonio." It was Jane Jared's voice.

"I, um, we are supposed to.... I can drop you off in Fort Stockton, Jane, but I...."

"Roger told me all about what you're doing, Judy. He asked me to help you since he can't be here. It was an unexpected lead, he said."

"But he didn't explain it?"

"No. Now you get some sleep. I'll wake you up in two hours."

...

The doc was driving., with Steve in the passenger seat. Seal leaned over the sink staring vacantly at Mara's back in front of him. Charlie brought the cell phone down from the comm bank and sat on the booth seat across from Mara. He called Jay Turner, told him Roger was dead, and asked for the carphone number in Roger's car.

Seal made himself as small as possible—would have crawled up into the faucet given enough magic—and listened as the tape turned to the sound of the ringing phone.

"Hello," said Jane.

"Is it Roger?" said Judy.

"Shhh!"

"Hi," said Charlie.

Seal was hearing both sides of the conversation. Charlie must know that. Something made Seal not want to draw attention to it, even though he had an urge to run and get Frank.

Jane paused before answering, "Michael," with no hint of surprise.

"Who's Michael? Ow! You don't have to hit me," said Judy.

"How did you know where to find me?" Jane asked.

Steve poked his head through the curtain. "Oh Shit," he mouthed silently.

Charlie waved him away. "I was there, Jane," he said into the phone.

With a straight face.

Another pause. "Then why didn't you save the poor schmuck?"

"What schmuck? Ow! All right. Stop hitting." Judy harrumphed and fell silent.

"Was it your first?" asked Charlie.

"No."

"Who gave the order?"

"You know who."

"Why?"

Silence.

"Have you been given the order for me?"

More silence.

"So is he a boyfriend? He had his hands all over you when you met that team with the white van."

"You can't be jealous. You promised, remember, no promises."

"I lied."

Jane laughed. It was a beautiful deep, merry laugh.

"He's like a pimp, Michael. I imagine your babysitters treat you that way."

"Not quite."

"Well, they will treat Mara that way."

Charlie looked up at Seal, who stopped mid-chew on a piece of pound cake, his gray-stubbled chin dusted with crumbs.

"I doubt it," said Charlie.

"This is the pits," said Jane. "I'm sorry."

"You don't have to be. Come to me."

"I can't. They own me."

"I'll buy you."

Another rumbling laugh, like an earthquake.

"Yassuh, Massuh!"

"You brought it up. You said they own you. Let them name their price."

"And our brown-eyed babies will be the scandal of your family."

"My family can handle it."

"You think so, Romeo? You come to me."

"I can't."

"Why?"

"You know I would not survive, and besides, your side is wrong."

"Oh, I see. I'm the one who has to change. I have to give up everything I've ever known, everything I've ever believed, to be your ornament, to be quasi-accepted by your people. Is that it, Michael? And why? Because you have a corner on the truth? What if my side is right?" Her voice had come up a note.

"It isn't. We are running out of time to argue, Janie. Meet me somewhere."

"I don't know what your procedures are, Michael, but if they're anything like ours, I don't want to do that. I don't want to spend months in a black hole having my brain vacuumed, not even for you my darling, not even for you. I'd go mad without sunlight. And after that, then what? Where do you guys lock up your women? Do you know how badly Volodya wants your sister? He foams at the mouth. He's rabid with Mara disease. Do you want to saddle me with an army of enemies like Volodya? My life is shitty, Michael, but yours is shittier."

Charlie's forehead rested on his left hand. His right hand held the phone to his ear. He paused long enough to stop the tape through silence.

"Goodbye, my darling," she said as she put the phone down.

"Why are you crying?" asked Judy.

Mara reached across the table and took Charlie's hand. He gave her a half smile and stared at the phone. He drew circles around it with his index finger.

The tape ran again, briefly.

"Shit," said Jane. "I should have said I'd meet him and got it over with. But I can still use it later. He'll come. God, that's low."

"What's low?" asked Judy.

"Did you ever prosecute somebody you were pretty sure didn't do the crime?"

"Sure."

"So he went to jail?"

"She. Yep."

"And you don't feel bad about it?"

"Why should I? I won."

"But how is that justice, if somebody else did it and is still free?"

"She probably did other things, would have done more. She was the type—and anyway, I won."

"Winning is all there is?"

"You got it."

"Thanks, Judy."

Seal wanted to say something about this conversation, but the RV was pulling over. He marked the place with cellophane tape and rushed to the first available bush. By the time he was empty, so was his head. Steve and the doc were back in the RV and Charlie and Mara had taken the car down the road to get fuel. Steve handled the radio link to the car. Seal and the doc found a deck of cards and played War.

After twenty minutes, Charlie's voice came over the radio. "This is not good."

"Shit," said Steve.

"What?" said the doctor.

Steve was pulling open the footlocker in the corner, telling the doctor to get his blinking blank over here and help by blinky blank. He handed the doc a Texas license plate, a screwdriver, and strips of red vinyl trim.

"He only said something isn't good," said John.

"It's one of the ways we practice radio discipline. The more understated the words, the worse the situation. You switch the back plate and put this trim over the wheel wells. I'll do the front. Seal, wake the others and watch the sensors."

In twenty minutes, after the RV had been transformed, they heard, "… on our way."

Mack and Louis were putting on their gear and were almost dressed when the fireball went up in a field about a mile away. They told Steve to stay behind and were out the door before the second explosion sent another red and gold plume into the night. Steve pointed his MP5 at everybody.

"Did you hear that?" Judy said in Seal's ear.

The infrared sensors picked them up on their way back ten minutes later. There were four figures on the screen, the smallest glowing brighter than the rest. Steve took no chances, covering the door even after all recognition signals had passed.

The first one in was Mara, propelled by her brother behind her. Then came the two older men. The cordite smell was nothing new to Seal, but he noticed the doctor wrinkle his nose at it. There was another smell, too, that Seal could not place. It took a minute for the confusion to resolve itself, on orders from Mack. He was sent to the wheel, Frank to the phone, Sergei to the radio to monitor the police nets. Charlie gave a quick and dirty in German. Everybody turned to the doctor. Seal paused on his way to the cab and saw Mara turn around. He saw the doctor's face as he looked at the glistening, muddy burns down one side of her back.

Shoved into the driver's seat, Seal started the engine and put the truck into gear. He heard Mara's cool, slow voice behind him, telling the doctor, "There were cows in the field. The manure put the fire out quickly. I was lucky. Don't you think so?"

THIRTY

John began cutting. He reached out his left hand for the box of morphine. Charlie snatched it away. John dropped the scissors and lunged after it. Louis turned him around and put the scissors back in his hand. "Not yet," he said. "She must stay alert."

"But it's filthy. The wounds are filthy. I'm going to have to get all of that out."

Steve sat next to her on the bench, his arm around her hips. "You shouldn't wear that chain, Mara."

"It won't garrote me. It will break easily. My father gave it to me. It's lucky."

"*Wie Vasily,*" Mack mumbled. He tore open another package of gauze and arranged it on the table with the others.

John gave her a solid dose of antibiotics, then finished cutting away her shirt and jog bra, his stomach turning at the sight of blistered and bleeding wounds covered in manure. Sergei unbuckled her holster and took it off her carefully.

Charlie brought a bottle of good scotch out of the coffee cabinet. He poured some into a Styrofoam coffee cup and handed it to Mara.

"She needs water now, not alcohol. It's dehydrating," said John. They all stared at him, appalled. *I know I'm right.* "Besides," he said aloud. "You said she has to stay alert."

"This much will not impair her," said Charlie. "And it is not the same as a drug." He began pouring scotch into more Styrofoam cups until everybody had one. He offered one to John.

John watched Mara as she drank it, matched her in tossing it down. It warmed him inside, reminding him that he had an inside, a welcome internal warmth that made the outside heat more bearable. Charlie was right. It was not a drug. It was a gift.

Sergei found a more or less clean tarpaulin in the shower and spread it on the littered floor. Mara lay on this, face down, her arms stretched out over her head. Louis lay along her arms so that his long legs touched the GPS in the cab. He held her shoulders, his head next to hers. He spoke to her quietly in French. Steve held her legs. Sergei relayed clean bandages from the table to John's outstretched hand.

John worked quickly, ruthlessly, to get the manure out of the raw wounds on her back. A splash of burning fuel had formed a mark that snaked down the right side from shoulder to waist. John pulled bits of clothing out of a charred hole, a piece of leather from the cross strap of her holster from another wound near the waist, and two small stones out of another gash, higher up. He cleaned and disinfected, killing every nest of bacteria there could be, he hoped. Then, he disinfected again. He laid on the burn ointment, then the anesthetic ointment, since that would not make her groggy, and he checked her vitals for signs of shock. There were none. She had not made a sound.

The men all turned away while he helped her sit up and wrapped her chest to hold the dressings. Charlie gave her a clean black T-shirt. Dressed and alert, she sat at the table, careful not to lean back against the booth, and demanded more scotch.

"John says you need water first," said Steve.

Sergei handed her an eight-ounce bottle of mineral water, cold from the refrigerator.

She stuck her tongue out at it. Charlie pointed at the water, and she drank it.

"You do the briefing," he told her as he poured more scotch into her cup. He put both babysitters in the cab and gave John the headphones. John had no idea what he was supposed to listen for but stood behind the sink feeling triumphant at this new expression of trust. The team began stripping and cleaning weapons, as usual. Charlie refilled the magazines for his and Mara's Glocks. Mara sipped her scotch and gave her briefing.

"When I came out of the bathroom," she said. "I saw nothing, but I felt something. I made eye contact with Charlie, who was at the pumps, and could see he felt it, too. There seemed no basis for it, though, so I went inside to pay for the gas.

"I was third in line at the counter. The line stretched across a crossway aisle and down a center aisle to the door. I edged to the left, near shelves of canned goods, to be closer to cover and also to use the surveillance mirrors in the far corners. There were other people in the shop, two women to the right at the soda machine, a man at the back looking at magazines, plus the two men in front of me in line.

"I saw them before they came through the door. No one in the shop was moving wrongly, so I concluded that everything would come from outside and kept watch there. I crouched closer to the canned goods and drew my weapon. I had already chambered a round. I was open on three sides, but there was nothing I could do about it without cutting off my escape.

"They came in four abreast, but the first three were quickly telescoped behind one another because of the narrow aisle. They carried Uzis. I decided this was not a robbery. The first one fired a controlled burst at the ceiling and shouted for everyone to get down. I do not think they expected me to be right in front of them because they were looking at the mirrors to see down the aisles.

"I am sure I hit the first man in the chest, but he must have worn soft body armor. He did not go down. I stood up and stepped partly behind the shelving, now on my right since I was facing the door. On the next round, I used a silhouette point at the head, and he went down. I knew the one behind him would be similar, adjusted the silhouette for his head (he was slightly shorter) and he went down.

"I did not think I had time for the third, as his muzzle was already bearing on me and his weapon was in full automatic, clearing the shelves to my left. Besides, I could see that Charlie was at the door, trying to acquire the target and I was in the way. I ducked behind the shelving to my right, thinking I would use the right-hand aisle to approach the door. I was quickly surprised by the fourth man, who was also surprised. We almost collided, and so neither of us had a chance to bring our weapons to bear. I used the opportunity to try to knock the Uzi out of his hands with an outside crescent kick. I was not successful. He was quite large. I needed height and power and so I chose a tornado kick to the head. He fell back into a display of soft drink cans, but I do not think he was dead. I met Charlie at the door."

"This took?" asked Mack.

"Three, perhaps four seconds," she replied.

"And did you get the third man?" he asked Charlie.

"Yes."

"We assumed there would be two more outside," Mara continued, "because we had accounted for four and Sergei said that Maximovich uses teams of six. We were correct. We covered each other to the car, but the windshield was blown out on our way to the highway."

"We did not have time to reinforce the glass in Reno," explained Louis.

Mara shrugged, then winced. Her face had turned a vivid crimson in the heat. John stepped over half a dozen gun parts and cleaning rods to get to her. Her pulse was steady, though, and she was not finished.

"Charlie drove," she said, "and I tried to read the map. The two remaining men pursued us in a dark-colored van. When the rear window of our car blew out, Charlie ducked, then swerved to avoid a slower car. We left the road and traveled through a barbed wire fence into a rocky pasture. A rock must have punctured one of the tanks because we began to smell gasoline rather strongly. Charlie told me to get out. I obeyed."

She paused for approval. Everyone nodded. Good girl.

"I landed in manure," she continued. "And the car traveled to the right so that it almost circled me before it stopped. This is why I was not far enough away when the first tank exploded. I rolled in the manure, and when the fire was out, I ran toward a ditch a hundred meters away on my left. I was in the ditch by the time the second tank went up.

"I heard Charlie's call and I answered. He found me in the ditch. We were deciding our location when we heard your call and we replied."

THIRTY-ONE

It fell to John's shift to solve the fuel problem.

"We have to turn on the air conditioner," John told Louis. "It must be a hundred degrees back there. Mara will be in agony." He sat in the passenger seat sipping his coffee and adjusted the air vent. It was already hot, and the sun was not yet up.

The dawn put lights and shadows on Louis's face as he drove the RV. It made him look more sinister than usual, which was considerable. His dark hair had long since slipped its bonds and its curls waved over his head in gray-flecked excursions. His beard was thick, coarse, and matted. He had a look in those almost-black eyes that would make any sensible person cross a street to avoid him.

John liked him the best of them all. Louis's jokes were usually crude but always funny. He was mercurial and violent but devoted to Mara.

"We must conserve the petrol," Louis said. "Until Misha decides the safest way to get more. Mara suffers now no more than a man would. She is all right."

"What? No more than a man?"

Louis then casually turned the switch on the back air conditioner to high. This was another thing John liked about him. You could never tell what he was thinking simply by listening to what he was saying.

Louis drank his coffee and glanced at the road once or twice while he watched John. "My Uncle Bertrand taught me from the time when I was eight years old," he explained. "He taught me to fight, to kill, to listen. These are important skills. He also told me about women. He told me all the ordinary things that boys learn, but the training he gave me was more than what is considered ordinary. He also taught me about the women in this business.

"Uncle Bertrand explained it is theoretically possible for a woman to be as effective as a man of her weight. He said with good training, a woman could be formidable in her class. We have now proved this with Mara.

"But, my uncle insisted, a woman is most effective when she is allowed to be herself. Use her for honey traps, he said. When she kills, she should do it with finesse, not strength, because she has more of the one than the other. She is subtle. This is her advantage.

"It also can be her disadvantage. When she suffers ordinary hardship and pain, she suffers them the same as any man, according to her strength. But add intelligence to the pain, let it target the soul, and here she differs. A man's response will be physical. He will be too angry or too busy to appreciate a subtle torture, but a woman will grasp its full impact.

"This is why, Uncle Bertrand insisted, while you may use a woman, or you may marry a woman, never have one on your team. If she is ever made to suffer as a woman, you will not be able to bear it. This is what I mean when I say that, for now, Mara suffers as a man."

John stared at him. "*You* will not bear it?"

"I will not. We will not. The men will not. Cannot. The relationships within the team are … I am at a loss." Louis looked at the road for half a mile, searching for English words written in the lane lines.

"During great stress," he continued finally, "the bonds between us are more important than all of the training and all of the equipment. We think, move, act, and suffer together. If we cannot, then there is no bond, or it is a foreign bond. In any case, it is useless under the conditions we face."

"Then what will you do about Mara?" asked John, incredulous.

"Do?" Louis raised an eyebrow. "Nothing. Wait for Mara to see it. It has been explained to her, but she does not know it. Some wisdom comes with maturity. We hope she hurries."

"But the risks?"

"There are always risks in bringing up children."

Mack spoke up from behind the curtain.

"Take this exit."

Louis parked the RV on a side road behind a few mesquite trees. Misha and Frank explained the plan for the shift.

"We will clean up the doctor," said Frank.

"Because he smells," said Sergei.

"So do you," said John.

"Get him a fresh shirt and jeans," said Frank, "and an electric razor."

John kicked Sergei. Sergei kicked back.

"Please." Frank exaggerated the word, spreading his lips like a chimpanzee.

With prodding, John stripped and dressed in the middle of the room and listened to his briefing while he buttoned on a starched blue and red striped shirt. He took it off again so he could shave without getting his beard all over it.

"There is a large truck stop about five miles further along the highway," said Mack. He pointed to the computer screen. Sure enough, there it was. "The vehicle is disguised. You are the least well-known of us all. The watchers will be looking for at least two people in the cab, and someone to watch the payer's back. They will expect the person at the pump and the person paying to be in the same condition that Charlie and Mara were in at the last stop, that is, dirty and tired.

"You will go in looking fresh and alert and completely alone. We will turn on the cameras and sensors, but we will be very quiet. We will give you three minutes to pay. After that, we will leave without you. We cannot risk staying longer." He looked at Louis. "In that event, we must assume that Sergei is blown."

"It does not matter," said Louis. "Charlie wants to jettison all the dead weight."

"All?" asked Mack. "Who else does he include as dead weight?"

"Sergei and Seal."

"Seal is not dead weight. He is a master of tradecraft. Charlie would profit from lessons from Seal. Also, Seal is guaranteed to put himself between Mara and any bullet. I will speak to Charlie."

John held the razor an inch from his chin, waiting for the rest of this 'dead weight' discussion to clear up. It didn't.

He cleared his throat. "There can't be that many bad guys out there, can there? And how can they find us at one particular truck stop?"

The four men at the table stared at him. Frank answered finally. "Doc, the FBI, or at least some part of the FBI, is unwittingly helping the bad guys. There are lots of them."

"But they killed Roger and he was FBI." John's voice vibrated with the razor on his jaw.

"Jay Turner runs his own game, too, you know, and if Roger was one of his, and if the bad guys as you call them found out, well, then Roger's dance card would naturally be canceled. As for them finding us in one truck stop, they will be looking for us in all truck stops. They know we're on wheels. They know we blew up a whole car full of gas, and they can put two and two together, come up with four, and put that many watchers at every station between here and San Antonio."

John finished shaving one side of his face and began on the other, gently over the bruises. "What do I do if they catch me? Will they shoot me, do you think?"

Mack shook his head.

"Tell them that Sergei is with us, and your FBI should guarantee your safety. Tell it to them, not to Maximovich. If he catches you, tell him you will talk only to the FBI."

Sergei shook his head. "It will not help. Don't you see, Mack, the only way you can jettison the doctor is to shoot him? John has spent more than two days with you. He knows your habits, attitudes, and working relationships. Everybody talks too much. He knows that Frank is forgiven, that Charlie finally made Mara obey him, and that you might give quarter, but Charlie never will. He knows Steve is in a lather over Mara, and Louis would march into hell for her. Volodya will ream our good doctor until he gets it all."

Louis snorted. "For what?"

Sergei stared back at the Frenchman for a moment, deciding how to explain this. "Have you told me how you plan to get the file?" he asked.

"No," Mack answered.

"Then I will tell you your plan. Charlie and Steve will create a diversion by going into the warehouse through the roof. While they pin down Volodya's teams from above, Louis will open the lock on a side door. You will run point for him, taking them out silently with the knife. He will open the correct safe while you set a diversionary charge. That charge will also be a signal for Charlie and Steve to get out. They will secure one door. You will exit together."

Mack and Louis were silent.

Frank spoke. "You figured that out from listening to Charlie and Mara bicker?"

"Among other things," said Sergei. "When Sobieski was alive, the three of them worked as a single team. Now, they have become effectively two teams, with twice the coverage and the ability to create diversions. The watch system alone during this trip shows this. The point is, that to a brain like Volodya's, the doctor is vitamin-enriched protein. He is not dead weight."

Thank you, Sergei Pavlenko. John put the razor on the table and almost shook his hand.

"He is poison," said Louis. He pointed at Sergei. "And so are you."

"All medicine is poison," said Mack. He pointed at John. "Put your shirt on and start driving. And do not get caught."

THIRTY-TWO

They've solved it, thought Seal. He opened his eyes and watched Steve slide off the bunk above him. The room was cool, almost cold. They got the gas, thought Seal, and the air is on high. He wondered if Mara had slept at all.

The doctor stood by Mara's bunk. He looked spiffy, all cleaned up, in a striped shirt and new blue jeans. Steve took this opportunity to ram his shoulder into him on his way out. Shift change was a series of thumps and bumps and shushes as everybody tried to get out at once and the other watch tried to get in and the doctor tried to look at Mara's back without waking her up. There was a long-whispered relay of 'Mara stays back this shift. Frank and Sergei stay up.'

Charlie was dragging mega-gear up front. Seal groaned. The guy was all work. Seal had now been days without play and was ready for a minor goof-off. No go with Charlie. Normally, Seal would not think about a boss's opinion in a decision to kick back, but normally the boss was not such a... Seal wanted to think the word fucking, but he had cleaned up his language considerably around Mara. If you think it, you'll say it, he always said. So his boss this trip was a damned error-free killing machine half his age. He was no good time Charlie, not by any stretch. Seal sighed and pushed the f...ing—damned—locker full of submachine guns in front of him into the galley.

This would be their last shift. At the end of it, they would be in San Antonio. After that, it was a straight go to the end. None too soon, in Seal's book. For a last shift, it was exactly like all the others, gloriously unexciting. He liked it that way. No f...ing cockups, no funerals. Seal took his turn on the tape machine, listened to Judy's stupid whining, and wondered why Jane didn't shoot her right then.

He also took a turn at the wheel, with Charlie as his passenger. Seal could have lived happily ever after without trying to make conversation with Sasquatch here, but Charlie became surprisingly civil. He asked polite questions. Seal would have been almost comfortable if this new warmth didn't make yesterday's dead weight talk stand out even more. The thought of ever being on this guy's bad side gave Seal the willies.

For the second half of the shift, Frank and Steve drove while Charlie and Seal checked the ropes and knots. Charlie asked for Seal's opinion. Seal gave it, carefully and showed Charlie a better knot. *Always ask a sailor.*

Sergei sat at the table next to Seal, trying hard not to be too visible to Charlie. He failed. While Seal re-knotted the ropes, Charlie pulled a long roll of white paper from between two radios overhead. He unrolled it on the table. It was a drawn floor plan of the warehouse containing the file.

"Let's go over this," said Charlie.

Sergei nodded. If we must.

"It's ten meters to the roof?"

"To the ceiling. Semianov said there is an iron catwalk, mid-way between ceiling and floor, all the way around, and that it is five meters from the floor. This suggests the roof is ten meters."

"How many rows of crates?"

"He did not say."

"How many rows of safes?"

"He did not say. He said to count the rows from the south staircase that descends from the catwalk. Fourth row of safes, from south to north, sixteenth safe east. The combination is 29-16-5-0. Look in the second drawer, sixth compartment."

"What does the rest of this look like?" Charlie swept over a wide white space on the paper with his hand.

"*Ne zhnaiyu.* Semianov said it is a U.S. Government temporary archive. Documents are held for up to eight years. He put the files in with documents to be retired to another archive in 1999."

"And Maximovich has the warehouse?"

"I am sure he has. Semianov told four of us about the warehouse. He told only me the exact location to find the documents. Maximovich interrogated the other two."

"He assassinated the other two?"

"Yes." Sergei squirmed. There was not much room next to Seal for squirming.

Charlie stared at him across the table, that still, blue stare that x-rayed you with maximum radiation. Seal didn't blame Sergei for sweating.

"I know why he wants the file," said Charlie quietly. "I know his plans for an American destabilization, and I know his underground alliances. I know his resources and his procedures. I even know some of his motivations. I appreciate that the KGB, or what was once the KGB, must find new work. I wonder what your plans were?"

"My future was assured. I escaped the chopping block and was designated for a directorate within the new foreign intelligence service, the SVR. My past success, my pre-Bolshevik family name." Sergei shrugged.

"But Maximovich was getting the axe?"

"Yes."

"And when he asked for your help, you refused because of the danger to Mara."

"Yes."

Charlie paused. "It's still not enough. Jane said 'rabid.' She said Maximovich is rabid about Mara. This is a personal thing, certainly related to you, but also having to do with Mara. What have you done to Maximovich that makes him target her, Sergei Nickolaevich?"

It was a direct, unavoidable question. Confession time. Seal wanted to leave the confessional. Lightning can miss. Even a close brush with it will burn you.

Sergei swallowed.

I bet he's remembering that iron. Not something I'd forget.

"Last year," said Sergei, "Volodya went to the Congo for several months on an operation. While he was gone ..." Sergei cleared his throat. "While he was gone, Nadhezda asked me to help her. She did black-market work on the side and...."

"Nadhezda is?"

"Was. Volodya's wife—what Americans call common law. They lived together. I think they planned to marry someday. While Volodya was gone, I helped her out at the flat, and one night, we celebrated something, a killing on the market, I don't know what, and with the vodka and her loneliness, and...." Sergei raised his eyebrows.

Charlie did not shift his gaze. "You seduced her."

Sergei shook his head and threw up his hands. "She seduced me! I was helpless, I swear it! But she died in childbirth in March. I could not deny it was my child. The little thing had no one else. But the baby died a few days later. I thought Volodya had forgiven me when he asked me for the file. He was civil, almost friendly. He was my friend. I had to tell him why I could not help him."

"*Sheisse*. Did you spell it out for him? The file, the plans to Vasily's Carpet?"

"No. Only that it could damage Mara."

Mara poured herself a cup of coffee behind them, not making a sound. Her hand shook as it held the cup. Her eyes had sunk into black circles in a dirty face. Medusa had a better hairstyle. The fire had burned the top of her braided knot so that clumps of hair hung down or stuck out on either side, no longer containable by a rubber band. Mara put her cup down and removed what was left of the rubber band. Six inches of singed hair fell to the floor. She looked at it and burst into tears.

Seal and Sergei were right there, consoling her with cluck clucks, trying to figure out how to pet her without touching the burns on her back. Charlie sat at the table and rolled his blue eyes to the ceiling.

"I can fix it," said Sergei. "I need a scissors. Where is the doctor's bag? I will fix it." He rootled through the doctor's bag, found the scissors, and began snipping.

"A comb. A comb will help."

Seal produced one from a back pocket. He rinsed it with hot coffee over the sink.

Sergei did an acceptable job. She looked adorable in their eyes, even with short hair, but she kept on crying, and they stood around helpless and distressed. She cried onto Sergei's shoulder. He held her as tightly as he could but for the bandages, and she shook with sobs.

Seal jerked his shoulders and shook his hands to loosen the tension in his arms. He looked at the ceiling, then returned Charlie's ironic stare. He remembered the big black bow. Charlie was right again.

Charlie smiled.

Seal shuddered. He hated this mind reading shit.

Mack was the next one to come forward, and this was the little scene that greeted him. Sergei tried to look nonchalant, as though he didn't know how the girl crying on his shoulder got there. When

Mara realized Mack was behind her, she stepped away from Sergei, forced her arms to her sides, and stood there, hub-chub-lubbing with tears streaking mud down her face.

Seal would not have believed it if he had read it in a file. Mack took a handkerchief from his pocket, gave it to Mara, and gathered her into his arms. The real sobbing broke out now, and with it came wailing and protests and reassurances, all in German. This is the guy with the knife, Seal told himself. *I've seen this. I'm a dead man.*

Charlie produced his usual helpful cup of scotch. Problem solved. The sobs subsided. Louis came forward and asked what the problem was. Steve pulled the van into a thicket on a side road and demanded to know what was going on. Frank came with him looking concerned. The doctor showed up last, rubbed his eyes, and wanted to know what's up. Mara smiled and hub-lubbed and sipped her scotch. Then everybody complimented her haircut.

Mack sent Frank and Sergei to the back to sleep. He told Mara she could sleep, too, but she had already taken the headphones and was making herself busy with the coffee machine. Charlie handed her the holster with her Glock in it and told her to put it back on. She found a new cross strap in the open weapons locker and had no shortage of people helping her put it together.

The room was in chaos, with Jay calling them on the cellular, the meeting beginning, and the plan prescribed for a reconnaissance. Seal made himself invisible in a corner until he might be needed, but the doctor had no clue and managed to stand directly in everybody's path. This wasn't hard to do in such a tight space, but the doctor contrived to do it with spectacular results.

At one point, Steve fell past him, tripping over his feet, but was up on the rebound and coming straight at the poor schmuck with only one thing in mind. Seal was the closest man there, so he had no choice but to play punching bag. He bore Steve down with his weight mostly, and a minor resurrection of the skill he once had. Even so, Seal barely held him, and it took Charlie and Louis to pull Steve off and a sharp word from Mack to settle him into a slow seething.

The doc's jaw never came up off the floor. Somebody pushed him against the wall, and he stayed there, staring at the chaos, feeling the swell of violence as the adrenaline began that would carry them through a killing night. Seal gave him a pat on the shoulder, but he did not respond.

Mack and Louis were stripping and shaving and dressing in suits, with white shirts and ties, wires and transmitters, soft body armor and shoulder holsters, backup holsters with little .38s at the ankle, knives carried horizontally inside their belts and more of them tucked into scabbards carried in the crotch. Mack slipped a slim, light, sharp little number inside his tie.

Louis tamed his wild curls with mousse. Mack brought his hair under control with just water.

"Jay is meeting us at Dick's in someplace called the Riverwalk," Mack told Charlie. "He is bringing a car and says he has a safehouse for us. We will need fuel in the truck. Use the doctor. It worked well last time and might work again. At least it will keep them busy while we look at the warehouse. Then meet us in the parking lot by the bus station next to the Alamo. Here. I have marked it." He pointed at a map on the table.

The doctor asked a lot of stupid questions that nobody answered. Seal shoved him into the driver's seat and climbed into the seat next to him. He navigated them downtown and onto Crockett Street. They let Mack and Louis out a block away from Dick's.

"I'm supposed to be alone in the cab to get the gas," said the doctor. "They won't be looking for somebody alone."

"We want them to see us, Doc," Seal said in his most patient voice. "We want them to gather round."

"Do you know what they'll do to me if I get caught?"

"No. Do you?"

"I understand it's not pleasant."

"That's probably a safe assumption. Turn left at the next light."

"But what should I do?"

Seal shrugged. "Don't get caught."

THIRTY-THREE

John could feel their eyes, their thoughts, their estimates. Two men with long hair and dirty white t-shirts edged closer to his pump. They were within twenty feet of him by the time the tank was full. He threw the nozzle back onto the pump and jogged to the shop.

The two men did not follow him.

He threw a fifty at the man behind the counter and said, "Keep the change."

"Hey! Is your name Jerry?" The man shouted over the heads of his customers.

John was already at the door. He paused with his hand on the door rail.

"She said he'd be a blond guy in a hurry," said the man behind the counter, still shouting. "If you're Jerry, Jane says call her at the Merriot. Merriot Rivercenter."

John waved at him and ran to the RV. The truck was in motion before the door slammed shut behind him. Seal drove. Seal would lose the bums, Mara told him.

After John tumbled around inside for fifteen minutes, Steve handed him another license plate and a screwdriver and pushed him out the door again, into the staff lot of the city zoo. It was faster work this time. They tore off all the trim they had put on before, then tore off the previous trim underneath it. The RV now sported a set of slim purple lines and Louisiana plates.

John collapsed on the bench across from Charlie as they returned to the road. Charlie was cleaning his Glock.

"Any problems at the gas station?" he asked. He wet a cleaning pad with solvent.

John's brow wrinkled, puzzled. "The guy thought I was somebody named Jerry."

Charlie stopped and stared. "The exact words. I want the exact words."

Steve had two bags of gear and clothing on the floor by the time Charlie finished dialing the Merriot. He put the phone on speaker, so they could change their clothes while he spoke to her.

"I'm so scared, Michael," said Jane.

Mara closed one eye, thinking.

"Okay. Stay in your room," said Charlie. "I'll come to your room."

"It's Judy's room," said Jane.

"Not another fucking hotel room," mumbled Steve. He adjusted the Velcro at the shoulders of his soft body armor.

"Get Judy out of there," said Charlie.

"I can't. It's her room."

"I hate clearing a fucking hotel room," whispered Steve. He buttoned a white cotton shirt over the armor.

"Tell Judy how to act," said Charlie. "Tell her to keep her hands in view."

"Full of god-damned hidey holes and the first one's right behind the mother-fucking door." Steve pulled on a pair of summer weight brown wool trousers.

"I know," said Jane. "I'll tell her."

"I will put you in a safehouse. You'll be okay." Charlie reassembled the Glock as he spoke.

"And you fucking never, never know which fucking side the fucking son of a bitch bathroom is on." Steve slammed a full magazine back into his Beretta and slipped it into the holster under his arm.

"Tell Steve the bathroom is on the left side," said Jane. She sounded amused. "Hurry."

Click.

Charlie waved away the wire Mara offered. She frowned. "It'll scare her off," he said. "We don't need the wires. We'll clear the room and disarm them both. Steve will take Judy down to the lobby, slip away from her there, and meet us in the parking garage. We'll walk across, climb in the van, secure her gently, and be on our way."

He scowled at Mara's doubtful look. "It's on the next block, Mara, and utterly simple. We will not take chances."

She watched through the cab curtain until they were in the Rivercenter parking garage across the street.

John was elated. It was the first time since Reno that he found himself semi-alone with her. Seal was there, but that was all right. Seal didn't exploit every opportunity there was to hit him. John was not sorry Steve had to clear a hotel room, fucking or otherwise. He was not sure what clearing involved, but if Steve found it nasty, it made John smile to think of him doing it.

Mara was not smiling when she turned around. Her solemnity almost put a lid on his sudden high spirits, but he had to take his chance. Now.

She was looking past him with wide eyes. John took a step toward her, but turned around at the same time, to see what alarmed her. Seal stood in the galley, staring with the same wide-eyed expression at the tape machine. He reached toward the bottom reel, pulled a cellophane tab out with his fingernail. It had folded itself into the magnetic tape, and the conversation it marked had never been reviewed.

John would have liked to ignore it, except for the looks on Seal's and Mara's faces. Seal cued the tape and pressed play. While Mara listened to Jane say, "God, that's low," Seal brought a nylon bag up from the back.

"I'll need three magazines of subsonic hollow-point," she said. She pointed to the box of assorted guns and cartridges.

Seal began rummaging.

"And the suppressor. Mine is in the red case."

Seal pulled out a red case.

"Mara," said John.

"Not now, John."

"But ..."

"It's a trap, John. Jane is going to kill them. I have to go. I don't have time for other things right now."

"Go? You can't! It's dangerous."

She was already stripped to panties and bandages. Seal handed her a soft body armor vest and helped with the Velcro at the shoulders. She grimaced as the weight settled on her back. Next came a powder blue knit skirt. She buckled a web belt with loops and pockets over the waistband, picked up her Glock and inserted a full magazine, then practiced attaching a suppressor and returning it to its pocket. Finally, she chambered a round and slipped the Glock into the holster at her back. She drew it twice, practicing a smooth extraction. Seal handed her two more magazines. She put these into loops at the front. Seal put the earpiece of a wire into her left ear and arranged the wire down the front of her body armor. He plugged it into a box and clipped it to the belt. Before she put on an oversized loose knit top in powder blue to match the skirt, Mara slipped a small knife into an inner pocket in the breast of her body armor.

She sat on the folding chair to tie the straps of a pair of white string sandals. John wanted to reason with her.

"I know what I'm doing, John."

"I never said you didn't. I'm only suggesting that you should wait."

"Makeup, Seal. I need makeup. I look like hell."

Seal made up her face: eyeshadow, mascara, powder, blush, and lipstick, while she checked the draw on her Glock again, drew back the slide, and looked in the chamber.

"Don't move your eyes," said Seal. He brushed an eyelash gently. "I'll monitor the normal frequency. If Steve and Charlie come back, I'll tell you. What do I tell the other two if they come back?"

"Tell them the room number, 557. My plan is to warn and interrupt. That's all. Then, I will do as Charlie tells me. They can contact us on my wire. We will be here within ten minutes. I'm ready. How far ahead of me are they?"

"Six, maybe eight, minutes."

"I will make up time by running."

"I can't let you do this, Mara," said John. He blocked the door, determined, but only until Seal's three hundred pounds removed him. He was still trying to hit Seal when Sergei and Frank came out of the back room.

Seal threw him off and stood over the door. John sat on the floor holding his head in his hands.

"Where is Mara?" asked Pavlenko.

"Gone," John moaned.

"Jared set a trap for Charlie and Steve," said Seal. "She went to warn them."

"No!"

Sergei rushed the door, but Seal was prepared for this, repulsed him, and tackled him as he fell against the weapons locker. Frank stood looking stupid until Seal swore at him to move his ass and help, damn it. Frank pinned the Russian's arms so that when John tried to get up, Seal could send him sprawling again with a kick to the abdomen while he kept the bulk of his weight on Sergei's legs.

"Now listen up folks," said Seal as they lay in a twisted heap on the floor, "Mara is a specialist backing up a member of her team. There ain't shit we can do about it except support her as her babysitters. That means we stay here, keep this vehicle secure, and afterward, clean up any mess she makes. That's our job. That's our only fucking job. If you do anything else, you asshole Pavlenko, you'll put her in more danger. If you get yourself killed or caught, you'll put the whole fucking operation in jeopardy. I declare myself to be in charge—no offense Frank—and I expect my orders to be obeyed here. Is that clear, doctor?"

"Yes." He pulled his knees up and rolled onto them.

"Pavlenko?"

A grunt that could be taken either way.

John and Sergei climbed into the cab and stared out in the direction of the Merriot. Sergei should be undercover, Seal shouted from behind the curtain. "*Idi nakui*," came the reply. Frank kindly translated, "Go fuck yourself."

Sergei sat with his arms on top of the steering wheel and his chin on his hands. He and John were silent for a full ten minutes.

Then the sirens began.

THIRTY-FOUR

Mara hugged the wall to the right of the door labeled 557. Doors alternated on either side of the narrow hallway. Mara chose the right side of the door because a specialist leaving the room would be oriented toward the emergency exit stairs on the left instead of the elevators on the right.

There was no sign of Charlie or Steve, nor any sound from the room. With her left fist, Mara pounded on the door. Nothing. She pounded again. She heard movement. An older couple came out of their room down the hall to the left, six meters away. The door beside Mara opened; two bullets came through it and into the opposite wall. The old couple was now three meters away, with puzzled faces. The noise was not excessive. The shooter had a suppressor. Jane ran out of the room and into the old people. Her gun was in her right hand. She wore a loose assortment of flowing cotton in an African motif that wrapped itself around the strap of the old woman's purse and set the two innocents hollering for the police.

Jane took the woman's purse with her for almost a meter before the cotton unraveled and let the purse fall to the floor. The old man ran to pick it up while his wife stood bawling and shouting in the middle of the hallway so that Mara still had the two of them between her and Jane. No unobstructed bead. Jane reached the door to the stairs.

Mara looked into 557, fearing the scene, but Charlie was up and about, more or less, tangled in bedclothes, but dressed and stumbling to the door, his Glock in his right hand. The suppressor was not on it. That meant the shots had been Jane's, random, to clear her egress. How careless Mara thought. She downgraded her estimate of Jane's abilities.

Mara decided that Charlie could fend for himself, and Jane would try for Steve next, in the lobby. She ran after her, knocking the purse out of the old man's hand as he tried to pick it up. She did not wait to see the blood on Charlie's hand or the hole in his coat. She did not hear him wheezing. The old couple did, though. They saw a blond man come out of that room, with blood on his left hand, a gun in his right, and his breath sounding like a bellows in a forge. The old man told this to the police later. The woman fainted.

The lobby was decorated for coolness in a hot climate, with re-frigerated air, tile floors, and southwestern colors. It was crowded with rough-hewn furniture and too many plants. Plants that con-cealed without providing cover.

Mara arrived to find Jane poking her gun through a fern.

"Steve!" She raised her Glock, using a geometric point. A woman in spandex with a big purse and sunglasses stood screaming in front of a chair two meters from Jane.

"Ah! Ahhhh!" She waved her arms over her head, centering her-self in Mara's sights.

Mara moved to the right. Jane fired and moved to avoid the re-turn. Her movement brought her around the plant in plain sight of Steve, whose Beretta was ready on the mark. Mara could see Steve and Judy plainly between the ferns to her left, and Jane to her right. Steve would fire before she could get another line on Jane, but she went through the drill anyway, just in case.

Sometimes, a just in case comes in handy. Other times, it's as useless as any other exercise. This was another time. Judy pushed Steve's arm upward and brought out her stupid revolver. Mara shift-ed to a point-and-shoot at Judy just as Steve's Beretta boomed, send-ing ceiling dust onto the reception desk. Judy died, and Jane ran out of the hotel and into the Rivercenter shopping mall.

Mara followed her. It was not hard to do. Jane was tall and had covered her beautiful cloud of brown hair with an orange turban arrangement that stood out above the crowd like a beacon.

Jane ran out of an exit beneath the IMAX Theater with Mara no more than ten meters behind her. They ran into the Manger Hotel, past the reception desk, through the old corridor, and onto the staircase. Jane climbed to the fourth floor, looking back once. She found a service door, locked. Mara was at the end of the hall, lifting the Glock. Jane fired twice at Mara, wildly, to keep her down and then once more at the lock. The door opened to a steep staircase leading to the roof. She took it.

Jane's magazine held only eight rounds, and these were gone. Her spares were still on the bed in room 557 where Charlie had put them when he thought she would come with him. Damn that girl, she thought. Mara was a positive professional hazard. Jane waited for her on the roof and evened out the match with a well-timed kick that knocked the Glock out of Mara's hand and off the roof.

Mara rolled away, losing the wire in her ear, and when Jane landed beside her, used a sweep to take her down, but Jane was up again and away before she could make this minor victory a major one. Jane came at her, preparing a punching combination that Mara could see a mile away. Jane was slow, her training not as thorough, but she had limbs far longer than Mara's, more strength, and greater weight. Mara could not get in close enough to land anything effective.

Jane could not land anything, either, because Mara was too fast and seemed to read her mind. Every lunge landed on air.

Mara's entire body was involved in every move. Hatred impelled her, without dilution, without reason. There were plenty of causes; Jane was a proven enemy, a devious one, and formidable, but the hatred had nothing to do with any of that. It was a pure intensity of physical, chemical, and mental concentration. She hated the person who was trying to kill her. Mara intended to win or die. There were no reservations in her, no restrictions.

They moved naturally to the edge of the roof, and the idea occurred to them both simultaneously. Mara's plan, though, was one grain more devious. She teetered at the edge and watched Jane gather herself for a big push. The tall woman came toward her, giving her enough time to read a manual of martial arts. Mara waited for her and then helped her over the side.

Celebration would have to wait. She saw them from the corner of her eye and had only sufficient time to break the chain and drop her lucky charm before they were on her. A signal, she thought, but she doubted anybody would look for her up here.

She was forced face down onto the roof, her arms tied behind her, her mouth taped shut. She was blindfolded. They half pushed, half carried, her down a metal staircase at the side of the building. She tried not to think about the height, was grateful she couldn't see it. At the bottom, she felt herself seized and thrown onto a metal floor, heard a door slam behind her, and felt movement. She was in a vehicle of some kind. Her ankles were being tied. There were instructions given in Russian. She understood them.

"Begin procedures," said a voice.

THIRTY-FIVE

Charlie and Steve were the first to come back.
"Where is Frank?" asked Seal. He could smell the cordite and the blood, and he did not dare ask about Mara.

John had no such reservations. "Where is Mara?"

Steve answered Seal's question. "Frank is fucking running rings around that cop. He's a damned good babysitter. Call Misha and Louis. Now. Tell them to meet us somewhere. Now. Jay said he had a safehouse for us. That will do. John, get your black bag."

Charlie sat on a folding chair and began peeling off the layers of his suit: coat, tie, holster, shirt, armor, undershirt. John knelt beside him and probed the wound in his side, across and between the ribs.

Seal spoke to Louis on the radio and punched Jay's directions to the safehouse into the computer. When Frank came in, Seal gave him the address and put him in the driver's seat. He stood by the computer as they lurched out of the parking lot. The air conditioning blew a few empty coffee cups off the top of the screen but made no headway in the heat that had built up from baking for ten minutes in the South Texas sun.

Steve and Sergei sat across from each other at the table. Charlie sat at the end of the table facing them, the doctor dabbing at his side. Steve put an elbow on the table, held his forehead in the palm of one hand, and let a gold chain drop to the table from his other hand.

Seal lost it then. He blamed that pussy-whipped asshole Charlie, pure and simple, and he would make the sucker pay. He would fucking grind him into the coffee stains on the floor. Seal was lucky that Charlie was wheezing and partly disarmed. He was lucky, but not sorry. Charlie got in some good licks, but so did he. Steve and Sergei held them apart and they continued the battle in screams.

"What the fuck were you doing? Trying to turn the enemy just because she has tits! You son of a bitch!"

"Why did you let her go out? Why didn't you keep her here with you?"

"What the fuck was I supposed to do, Charlie? She's a specialist. I'm a babysitter. We both did our jobs. I supported her and she saved your sorry ass, yours and Steve's."

"You don't know that."

"I do know that. You're sittin' here, stuck like a pig but still breathin'. You shoulda never gone out on that goatfuck and you know it!"

Sergei joined the discussion. "You should have let me go after her!" he shouted at Seal.

"To do what? You think you could save her when Charlie and Steve couldn't? What are you, the fucking kung fu kid?"

John stood up between the parties. "I need some room here to work and some information. Steve, why don't you pour us all some scotch?"

The first round went down right away, the second more slowly. While he sipped his second cup, Charlie briefed them, gasping and puffing at intervals.

"We cleared the room with no problems," he said. "I took half a dozen weapons off Jane: a primary, a backup, three spare magazines, a couple of knives. I put them on the bed. Steve took the cartridges out of Judy's .357 and let her carry the gun empty because she wouldn't leave the room without it. He took her downstairs to the lobby. I told Jane we would give him five minutes to dump her and then meet him behind the hotel."

Charlie paused to drink and catch his breath.

"Jane kissed me. To pass the time, she said. I felt her hand come up my right side, where the armor does not meet. It was an odd movement, but her hand was nowhere near my gun on the left, so I was slow to be alerted. Then I heard somebody banging at the door. I turned suddenly and felt something cold rip the flesh over my rib. Whatever it was went in above the rib, but I was alerted by this time and able to stop Jane's hand. There was more pounding on the door. Jane wriggled free from me, grabbed her primary off the bed, and ran for the door. She opened it and fired two rounds towards the hall before running out. I drew my Glock, but I was tangled in a bedspread that had been on the floor. I took the knife out of my side. It was an eight-inch stiletto. Two inches were bloody."

"Only two?" asked John. "You're sure?"

Charlie nodded and gasped for air. "I saw someone look inside, then run after Jane. The light was behind her, so I did not know it was Mara. I followed but couldn't catch my breath enough to run. I heard a shot in the lobby and got there in time to see Steve running through the mall. I followed him but lost him in the crowd. I left the mall through an exit that faced another hotel. There was a street to my right. A crowd had gathered in it. I pushed through and found Jane at the center. She was dead. Her legs were broken. She must have fallen. Steve pushed through to me and began pulling me out of the crowd. A policeman stopped us. Frank came out of nowhere and played his US Government official line. He was brilliant."

"Thank you," came a voice from behind the curtain. Frank pulled the RV into the driveway of a house on a residential street. It was a fairly well-to-do neighborhood, with large trees and manicured lawns, but the houses were older, and graffiti decorated the wooden fences at the end of the block.

The safehouse had a heavy door with good locks. The perimeter was covered by motion and infrared sensors. The house also had three toilets and two showers, a full refrigerator, and a large dining room table. John claimed first use of the table. He put Charlie on it and widened the wound enough to get at the lung to repair a nick. In the first five minutes, there was no mention of Mara. Mack and Louis came in and sat on dining room chairs, watching without expression as John worked. Sergei held Charlie's shoulders down.

While John stitched the muscles in Charlie's side, Steve began his briefing. "Judy talked my fucking ear off in that lobby. I heard Mara shout my name and I knew it was a warning, so I rolled and came back to my feet as two rounds whizzed right past me. I had my gun in my hand and pointed in the direction the shots came from when Jane stepped out from behind a tree. I had her. Shit. I had her, and that bitch Judy bumped my arm up, so I shot the fucking ceiling. Then she pulls out an empty revolver. How stupid can you get? There wasn't a damn thing I could do for her. She was down before I could blink, and I saw Jane heading for the door and Mara going after her. I ran after Mara. I lost her but kept going to the other end of the mall. I found a door and went through it. Mara's Glock hit the sidewalk in front of me. It almost beaned me." He pulled it out of his pocket and handed it to Mack.

Mack looked at it, still without expression.

"I figured it came from the roof of an old hotel in front of me. The windows were all shut, and I couldn't see shit going on. I went inside and climbed the stairs. I found an access door on the fourth floor with the lock blown off. It led to the roof. The stairs were steep like a ladder. While I was climbing, I heard scraping sounds on the roof, but when I got there, there was nothing. No sound. Nobody. I heard people in the street below, ran to the edge, and saw Jane smashed in the street. There was something shiny on the roof. I picked this up." He handed Mack Mara's lucky charm.

Everybody had gathered near the table. Some sat on a long, low counter that separated the dining room from the kitchen. Others were in chairs. Sergei and Seal stood. Everybody watched Mack and Louis. They did not move. Mack gazed at the gold chain and charm in his hand, then looked up at Steve. "Go on," he said.

"I decided I would run to all four sides of the roof," said Steve. "At the very first one, to the left of where I found the charm, there was a fire escape to the street. I saw a green van below me. It pulled out and squealed around the corner."

John finished the dressing, and Charlie got off the table and repeated his account for Mack and Louis. He received the same quiet attention. The doctor took a chair next to Seal in a corner. Nobody seemed to be breathing. The violence in the RV had been less creepy than this airless stillness.

When Charlie finished, Mack put Mara's Glock in his pocket and gave the chain to Louis. He pulled his chair to the center of the table and began pointing to people and then to places at the table where he wanted them to sit. Everybody did as they were told. With alacrity. Louis sat next to him, Sergei across from him. Charlie and Steve sat on either side of Sergei. Mack put Frank at one end of the table, and Jay at the other. He did not point to Seal or the doctor, and they did not volunteer to move from their corner. Anyway, the only places left at the table were next to Mack and Louis. Nobody wanted to get that close.

Mack took off his coat, loosened his tie, and looked at his watch. "It requires twenty-five minutes to reach the warehouse from downtown. They should be there just now. I assume they are going there?" He looked at Sergei, who swallowed and nodded.

He looked at Jay. "What about FBI presence? Will they be there?"

"I'm afraid not," said Jay. "I took a look at some of the message traffic in the local office. The Special Agent-In-Charge here is a friend of mine, though he doesn't work for me. The word he got from Justice was to support this guy's operation with watchers and intelligence, but to stay out of his way."

"Then Maximovich is free to do as he pleases." Mack looked at Sergei again. "Begin with the extraction itself. You are Maximovich. Begin with procedures."

THIRTY-SIX

Sergei spoke quickly. "If there was only one van, then he is using one team. This was an opportunity, not planned, so there must have been only one team available. Place the subject on the ground, in this case on the roof. One ties the hands, another tapes the mouth, a third the blindfold. They must get her off the roof, so they will leave the legs free until she is down. In the van, the legs are tied, with a connecting rope to the wrists to restrict movement."

He paused. Then he continued as if reading from a textbook. "Check her for weapons. Check her everywhere. Remove the tape to check the mouth if it has not been done. Replace with fresh tape."

"Will Maximovich do this himself?" asked Mack.

"No. A subordinate will do it and tell him that... she is innocent."

"And when they come to the warehouse?" Mack looked at his watch again. "They are there now."

Sergei looked him in the eye.

"He will rape her immediately."

"And the others?"

Sergei hesitated. "No. Not until the interrogation."

Mack looked at Seal. "What was she wearing?"

"The blue knit outfit, white sandals, body armor."

Back to Sergei. "Will he strip her?"

"Only what's necessary. Apart from cutting the leg ropes, no. Not until interrogation."

"When will that be? Why not interrogate now?"

Sergei hesitated again and looked away. "He will be eager to set a trap for you. He knows he will need every moment to prepare."

"How does he know we know where they are?"

Sergei looked at his hands on the table. "I gave her a ring. It once belonged to my great-grandmother. Volodya knows the ring. When he sees it, he will know that I am with you and that I will give you the location. He will want to be ready."

Louis spoke. "She was taught not to wear jewelry at such times. This charm from Vasily was an exception." He looked at Seal. "Did she take the ring off?"

"I didn't know she had a ring."

John spoke up. "No," he said. "She wore it. I saw it." He kept his face expressionless in the unwelcome heat of Mack's stare.

"If it delays the interrogation," said Mack, "it is good news." He held out his hand to Jay, who put a large white roll of paper into it. He spread the paper on the table. It was a diagram of the warehouse. "Now, Sergei, set the trap for us. Procedures."

Sergei stood over the table and considered this. "I will put her in the center rear of the warehouse, on the floor, not in the offices." He pointed at the large white space on the paper. "I assume you will come in through the large doors at the front. I may even leave them open for you. I want to make you run the gauntlet. I will take the tape off her mouth, I want her to tell you where she is, and I will leave her body armor in place so that my snipers don't kill her too soon. Then, I will have her hug a crate. Semianov told me that the back portion of the warehouse contains mostly crates. Old Dunovski taught us to make rescues as complicated as possible. Tie everything separately, he said. If you tie her hands and feet to opposite sides of a packing crate, the cutter must negotiate at least three faces of the crate, at each face will be a sniper, behind good cover. With two ropes to cut on each side, a rescuer will not survive." Sergei looked up from the paper. "There are only four of you."

"How many of them?"

"Volodya traveled with five teams, so that is thirty, plus drivers and extra watchers, but these are useless as fighters. You destroyed one team in the desert, and Charlie and Mara decimated another, leaving three teams intact and two extras."

"And where would you place these twenty men?"

"Besides at the sniper positions, I would put them throughout the building but especially on the catwalks. Once you enter, they can watch your progress and support the others on the floor, who will try to converge on you when they hear firing and can determine your position. I doubt that more than one or two of you will make it to the snipers."

There was a long silence.

Charlie finally broke it. He held his forehead in one hand, the elbow on the table. "I made a terrible mistake. I am sorry."

"So it is your first," said Louis. "Your father made a dozen mistakes by your age."

"That is an exaggeration," said Mack.

"None was this disastrous," insisted Charlie.

"One was nearly so," said Mack. "It cost Vasily a portion of his liver."

Charlie looked up at his father. There was another long silence.

The doctor broke this one.

"Look, ah, I can use a knife. I can cut a rope. You could cover me or something like that."

"I can do that," said Seal, "and I can fire an MP5."

"So can I, for that matter," said Frank.

"Ditto." Jay raised his hand.

"They would cut you down within the first ten meters," said Louis.

"Not if someone ran silent point ahead of them," said Sergei. "While you keep them busy at one end of the building, we can run in at the other, find her, and cut the ropes. With four of them cutting, it will be fast enough. I will run silent point."

"These were your men," Mack told him. "How many have you ever killed?"

"There were the two I shot the other day."

"And you think you can run silent? One hesitation and you will all die."

"I killed plenty of the VC in Nam," said Seal.

"That was twenty-five years ago and in battle. There is a difference."

"Uh. this is going to be a fucking battle," said Seal defiantly.

Mack rubbed his forehead. He looked at John, sat back in his chair, and loosened his tie again. The leather of his holster creaked as he shifted. "Doctor," he began, "I must say something to you especially, but this applies to all of you." He looked at Jay, Seal, and Frank in turn. "Your intentions are noble. I acknowledge that you are brave, but in your case, Doctor, also a little stupid. I tell you again, this is not television. Mara is not the pure maiden held by a dragon. She is a specialist who knew precisely what the risks were when she began this operation and when she went up on that roof. She does not expect anyone but her team to risk anything for her.

"You have known her for a few hours. If you succeed in helping to rescue her, and that is not likely, and if you live, which is even less likely, you will probably not see her again. You are a fine surgeon and a good man, Doctor, but I do not think you will win her. I am being very truthful. I will use whoever offers to help, but some of us will die. Each of you must make this decision with the understanding that it will probably be you and that it may be for nothing."

"We're all in, Mack," said Frank. "Let's not waste time. What's your plan?"

Mack took a pen out of his shirt pocket and used it to point at the diagram on the table. "They expect the team to go in together, through a door. We will climb to the roof, use plastique to blow holes in the roof—Sergei said he can prepare them—and fast rope down in four places onto the catwalks, firing as we descend." He pointed to points at roughly the four corners of the main part of the building.

"They are expecting to see four of us, so we must not disappoint them." He pointed the pen at Sergei. "You will be the fourth. If you hesitate on the catwalk, you kill only yourself. I hope. You go in here, near the safe, and make your way to the file. Louis will be on the other side of the front of the building. He will move to support you. Steve, here at the back, and Charlie at the other side."

"And you, Misha?" asked Louis.

"I will lead the babysitters in through this door, here." He pointed to a small door marked at the back of the building, labeled offices. "I will run silent point. Once we find Mara and cut her free, I will lead them out by the closest door."

Louis studied the paper and looked at Charlie. "Can you climb twenty meters with fifteen kilos of full body armor and weapons? You still do not breathe well."

"I can do it."

"Can you fast rope down ten meters, firing, in all that gear?"

"Of course." The wheezing was audible.

Mack looked at the Doctor. "Can he?"

"He's in very good shape. It's amazing what a man can do when he has to."

"Can he, Doctor? I am asking you for a professional opinion."

"I don't see how he can."

Charlie threw him an eyeful of venom.

Mack rubbed his chin and shook his head, thinking.

"Papa. I can run point." Charlie's voice was quiet.

Mack stared.

"I have done it before. That is how Steve and I got out of Tbilisi."

Sergei nodded. "It's true."

There was an awkward silence.

Mack looked tired. He rested his arms on the table in front of him, as if worn out, and sighed. "Then you will be point."

Steve cleared his throat. "Ahem. If the babysitters are coming in here," he pointed at the back door on the paper, "and coming through my area under the catwalk over here, then I'm going to shoot them, because I'm going to shoot anything that fucking moves, except for Seal, maybe, in his dippy shirt. I can see that stupid shirt a mile away."

"Do you have more of these shirts, Seal?" asked Mack.

He nodded.

"All babysitters and the doctor will wear one of Seal's shirts."

"Give me about seven meters in front of the first shirt, Steve," said Charlie. "Do not shoot at movement in that space."

"Sensors?" Mack asked Louis.

"I will take care of them."

"May I make a request?" said Jay. "Once Mara is free, I would like to move to the safe. It will help if I ever have to testify in court that I can say I saw the list in such and such a place and removed it from same. It would be best if I am there when the safe is opened. Of course, I know it will depend on how it goes with Mara."

"If Mara is able," Mack told Charlie, "tell her to lead the others out. You take Jay to the safe."

Charlie nodded.

The neighborhood was nearly deserted in the early afternoon heat as they walked out to the RV. Only two boys on bicycles watched them leave. Jay Turner pulled John back to the end of the procession.

"You can stay in this house safely and I can get you out on the next flight, Doctor."

John looked at him in horror.

"You can stay on the RV and support the operation from there if you must help," Jay insisted.

Horror was fast becoming anger.

"I don't mean to insult you, Doctor. I'm just trying to keep you alive."

THIRTY-SEVEN

John did not regret his decision, but he complained like everybody else. Seal's shirts smelled like fetid mustard. They should turn up the air. Complaining was important. It made him feel alive, a precious feeling he savored.

"I am not wearing full body armor," Louis said in French.

Steve put it back in the shower and pulled out his full armor.

"Louis, we have discussed this," said Mack.

"I must climb a pole to set the fuse and cut the power, sprint two hundred meters, roll under the sensors, disable the backup generator, and sprint fifty meters to my rope. Then, I am only beginning, and you want me to wear an extra fifteen kilos. No, thank you. We never wore that crap in the old days, and we survived."

"We were constantly shot to pieces. And we could never attempt this."

"I don't like all this modern nonsense. I am more effective without it. I will wear the soft armor to make you feel better."

Charlie also wore the lighter soft body armor under his black shirt. John noticed nobody said anything about that.

Somebody handed him Steve's soft armor. Jay had his own and Frank wore Mack's, considerably adjusted. Seal hoped for luck; there was nothing to fit him. Mack, Sergei, and Steve looked like a human armada, with full body armor over their black clothing, vests over the armor, Kevlar balaclavas, and in the vests, spare magazines, ropes, and small, neat packages of plastic explosive, detonators arranged by Sergei. They also carried an assortment of handguns and knives along with Heckler & Koch MP5 submachine guns, two each, strapped across their backs.

Everybody received a wire and the radios were tested. Charlie handed John a Spyderco knife and a wire cutter, in case they had her tied with cables. Jay and the two babysitters each had an MP5 and a spare magazine in every pants pocket. There was a short debate about giving the doctor a gun. Seal objected; the doctor was directly behind him in the lineup. The idea didn't go anywhere.

"Once we're in, we use hand signals only," Charlie briefed them. "Silence must be perfect."

"Won't there be all kinds of shooting?" asked John. "Who cares if we make a noise in that?"

The other four stared at him until Frank answered. "They won't be expecting a bunch of babysitters coming in just to cut the ropes, Doctor. We don't want to announce ourselves. We want them to concentrate on the team coming down from the roof."

"And it's a fucking rule of nature that the smallest sound will find a nanosecond of silence," said Seal.

"Oh." John sensed that he was supposed to know what they planned to do about the snipers, so he did not ask any more questions.

...

John craned his neck around Seal's fat head, trying to see beyond it to the Kevlar balaclava that covered Charlie's. Behind him, he heard Frank breathing and Jay shifting his weight as they leaned against the wall in the shadows. Behind them, the RV was parked for what Steve called a quick egress.

Steve was now halfway up the face of the back wall of the warehouse, fifty meters ahead of them. The other three specialists— even Charlie now referred to Sergei as a specialist—were also on ropes at the same level as Steve. This was the office end of the building. It had windows in it but was judged the safest approach for them because no other building looked onto it.

Charlie's team waited in the shadows until Steve gave the signal from the rooftop. Then they moved forward. The door was locked. Charlie brought out a narrow tool and opened it quietly. The first room was empty and dim, with only a thin stream of daylight from a high window. They walked to the opposite end. Charlie stopped and gave them all a murderous look, telling them with signs to pick up their feet. The shuffles had been deafening, even through the noise of explosions on the roof and the beginning of a gun battle.

They made it to the warehouse floor. They made it around the first crate, ten feet past the last office. John could see the catwalk on the far wall to his right and a constant flash from something moving around on it. He did not have time to look up to his left, but the sounds of gunfire were constant there and in the distance toward the front of the building.

Charlie gave them the signal to crawl. John tried to crawl quietly, though the gun battle filled his skull with both primary and echoed booming, making him unsure what was noisy and what was not. In the next five feet, he learned what running silent point meant. His hand stuck in a warm puddle, and he saw a bloodless corpse not more than three feet away, the carotid still glistening. John understood, finally, what Charlie planned to do about the snipers. He followed the ballooning form of Seal in front of him. They paused, two, then three, times, and after each pause, they passed another body, though these had been killed more bloodlessly, which is a relative term, he thought, in the circumstances.

Windows high above the catwalk and the holes in the roof allowed them enough daylight to see where they were going, but their crate canyon route kept them in perpetual gloom, welcome when they were moving, terrifying when they sat waiting.

They waited again in the murk. John heard Mack shouting.

Mara's voice rang out. "Don't! It's a trap!" It was not far away.

"Of course it's a trap, you silly girl," muttered Seal.

"Silence!" Charlie's whisper came over the wire. They could not see him. "Left, then forward," came the next whispered order.

They stopped again. To his left, John could see a shape sitting high on a box, supporting what looked like a broom handle over the lip of another box. A dark form moved toward it from behind. The forms converged, the second laid the first one down and caught the broom—John recognized a rifle—before it hit the floor. Charlie slid off the box and gave them the hand signal to wait. Seal acknowledged. Charlie disappeared to the right.

They squatted along a long wall of crates and boxes leading to the dead sniper. This time was the longest wait. Altogether, they had been inside the warehouse for two minutes, by John's watch, yet this wait seemed to have gone on for hours already. They heard a steady foot-pound and pushed themselves closer to the boxes behind them, wishing they were chameleons. The steps became louder and were coming from an aisle that opened to the left and in front of Seal.

The man rounding the corner got over his surprise quickly. He swung his submachine gun in a wide arc, firing as it moved. John watched as the bullets hit the concrete floor, ping, ping, ping, chewing up little bits of concrete and puffs of concrete dust, as each pit appeared a foot closer to Jay on John's right.

Everything was clear and slow, yet John had no time to think about it before the noise exploded next to him and he was hit by something hot. He looked at his arm. There was no blood. Pieces of brass were scattered at his feet and Seal's gun was spewing more. The man in the aisle was dead.

"Shit!" said Charlie.

"Had to," said Seal. "I got him."

"You're going to have twenty more. Keep them busy."

Frank took his Walther PPK from under his shirt and put it in John's right hand. He molded the fingers of his left hand around the bottom of the right and made him sit on the floor, knees up, forearms between the knees. He moved the wire away from his mouth. "Point that way," he whispered in his ear, moving John's hands until the Walther was pointing at the intersecting aisle. "If you see anything, squeeze the trigger."

John glanced at Seal on his left, who nodded. They heard the sound of several feet running. In the next instant, the gun battle was a reality, a practical occupation, not an abstraction. He smelled the cordite, heard the constant boom in every aural nerve, saw the muzzle flashes, his friends' and his enemies', and felt the Walther throw him into the crate behind him every time an enemy poked his nose out of that aisle. He hit nothing but crates, and occasionally the floor, but the enemy behind that corner could not stay long enough to take aim.

"Now!" came Charlie's voice over the wire.

John wanted to ask, "Now what?" But Frank was already nudging him to follow Seal to the left.

Frank followed, facing backward. Jay moved in front and to the right of John, firing into the aisle until they cleared it. They sprinted then, firing behind them occasionally, following the constant stream of Seal's gun. He stopped firing as they flew around a corner and there in front of them sat a single, narrow crate. They were at its empty face. On the left-hand face, John saw fingers.

He took a step toward the fingers. Seal yanked him back and pushed him to the right side of the crate. John saw a rifle barrel extending over his head from the top of a taller crate. A dark head moved behind it. John raised the Walther. Seal slapped his hand.

"No, stupid. That's Charlie."

Charlie fired and they cut. There was a lot of rope, much of it tied in independent knots. John had an ankle. Seal cut the rope around the wrist above him. There was a burst of submachine gun fire from behind them. John heard the boom of Charlie's answer. Another burst came from their left. John was almost through. The knife slipped in his hand, and he realized his hand was wet. He gripped it tighter and cut the last strand. Her foot moved back immediately. Seal's knife fell on the floor by his knees and the wetness was everywhere. Seal leaned on him, and John struggled to shrug him off. He knelt high on his knees and finished cutting the last few strands around her wrist.

She was beside him in the next instant, cradling Seal's lifeless head in her hands. She kissed his forehead and picked up the MP5 at his side.

Charlie, Frank, and Jay were already there. Charlie handed her three spare magazines. She put them in the belt under her blouse and slipped the wire he gave her into her ear.

"Jay and I are going to the safe. You take them out."

She nodded.

They met Mack on the way. He took over from her as point.

They stumbled onto the backs of at least seven men firing into a cubicle formed by eight-foot safes. Mara and Mack shot most of them in the back. Only one or two had time to turn around. Inside the cubicle, they found Louis, smiling. He sat in a snug corner under an iron shelf. John could feel the heat from his gun. Mack moved his wire and spoke into Mara's ear. She nodded and left the cubicle, pulling John behind her. They ran for a green exit sign.

Outside was just that. It was outside. Glorious, sunny, blinding, hot, free, safe. John ran beside Mara. He could still hear gunfire coming from the building beside them. They ran to the RV. Once inside, he wanted to kiss her, to celebrate. He wanted to shout and whoop and beat his chest. He was not only alive; he wasn't even hurt. She climbed into the cab before he could catch her, started the engine, and set them on a course careening toward the front of the building. He fell against the table as they turned. She shouted at him to put the table away.

"Make it into a bed," she said.

"A what? Oh." He folded up the table and pulled out the seats, making one seamless single bed.

They skidded to a stop. She set the brake but left the engine running.

"Get your bag," she said as she threw open the door.

He brought both eyebrows together in a 'v' over his nose.

"Louis is hit," she explained. "Louis is hit bad."

And the euphoria was gone. He could barely move his arm to pick up the bag. Seal was gone. John looked down at the shirt he wore. He only met these guys a few days ago and they felt like an anvil in his stomach. Mack came through the door, supporting Louis behind him. Frank pushed from behind. They put the Frenchman diagonally on the bed because it was too short for him.

John tried to pull Louis's black shirt away from the wounds in his side. He could see the entry holes in the wet fabric, black and red. Louis grabbed his wrist with incredible strength, said "No," soundlessly, and looked at him with an expression that reminded John of a patient he once had as an intern.

She had been a middle-aged woman, terminal with cancer, who would not let the nurse insert a catheter for a test he'd ordered. "You're not touching me," she said to him when he tried. He called in two orderlies to restrain her while the nurse did her job. The memory made John close his eyes in shame.

He opened them again when Mara touched his sleeve. She held the box of morphine vials. He drew up the dose. Louis let him administer that.

Charlie and Jay both fell through the door, Charlie wheezing, Jay bleeding. Jay held to his chest a flat packet, the size of a patient's chart, in a zippered black plastic pouch.

Mack took the pouch from Jay and waited while Charlie lay on the floor, finding breath. "Where is Steve?"

Charlie shook his head. He didn't know.

"Sergei?"

"Reminiscing with Maximovich." Jay pushed his back up against the seat. He pressed his right thigh and blood seeped through his fingers. John brought his bag over. It was a jagged wound, deep and bloody, but major vessels and bones were not involved. John pulled out a splinter of wood, cleaned the wound, and began stitching.

Jay made him stop and crawled to the open door. John followed him, protesting. Frank said, "Shhh!"

Charlie picked up his rifle and used it to help himself up. He pulled the curtains off the window next to the RV door, opened the louvered glass, and used the barrel to break through the screen on the outside. The entire screen came off in one piece and clattered to the ground.

The attraction was a silent, rolling battle that poured out from the loading door at the front of the warehouse, off the loading ramp, and onto the broken cement in front of them. Sergei and his friend Volodya were locked together in a mutual determination to annihilate each other. Maximovich's face and neck glowed red, glistening with sweat. Veins and muscles bulged in Sergei's neck as he held Maximovich's wrist and tried to twist the gun out of his hand. They each scrambled for a foothold, first Maximovich on the bottom, then Sergei. Sergei's left hand remained locked on that wrist, but his right sought an opening, any opening, in which to do damage.

Mack looked at Charlie, who shook his head. No clear shot.

Sergei found his opening. Maximovich's gun fell out of his hand as he flew backward into the raised loading dock. Sergei landed a kick to the chest and Maximovich's back hit the concrete with a thwack. He fell, sitting up. Sergei held a knife to his throat. They could see only half of Maximovich's face and in that half, defeat.

Sergei paused, then turned and put the knife away, laughing, and began walking the seven remaining meters to the RV.

Maximovich began to move.

"No!" whispered Mara.

"I can't get him. Sergei's in the way," said Charlie.

Volodya stretched himself to the right, grabbed the gun, staggered to a stand, and pointed it at Sergei's back.

They heard a single shot.

Sergei turned; Volodya fell. Steve stood swaying in the doorway on one leg and lowered his Beretta.

"Pavlenko, you son of a bitch, there was no fucking catwalk in my corner. Get your stupid ass over here and help me."

...

The RV rolled away from the warehouse twelve minutes after Charlie first picked the lock.

THIRTY-EIGHT

A twelve-year-old single malt scotch made the rounds and Mara was grateful for it. She sat on the floor by Louis's bed, holding his hand as he slept. She did not sip the amber liquid in the white Styrofoam cup, she drank it in hungry gulps. One, two, and it was gone.

The RV took a sharp turn in the road, rolling Louis on his side. He groaned in his sleep. He was not gone, but he was going. Mara watched the doctor's face as he inspected the neat, round holes in Louis's side, where the soft body armor did not meet. John's lips were pressed together. They became seamless as he took the pulse. He gazed at the skin. It had a yellow tinge. He looked under an eyelid, then turned away quickly without looking her in the eye. She began to cry, silently, allowing only a few tears at a time.

Misha was on the computer arranging their egress. He called their pilots on the satellite link up and told them to bring the jet to an airfield in Mexico.

John sewed up Jay's leg as the FBI man made frantic phone calls on the cellular, cashing in chips, he told one person. He was beginning to sound like Frank.

John sounded like Steve. He called Mara away from Louis to assist because these scissors were fucking useless, that needle was a piece of shit. Jay covered the phone with one large hand and pleaded with her with his eyes: come and help this doctor before these people hang up on me. She helped and John was quiet, but still ruthlessly exacting. She gave up the idea of having him look at her back whenever the dust might settle. Jay gasped more than once, despite the local anesthetic, but of course, the stitches in his leg were flawless.

Setting Steve's broken leg was a wrestling match and a profanity contest. Mara had no idea that so many of Seal's words could be strung together so artfully, the same word used as noun, verb, adjective, and adverb in the same sentence. John held his own in the word battle and managed to hit Steve twice physically, in the stomach and chest, for fucking interfering with fucking medical treatment, he screamed, as Sergei held Steve's arms and shoulders to prevent the reply. Mara wondered if the word was used here first as a helping or linking verb, or was it a gerund? She decided it was a participle modifying the gerund 'interfering'. And the second was certainly an adjective.

Misha had a ricochet round in his arm. He told John to go away.

John approached Michael cautiously. Mara's brother sat on the floor with his back against the refrigerator and his feet stretched out before him. His lips were blue, and he breathed in short, noisy gasps. He held his rifle across his lap. Dried blood caked his fingernails.

It is as difficult to see a loved one through a stranger's eyes as it is to look in the mirror and pretend you see someone else. A magic mirror might tell a few truths, but these are hard to come by. Michael was revealed to Mara through the change in John's eyes. Two days before, the doctor had been careless, confident, and even impudent with everyone he met. Now, he showed more respect around Misha, a thing remarkable only because it took him so long to catch on. But with Michael, he was more than respectful; he was careful.

The stitches in Michael's chest had torn out and three ribs were broken. The soft body armor had taken six rounds. The lung repair held, though, and Michael found it easier to breathe once the ribs were bound.

Mara sat next to her brother and handed bandages to the doctor until every movement of every finger required every last effort from her. She slumped against Michael's undamaged side and laid her head against his shoulder, staring at John without seeing him, seeing only the ridiculous shirt that tented him in green, yellow, apricot, and azure, like a painter's smock, a painter more than normally clumsy. The shirt reminded her that Seal was gone, and the tears began again, more noisily than before because she did not have the strength to control anything. Nor did she have energy for a full deluge, so when Michael put his arm around her shoulder, she took the comfort offered and promptly fell asleep with him, blocking the aisle with two bodies no one dared disturb.

She did not sleep long. Her back was on fire, a fire hotter than the one that had burned it, and every bump in the road moved the floor, refrigerator, her brother, her body armor, the bandages, in a chain reaction that scraped each wound, deep or shallow, adding friction to the flames.

Michael was sick beside her, and it triggered the same response in her. She dabbed at the mess on her skirt until it occurred to her to just take the thing off. She had put on a pair of jeans under the skirt as soon as she climbed into the RV because Maximovich had cut away her underwear. The skirt was redundant.

She thought she was doing all of this gracefully, but it woke Michael and attracted John and Sergei. She said no, but they made her let the doctor look at her back. He dabbed something cool on it and stuck in a needle and everything felt better. She fell asleep again.

The RV was slowing down when Mara woke the second time. She stood up and leaned on the computer. Jay had opened the black curtain behind the cab and was standing behind it, steadying himself at the comm bank. Mara read the sign as they entered a place called Hondo. "This is God's Country," said the sign. "Please don't drive through it like hell." They drove through this piece of Texas heaven, past a golf course, and onto an airfield. Jay directed Frank to a metal hangar where two men were sliding the doors open. Frank drove inside, and the doors squealed as they closed after them.

Nothing now was good, right, or pleasant. Everybody bumped, groaned, and swore, at life, at each other, at themselves. There was an argument Mara did not even try to understand. She was disgusted. There was nothing to look forward to. The flight home, the cool mountains, a hot bath, were all too far away to appeal or to lessen the prospect of the burning in her back at every next moment. Yet that was not the worst of it. Her heart had been dipped in hot lead and as it cooled it dropped, gaining mass and weight until she thought she could never carry it all. Seal was forever gone. Louis was going. And Sergei?

Sergei was talking to Misha.

Misha said something to John and John led her by the arm out of the RV. She needed a walk, he told her.

They strolled around the hangar looking at antique airplanes without seeing them. She saw Sergei and Misha step out of the RV and around to the other side, out of her sight.

John stopped by an airplane engine on a maintenance stand. Oil dripped into a bucket on the floor. Mara stuck her finger in the oil drip absently.

"I ..." said John.

She looked at him and waited. Her tears had streaked the dirt into striped rivulets down her face. There was blood and now oil on her powder blue knit blouse.

John wanted her more than ever, but she did not see his longing through the multicolored hues of his face. She did not see much of anything through the litany of names that sang the grief in her soul, Seal, Louis, Sergei.

She was unprepared when he took a deep breath and said, "Will you marry me?"

"Oh, John, you flatter me too much." *Was he blind?*

"That means no."

Was there a hint of relief there?

"But what would you do with me?" she said. "Think, John. Where would you put me? Imagine me as a doctor's wife. It should make you shudder. What will happen to your career if Mrs. Fleabottom insults the color of my shoes at a coffee morning? Think of the scandal. Surgeon's wife purees boss's wife. I won't have my shoes insulted, you know."

She grinned. She meant to cheer him, and such a smile would have improved any moment but this one. But she had added to his share of lead weight and could not help him carry it.

He looked away. She wiped an oily finger on her jeans.

"There is one other thing. Mack asked me to ask you," he said awkwardly, "to offer you medical help if... if there is damage...." He did not look at her.

"I'm sorry, John. I am sure Misha did not mean to put you in such a position. Please don't turn so red." She put her hand on his shoulder, smearing grease on Seal's shirt, and looked him directly in the eyes. "I am all right. You can tell Misha. Maximovich was about to, but he saw Sergei's ring." She held up the ring on her right hand. "He knew he did not have much time and he was smart enough to use every moment. He was very, very good, and would have succeeded if it weren't for you and the others, John. I owe you a great debt."

"What will you do?" he croaked. "Will you join the team?"

"I am on the team. But I will try to stay home at times like a good girl. Maybe I can make myself useful in the computer room."

She turned to the engine again, played with new oil on her fingertips. "Some victories are too expensive. Some victories are shams, deceits, chimeras that dissolve when you try to celebrate them." She looked at John, not noticing the tears that threatened his eyes because he was so good at stopping them.

"Misha is hard and sour and dutiful and dangerous," she said. "But he is also right. My mother says that is the most infuriating thing about him. I agree. He says—he lectures me—that life is not always arranged the way we want it, that selflessness takes many forms, that boring old caution, like wearing your gun when you'd rather pretend you don't need it, or wearing full body armor even though it's heavy, or staying home when that's not very exciting, sometimes takes the highest courage, is the greatest sacrifice we can make for people who love us. I wish my father had made it. I wish Louis had made it. I will go home and try to behave myself."

John looked around the hangar, fighting the stupid tears. She saw them now, at the corners of his eyes. Jay and Frank counted money from a suitcase onto a small table, and the man selling his airplane counted it again.

The shot was not very loud, but it echoed in the metal building. Mara did not have John's control. Her tears fell immediately. The lead in her heart gathered mass, at least nine millimeters more, and her heart sank under the weight. She ran to the RV. John followed her, trying to reach her arm, tugging at her shirt, babbling something about waiting. They rounded the far corner of the vehicle together.

Misha held his SIG at his side, and there was a new hole in a trash can near him. Sergei stood next to him. Mara threw her arms around Sergei and laughed and cried.

"He requested that I shoot him," said Misha. He shrugged and reholstered the SIG. "I missed."

Mara flung herself around Misha's neck, laughing with more tears and kissing his cheek. He smiled an almost smile and returned her hug.

"The bad guy is not supposed to get the girl," John said to Misha.

"I told you before, Doctor, this is not television."

EPILOGUE

Janine Fairfax tapped her finger impatiently on her breakfast plate. "When do you suppose he will come downstairs?" she asked the newspaper across the table.

"Hmmm?" Her husband Jack put down one side of his paper. "Who is that, dear?"

"John. Our son. He has been asleep for three days now. And that eye! Are you sure he is all right? Could he have a brain concussion?" She pushed a wiry red curl away from her eyes. Another took its place.

"He is all right." John Fairfax, Senior, returned to his newspaper.

"But he does not talk about where he has been." She stared at the paper. There was no response. She picked up the mail beside the butter and began leafing through it. She found a letter with no return addressed to her husband. It was postmarked Chicago. She opened it, curious.

Dear John,

We landed safely in Mexico. Louis requested a priest and was given the sacrament before we took off. He passed away peacefully in our jet on the way home. Before he died, he asked me to tell you he was sorry he hit you. He was anxious for your forgiveness. He also wanted me to thank you. You are the first man of peace he ever met, he said, who truly behaved as a man.

We are healing quickly and send you our deepest gratitude and best wishes.

With great fondness,
Mara
P.S. Please remember how deadly a piece of paper can be.

Janine's brow was still furrowed over this puzzle when her son plopped into the seat beside her. "Who is Mara?" she asked.

He took the letter from her hand and read it quickly. She watched his face change colors beneath the yellow tint that surrounded one eye. He stood and walked to the kitchen stove, lit one gas burner, and set the letter on fire.

"What are you doing?" she asked.

Her husband put down the newspaper to watch as their son dropped the charred corner of the page into a pot of cold oatmeal. He left it there. He inspected the coffee pot, poured some old coffee into a dirty cup out of the sink, and sat down at the table. He wore the most horrible shirt Janine had ever seen. It was not only horrible, it was filthy, smelled to high heaven, and she was sure that some of the red-brown stains on it were blood. This did not particularly distress her as the wife and mother of surgeons, but she wished he would wash and shave. He stank.

"I'm glad to see you have emerged," she said. "Is Mara a girlfriend? Someone important?"

He did not answer.

She had another way to get a response.

"Clarissa Sonsten is coming over this afternoon. Mary Beth is in town, and I invited them both. You remember Clarissa's daughter, don't you? The pretty girl you took to the senior prom. She is a very successful lawyer now." She stopped when she saw him close his eyes and wince.

"Why do you keep trying to pair me up with women who are nothing like you, Mama? They all come off an assembly line. Suitable for doctor's wives. Conventional, rational, and above all, polite."

"She's a pretty girl, John."

"Yes. But what would she do if Mrs. Fleabottom insulted her shoes?"

"Who is Mrs. Fleabottom?"

His father put the paper down again to look at him. "We want grandchildren, John."

"Yes, Dad."

"Will you please make yourself presentable for the Sonstens, *mon cher*?

"Yes, Mama."

His father raised an eyebrow and squinted at the same time, a difficult maneuver for other faces, but not for one trained to freeze scrub nurses with a single glance over a mask.

"What makes you suddenly so agreeable, son?"

John shrugged. "I guess if I need somebody to plead for me, it may as well be a lawyer." He drained his cup and stood. On his way through the dining room, he suddenly leapt into the air, swinging his foot in a high arc and upsetting the lamp on the buffet.

"What are you doing?" Janine cried.

"Just wondering," he said, "if Mary Beth Sonsten can do a tornado kick."

The End

VORY

A Year Later

Vory (Воры)
Russian thieves under the law 307

PROLOGUE

He found her. It had taken him almost ten years, but he had her where she belonged—in his sights.

They were careful to maintain a distance after his father's murder. So careful. And she changed colleges, with no word where. She seemed to drop out of sight, but he knew better. This had the marks of protection. From what? From his father's murderer? No. It had to be from him. From his revenge.

He printed the address, placed it in his planner, called his travel agent, and booked a flight to Florida.

The airplane was crowded, a regional jet out of Atlanta. He sat next to a blond man around his own age, who was packing. It took a practiced eye to know the cut of a sports coat meant to conceal. David Bertram knew because he, too, was armed. He studied the man carefully, in small glances, a snapshot at a time. First the eyes: blue. Scars on the left hand, some of them significant.

He wondered what the man could be. Not *vor*, he decided, not a thief under the code. The man had a Slavic hint about him, but no tattoos. There was a federal prison in Fort Walton Beach. Maybe he was connected to that. David rejected the idea. The coat had cost a pretty penny, too expensive for a civil servant of any kind. David should know. He was the son of a civil servant. A murdered civil servant.

It was the murder that had changed his life. He was seventeen when Nick approached him at the funeral. He became like a father figure, urging him to transfer to MIT, and helping him apply for financial aid from a number of organizations David had never heard of. He never would have been able to manage it otherwise, especially without his dad.

Nick guided him through his graduate work and encouraged him to take his present job working in cyber security for a firm based in Eastern Europe. It meant he traveled enough to know a European coat when he saw it sitting next to him, but the guy spoke American English to the flight attendant. A diplomat maybe? Going to Fort Walton Beach? Maybe the guy was Canadian. David listened for clues, like the use of eh, or his pronunciation of the diphthong 'ou.' He heard nothing, but then, the only languages he had any real facility with were computer languages.

It had been a year now since Nick told David what he discovered about his father's murder, about how Dad's boss had been involved, and not only him but his wife and daughter as well.

David started the search then, once the dust settled after the fracas down in San Antonio that had his office scrambling to protect the company's servers from being crippled by exploits. He scoured the World Wide Web for any information he could find on those three people and found nothing at all, though recently he thought he had them up north, but the lead turned up empty. It was as if they pleaded guilty to his father's murder. Innocent people do not hide, decided David. The Vilsecks were a large family, but most of them seemed estranged from the three he sought. The three murderers.

And now he had her, the bitch. Now he had her. He had long dreamt of fucking her. Now he dreamt of making the experience even more memorable. He would fuck her, and then he would fuck her over.

...

David saw one of Nick's men at the baggage carousel. He was careful not to let on that he recognized him. Nick was lending him one of his teams to assist David on this operation. As a vory associate he had been trained for it, but this would be his first actual use of those skills. He was truly grateful to his mentor for any help he could get but wondered how difficult it could be to kill one old man and two women.

As he stood next to the blond man from the airplane, David spotted his suitcase on the carousel. He set down his briefcase to take half a step forward and grab the bag when a commotion began not twenty feet from them. The blond man remained very still, unimpressed by the hysteria, but David could not help being curious. He squeezed into the crowd and moved toward what seemed to be the center of everybody's attention.

Nick's man lay on the floor, his eyes staring upward, unseeing. David did not see any blood, but he knew death when he saw it. He pushed his way out of the crowd, saw the blond man leaving with just one suitcase, found his own, and looked for his briefcase.

An hour later, after the police interviewed everyone who had been near the scene at the time of the death, after the EMTs took Nick's man out on a wheeled stretcher with a blanket over his face, after David had made a pest of himself at the baggage office, then again at the airline counter, and finally at lost and found, he was handed his briefcase, still locked. They asked him to open it and inspect the contents before signing for its return. Everything was in place.

He called Nick from the safehouse.

ONE

Theresa Vilseck turned the lock on her apartment door and noted with satisfaction as her alarms, a hair and a speck of paper, fluttered to the floor. Daddy had taught her well. She threw her keys onto a little table next to the door, kicked off her shoes, and took a long stride into the living room.

"Hello, Theresa."

She spun around. "Charlie..." But he was already upon her, wrapping his arms around her and parting her lips with his tongue. His hands migrated to her bottom, pressing her to him, to a rapidly rising erection that she could feel like a beacon of need. She responded instinctively, as she had when she was eighteen. Her bra strap presented no obstacle to him. She noted other things that spoke of the experience he must have gained in nine years, like the command of his kiss, the tweaking of her nipple, the thigh pressing between her legs, and she wondered if the men she had known in that time had changed her also and, above all, if he would notice.

He broke off the kiss, but kept his hands where they were, searched her eyes, and said, "How many?"

"Two," she lied. If pressed, she would mention her least favorites. He was a dangerous man, no doubt even more dangerous than he had been then, and she did not want her former lovers molested.

He regarded her with alarming stillness, and she remembered what could happen when he became so motionless.

"And now?"

"No one."

This, at least, was the truth. Nobody could match Charlie, let alone excel him. Her father looked on their liaison back then as a tragedy in his life, a despoiling of his youngest daughter. She considered herself spoiled, not despoiled by what remained the greatest joy of her life so far, forever making her unable to accept a mediocre relationship. Charlie had never been far from her thoughts—and desires.

He resumed the kiss and swept one arm under her legs, lifting her without breaking it off. He carried her into the bedroom, laid her on her bed, and stripped off the barriers presented by her clothing, piece by piece, all while pressing into her mouth with his tongue. She had no opportunity to object, her mouth being fully engaged, and by the time there was a break in the proceedings, other parts of her were fully involved. With one long kiss, he filled all the empty spaces left by an almost nine-year absence, and was still the most exciting thing ever to happen in her life. If anything, his appeal had only sharpened.

When he entered her, he was not as gentle and patient as he had been when she was a virgin. He was insistent and pounding and she gloried in his power.

They lay side by side and were barely finished gasping when he said, "You know, I've been paying attention. I count four significant relationships and one possible affair with a professor. Which two names were you going to give me?"

It took her several seconds to form a reply. "You're as scary as your father."

"I have been told I'm scarier. Which two?"

"What about you?"

He took a moment. "There was a brief infatuation last year. It ended when she tried to kill me."

"That would do it for me, too."

"So, names?"

"Her name?"

"It would do you no good. She's dead."

She had no reply for this.

"And no, I didn't kill her," he said.

"I wasn't...."

"Yes, you were. But we don't have time. Get dressed and pack a bag. We are leaving now."

...

Leo and Maryann could not see the approaches to the house or even its facade. Blindfolded before they deplaned, exhausted and still terrorized by the spray of semi-automatic gunfire across the back of the house they had been renting in the North Country of New York, they were unaware of the time and ignorant of the place where unseen hands helped them climb down the steps. The jet had picked them up at midnight from a small, secluded airfield in Quebec and made one refueling stop in Reykjavik, where they were told not to go outside, not even to stretch their legs. The shades at the windows stayed down the whole flight.

After a short ride on the ground, they knew they had been led inside when a door closed behind them. Blindfolds off, the light of an overhead chandelier made them blink until they could see a large hallway with a parqueted floor at their feet. A wide staircase before them swept upward and to the left. A small woman in her early forties smiled at them through sad eyes. Not exactly a beauty, the woman's brown curls were lightly sprinkled with gray at the fringes of her face, adding a soft attractiveness to her appearance.

"Hello Alex," said Leo. It's been a long time."

"I hope you don't mind if I use your game name, Frank," she said. "It is the one I've always known you by and this being a serious play of the game, I think it appropriate that we remind ourselves of the fact."

She turned to Maryann. "How do you do? Call me Alex. You and I, at least, are allowed our own names. I know you're exhausted, but I must beg you to meet with my husband. You know him as Mack. Once that ordeal is over," she said with a confidential twinkle in her eye, "we can leave Frank behind in the office to talk strategy. I'll take you to your apartment for food and rest. Is that agreeable?"

Maryann nodded dumbly. She had seen the man named Mack slap a woman twice, years before. It happened in her kitchen while she made lunch. She croaked out the most important thing on her mind, having nothing to do with the woman in her kitchen, and everything to do with the chief concern of her life, the safety of her daughter.

"Theresa...," she said in a voice half whisper, half plea.

Alex nodded. "She is the topic foremost in everyone's mind right now. Don't worry. Come with me."

She led them up two flights of curling staircase and along a wide, empty hallway, its sole decoration a narrow carpet with an intricate pattern. After going through a series of locked doors, Maryann recognized the brilliant blue eyes of the man behind the desk. She was invited to sit but would rather run—out this door and all the others that led them to this office. She wondered if they had landed from bad to worse. Leo usually knew what he was doing and she would have to trust him, but what she knew of the man behind the desk made her acutely conscious of his dangerous power.

"Will you be coming with us, Frank?" asked Mack after acknowledging Maryann with a minimal nod.

Frank said yes, of course. Nothing would keep him from being present to protect his daughter—alone if necessary. Mack's question, suggested he would not be alone. Nine years before, it had been a revelation to Maryann when she learned what her husband had been doing all his career. The name was Charlemagne, not a dead monarch but a team of the most competent and deadly operatives in the business. It should make her optimistic to have such allies, but if Mack thought the team's involvement necessary, more danger stalked their daughter than they realized. Frank blanched, his shiny scalp turning white and his eyes bulging even further from their sockets. Maryann moved closer and touched the sleeve of his coat.

"I retired last year when you sent word that David was looking for us," Frank said. "My successor in The Section is Skosh. You met him during the op at my house. He is very able, but I want to participate."

"Naturally. We will take you with us when we leave for Fort Walton Beach in two hours."

"Fort Walton? In Florida?" said Maryann. "That's where Theresa is. She's a surgical resident there, at the Air Force base. We picked public fights with the rest of the family and tried to make it look like our youngest was with us in New York." She rubbed under one tired eye and noticed with dismay the mascara on her finger. "I'm so worried."

"Would you like to contribute to this operation?" Alex asked her.

"Of course, I would."

"Do you think you can run a household that you do not know, listen to and obey our security experts, and care for the staff and our dependents while we're away?"

Mack gave his wife a sharp look. "I have not decided this."

"But surely this is part of the calculation?" said Alex.

Was her manner just a touch too sweet? Would such a man respond to it? Alex added a coy smile. *Frank would never fall for that.*

"Maryann has seven children and four grandchildren," said Alex. "She is experienced and knows how to run a household. We can trust her in Vasily's Carpet. And she speaks German."

"We will discuss this later," said Mack, hissing between his teeth.

"I'm sure we will." She turned to Maryann. "Let me ask again. Are you willing to run the house for me?"

"I am." Maryann kept her answer short and definite. She knew there was an argument going on, that she was instinctively on Alex's side, and that the least said gave Alex the most leverage. Besides knowing how to manage a household, Maryann was also adept at managing a husband. She left Alex to it.

TWO

"Will Alex come with us, then?" asked Frank as the women left the office.

By way of reply, he was treated to the cold blue stare he had known so well for almost thirty years. Mack's hair had turned a bit gray, especially at the temples, but this glare remained undiminished in its power to intimidate.

Frank raised his hands, "I know, I know. It is not my business." He resisted the urge to mimic Mack's Austrian accent. Something else must be at stake here, he knew, or no discussion on such a topic would be taking place. Alex did not leave home often. Did the word 'dependents' mean children? The question gave him an intelligence itch. Did Mack and Alex have more children?

Mack brought out maps of Fort Walton Beach, Eglin Air Force Base, and several of its auxiliary fields, most notably Hurlburt Field.

"The team brought the jet into North America to pick you up," he said. "They are in Florida now. We need you to contact Skosh to arrange a reason for us to be there. It will be after the fact, but we do not want complications with authorities. Jay Turner suggests the Special Operations School here." He pointed to a spot at the western end of the city, just north of the Santa Rosa Sound. "Perhaps one of us could be invited to give a lecture there. Jay says he does not have the necessary connections to arrange it."

"In front of an entire auditorium?" asked Frank, eyebrows raised high. He knew that auditorium, secure only up to top secret, but rarely used to that level, mainly because information with a classification that high did not tend to be shared with so many people at a time. The room was large enough to make the members of Charlemagne far too well known, and they had been there before. It was long ago, but they were memorable.

"Sergei is already known to the vory," said Mack, reading his mind as usual. "They are the enemy in this operation, so there would be no harm done if they were to notice him. We think they do not know his current association with us."

Frank's blood froze, his bulging, bloodshot eyes wide open. "The vory? I thought maybe it was Bertram, David Bertram, I mean." He heard himself beginning to babble.

"It is Bertram. He has become a vory associate and bears the white and black tattoo. His sponsor is Nikolai Beridze, a thief under the code, now working with Russian intelligence. David has his own team, but it is untested. Beridze has given him another, more experienced team in support. We presume he will be supervising his protégé."

Mack looked at Frank's face and wondered why the man's bulbous eyes did not dry up. They bulged further than usual with this news and were unrefreshed by blinking. He debated snapping his fingers to bring Frank back to the task at hand.

"You will be able to call Skosh from the airplane."

"Yes, yes, of course," said Frank with a shiver.

They traced the possible routes between Hurlburt Field, the hospital at Eglin where Theresa worked, her apartment, and three safehouse sites that Jay Turner, their FBI contact, proposed. Mack produced topographical maps of the area, ordinance surveys, reconnaissance photos, and street-level photos. Lack of sleep interfered with Frank's ability to see fine details through his streaming eyes. He did get the overall picture of way too much highly classified photo intelligence spread across a desk in a place he was sure could not be in the United States. Mack knew how to gather intel; he had to give him that. He stifled a yawn.

"You will want to repack your suitcase now and say farewell to Maryann," said Mack. "We will leave presently and discuss this further after you have slept awhile on the airplane." He pulled a bell cord, producing a butler at the door almost immediately, followed closely by Alex.

Their argument began before the door fully closed behind him, but Frank heard very little of it. Once closed, the thick security door emitted no sound.

He hated to wake Maryann, but could not find his suitcase. She lay nestled in an enormous, canopied bed surrounded by the opulence of a palace.

"It doesn't matter," she said with a yawn. "I would have been angry if you left without letting me say goodbye."

She opened a wardrobe where all his clothes had been organized—by a servant, she said, eyebrows raised to her hairline. Servants had never been part of their experience. They found his suitcase in a closet on one side of the bathroom.

Maryann packed for him, as she had for the past forty years, and they held each other while they waited for whoever would be sent to fetch him. A single knock alerted them. They separated as a servant opened the door and Alex walked in.

"I'm afraid I must move you, Maryann," she said.

"You convinced him then?" said Frank.

She smiled, again with a twinkle. How did her eyes do that? "Of course. Or maybe I just wore him down. Come, Maryann, I'll take you to Vasily's Carpet, explain some of the procedures, and introduce you to the interior staff. There are only three. It's excellent that you speak German. You won't be at a disadvantage."

The two women fast outdistanced Frank, talking as they took a path through the mansion that soon diverged from the one taken by the footman carrying his case. He had been made to understand he should follow the suitcase.

He climbed into an armored limousine and sat across from Mack. Incredible wealth, servants, luxury, and a very angry Mack, eyes narrow and jaw set, as they waited for the wife who had bested him in a private argument and was now late. Frank commiserated silently.

There was a quiet but sharp exchange of words in Russian as Alex sat next to her husband. Frank's Russian was rusty. He had not used the language in over a decade and had difficulty piercing the odd mixture of aristocratic and Chicago accents enough to understand entirely, but he got the distinct impression they were discussing Mack's son, Michael, who operated under the game name Charlie. Frank considered the only intelligent thing Steve Donovan's ex-wife ever said was her description of Charlie as 'son of Satan'.

The operation was shaping up like all the others: danger, uncertainty, and disagreeable associates, but this time, Frank had a personal stake in the outcome.

THREE

"Dad!" Theresa ran into the arms of the bald man with bulging eyes who stood up when she came into the safehouse. "Where is mom?"

"Safe."

"What do you mean? Why aren't you in New York?" She looked past him as they each stepped back from their hug. Jay Turner, the FBI agent, stood there with a considerable amount of premature gray in his black hair, also Steve Donovan, but no sign of his wife Sally, thank heaven. A man and woman she did not recognize stood close by, and finally Satan himself, Mack. He was the older blond, blue-eyed killer with a talent for stillness, she remembered, and the father of the younger one of that description who held her heart.

"Where is Louis?" she asked.

Silence and dropped glances answered her.

"When?"

"Last year," said her father.

She had only a moment to register her internal regret before Charlie introduced Mara and Sergei Pavlenko, new members of the team. She looked at the young blonde woman before her and again at Charlie. "You are related," she said.

"Mara is my sister."

"And you're on the team?" Theresa was not sure she liked the breaking of this particular glass ceiling. The woman did not look old enough to have graduated high school. Theresa would have assumed Mara acted as some sort of support staff but for the wicked-looking gun hanging in a holster at her hip. Sergei was older than his wife, about ten years at least, with light, almost colorless eyes, a Slavic brow, and a nose that had been badly set after a break or, Theresa suspected, several breaks. He had the same predatory gaze as the other men though, convincing her that the weapon in his shoulder holster also was not a decoration.

Mara smiled without answering. It was as if she knew the progression of thoughts in Theresa's mind. A family trait, along with the stillness in all of them.

Another woman entered the room from the galley kitchen to the right. She wore jeans, a tee shirt, and sneakers in a completely ordinary way, with a cloud of curly soft brown hair, light eyes, and a sparkling presence that was anything but ordinary.

"This is my stepmother, Alex," said Charlie.

A stepmother not much older than Charlie. And wife of Mack? Of course, she could not be ordinary, thought Theresa.

"I am so happy to meet you, Theresa," said Alex, taking and pressing her hand warmly. "Or should I say, Dr. Vilseck? Have you finished your training?"

"Please, call me Theresa. I am almost finished with a surgical residency, but I am fully qualified as a physician."

"Splendid. Come in and sit down. Would you like coffee?"

They gathered at a conference table in a back room of the house, devoid of windows and with steel double doors that had replaced a glass sliding door to the rear. The house was set back from the road on a narrow half-acre of land in an unincorporated section of Okaloosa County. Its keepers mowed all vegetation around it to no more than an inch high to deny hiding places to intruders. The result was essentially a sandlot with a few low patches of struggling Bermuda grass, bordered by decorative neighbors on either side who seemed more fond of vegetation.

Besides the windowless Florida room downstairs at the back where they gathered, the house offered three bedrooms upstairs and a combination living and dining room off the galley kitchen. Another heavily bolted steel back door led from there. The armored front door opened directly into the large living room dominated by a restaurant-sized coffee-making apparatus.

Theresa still did not know why she was there.

Jay Turner began proceedings. It was an FBI safehouse, so he was their host. Frank sniffed a bit with the superior air of a retired member of a sister service with a bigger budget. The unspoken consensus among those who enjoyed this hospitality was that the FBI had put its more limited budget to good use, dependably providing

the most important amenities. There were two full bathrooms upstairs and a half bath downstairs. And then there was the coffee.

Jay led with coffee instructions: if you finish a pot, make a pot,
to which the more experienced in the room added the silent caveat,
unless you are Mack or Charlie.

Theresa knew none of the subtext going on in people's heads
and would not have understood it if she did. She noticed that she
seemed to be the only person present who had slept the night before.
Baggy eyes and coffee jitters were the rule.

"We were unable to find a second suitable house for support
staff, so there are nine of us...," said Jay.

"Ten," said Frank, interrupting. "Skosh is on his way."

"What? We don't need another babysitter," said Jay. "And anyway, this is an FBI operation. It is domestic and involves counterintelligence and organized crime. Both lie fully in our wheelhouse."

"I am retired and have no authority to help you," said Frank.

"That's not the point."

"The point is," said a quietly sinister voice at the head of the table, "I make all operational decisions." Mack was leaning back with
his coat open. The spotless SIG Sauer gleamed in his shoulder holster, black against a no longer spotless white shirt. He had been
without any rest worthy of the name for more than twenty hours
now.

"You may resume your bureaucratic bickering when we are
dead or out of the country," he said. "Skosh and Jay will behave as a
team." He reinforced the finality of the statement with a pointed look
at Jay.

Theresa remembered Skosh, a hard man who had worked for
her father and was briefly responsible for her family's security when
she was eighteen.

Jay resumed a recitation of what he called administrative and
housekeeping details. "Women will use the master bedroom and its
en-suite bathroom. The men will have exclusive use of the other two
bedrooms and the main bath upstairs."

He had begun explaining the watch schedules when Skosh arrived.

Everybody took this disruption as an opportunity to refill their
coffee mugs. Theresa noticed that despite Jay's insistence minutes
before, absolutely nobody, including Jay, made coffee as the four pots

on their burners emptied steadily. All were depleted by the time she reached the machine. Remembering how essential coffee had been to her in medical school, she expected the need to only increase as she filled and restarted both halves of the machine with fully caffeinated coffee, giving the lie to the decaf label on one of them.

Silence reigned in the conference room as she returned, all of them watching the door, apparently waiting for her, judging by the impatience on several faces and the set jaws and glowering looks of Mack and Charlie. It occurred to her that no good deed could provide penance enough for the ultimate sin of keeping Mack waiting.

FOUR

"We lost touch long ago," said Theresa as the meeting resumed. "Surely David has his own life, like I do."

"David's life now lies with the vory," said Charlie. "Thieves under the code. I sat next to him on the flight he took in from Atlanta. He has the half-black, half-white finger ring tattoo of an associate. Nikolai Beridze sponsors him. One of Beridze's men was also on the flight. They did not acknowledge each other."

Theresa saw the others in the room raise their eyebrows at this. She wondered why they found it significant.

Steve took a passport and wallet from his jacket pocket and slid them across the table to Mack. "A made man and a real threat. Bertram was distressed at the death."

"Are you saying you took him out?" said Jay. "You made a bloody mess in a local airport terminal and didn't tell me?"

"At the baggage carousel, not in the main terminal," corrected Steve. "A new technique I learned recently. Very little blood. Relax. It gave Mara the opportunity she needed to get Bertram's briefcase, and it's one less tango we'll have to kill later."

Mack inspected the passport and wallet and gave them to Skosh, who looked through them and passed them on to Jay.

"I think it would be good if you and I met with the local constabulary," Skosh told Jay. "I mean, before more bodies turn up, that is. It's best to have a professional relationship already in place."

"Don't tell me my job."

Mack slapped the tabletop to stop them before they could start and turned to Mara. She brought out a sheaf of photos from an envelope Jay handed her. She gave an overview of the intelligence con-

tained in documents from Bertram's briefcase that she had pho-
tographed.

Theresa was still trying to work out the new technique that kills
with little blood and decided on three possibilities while contemplating the man with eyes like melting chocolate across from her. She
wondered where his silly wife and little boy might be now. Steve
Donovan returned her gaze with a mixture of threat and desire that
made her gulp and switch her attention quickly back to Mara. She
noticed Sergei register the entire silent communication. *Geez, these
people say nothing and everything with just their eyes.*

Mara's briefing had to do with a bug planted in the lining of
David's briefcase and the need to set up a rotation of listening duty
as the tape reels on a machine behind them began to turn. A shabby
credenza had been shoved against the wall and burdened with two
computers, a printer, and extensive listening and recording equipment. A separate communications station was set up on what looked
like an old half refrigerator turned on its side in a corner. The
perimeter sensors would sound alarms when breached. Mara
demonstrated the separate sounds of sensors at the front, back, and
each side of the property. Technology had changed since Theresa sat
in her living room wearing a headset to monitor these gadgets. The
professional sniping was the same, though.

Also, shoved against the walls of this room and the living room
were foot lockers in various sizes, containing weapons, accessories,
and the equipment needed to repair, maintain, and clean them.
Theresa knew enough to steer clear of these.

She was assigned to a watch like everyone else, always with
Mara, Mack, and Jay, and spent most of it on a headset once again,
this time listening to David as he spoke to one creep after another, all
of it in English because he knew only a few greetings in Russian.

At first, she felt dirty and sneaky and bored out of her increasingly exhausted skull. Then she heard David, in a drinking session
with members of his team, presumably taking in more than one bottle of vodka judging from the increasingly boisterous and profane
language, describing in lurid detail how he planned to fuck her over
when he caught her. It was not the initial description, which was bad
enough, but the advice he got from his companions that chilled her,
the enhancements to the terror, and finally, the way they spoke her
name.

She was a fully qualified physician for heaven's sake, a trained surgeon. She knew about filth and pain and body fluids and she retched over the floor of the conference room again and again until empty of lunch, breakfast, and every molecule of coffee anywhere in her alimentary tract.

Mara helped her up, handed the headset to Jay, took her upstairs, and woke her mother, Alex. Mack woke Frank in the other room, none too gently—out of policy. Alex and Frank tucked her in as Sergei injected a light sedative. She objected but was firmly overruled. Everybody went downstairs to listen to the tape as soon as she was asleep. They did not want her to hear it again.

FIVE

Mara switched off the tape in a deeply silent room. Frank was the first to speak. He looked at his hands then at Mack. "You son of a bitch. Why do you always have to be so fucking right?" His next target was Jay. "Not a word of 'I told you so' from you either, my friend. I will throttle you if you so much as hint it."

Questioning looks crossed the room as Frank hung his round head in his hands. Steve explained to those who had not been present in Frank's dining room nine years before.

"Theresa pleaded for David's life because he was her friend and only seventeen at the time. He had been his father's accomplice. More than that, he was the instigator of a murder. Misha and Jay argued for a commission on him as well as on his father."

"I should have killed him nine years ago without the commission," said Charlie with a slow blink of hindsight. "I wanted to."

"So let us do so now," said Sergei. "Together with his vory friends."

"We have to find them first."

"This may help," said Mara, who had donned the headphones. "Listen." She reversed the tape and switched to speaker. There was a two-second gap in the drunken revelry. She pinpointed the gap, slowed the tape, and played it again. They heard a deep rumbling drone.

"Air conditioner?" asked Jay.

Steve tilted his head forward. "No. It's an engine. Play it again, regular speed." Mara did so three times until he said, "It's a C-130."

There began a brainstorming game with Steve saying no to each suggestion. Not the airport, how stupid can you civilians get, Skosh? Not Eglin; it's not their mission. It has to be special ops. It has to be

Hurlburt Field. As this was digested silently, it was Mack who voiced the suspicion that rose in everybody's mind.

"They have an asset on the special ops base."

"Skosh," said Jay, "is there any progress on getting Pavlenko scheduled to lecture at that school? I appreciate that the invitation allowed us to let them in the country post hoc, but the lecture itself might be helpful."

"A new class started today. I can probably get him in tomorrow or Wednesday. What are we billing him as?"

"A KGB defector, of course. Just don't use his real name," suggested Frank.

"What are you suggesting as a substitute? Igor?" Skosh pronounced it eye-gore.

Frank gave him his roundest frog stare. "Don't take that tone with me, junior. I had to retire. You were the best man for the job, hands down. I couldn't stay forever."

"It's a fucking nightmare, old man. I'm losing all my Asian contacts and haven't had a decent plate of sushi in six months. I blame you for refusing to be immortal. My successor is Korean. How do I supervise him with any semblance of fairness? Tell me that. And I have no fucking idea what's going on in Argentina, nor do I care. You've ruined my life."

"I tire of babysitter squabbles," said Mack in his iciest voice.

"Geez, you scare the shit out of people when you stop moving like that, like an Okinawan habu snake about to strike. Fucking move once in a while. Please." Skosh tried to return Mack's stare until the man's lip turned up at one corner in a half smile making Skosh suppress an involuntary shiver. "Okay, that's worse," he said. "You've made your point. I'll arrange the lecture for tomorrow morning."

...

"I do not know what I am to say." Sergei fidgeted as Mara knotted his tie. "And I must give this speech in English. My English is excellent. I was always getting the compliment."

"No 'the' sweetie," said Mara, "and use the plural. You were always getting compliments."

"Yes, I was. And you have now, this minute, used 'the' with word 'plural'. I do not understand distinction. Also, why do you have such useless things, these articles? They give me the nightmares."

Mara kissed him and he took it as an invitation, extending and deepening the kiss until Frank cleared his throat at the bedroom door. Sergei and Steve checked their weapons again before leaving the safehouse. Jay and Skosh were also armed but not as nervous because they did not feel as exposed as two specialists out in the cold without the rest of their team.

...

It did not go well.

Skosh likened it to letting wild carnivors run free in a shopping mall. It simply should not be done. They were met by a colonel who wanted to know Sergei's name and the topic of his speech.

"Igor Stravinsky," said Skosh. "He'll speak on the historical role of the AK-47 in Soviet intelligence strategic planning."

The colonel nodded, made a note, and showed them to a room where they could wait until the time came to introduce the speaker.

"Igor Stravinsky?" said Jay and Sergei simultaneously.

"It's the only Russian name I know," said Skosh. "What the fuck was I supposed to say?"

"The role of the AK-47? Really?" This from Steve.

"Well, I could hardly say we're here to check out the lay of the land where we have good reason to believe that an asset of the Russian Federation is harboring two hostile specialist teams now, could I?"

They simmered into a low grumble. Nobody sat down. The specialists were decidedly edgy. Sergei paced. Steve unbuttoned his jacket and opened and closed his right hand. As an experienced babysitter, Skosh knew these two were feeling visible and at risk and were showing all the chaotic signs that Skosh's Asian team had displayed on a regular basis. He grew concerned.

It did not get any better. A young woman in a well-fitting uniform came to collect them from the waiting room and lead them to the wings of the stage. Steve gave her a lascivious smile and Sergei smacked him in the arm. They waited off stage while the colonel introduced Igor the KGB defector and Steve tried to talk to the woman in uniform. Jay pushed Sergei onto the stage where he was sure to feel perilously vulnerable in front of an audience of more than a hundred people he could not see because of the lighting. Skosh wondered who came up with this plan. Surely not Frank. Maybe Jay. Must be Jay. *He does not understand the psychology of these guys.*

"Get him the fuck off the stage," he said to Jay. "Now!"

But it was too late.

A voice came out of the crowd, screaming in Russian. Sergei unbuttoned his coat to reach his Makarov. As if connected to his partner by a wire, Steve's hand went to his Beretta. Jay and Skosh reached into their coats. The colonel hissed something about no weapons being allowed in the building. Skosh asked him why there was a Russian in the audience. Foreign exchange, said the colonel. Russians? In special ops? Terrorism, rejoined the colonel, everybody's problem and the wall is down, hadn't he heard?

Steve brought his Beretta fully out of its holster, and translated, roughly, that Sergei was being called a mother fucking traitor to his country. He was just off the stage and Sergei gestured that he should stay there. Sergei engaged his heckler in a shouted conversation in Russian, while Steve translated quietly in the wings.

Sergei invited the heckler onto the stage as he signaled his partner to put away his weapon. Steve merely dropped it to his side and turned so that it would not be visible. After getting the man's name and shaking his hand to check for tattoos, Sergei began a spirited discussion in not always accurate English on what it means to be patriotic, all of it prime bullshit, but the episode ended with a promise by the heckler to share vodka and herring and discuss the philosophical bases of true patriotism at an undetermined place and time in the future.

Sergei buttoned his coat as he left the stage. That he had unbuttoned it was not lost on any of the audience in the first two rows, or on the colonel.

"When did we start letting KGB defectors walk around armed?" he asked.

Skosh shrugged, "Around the time we invited Russian operatives to our special ops courses."

He helped Jay usher their charges out the back door. Steve holstered his Beretta and asked the young woman for her phone number. She responded with a terrified stare.

"Whose idea was this?" demanded Skosh.

"Mine," said Jay as he put the car in gear. "You have to admit it got us on base."

"Couldn't you just flash the magic badge you guys carry oh so proper?"

"That would get me and maybe you in, but they have to be invited, just like they had to be invited into the country."

They—the invitees—were busy checking behind them every few seconds. Another mannerism of wired specialists that Skosh knew enough to be alarmed about.

"Hey guys," said Jay, "as long as we're here, we'll ride around for a while and you can keep an eye out for anything you find interesting."

Given a task to do, the two in the backseat sobered up and calmed down but saw nothing of interest until the car skirted a vast cemented area of hangers, maintenance vans, and military police carrying M16s.

"There," said Steve. "Plenty of places in there. In the hangars."

"But that is a secure area," said Jay, citing the evidence of the M16s.

"Steve would know," said Sergei. "He was Air Force pilot."

So the trip was not a total loss after all.

SIX

Misha called a meeting as soon as the four men walked through the door. Alex was glad Theresa had recovered sufficiently to attend. She was not happy about the state of her husband. They had met on an operation, the details of which were etched in her memory. The man at the head of the table was not the Misha of home. She recognized instead the operational Mack of her darkest memory, at hazard, efficient, and ruthless. She was always a little afraid of him, but even more when he was like this.

She watched as he quashed another internecine quarrel between Jay and Skosh and then glared Frank into silence before he could come to Skosh's defense. Not five minutes later, Steve and Sergei made insolent remarks when Theresa complained about being the only person making coffee. All Alex could see was Misha's glance directed their way but it was enough. Both men apologized and looked away.

For her, the hardest thing of all, though, was that she had no time alone with him. They had not spoken above a dozen words in the past twelve hours. Each knew the other's purpose in being here, the two missions whose importance intertwined into an imperative that raised the stakes to almost unbearable levels. Both would use cunning and manipulation to achieve their aims, though she liked to think she would be less manipulative. She considered herself nonviolent, while Misha… well, not so much. Their goals required the success of Misha's violence before anything else could have any meaning, a fact she found difficult to reconcile.

They must survive the beginning to have a chance of survival in the end, he told her in his office—at volume and at length.

She agreed and thought she would never convince him about the reality of a thing called future. Then suddenly, he capitulated—without grace to be sure—and allowed her to join him on this trip. Present now in service to the future, Alex watched, listened, and allowed Theresa to make the coffee.

Skosh briefed them on their trip to Hurlburt Field. Alex felt for the man. He had been plucked from a happy job to a hellish one in the run-up to this op. Frank had no choice but to retire, cut all contacts, and disappear with Maryann when the intelligence on Bertram's activities came in almost a year before. Everything that could be done to hide Theresa had been done. It was more difficult for her because professional requirements required that she maintain her name.

"The colonel was not pleased," said Skosh in typical Japanese understatement. When all eyebrows around the table rose at this, he said with some exasperation, "For fuck's sake. They're all special ops. They knew damn well we were packing the minute Sergei put his hand in his coat."

"Especially when Steve drew his out of his holster," said Jay.

"Don't act so superior, Turner," said Steve. "You were ready to and you know it. Nobody could see me anyway."

"All special ops?" said Misha. "The Russian in the audience as well?"

Sergei nodded. "Spetsnaz. Or GRU."

If it were possible, and Alex did not think it was, Frank Cardova's eyes bulged even further than usual from his head. "A GRU—a military intelligence operative on a classified American military course?"

"That particular course is only rated up to Secret, and only in parts," said Jay.

"Only?"

Sergei smiled. "I told you last year when we went after Semianov's list of assets, that you should not be so sure you won the Cold War. When the wall came down, we sent you ever more vory, and now you invite even our technical specialists to your 'only' secret study courses."

"What do you mean ever more vory?" asked Skosh.

"We, I mean KGB, have been sending them at least since the early 1980s. Your immigration did not well distinguish between political and criminal prisoners. When they were released, you often accepted them. They are very patriotic—to Russia. They do as KGB tells them. They are experts at dirt and they live by pressure. They find dirt and exert pressure. Their pressure is for money. KGB's is for information and obedience. They work....," he lifted a hand and furled his fingers, looking toward his wife.

It was Steve who filled in the phrase, "Hand in glove."

"I have managed to neutralize one hundred thirty-six names on Semianov's list of more than two hundred," said Jay. "Are you suggesting there are more?"

"Not on Semianov's list," said Sergei. "But there are more lists."

"As long?"

He shrugged. "Some, perhaps, or longer. We were not the only directorate using the vory."

"Then why did we go after only one of these lists?"Jay said through his teeth.

"Because Semianov included information that would endanger Mara. I do not care what happens to you. I care what happens to Mara."

There could be no better explanation in those nearly colorless eyes.

The Americans in the room, among whom Alex counted herself both by birth and education, sat stunned and silent.

"But Russia is no longer communist," said Frank, grasping at straws. "It's not even KGB now. It's called the FSB and the foreign activities branch is the SVR."

Sergei answered with a smile. "Correct. It is now only a mess and you need not worry." He paused. "Until someone takes power who is both sober and knows how to exploit the assets we developed."

After a short break when dinner arrived, the meeting continued while they ate a starchy meal full of fats and preservatives, catered by FBI contract and eaten with plastic utensils. Questions tabled for further study included how David Bertram was getting access to

Hurlburt Field, the possible nature of the asset who arranged to house his teams, that is, male, female, military, civilian, and so on, and how Charlemagne would gain access without alerting any unknown Russian assets in either Jay or Skosh's hierarchies now that Sergei's revelations had sunk home in their minds.

Alex caught herself nodding off and looked up in time to see a tear fall from Theresa's cheek. This would not do. She stood quietly, triggering an automatic response from Mack and consequently from the other men, making them all stand as she led the younger woman into the living room.

"What is it? What's wrong?" she whispered.

"It's nothing. It's silly, and you are so kind. I...."

The tears came faster.

Alex remained silent, looking up into Theresa's tired eyes searching for answers there.

"I left Wooly." Theresa was sobbing now.

"A pet?"

"No. I am so silly. It's just a stuffed animal. I think it was a lamb. I'm not even sure. It might have been a dog. His fur has worn away now. Please don't think I'm an idiot female. It's just that I've had him all my life and...."

"You're tired, my dear. The meeting will be over soon. Why don't you lie down a moment here on the sofa?"

Alex went back to the conference room, entering as silently as possible but managing to catch Charlie's inquiring eye immediately. A lift of her chin told him he was wanted. He lost no time in slipping from the room during a rousing description of Beridze's known tradecraft practices. The exchange was not lost on Misha. Nothing was ever lost on Misha. He set his jaw and narrowed his eyes at her. She gave him a noncommittal smile.

Intelligence professionals populated the room. They noticed all of it.

When Charlie returned a minute later and asked Misha to meet him outside the door, the room heard, in German, "A what?" At volume and even louder, "Are you mad?" Charlie came back in and sat down coolly, while Misha, with a face full of thunder, pointed upstairs and held the door for his wife. Alex knew better than to disobey.

They heard him shouting, then two voices talking, then a somewhat long silence, then an upstairs door opening and footsteps on the stairs.

Steve said quietly what everyone was thinking. "He's had her."

Jay's eyebrows rose.

"No surprise to me," said Frank. "None of them missed an opportunity when they were younger. At least she's his wife. Presumably, he can trust her not to shoot him."

As a blushing Alex resumed her seat, the men became sure of it. She noticed the way Sergei was looking at Mara and knew they had been discussed. Misha sighed and said, "Charlie, tell us what you propose."

SEVEN

Skosh had been awake twenty-two hours. He caught himself momentarily contemplating a career change from a job he had always loved. Sure, he had skirted a few rules in his time with some of the murdering thugs he had handled in the Far East, but he'd never been this close to it. He wanted to vomit. Only pride kept his cookies down his gullet.

They walked into the conference room where everybody else had gathered. It occurred to Skosh that they were gone only an hour, and the apartment was a twenty-minute drive away. The entire little mini-rescue of a fucking toy lasted less than five minutes, and that included ground reconnaissance.

The two he had begun to refer to privately as 'the delinquents', Steve and Sergei, plopped into their chairs side by side. Charlie came in and found Theresa once again on the earphones. Brave girl, thought Skosh, forgiving her for this most recent shit show. It wasn't like she had anything to do with it other than being the source of misapplied mercy nine years before.

Charlie held the thing out to her while Mara took the earphones.

"Wooly!" Theresa's eyes teared up as she held the worn, faded toy to her chest. She reached up to kiss Charlie's cheek and kept hold of her old toy while she put the headphones back on. Charlie walked behind her back to his seat, turning up the volume of the machine as he went by.

Skosh felt, rather than saw, the silent communications bouncing around the room. He wished he could go upstairs, find himself a bed, and close his eyes for five minutes. Just five minutes. Frank's face broke through his watery gaze. The man's froggy eyes were looking daggers at Charlie as he sat down across the table from him.

Jay spoke first. "How many?"

"Three," said Skosh with a soft belch.

"Do you want to come with me to contact the sheriff?"

"I kinda feel like I've done my part, to tell the truth."

"Are we blown?" Mack asked Charlie.

"No. We used Steve's new method. I think we have more time before it becomes associated with us."

"Tell us."

"They did terrible things in her apartment, destroying her things," said Sergei. "They shit on her bed. It was a pleasure to kill them."

"Except we didn't know about that until after we killed them," said Steve, looking at his friend.

"Then it was a pleasure to have killed them" said Sergei, smugly proud of his tenses.

Skosh watched for signs that Theresa heard what was being said. There were none. The young woman seemed to be asleep with her eyes open. *Must be something they teach you in med school.*

"The toy escaped by being kicked under the bed in their frenzy to destroy everything in sight," said Charlie. "You were right, Papa. They were watching for her. I took one out beneath the stairs. I think he was just a watcher. A big man, though. It's an effective method."

Skosh belched again at the thought of effective methods.

"The other two were sitting in a car," said Steve. "We needed the driver to get out because we didn't want him falling onto the horn or anything, so we had Skosh approach with jumper cables."

"We unlocked a car parked close by and lifted the bonnet," said Sergei.

"Hood, Sergei," said Steve. "Bonnet is British. So when the guy got out to take a look, I took care of him and Sergei opened the passenger door and slipped it to the other guy. Then we went inside and saw the mess in the apartment."

"Charlie found the toy," said Sergei. "Then we left." He slid passports and wallets across to Mack.

"No blood?" asked Jay.

The delinquents shrugged a negative.

"Are you sure you don't want to come with me, Skosh?"

He received another belch and gulp in answer.

"Is this one of those babysitter objections to being too close to it?" asked Jay. "Shit, it was positively brilliant. You should be proud of a job well done."

Skosh was too busy keeping his stomach down to speak. He pointed meaningfully at Charlie and croaked, "His plan."

Frank held his round, bald head in his hands. Probably, thought Skosh, in conflict between gratitude to Charlie for taking out three more bad guys who were after his daughter and thinking of Charlie as a bad guy who was after his daughter.

Mack finished with the passports and wallets and slid them down the length of the table to Mara. She turned around to one of the computers and began typing in names and passport numbers.

"Charlie is correct," she said. "One is a watcher, a rental, American. The other two are Georgian. Not American. I will see if I can find out if they are Beridze's or if he has given them to Bertram. Do we know how many are usually on one of their teams?"

"Six," said Sergei. "Same as KGB."

"This is a new concept to me," said Jay, "at least its political implications, not the organized crime, but their deliberate use by intelligence. I will ask someone I know in DC. There is bound to be an analyst somewhere who has been jumping up and down trying to get people to listen to him about this threat."

Mara turned from her keyboard. "The American belongs to a violent anti-government group with headquarters in Crestview. It is about forty minutes north of here, depending on the roads taken. I have found no other groups or gangs closer than Tampa or Mobile likely to offer rentals."

"Jay, can you make them close down for one week?" asked Mack.

Turner sucked air through his teeth. "Perhaps we can use a firearms charge," he said reluctantly. "They always have illegal weapons, but it has not turned out well for us at times because of reactions in the press. Maybe it would be better if you could."

"I have only one method of dealing with such problems. Your press may find my results extreme and of course, quite permanent. I want only existing rental agreements to end now and no new agreements made for one week. Without attribution of the cause."

"Of course," said Jay. He looked at Skosh, who answered with a glare translatable as 'How the fuck would I know how to do that?'

"We'll be sure to get that done," Jay said, with emphasis on 'we'.

After the shift changed, Skosh joined Jay at the coffee machine to hash out ideas for mission impossible. "You know," he said as he poured coffee into his mug, "if we tell them how their guy died, they might be willing to listen to us about cooling it for a week."

Jay's brow registered scorn and disbelief. "You don't get it, do you? Have you ever lived in the South?"

"I visited southern California a couple of times and I live in Virginia."

"You live in a DC suburb. Let me put it to you as plainly as I can, Skosh. The only people these boys hate worse than the government are blacks and Asians, and guess what we are?"

Skosh rolled his eyes upward and threw his head back. "Together, you and I are all three," he said as his head came back down with a nodding bounce. "What about Frank? He's white and retired."

"What about Frank? Do I hear my name being bandied about for a suicide mission?" Frank poured the last of the last pot of coffee. Alex swept by them, taking the empty pot from him. She returned with a pot of water and poured it into the top, standing on tiptoes. They explained their idea to Frank.

"Sure, I can do that," he said, rubbing his hands together. "I'll do anything to stop thinking too much."

"You can't, Frank," said Alex.

They all glared at her interference. Skosh began to understand Mack just a little bit.

"Have you forgotten?" she said. "It's not just Theresa that Bertram is after. He's looking for you, too, Frank. And you're distinctive, Frank. These people in Crestview could easily describe you. The only thing we have going for us right now is that Bertram doesn't know we're here and that advantage would be gone."

The three of them stood stunned. Her soft brown hair, dimpled smiles, and besotted knife-wielding killer of a husband had made them underestimate her overall grasp of the situation.

"I am the only one here who is completely unknown and whose description would say nothing. I must be the one."

"The one what?" said Charlie walking up to the machine. He gave her a narrow look as she explained.

"Are you mad?"

"You sound just like your father."

"For good reason!" Charlie's volume was rising.

"Think about it, Michael. I mean, Charlie. Even Mara looks like you and would be very memorable in her own right. Bertram did not see you that day, but his mother did and will describe you to him if she hasn't already. I am the only person in this house he has not seen and whose description is ordinary."

Her description might be ordinary, but the woman was any-thing but, thought Skosh.

"Papa will never agree."

She patted Charlie's arm. "Leave that to me. Is he alone?"

He nodded. "He's gone upstairs. Steve and Sergei are sleeping in the next room."

The four of them stared after her as she climbed the steps. It took five minutes for the shouting to begin.

"What's going on?" said Steve ten minutes later, his voice still groggy with sleep. Sergei stood behind him.

They explained.

"Shit."

"Misha will have very good sex tonight, I think," said Sergei. Then, as the thought took hold, "Where is Mara?"

"Welcome to my world," said Charlie. "My father almost never shouts. Except at Alex."

"Why is there shouting? Is something wrong?" Theresa walked down the stairs, her dark hair standing in knots around her head.

They were too tired to explain again and she was too tired to listen anyway.

She made more coffee.

EIGHT

They reconvened at dawn. Everyone, except Frank, had enjoyed at least four hours of sleep in the last twelve so that, considering the overall misery of their situation, they were reasonably fresh. Frank felt overjoyed to have made himself useful and relevant for the past two hours, maintaining indoor perimeter checks every fifteen minutes, with the exception of only one room, and outdoor sensor checks—carefully skirting the couple sleeping on the conference table—to check the bar of sensor lights next to one of the computers.

As the safehouse came alive with the waking of slightly less exhausted but hungry people, Jay took delivery of tubs of scrambled eggs, biscuits, bacon, sausage, grits, gravy, and hash browns, and laid them on the conference table in no particular order. There was a discussion about the grits. Some of the Europeans had never seen it. Alex had never tasted it, though she had read about it. She was from Chicago, so the more experienced among them excused her ignorance. They ate on paper plates with plastic spoons because they were out of forks, while Jay tried to explain the difficulties of entering an Air Force base for purposes of a firefight with the Russian mafia.

"It's not just...." He could not conjure a large enough thesaurus to convey his meaning, but tried again. "It's not just the absurdity of the concept. It's the flightline full of eighteen-year-old military police carrying M16s. Those airplanes are classified. Well, the airplanes are older than dirt and used all over the world, but what's inside them is not and Uncle Sam is not about to share that anytime soon. Shit, I'm beginning to sound like Donovan."

Mack tabled the discussion in preference for the task that held first place on everybody's mind: how to manage Alex's meeting with the rental agency. Once again Jay provided initial intelligence.

"They meet every morning for coffee at a diner on the main street of the town. The head MFWIC is a bubba named Earl Smith, age 72, divorced and estranged from his children. He owns a shrimp boat."

"You sure are beginning to sound like me," said Steve.

"What is miffwick?" asked Sergei, voicing the question in everyone's mind.

"Mother Fucker What's In Charge," said Steve. "It's a military title."

The questions they thrashed out included who was going to Crestview, in what car or cars, who should drive, who should be seen, who not, who should stay in the safehouse, who would be in charge of the safehouse, and who would be in charge in Crestview? That done, largely by Mack's edicts because time was pressing, there came a brief argument about how Alex should approach the subject. This was more of a lecture by her husband to her. Nobody argued with him.

"You will make no jokes. You will not smile." She suppressed her smile at this. "You will walk in, sit down, and say what I tell you to say, nothing more. You will not engage in philosophical discussions. You will not speak of morality. You will not tell them their eating is unhealthy. You will not criticize their wearing of hats indoors. Americans do this all the time. You will not say anything about it. You will wear a wire. You will wear a weapon. I told you to bring your weapon. Did you?" She nodded. "Did you bring the holster?" He looked like thunder when she had no answer.

"I have one you can borrow, Mama," said Mara.

Was that relationship in the file, wondered Skosh. Why hadn't he connected Mara with Alex before this? Because Mara looked like Charlie, not Alex.

Discussion did take place over what she should wear. Mack had never noticed what women wore back at his home, let alone in the forests and bayous of the Florida panhandle. Frank and Skosh had the same disability regarding the mysteries of women's clothing, and the height of fashion for Theresa was a new set of green scrubs. Alex had lost all cultural understanding of her own country two decades before and had no experience outside Chicago to begin with. Steve and Jay were sufficiently American, but not sufficiently female to advise on some things, so after Mack ended the argument by banging on the table, Sergei produced a tape measure from his bottomless Footlocker of Useful Things (FUT) and Jay gave the measurements to one of his watchers on duty outside with instructions to go to a local twenty-four-hour discount store for a pair of cheap jeans, sneakers, and a flannel shirt. They cut the sleeves off the shirt because it was summer in Florida, and they rolled the shoes and clothing in sand and a little bit of mud. Until then, it never occurred to any of them to ask advice from a watcher who lived in the area.

The same watcher who advised Jay to roll the sneakers in mud was sent back to the field office and told to bring them his own car, a very used Chevy of no description and doubtful color or cleanliness, but with plain, faded Florida plates and bubbling tints on the windows that obscured, probably illegally, everything inside.

Jay drove. He pointed out that in the South, he would be less conspicuous than Skosh. Steve rode shotgun. Mack and Alex sat in the back. Steve and Mack got out first so that when Jay dropped Alex off a thousand feet from the diner, they were behind her. Jay parked where he had a good view through the diner's big picture window and watched as Alex and then the other two entered. This was Alex's first op in more than twenty years. According to Frank, that first time had been a disaster for her. It explained why Mack was unhinged the entire morning. Frank mentioned that Mack made all the decisions on that previous op, too.

Jay heard the sounds of people in a diner and turned up his earbud.

"Mr. Smith? Hi, my name is Jenny."

Uh oh. Jay remembered one of the many instructions Mack had given her. *You will stay exactly on the legend we give you. No exceptions. You will not ad-lib.* So much for that one, he thought. She had been made to repeat the name Jennifer three times. She was right though. Jennifer would be too formal in this setting.

"May I sit down?"

Her English was too good. She was too polite. Jay felt the sweat beading on his brow and pouring down his back.

"Sure thing, little girl," said Smith. "Can I get you some coffee?"

"That would be lovely, thank you."

Jay groaned inwardly. *You will not accept anything to eat or drink.*

"Mr. Smith, I have something a little delicate I need to discuss with you."

"These friends of mine are trustworthy. Ain't you guys?"

General grunts of acknowledgment.

"Nonetheless, it is vital that we speak privately."

There was a brief silence, and then Smith said, "Scram, you guys," followed by the sound of chairs scraping the floor.

Jay imagined her smiling at the guy. That was on the list.

"Now what is it you wanna talk to your old Earl about, honey?"

"Do you know a man named Cory Lowell?"

"Yeah, what about him?" Jay heard a note of caution in the man's voice.

"Well, I'm so sorry to tell you, Mr. Smith, that Cory is dead. He died late last night. I am here on a quest to save lives, Mr. Smith. Please believe me when I say that in all sincerity."

She had begun to sound a little bit southern. *You will not use dialect or accent like you are an actress in a bad American movie.*

"How so?" said Smith.

"I heard that Cory was working for somebody else when he died and that he was on loan from you. I don't think that's a good idea, do you?"

"I think that's my business, little girl." He sounded hostile.

"I agree entirely, Mr. Smith. But I think in this instance, it might not be the best business to be in. I think maybe you shouldn't be lending anything more to those people, and I'll bet your folks who are already down there will feel a lot safer coming back home after what happened last night."

"I don't know nothing about what happened last night. If this is a threat, I want to know who sent you and I aim to find that out right now."

Jay saw Mack stand up from his seat at a booth in the window. Alex was in a back room.

"I am not threatening you or anybody, Mr. Smith. As I said, I only want to save lives. Please believe that. As a mark of my good intentions, I will tell you something important so you can check with the sheriff's office to see if it's true before you make your decision. Cory died because somebody stuck a stiletto between his ribs and into his heart. I appreciate your time sir, and I'll be on my way."

She wasn't supposed to tell him the manner of death. She wasn't supposed to know the manner of death.

"Now hold on there!"

But she was already at the door, and two men, who were slowly leaving the diner at the same time, blocked Earl Smith's effort to catch up with her.

...

"What're they doing?" Steve murmured through the side of his mouth.

Jay checked the backseat in the rearview mirror. "Kissing," he said, very low, and not moving his lips.

Silence reigned during the hour it took to safely reach the safehouse without a tail while Skosh covered their backs.

NINE

Charlie looked up from the rifle components spread out before him on the conference room table. Mara sat at the other end of the table reading Vogue Magazine and wearing headphones. The reels were not turning, which meant nobody near David's briefcase was talking.

"How did it go?" asked Charlie as the babysitters came in. He began putting the now clean weapon back together.

"Time will tell," Skosh said with a shrug.

Jay followed him in, carrying a fresh mug of coffee and a half smile, which was akin to boisterous laughter for him.

"Time is finite," said Charlie. "We need a break and we need it soon." He popped in a magazine.

"If what she did works," said Jay, "our odds will improve by a third."

"What did she do?" Charlie narrowed his eyes. He chambered a round.

"Broke about a dozen of Mack's instructions. But she made them sound ambiguous and had excuses."

"She learned from the master of ambiguity," said Frank also carrying a full mug of coffee as he took his seat. "Her husband. He'll make her pay, though."

"I imagine that's what he's doing now," said Skosh. He spilled some of his coffee putting the mug down hard when he noticed Mack in the doorway giving him an unblinking stare. He did not know how much of the exchange Mack might have heard and was unpleasantly aware that he had spoken the last words in that conversation. *Damn the man's silent stillness.*

Mack was not yet in his seat when Mara raised a finger. "David Bertram is awake and has a telephone call," she said. She flipped the switch on the external speaker as the tape began to roll.

"You're what?" said Bertram. "You can't. You can't come here. I'm not ready." After a pause, "I have no place to put you for one thing. You'll have to stay in a hotel. No, the place isn't suitable for my mother to stay in. Yes, Kenny set us up in an excellent location, but my guys are pretty rough, Mom. You would not be comfortable there either." Another, even longer, pause from the speaker. "No, I haven't found her yet, but I'm real close. Okay, I'll reserve you a room. Someplace nice. Two? Who else? Oh, her. A double? Is she bringing a boyfriend? Okay, okay already. Actually, that might work out. Two rooms and one's a double. I got it. Give me the flight info and I'll meet you." They heard a knock on the door. "I gotta go. See you soon. Yeah, yeah, bye, love you."

By this time, the conference room was full, and the last to be seated was Alex. Mara raised her finger again and the tape resumed its roll.

"Shit, David," said a voice as the door opened. "Shit."

"Beridze," said Mara.

"What? Tell me," said Bertram.

"It's the fucking Italians. Has to be. That guy—the big one we got from the shrimp guy—he had a fucking stiletto through the heart. I bet that's how the others died, too."

"Others? What others?"

"Last night. Two of your guys. At that bitch's apartment. Fucking dead in their car. And the rental. That really big guy. Remember him? Fucking stiletto to the heart. I'm telling you it has to be the Italians. I thought we had an agreement with them. Fuck."

"My guys? Shit. But we're still good, right? I mean, do we still have enough?"

"Sure, yeah. I'll find some more rentals."

"Why? There're still four more of them, besides all our guys."

"No. The shrimp bastard told them to run, the fucking cowards. Come with me. You need to talk to what's left of your team before they disappear, too. Like the wind. Like the fucking wind."

There was a moment of profound silence. No secrets exist in a safehouse or isolation cell full of operatives in the middle of an op. All relationships are public. They wanted to cheer; they wanted to carry Alex around the table on their shoulders, her victory had been so complete. But they knew about the rule-breaking and they knew how Mack dealt with disobedience in all its forms. None of them wanted to be on the wrong side of him.

Alex blushed and looked down. Mack smiled slightly. The room erupted into applause, having been given license by that half smile.

When the noise died down, Charlie asked Alex, "How did you know?"

"I saw a book Steve was reading for research on a table at home, and I remembered the injury you suffered last year." She shrugged. "I connected them."

Frank polished his knuckles with a superior smile.

"What, old man?" said Charlie, giving him the blue gaze that was somehow worse than his father's.

Frank was tired and retired and overwhelmed by the many personal threats he faced. He never liked this young man in the first place so he gave his best bulging stare with a smile as he said, "You have to expect extraordinary talent in a babysitter's daughter."

They were locked in a mutual glare as Charlie replied, chopping the ends of his words, "I'm all about the talents of a babysitter's daughter, old man."

Frank broke the stare first, seething.

"Jay," said Mack, "we will need Linda Bertram's flight information. His team members will be present to help the son greet her. We should continue to improve our odds. Who is her friend and who is the friend bringing? Can you find the manifest?"

Jay nodded. "I will call the field office and get them started."

"Use the secure phone you installed in the kitchen. I do not want Beridze to know about us yet, or our interest in Linda."

"Are they that sophisticated? I mean they seem like just a bunch of bruisers." Jay realized too late that he had said this in a room populated primarily by a bunch of bruisers.

"Bertram is sophisticated and an expert with computers and telephones," came the quiet purr signaling displeasure from Mack.

"In fact," said Mara, "he has tried getting into our system three times. I don't know if he's been into your system, but as we share a modem ..."

"What?" Mack brought a fist down making everything on the table bounce. Non-team members jumped in their seats. The team was used to it.

"When were you going to tell me this?" he said, well above a purr, to Mara.

She swallowed hard. "He did not succeed. I ordered another hard drive in case, and Jay said...."

The blue mind-reading eyes turned back to Jay. "What did Jay say?"

"I ordered it. It'll be here soon. It was just a precaution; in case we detect anything on your computer."

"On our computer? Have you detected anything on your computer?"

There was an ominous silence. Everybody thanked God or heaven or karma that they were not Jay.

"Um. I am not very good with these things."

"Then get someone who is." Mack was back to the purr, which was infinitely more menacing to anyone who knew him.

"May I point out," said Skosh, not necessarily coming to Jay's rescue, "that most FBI field agents don't have the level of clearance necessary to be here at all, we cannot let him leave once he's here, and we are already overcrowded."

Jay never missed an opportunity to look a gift horse in the mouth. "Our special agents have top secret clearances and take regular polygraphs."

"We're talking SCI clearances here, Jay, sensitive compartmented information with a WEDGE caveat and...."

Mack exploded. "I do not care about your clearances. I will cut the throat of anyone who poses a danger to us. That should be enough to ensure silence. You," he pointed at Jay, "will go to the field office and bring back an agent with computer knowledge and a packed bag. Also, bring two new hard drives, and...?" He looked at Mara.

"A KIV-7. Also a couple of CIKs, a TEK, and a filler."

It was Sergei who produced the technology Jay needed to make a list of these mysterious apparatuses to take with him. The FUT included paper and a pencil.

"I'll just accompany Jay to make sure his computer guy meets at least minimum standards for this situation." Skosh maintained the bullshit as he made his escape, closing the door behind him on the word 'situation,' and caught up with Jay at the front door.

"I'm going with you."

"What for?"

"So I can tell you what an idiot you are. I practically handed you an excuse to give him and you had to get all defensive."

Jay started the car. "You heard him, Skosh. He cares about security, not security clearances. No amount of bullshit was ever going to get me out of this."

"I suppose you're right, but where the fuck is this new guy going to sleep? It's bad enough sharing a room with those two delinquents."

"Delinquents? You mean Pavlenko and Donovan? Very apt. They do belong in juvie. But Mack is right. We need professional help with this. Bertram is a true whiz kid. And nobody is getting any sleep anyway. I know I'm not."

"Mara seems like a whiz kid as well, couldn't she…?"

"I can't put her on an FBI computer, Skosh. Mack doesn't care about such things but the FBI sure as hell does."

"Why are we turning around?"

"I forgot that the caterers will be there with lunch. You'll need to be at the door to receive it while I'm doing this."

Skosh thought for a moment. "Jay," he said before getting out of the car at the safehouse, "is this computer guy kind of junior to you?"

"Yes. Quite a bit junior. Are you thinking what I'm thinking?"

"I'm thinking it would be nice to have some assistance with all the housekeeping in this house of horrors."

"I think, Skosh, that you and I are in complete agreement on this issue."

TEN

J ay walked in and stepped on a tray of hamburgers.

"Shit, Jay. Watch where you put your feet for fuck's sake," said Skosh.

"There is no place to put my feet. Why didn't you have them put these trays in the kitchen?"

"Have you seen the kitchen?"

"Did you give them the empty breakfast trays so they could take them away and make room?"

"That's FBI shit. How am I supposed to know about that?" Skosh cleared a path for Jay and the new agent to get in the door inconspicuously—if that were possible.

He looked at the young man carrying a large bag of computer parts and a smaller backpack that might have room for a toothbrush. He wasn't a kid, Skosh decided, but he was pretty young to be stepping into this job.

"Hi. I'm John Nakamura. Everybody calls me Skosh." He did not offer his hand because there was no place for the new agent to put down his bags. "Did Jay brief you on the situation?"

"Some," said the young man.

"Not really," said Jay simultaneously. "Some things just have to be experienced."

…

Justin Goodwin's experience began as he ferried food, paper plates, and plastic utensils into a back room filled with a huge table, computers, equipment, footlockers, and armed people, mostly men. A small woman with brown hair made sure everybody had access to the food. There was a tense conversation going on in German. Justin had grown up in a midwestern suburb. He knew the language was

German because he took a few classes in high school and anyway, everybody knows that nein means no. This was being said a lot. The noise, the languages, the equipment, and the guns were as far outside his experience as he had ever been.

He scanned the room, trying to understand what he was seeing. It was highly classified. *Got that much.* It looked more squalid than secret, though the steel doors and lack of windows were an indication. His eyes came to an exquisite blonde at the other end of the table and rested there because this, at least, he understood. He also grasped the nature of the stare from the man with colorless eyes sitting next to her. The man pointedly covered her hand with his own, and the communication could not be more clear. Justin's eyes moved on.

Everybody was armed, as was Justin himself. Jay had insisted, though he did not find it comfortable. He preferred weapons of the mind, manipulations of ones and zeros moving at the speed of light. He had skill in that arena, he knew, and his lack of significant prowess with firearms made him more arrogant about the fact, not less. Any brute can pull a trigger.

The logical conclusion, therefore, was that he was in a room full of brutes. They lived by their guns. Most needed a shave. All were coatless and had loosened their ties and rolled up dirty cuffs on their less than white shirts, but their holsters gleamed with polish. The visible stocks of the various weapons seemed to sparkle. These guys pulled triggers on a regular basis, and not at the range.

He could tell that the older man at the head of the table, the blond one with blue eyes, was in charge. Justin sat down as far away from him as he could, between the blonde and the small brown-haired woman.He felt that blue gaze travel his way as it shifted from Jay.

"Um," said Jay. "This is Special Agent Justin Goodwin, our computer specialist."

The man was sizing him up, Justin realized with a shock. He saw the glance move from his hands to the pistol in its holster peeping out from his jacket. Justin was being evaluated not as an engineer, nor as a law enforcement professional. This was a cold assessment of his capability as a man of violence, his capacity in the use of that pistol.

"We require first to know if Bertram has succeeded in examining your computer," the man said to him in English heavily laced with a

German accent. "Then you must guard against his intrusion. Finally, I need all the information you can retrieve about several people."

There were more instructions. Justin wondered if he should get his notebook and take notes or was he expected to remember all these impossible foreign names? Getting the notebook would suggest he could not instantly memorize them and he did not want this man to know that.

"Jay will give you a written list," said the man.

Had he been reading his mind?

"Misha, let him eat his lunch first," said the small brown-haired woman sitting next to him. She spoke English with an American accent.

The guy in charge, whose name must be Misha, pointed toward her with all the fingers of his right hand and an exasperated look. "Alex, we have discussed this."

Justin noticed that everyone stopped eating. The woman lowered her eyes. "Yes, we have. I apologize."

Everybody picked up their forks.

He was about to get up and go to the computer, but she put a hand on his arm, restraining him with a smile. Jay produced no list for him until lunch had ended.

...

Skosh chewed his Western institutional meal slowly, musing upon the education of Justin Goodwin. Not the master's degree from MIT, but the education going on right now in this room as the young agent reviewed the faces of those around him and rested on the pretty surgeon with deep auburn hair and almost black eyes.

After three days in crowded quarters, everybody knew important truths internally without realizing their meanings. They knew, for example, that of all the dangerous men in that house, and Skosh had to include himself, Jay, and Frank in that category—if only to criminals and terrorists—of all of them, then, the most dangerous by far was Charlie. Everybody also understood Charlie was wooing Theresa, and her father, Frank, hated the very thought. He had no choice but to behave himself, because Charlie was among those trying to save her life and because Charlie could kill him instantly without an ounce of compunction. Also universally understood was that the purpose of Alex's presence was to encourage the match so that Charlie might win his fair lady and take her home with him to whatever secure dungeon he infested as the dragon he most surely was.

Skosh amended that last thought. Alex would not condemn anyone to such a fate. Maybe it wasn't a dungeon, and maybe at home, Charlie wasn't a dragon. Maybe. He breathed fire here, though, and Justin, as he encouraged everyone to call him, would be severely scorched if he continued to smile at Theresa like that.

…

After lunch, Justin turned to his computer and stayed busy enough with his long list of tasks that he had no time to smile at anybody. Working on one name after another, he checked off the list until he noticed a change in the noises behind him. He surfaced from the monitor before him and turned around.

The blonde woman whom they called Mara stood shirtless in capri pants, sandals, and sports bra while the older man with bulging eyes secured a wire to her bra strap and into her ear, with a microphone hooked to the bridge between her breasts. He hooked a small receiver transmitter to a belt around her waist. Other pockets on the belt held magazines, a set of lock-picking tools, and a Glock 19 at her back. He helped her slip on a long, shapeless tee shirt to cover the belt.

Jay Turner, his boss, was busy clipping wires to his undershirt, then buttoning a crisp white shirt over it. He had trouble with the buttons. Justin figured he must be nervous. Across the table, the Russian with the light eyes, who had claimed ownership of the blonde and made sure Justin knew it, was being wired up by Skosh over a Kevlar vest. Once wired, he practiced drawing his weapon half a dozen times for a smooth extraction before putting on a sports coat.

The man with brown hair and eyelashes like a girl was already dressed and wired and practicing letting a stiletto drop into his hand from his sleeve. Justin decided he would never mention the man's eyelashes to anyone. Ever.

The two blond men stood by the door in deep consultation. Alex squeezed between them from the living room and spoke to Mara, then gave her a hug. Mack, the name Jay used for the older man in charge of everything, came to Alex and began a point-by-point list in German. She nodded at each numbered item. He blew out an exasperated sigh, noticed Justin, and pointed at him. Justin opened his eyes wide.

"I will cut your throat if anything happens to Alex because of you," he said in English.

"I'll be here, Mack," said Frank.

"You already know that threat." He turned back to Justin. "Also the same goes if something happens to Theresa. Is this clear?"

Justin swallowed. "Yes, sir."

"Jay?"

"Understood, Mack."

"Mara, can you do something to your hair? It is too distinctive."

"Yes Misha, I will make it messy." And she proceeded to do just that, before picking up a cloth bag full of small devices.

"Steve, stop playing. I want to hear each of you first in my ear, then Frank will turn on the main receiver here. Go."

There began a rapid-fire single word from each person who wore a wire, with only one glitch because Skosh had not yet turned on the transmitter at his belt. Mack expressed his displeasure with a curled upper lip. Frank turned on the receiver that sat on top of an old half-sized refrigerator lying on its side and the exercise began again, this time flawlessly. Frank left the radio on.

Mack pointed at Alex. "You will stay in this room with these two at all times."

"Yes, Misha." As he led everyone out she whispered, "Be careful."

ELEVEN

"Justin," said Alex, "would it be possible to arrange for that hotel where David Bertram reserved rooms for his mother and her friend to not have any other rooms available in case they want to change their reservation?"

"I think so, yes. Why?"

"I remember how funny my father was about hotels. He never reserved a room at all, but he also never accepted the first, and sometimes even the second room they offered. This made it difficult to set up surveillance against him."

"Fred was a master of tradecraft, Alex," said Frank. "He taught me a lot."

Alex smiled. "Nobody brought this up, so I hesitated to say anything during the meeting. I just don't want Mara's work to be for nothing."

"You know," said Frank, "it might be a good idea to leave two other rooms open and wire them as well. That way if they make a change, they will think they've been successful."

"Deviously excellent. But do you think it will put Mara at greater risk?"

"Let's call Jay privately on the car phone and ask him."

The answer was yes let's do it; it will not add risk. They were rolling into the hotel parking lot when Justin gave them the extra room numbers he had allowed the hotel computer to see. "Switching back to network now," said Jay.

"Should that tape be moving?" asked Theresa, pointing to the recorder. "Isn't Bertram on his way to the airport?"

"He must have left his briefcase. It might be ambient noise. Flip the switch," said Frank.

They heard seagulls, then a motor with a low sound, then another.

"Those are outboards," said Justin. "My dad always has a boat on the lake near our cabin." They heard another motor. "I'd say they're coming into a marina or a public slip. Very low power, no wake."

"Justin, find small craft marinas," said Frank. "Is there anything else to narrow it down?"

Theresa donned the headphones and flipped off the external speaker. "Traffic," she said. "Moving fast, so I'd say a major road."

"There is only one major road through this area that is near the water and it runs right by Hurlburt Field," said Alex. "I imagine he would prefer to be near his team if they are on the base. That reminds me, didn't he mention a name when his mother called?"

"Kenny," said Theresa.

"The safehouse will be small, isolated, near the highway, near Hurlburt, and near a marina for small craft," said Frank.

Justin began the search.

Alex watched the monitor from behind him as he worked. "After you find that, can you search for a friend or more likely a family member of Linda Bertram from Virginia named Kenny or Kenneth, who may be military or perhaps a civilian working at Hurlburt Field? Probably someplace near the airplanes."

They reached Jay on his radio channel as he left the hotel parking lot and gave him the address of a house advertised as a short-stay rental that fit all the criteria.

"Shit, Frank," said Jay, "It was made clear to me that my instructions—our instructions—were to take no risks."

"Just look at it, Jay," said Alex. "Mara can assess the risk."

"Misha will kill you, Mama," said Mara, laughing, "and after the loud argument we will know you are making up."

"No! Do they? Do you all…?"

"Do not dare tell him, Mama. You will spoil it for all of us."

"Jay," said Frank, "if this works, call your people and tell them we'll need more machines and tape capacity and some kind of table to put it on."

They began the long wait, no more than ninety minutes in the end, but endless when it stretched in front of them. The only sound was the clicking of Justin's keyboard.

"Alex," said Theresa, "I heard your dad was a babysitter."

"Yes, he was your father's boss."

"A damned good one, too," said Frank.

"May I ask," said Theresa, picking her words carefully, "what your dad's reaction was when you told him you wanted to marry Mack?"

"You should call him Misha now, Theresa. My father died before I married him, but he was not pleased when I married my first husband, Vasily. He was also a member of the team."

"I didn't know you had been married before," Theresa said, confused.

"That is a long story better left for another time, my dear."

"May I ask what happened to Vasily?"

"He died about ten years ago. I will tell you, though, that I have never regretted either one of my marriages. It helped my father to know this about my marriage to Vasily."

Frank made a sound somewhere between a snort and a snarl. Justin stopped typing to listen.

"Were you able to stay in touch with your family after your marriage?" asked Theresa.

Alex sighed. "Not as much as I would have liked. But I think technology has changed things dramatically. Justin can probably tell you more about secure communications today. I wish it had been easily available twenty years ago."

The radio squawked. "On our way," said Jay. "Success. Switching to network."

...

"It's a good thing I brought plenty of taps," said Mara as she walked into the room not long after. She showed them her depleted bag. "Four hotel rooms and it was indeed his safehouse. I saw the briefcase, so I touched all three of his rooms and the telephone."

"Not good. On our way." It was Sergei's voice. "Open my locker. Tell Theresa."

"Tell me what?" she asked.

"Who?" said Frank into the radio, "what, and how bad?"

"Steve. Several rounds. Collar bone, I think. Maybe more."

Mara opened the FUT and handed Theresa the medical kit. "I'll start water boiling." She came back ten minutes later with a basin of hot water and a stack of clean towels.

Theresa, rummaged through the kit she had been given, "I see some antibiotic and morphine, but no anesthetic. Is it kept somewhere else?"

"We don't use it," Mara said with a solemn tone. "Not during an op. We keep the anesthetic on our airplane. It's reserved for when we are out of the airspace."

"What if I have to do surgery?" Theresa let the shock register on her face.

"We will hold him down so that he will be still for you."

Theresa remembered a history of medicine class from long ago in her training. The professor pointed out that before the advent of anesthesia, a surgeon had to be very sure and very fast for his patient to survive. She prayed she would be sure and fast.

Confronted with the rapidly cleared and disinfected table, she left shock behind her as training took over so that her instruments were organized and the antibiotic drawn up and ready when the team exploded through the door.

This was not the sterile, hushed operating room she was used to. Theresa had seen two similar events nine years before, but she had not been the attending surgeon then, just a kid, helpful but unaware. Everybody was dirty and loud. The patient swore a blue streak, beginning and ending every remark with 'fuck'. She scrubbed up as well as she could and did not want to contaminate her hands. She wondered how she would prepare him without touching him. Just like before, she did not have to. The other men stripped him, not always gently, and Alex stuck the syringe of antibiotics into him immediately.

The noise and disorder were not a hysterical reaction to an emergency. They were purposeful in their actions and knew what they were doing, but it was as if they were on a kind of hyper-drug. Every move was rational, effective, and violent. She watched Charlie tear off the Velcro tabs of Steve's Kevlar vest and remove it roughly. He took out a wicked-looking knife, slit Steve's tee shirt down the middle and through the sleeves, and pulled it from under him, shoving him back down onto the table.

"Fucking stay put, will you Steve?"

"How do you want his arms?" asked Mack, whom she had been instructed to address as Misha. It would be a very long time before she could do that, she decided when she met the man's eyes. He was as wild as any of them. Even her father seemed infected. He seized an ankle and anchored it to the table.

Theresa forced herself to look at the patient. *Don't call him Steve; just refer to him internally as the patient.* She told them to keep his arms by his side but not touching the ribs. Severe bruising covered his torso. The vest had done its job there. At least one bruise over a rib looked bad enough for her to suspect a break, but it appeared to be in place. She touched that place and he winced but the rib felt intact. The major wound was a hole just below the prominent blade of the collarbone on the left side. She repeated to herself the mantra 'sure and fast' and reached for a scalpel before she realized Alex was already handing one to her and doing so properly. Someone had taught her.

Steve screamed obscenities as she widened the hole and the others were no quieter. Now she understood the leather gags they used way back when. She took a deep breath.

"I need you all to shut the fuck up!" she shouted at the top of her lungs. "Especially you, Donovan. I'm not used to patients who can talk. If you want a shoulder when this is done, you have to let me concentrate."

The entry point was not far from another scar, though that one did not look like a bullet wound. It reminded her of the scars she had seen on Charlie's body yesterday. He had none when they first met. It made her pause. How else had he been damaged during these years, she wondered as she inserted a probe.

Somebody fished a tongue depressor out of the medical kit and put it between Steve's teeth. He bit through it and the great straining began. Not only Steve's muscles bulged as his face reddened, but so did those of the men holding him down. But they were all silent and she had the bullet out in two minutes. It took another three to clean and disinfect to her satisfaction. She began the tedious closing.

"He should have some morphine now," said Theresa, looking for the vial she had laid out.

"No," said Misha. "We are live. When we dislodge those tangos from the base we will attack or be attacked. He must be lucid."

"It's not as bad now," said Steve through gritted teeth. "Just get on with it."

Even as he spoke, the new tape machine began rolling and Justin flipped the switch to the external speaker.

TWELVE

They heard three voices, David Bertram, his mother Linda, and a man they called Nick, older, with a Russian accent.

"Beridze," said Sergei.

"It was horrible, Nick, just horrible," they heard Linda say. "I could tell he was dead, staring straight up like that, but there wasn't any blood that I could see. Then Sally saw him and started screaming and we turned around and there was another one! What's going on Nick?"

"It's the Italians, I swear. And I saw the guy, too, walking out very cool. Nice suit, just like a wise guy. I went around a side door and had a good look. Brown hair, lots of it. Deep brown eyes. Definitely Italian. I let him have it. I could have sworn I hit him. Almost emptied the clip, and would have finished it, but then somebody was coming and I ducked in the doorway and when I went back out, he was gone. No blood. Then the sirens started and I was armed, so I left."

"I didn't fire," croaked Steve from the table, "because I thought then they would know we're here."

"Very good," said Mack. "How is it we are hearing this?"

"We'll explain later," said Alex.

The look he gave her would have made it snow in hell.

Linda was talking again. "Sally is a basket case, as usual. She is such a trial sometimes, but I'm glad I kept up with her, or we never would have known how that horrible family betrayed and killed Richard." She sniffed. "She's told me everything. I think we can use it and her. I'll let her sleep off the sedative I gave her and in the morn-

ing tell her it was all play-acting for a movie or something. The boy
is with her, which is another trial, but he'll look after her and he may
be useful later."

"Danny," Steve whispered.

"You will retrieve him this time," said Mack. "She has broken the
agreement." He did not mention the decision he already had made
when he learned from his sources that she had left North Carolina.

"She has to go, Mack," said Steve.

"Yes. I will take care of it."

"I should."

"No. She is Danny's mother."

"He won't know."

"Such things never remain secret. I will take care of it. I
promised her I would."

Justin thought the sentence should have ended with, it will give
me great pleasure, because of the way it was said. He noticed that
Jay and the babysitters shuddered.

The table was cleared of medical detritus and Steve sent upstairs to sleep after Theresa had wrapped his chest to immobilize
what she suspected was at least one cracked rib. Within twenty minutes, dinner was being quietly consumed as they listened to Linda
Bertram prattle on with David about gossip concerning sundry people they did not know. Then she mentioned Kenny.

"That reminds me," said Justin through a mouthful of bland
casserole. "I found him."

Forks went down in silence.

"You did what?" said Mack.

"I found Kenny. Alex suggested I look for him, so I did and I
found him. He's Linda's cousin."

"Did she? What else did she suggest?" Mack gave Alex a cold
stare. Her face was a study in expressionlessness.

"Well, the hotel rooms and Bertram's safehouse."

"His safehouse?"

"Yes, we found it and so Frank called Jay, and then Mara put
some serious touches on it, and...."

Frank received the glare briefly, then Mara, then Jay, and it rested finally again on Alex.

"I will speak to you upstairs," said Misha with a kind of softness
in his voice that was anything but. He put down the knife and fork

and turned to Justin. "You will give Charlie all of this information. Now."

The shouting upstairs was loud. They heard only one voice.

"I hope Steve will be able to sleep," said Theresa.

"It will stop soon," said Sergei. "This will not be long. The information gained is vital."

"She was disobedient. Again." Charlie's voice suggested severe disapproval.

"If you ever...." said Frank, his face reddening.

"What? What will you do?" Charlie looked away and took a deep breath. "He does not hit her and I have never struck a nonoperational woman, old man. Do not insult me in this way again."

As if emphasizing Sergei's point about vital information, Linda's voice on the speaker stopped its prattle and became serious. "Listen, David, do you remember Arkady from the embassy?"

He must have nodded. There was no sound, at least none that rose above the din from upstairs. Justin gave Charlie an empty disk envelope he had used to jot down the information on Kenneth Schott and the address of Bertram's safehouse.

Linda's voice continued. "Well, he sent you two more men. They were on the airplane with us, but of course, we had no contact with each other. We were very careful. They are here in the hotel. I was able to get them into the last two rooms available. I will introduce you before we leave."

Sergei shook his head. "We were focused on the two greeters, not on other passengers. We never saw these."

Mara was in sudden motion as she scrambled to her computer and dug into the bag of wafers, pulling out an index card where she had jotted down names and locations. After some furious tapping at the keyboard, one of the tape machines began turning. She handed the headphones on Linda's machine to Theresa, flipped switches, and they heard a deep rasping voice speaking Russian. A higher male voice replied. Three people present in the conference room spoke no Russian. Two others, Frank and Skosh, spoke some. The team members were fluent. A single word was enough, though, to make both team and babysitters turn pale.

"Komodo," said Skosh, as Alex and Mack came through the door. Alex did not react. Mack did.

"Where is he?" he asked Charlie.

"Here. In the hotel with Linda Bertram. She got him a room there, one of the rooms Alex asked Mara to touch."

"We have a touch on Komodo's room?" Mack's eyes opened wide.

"And his phone," said Mara.

"It is good that we know," said Mack with a half-smile at Alex. "It is terrible that he is here."

THIRTEEN

What followed would have been a great movie night if the room was filled with friends and if they brought beer and popcorn. None of those conditions applied as a specialist team and their enablers listened in on the private lives of their enemies. They did have coffee.

When necessary, Sergei or Alex translated for those with limited or no Russian. The only person not present was Steve, and no one begrudged him the luxury of extra sleep. Everybody who needed sleep, which was everyone, forgot their exhaustion in the fascination inherent in being unknown listeners to people who think they are speaking and acting in private. It was irresistible.

The new tape machines had arrived earlier and Mara set everything up so that all touches were monitored in real time. The table to put them on did not arrive, so they used the far end of the conference table, making all seats, except Mack and Charlie's, uncomfortably crowded. Nobody wanted to sit too close to either of them.

· · ·

Marathon Movie Night began with Horrors of the Komodo Dragon.

"He is describing me," said Sergei as they listened to the other man who had arrived with Komodo. "He is GRU. Major Gennady Tsaplin, I recall. He says he spoke to the officer in the auditorium. He wants to know who I am and is not stupid enough to think I am Igor Stravinsky. He will not remember me."

You mean you didn't sleep with his wife, thought Jay.

"Who else was in the auditorium?" asked Mack.

Jay was about to use a sarcastic tone to say the audience number when Sergei interrupted, "A young woman named Sergeant Andrews and a colonel called Durring."

Mack turned to Jay. "You must find these two and move them. And their families. Now. Go. Or they will be dead."

It took Jay only a fraction of a second to follow Mack's thinking before he ran to the secure line in the kitchen.

"Gennady is giving Komodo his orders," said Sergei.

Jay took his seat again quietly.

"He is to kill Linda and the boy Danny after they have destroyed the Vilsecks."

"Linda?" said Frank.

Sergei held up his hand for silence and nodded.

"Yes," said Alex. "He did not say Sally."

She turned pale as they listened to the rasping deep voice of the dragon and Sergei resumed the translation.

"He is saying he wants to be allowed to do what he pleases with the young woman. He wants to...."

He could not continue and did not need to because the translation was visible on the faces of the two babysitters with rusty Russian, of Alex, who had covered her face, of Mara whose stoic, inherited icy countenance was not entirely proof against what was being said, unlike the still faces of her father and brother. Their expressions did not change, or if anything, they became more hardened.

"Gennady assures Komodo."

"Komodo presses for carte blanche."

"Gennady reminds him who is boss." Sergei's eyebrows rose. "Ah. He mentions Komodo's sister. He begs to remind him how unpleasant it would be for her to be in prison. How painful for her would be any interrogation. How delightful she would be for the interrogators they would employ." Sergei sighed deeply. "The GRU are not subtle. They should stick to technical intelligence. Such explicit threats ..."

Mack interrupted, with an impatient gesture, a looming discussion of the internecine squabbles in the enemy's camp.

"There is a telephone call," said Sergei, his eyes wide. "Moscow is calling. Gennady says that he understands. The connection is not clear and he has difficulty. We are having difficulty. It amazes me that we needed only to let the Germans bring down the wall in order to make simple telephone calls to operatives in this country, but perhaps there are still obstacles...."

Another impatient gesture cut him short. The room became silent as static interfered with the voice coming over the telephone line into Gennady's hotel room, but the name Beridze was clear enough. His mission had priority.

"Gennady is now speaking to Beridze by telephone in Linda's room," continued Sergei, "and wants David to search the computer for a KGB defector, probably first directorate he thinks. He is wrong."

"Stick to translating, Pavlenko," said Skosh. He received in reply a filthy look as only an operational specialist can give, a look Sergei never dared give his father-in-law Mack. Skosh returned it with interest.

Mara switched the machine back to Linda's room.

"What did Gennady want?" asked Linda as Nick hung up the phone.

"He wants David to find somebody for us. I'll see your boy later and tell him." After a long pause, Nick asked, "The guy who recruited you, was he KGB?"

"Mm hmm," said Linda.

"What did he look like?"

"I don't remember. Just some kid."

"Did he sleep with you?"

All eyes in the room turned to Sergei. He looked away from Mara's cool green-eyed stare.

"No, of course not," said Linda.

"She is lying," said Sergei. When Mara's face turned from ice to fire, he said, "It was my job!"

"Nice work if you can get it," said Skosh. "May we presume she was better looking at the time?"

"Not much."

"You're lying, Pavlenko," said Steve from the doorway. He made Frank move to the other side of the table and took his seat. "You never did anything you didn't want to do."

Linda's voice put a stop to Sergei's retort. "You know I have been only yours since you were assigned to me, Nick. After all, you got rid of the idiot I was married to."

"I did not do that, Linda. You did."

"Those horrible men did."

"You arranged it. I almost did not survive the loss of that asset. He was important to my directorate. You are too reckless sometimes."

"Well, David will be an important asset, now that he knows who to blame. Thanks for convincing Sally to tell him. With any luck they'll take her out, too, and her brat. After the Vilsecks are dead, we should use the kid to trap Charlemagne themselves."

"Whatever you suggest, my love. I am sure we can arrange it. Especially the kid."

FOURTEEN

When Nick and Linda reduced their conversation to long sighs and low moans, there was a run on the coffee machine and its necessary corollary, the toilets. Frank was the last to return because he had been unlucky enough to arrive at the machine when all pots were empty. Mack had stopped Alex and Theresa from making coffee by edict, a prohibition everyone else found unfair, since neither Mack nor Charlie ever made a pot, and Sergei and Steve made coffee only when they couldn't bully a babysitter into it.

Frank sat down in the smug complacency of a man whose coffee was both hot and fresh. "What did I miss?"

Jay shrugged. "They finished what they were doing and Beridze left." Even as he spoke a reel began turning on a neighboring machine, and Mara turned it to speaker.

"Hello, my beautiful Sally."

"Is that Beridze?" said Steve.

Nobody wanted any part of that question and left it to Mack to answer. He raised one eyebrow in a minimalist form of yes.

"Nick, stop." Sally giggled. "Danny, why don't you go downstairs and get a soda?"

"Mom...."

"Just go. Just for a little while. Go on."

They heard the door slam.

"Come here, Sally. How much time do we have?"

"Maybe twenty minutes. But he doesn't have a key." She began giggling again.

"That is enough time for me," said Nick.

"He's mine," said Steve.

Mack agreed with a slight nod.

They sipped their coffee, taking advantage of the time to attend to ordinary tasks, like cleaning their weapons. Finally, intelligible words again met their eavesdropping ears.

"Sally, I think we will find them tomorrow and we will move quickly. You and Danny must be ready first thing. Wait for me to pick you up."

"You'll kill that awful man who hit me, Nick? You will won't you? Then we can go away and be safe. What will you tell Linda? Do you think she'll be mad about you and me?"

Nobody looked at Steve. They suspected it still rankled him and sensed that he would not appreciate their pity. Those who had never seen Sally knew instinctively that she had to be beautiful to have attracted a man like Steve despite her glaring lack of common sense. They commiserated, but silently.

Mack turned to Justin. "Can you make his research into the KGB defector difficult? Not stopped, just difficult. You have the address of his safehouse."

Justin was about to try explaining the difference between physical and computer addresses when Mara said, "It will be better to place a device at the junction box, but this time not to listen. It would be to interfere with the modem on his line. Louis often listened at junction boxes. I know how to do it if Justin has a device that will interfere with transmissions or perhaps reroute them into oblivion."

"I do, but it's tricky to put on a line like that."

Mack nodded at Charlie. "Take them, now." To Alex, he said, "Bring Theresa upstairs and get some sleep."

Alex opened her mouth as if to object, but closed it again when he narrowed his eyes in an unmistakable command.

When they had left, with a low voice he asked Jay, "Do you have someone reliable in the local office?"

"Ye-es," said Jay, hesitating as though he did not fully trust the question or the questioner.

"Can they hide the boy safely for a few hours?"

Steve looked up. "Misha—"

Mack silenced him with a gesture. To Jay, he said, "Call them on the secure line. Do not use anyone you are not perfectly sure about."

Jay left for the kitchen.

As they waited, Skosh was the first to lay his head on his arms to resume the nap he had begun during dinner. Frank, Steve, and

Sergei followed suit. Only Mack stayed awake, thinking, so that when Jay came back at the same moment as the three who had been to the junction box, Mack barked instructions, waking the sleepers.

"You," he pointed to Frank and Skosh, "go upstairs and rest." Justin turned to follow them.

"No. You stay here."

He obeyed and sat down warily. Charlie was in the room. Relations between them, never better than indifferent, had become decidedly antagonistic during the ride to the junction box. Justin took the wheel with Mara as his front passenger and Charlie in the back. As he drove down the highway, he made the mistake of asking Mara's advice on how he should approach Theresa. She raised incredulous eyebrows but before she could say anything, that fucking huge knife had appeared before his eyes so suddenly he nearly ran off the road.

"Put it away, Michael," she said.

"For the millionth time, use the name Charlie." He put the knife away. "I was only helping Justin think again about approaching Theresa."

"Men don't think at all when it comes to women," said Mara.

"So now you are playing the sage matron?" He paused. "Sergei is not hurting you, is he? He better not be. I saw that hickey on your neck."

"That is none of your business."

"It will be Papa's business if I tell him."

"You'd better not, Michael Joachim. Misha is just being a typical papa. You might consider that when you deal with Frank. Sergei always shows respect."

Charlie snorted.

Squashed back into the conference room half an hour later, Justin made himself as inconspicuous under Charlie's blue gaze as he could become, schooling the muscles of his face into impassivity. He was not fluent but had taken enough high school German beyond nein to understand when Mack asked Sergei if he still had any Russian ammunition. Yes, was the reply. Justin concentrated so hard on understanding what was said that he did not realize the next words were in English and also directed at him. He shook himself.

"I'm sorry, could you repeat that?"

"Can you find a photograph of Kenneth Schott?" said Charlie, slowly, as if talking to a two-year-old.

Justin did his best to keep his temper, but could not suppress a sneer. "Of course I can." This was a pleasure. He knew just where to look, and he had it on the screen in fifteen seconds. Charlie and Sergei stood looking over his shoulder for about thirty more seconds. They nodded at Mack.

"Can they find our safehouse by tracing the computers?" asked Mack.

"Yes," said Justin. "But we can make it more difficult by varying the routing through other cities and universities. I will show Mara how if she doesn't know the technique." He smiled at her hoping he had not insulted her knowledge. She smiled back, briefly, until she looked over his shoulder. He glanced up and found Sergei's glare almost as disconcerting as Charlie's.

He felt like dinner in the big cats pavilion at the zoo, and desperately wanted to go upstairs to sleep. The four men on the team left for god-knows where, taking Jay with them and leaving Mara in charge, with Frank responsible for security. But Justin still had not been dismissed, did not feel safe leaving, and did not feel safe asking. In fact, he did not feel safe, but fatigue became more important than security. He put his head down on his arms and fell asleep instantly. It felt like no more than a minute later when a fist pounded the table just beside his head.

FIFTEEN

"Call the fire department," said Charlie.

Justin jumped to his feet out of a dead sleep, confused and thinking he was dreaming.

"On the base, stupid. There's a fire in a hangar." To Sergei, standing at Justin's other side, he said, "What number was it?"

The unsafe feeling returned. They stood too close, using the proximity of their mass to intimidate him. He considered himself duly intimidated.

"He said it was the depot maintenance hangar, in the old quality control offices," Sergei answered.

"Call them," ordered Charlie.

Justin sat down and typed a report directly into the base emergency line. Using the modem, he sent it on via San Francisco without including his name. He added a line about many casualties.

"Nice touch," Sergei murmured.

Justin was not fool enough to think the compliment would help him.

They were still there dwarfing him as he hit send. He turned around. "Where is everybody?"

"Sleeping," said Sergei.

"They're out," said Charlie.

He sensed impending violence and knew he was the intended recipient. He tried to stand, but that power was taken from him. Instead, he was raised to his feet, shoved against the wall, and held by Charlie's fist in his gut while the other hand twisted his wrist. He was wearing a gun in a shoulder holster, but couldn't think how it might be possible to get to it, and anyway, wouldn't that escalate

things into a handy excuse to shoot him? And who would be the better shot?

"You will not approach Theresa."

"Or smile at Mara," said Sergei with a mischievous smile to
Charlie who looked at him with death in his heart.

"A girl like that doesn't deserve a thug like you," Justin said to
the man who had him up against the wall.

Charlie worked him over pretty good, adding liberal numbers
of bruises to his face and ribs, but Sergei was laughing too hard to
help him do it. They both shoved him toward the door smirking, "Go
get some sleep. You look like you need it." Mack and Steve were just
coming in through the front door. Mack raised an eyebrow when he
saw Justin head for the stairs holding his gut, but he said nothing.

"What the fuck happened to you?" asked Skosh when he
reached the back bedroom.

Frank's round eyes bulged further than ever. "Let me guess.
Charlie happened to you. What did you do, smile at Theresa? I noticed that at least you knew better about Mara and kept her out of
your calculus."

Justin could only nod. His lips were still too swollen to speak.

"They're wired now, Goodwin," said Skosh. "The adrenaline is
on its way up. They were always dangerous. Now they're fucking
dangerous."

"What happened besides your exclusive spa facial?" asked
Frank.

Justin mumbled about the device they put in Bertram's junction
box.

Skosh left the room and came back with a damp, dirty rag from
the bathroom. He handed it to Justin, who declined it, deciding he
preferred to stay swollen than add infection to the misery.

"What else?" said Frank. "Why did Mack want you there and us
out? What did they say?"

"I don't know what they talked about. It was all in German—
way above my head. They asked for a picture of that cousin of Linda's. Charlie asked for it. They looked at it on the screen for about
thirty seconds."

"They? Which ones?" asked Jay, who stood in the doorway.

"The delinquents. That's what Skosh calls them. No, that's not right." He squinted to focus his memory. "It was Charlie and the Russian guy."

Frank gave Skosh a frog stare of approval. "What else happened?"

"They went out. They all went out, except Mara. I fell asleep with my head on the table and they woke me up. I don't think they were gone long. And then this." He pointed to his face.

"That's it? No other requests?"

"Oh, yeah. They wanted me to call the fire department about a fire. I did it by computer. Then Charlie beat the shit out of me and told me to come upstairs and get some sleep."

"Why the fire department? What fire?" asked Skosh.

"On the base. In a hangar somewhere." Justin struggled again to remember, but his need for sleep had sapped the ability.

"They hit Kenneth Schott," said Jay. "That's why Mack got us out of the way. This is unacceptable. They even sidelined the babysitters. They don't have carte blanche to hit Americans who are ancillary to the operation."

"Are you telling me my job now, Turner?" said Skosh. "It is part of our normal terms and conditions. Mack's discretion rules, and he does have the commission on both Bertram and Beridze. Anybody ancillary, as you call it, is fair game."

"You don't want to know what I think of you and your fucking terms and conditions, Nakamura."

Jay had never been this rattled and Skosh was a convenient target for his acute distress. He had ridden in the passenger seat, with Steve in the back as Mack drove them in silence to the hotel where most of their primary targets were staying. In the lobby, Mack directed him to stay behind. Five minutes later Steve and his eleven-year-old son joined him. They bought the boy a soda.

The transaction upstairs in the hotel was on tape back at the safehouse. Jay heard it when they returned. It filled in the gaps left by his brief interrogation of Danny as he dropped him off in the care of the local FBI field office manager.

Danny had opened the hotel room door at the first knock. Room service took forever and he was starving.

"No, Danny, don't!" said his mother. But it was too late. Mack and Steve pushed in, closing the door behind them.

"Hello Sally," said Steve.

"Hello Dan." Her tone was flat.

"Dan?" said Danny. "Your name's Dan, too?"

"It was," he said. "It's Steve now. You can call me that, or you can call me Dad."

Danny looked at the man's eyes and wondered if the kids had made fun of him for those eyes like they did of his. He had the same eyes, but he still wasn't buying that this was his dad.

"My dad was a terrible person and he's dead."

Sally was about to say something but Danny saw that a warning look from the other man silenced her.

"Well," said Steve, with just a hint of a Texas drawl. "The first is probably true, but the second isn't. Last I checked, I was still alive."

Danny turned to his mother, who reluctantly nodded in confirmation, then back to Steve.

"Dad?"

Steve nodded. "Why don't we go downstairs for a soda? We can talk there while your mom and my friend discuss other business. What do you say?"

Danny looked again at his mother. She nodded numbly, giving him the approval he wanted.

"Danny," she said as he turned away.

"Yes, Mom?"

"I love you, son."

"Me too, Mom."

The door closed behind the boy as his mother looked up into the blue eyes of the man she called Satan.

"Are you going to gut me like a fish like you promised?"

Mack drew out his SIG Sauer and screwed a piston and suppressor onto the barrel, shaking his head. "No. You are still Danny's mother. For the moment."

Downstairs, drinking the soda in front of him took a backseat to Danny's rampant curiosity. He spent most of the time excitedly peppering this man who looked like him with question after question. Some questions, but not many, were answered if he paused long enough between them.

"Why did Mom say you died? Where do you live? Why did it take so long to come for me? How come you didn't call? Did Mom tell you not to call? Or was it Linda? I bet it was Linda. She's bad news, Dad. She wants to kill me. Can I live with you for a while? Can you tell Mom her friends hate me? Maybe she'll believe you."

The unanswerable torrent ended when the other man walked into the lobby and signaled to Steve.

"Let's go, son."

"Where?"

"Mr. Turner is going to take you to a person who will take care of you and keep you safe while I finish my business here. Then we'll be getting on a fancy airplane. How does that sound?"

"Cool, but Mom...."

Jay saw Danny's eyes widen when the other man said, "She agrees that the best thing for a young man is to live with his father."

"Mister, you're not Russian like Nick, are you?" said the boy. "But you have a funny accent, too."

He nodded. "Call me Misha, but I am Austrian, not Russian." He patted a pocket of his jacket. "Your mother has signed the paperwork. That is why she brought you down here. It has been arranged. After you."

He held the door open and Danny walked through it knowing by instinct that his life had forever changed, and for the first time in a long while, he was not afraid.

SIXTEEN

Jay was about to inform Skosh they would have a date with the local authorities at Sally's room in the hotel next day when Alex appeared in the doorway with Theresa behind her.

"You may want to see this, Frank," she said, then held a finger to her lips.

They doused the light and filed silently out the door to a short gallery railing overlooking the living room. The team stood below, panting and checking their pulses. They had stacked the foot lockers against a wall next to the coffee machine to maximize usable floor space. A table and lamp were missing, probably stashed in the kitchen. The biggest item in the room, a sofa, had been upended and stuffed into the kitchen doorway. The otherwise small space was now sufficiently clear to allow two or three of them to spar in the limited space.

The men were shirtless. Mara wore a sports bra. They had been working for some time and all gleamed with sweat. Alex and Theresa sat on the floor of the gallery in the shadows cast by the downward-directed pendant light hanging on a long cord from a vaulted ceiling overhead. The two babysitters and two FBI agents arranged themselves silently around them.

"Komodo is Kyrgyz," said Sergei. "I was his babysitter on two occasions. He is not pleasant to anyone and is very cruel to his target. He has so many prison tattoos on his face, it is difficult to see his expression, but it is always evil, so there is no need to know how he is feeling. He will telegraph what he is thinking. He is very large, maybe one hundred fifteen kilos, and carries a Yakut knife, about a centimeter longer than Misha's. He screams when he attacks."

Mack brought out his knife. Charlie drew his. They compared, and Charlie's was slightly longer. He handed it to Mack, who put his own away. And immediately attacked, screaming.

Theresa gasped. Alex grabbed her hand and squeezed. Fortunately, the gasp had been covered by Mack's scream.

Charlie defended with a straight arm, blocking the knife hand. Mack corrected the arm to ninety degrees, for power and position. Also, step to the side, he advised. Prepare for him to try again. They practiced at least twenty times and went on to practice different angles of attack. Then they began again from the beginning, adding technique.

"Force his arm behind him," said Mack.

Again, they practiced repeatedly before adding the offensive moves. Alex looked at Theresa's face with concern. Would she be appalled? Theresa winced at some of the more vicious blows but stared at the spectacle with fascination. Then Mack advised his son to cut the man as soon as he disarmed him in a manner that used the natural movement of the act to inflict maximum damage. He should then press in to finish him. Mack gave examples.

"Take him down and cut him," he said. "He has thirty kilos on you. Sergei says it is fat, but fat is useful in a fight. Cut him. Immediately."

Theresa had learned enough German from her parents to understand most of it. Her eyes opened wide at such ruthlessness and Alex sighed inwardly. Theresa must be made to know what she would face as his wife, but Alex prayed she would not turn away in disgust. Michael would not have a better chance than this.

The sparring they saw lasted almost ninety minutes, all of it between Charlie and Mack. The others had toweled off and put their shirts, holsters, and weapons back on before forming a downstairs gallery of their own to sit and watch.

"I know you are all up there," said Mack, still panting from the exertion as he picked up a towel. "You will go into the conference room now and begin listening to any tapes that have been recorded tonight. Take notes, not about what you think is important. Take notes of everything you hear. Alex, I will see you upstairs."

The watchers in the upstairs gallery flattened themselves against walls as the team took possession of all the upstairs rooms. Mack shut the door behind Alex and began the ritual lecture. Nobody was in a mood to joke about it this time, and Alex followed them into the conference room in less than five minutes, looking solemn.

SEVENTEEN

"It's been four hours," said Justin. "Why do they get extra time?"

Theresa also wanted the answer to this but did not have the courage to ask. She had never been so tired, not ever, not even in finals week. The tapes had finished an hour before. Skosh promptly put his head on his arms and fell asleep. The man could sleep anywhere. Jay's approach was more dangerous. He leaned his chair against the wall, threw his head back, and snored. Alex curled up on the Footlocker of Useful Things.

"Because pretty soon this is going to end," said Frank, "and if we want it to end in our favor, they must be well rested." He was about to rearrange his head on his arms to force the crick to the other side of his neck when Mack walked in, gazed for only the briefest moment upon Alex, and picked up the sheaf of notes in front of Skosh. They had stripped the printer of its paper.

Charlie and Mara walked in quietly, displaying that unsettling stillness common to their family. In contrast, the delinquents brought all noise and chaos. Sergei punched Skosh's shoulder. "There is no fucking coffee," he said. Jay woke and put the front feet of his chair on the floor just in time as Steve came by. Theresa stood up to make coffee, Mack's earlier edict notwithstanding. She wanted to be out of the room.

"What is this?" said Mack. "I cannot read it."

Skosh looked at the page, trying to focus. "We took turns. That's Theresa's handwriting."

Theresa would have been happier to escape Mack's notice. He pointed to a line on the paper. "My dad said to put down 'no pillow talk,'" she said. "That's what it says. There was no pillow talk."

Mack raised his eyebrows and remained perfectly still, which Theresa had come to regard as a warning.

Jay came to her rescue, yawning. "Nick and Linda are spending the night together. There was no pillow talk. Only an hour of heavy breathing. He snores."

Mack divided the pages among the four other team members, stood by the FUT, and gave Alex his hand to help her up.

"I translated for them," she said, "when the GRU man and Komodo spoke. He is an evil man, Misha."

He nodded.

The room was silent; even the delinquents became still. Mack went back to his seat and the moment passed, another example of the mad operational pendulum swing between boisterous chaos and solemn watchfulness before facing formidable foes.

Jay took delivery of breakfast amid the usual noise, but the team ate very little, concentrating on protein in the form of scrambled eggs, oatmeal, and grits, but no biscuits, butter, or jam. They read the notes as they ate, requesting certain tapes and locations, all provided by Justin so that nothing on his plate was hot when breakfast ended. Theresa saw him look longingly at the food left on the trays and hoped he would have a chance at it before it congealed. Several of the tape locations were replayed a few times. Theresa made no sense of it, but then, she had not had the recent luxury of four hours of sleep, lying down.

Again and again, they heard the snippet of tape in which Komodo, translated first by Alex and confirmed by Sergei, said to Gennady sometime after midnight, "It is a dump. Worse than the last place you put us. Fucking hot and falling apart. Prison rats were smaller than these monsters. I cannot believe they once sold American capitalist crap there. No air. No windows. Only empty, baking parking lots."

Mack sent his icy gaze around the Americans in the room, looking for ideas. Any thoughts at all were tough to come by without sleep. Frank shook his head. Justin stared straight before him.

"I got nothing," said Skosh.

Jay threw his large head back, brought it down again, blinked, and said slowly, "Could it be a shopping center? An abandoned, boarded-up strip mall?"

The other Americans groaned. Yes, of course, that was what it was, crumbling capitalism at its finest as seen by a Russian, with plenty of asphalt and decay. Justin turned to his computer and began a Boolean search for such places in the city, then expanded it to the county. Mara looked for commercial real estate listings.

David and Nick had a few interesting exchanges. Nick seemed irritated with the younger man. David kept pressing for answers. "When will we meet? Should I come to your hotel? You keep saying it will be soon. When is soon?"

"Listen, David. I don't know yet. We are working on some things. Have you had any luck with the computers?"

"No. But we should meet. I need to know when we will move on them. I can hardly see the screen anymore, I'm so tired."

"We cannot move on them until we know where they are until we know who they are. Are you still looking for the Russian who was at the school on the base?"

"Yes, but my Russian isn't good enough for this. I don't think I'm looking in the right places."

Nick sighed through his teeth. "Wait," he said. "Wait. I remember something recent. It was not in my department, but it was in this country. Let me think."

The room, with the exception of Justin, who appeared happy in his ignorance as he tapped his keyboard, stiffened.

"Try San Antonio," said Nick. "Last year. See what that provides."

Two hours later, as Linda and Nick met in her hotel room the tapes rolled and Charlemagne's machines listened in. "David says we are meeting tomorrow morning," said Linda. "He thinks he found where they are, but not yet who they are. He doesn't think they're Italian, but the location is close to our teams."

"He knows nothing. But the Russian bothers me still. I struggle to remember what I heard about last year."

"When will he be able to attack? He's so anxious."

"I think we will be ready by ten o'clock. We will meet at his safehouse at nine and just walk to our teams to give them their instructions."

"Why not go now?"

"Because we know nothing about them, their numbers, their identities. We need intelligence."

Then as the tape began rolling again, this time live during the team's breakfast, they heard Gennady the GRU man and Komodo as they finished a breakfast pot of coffee laced with vodka in Gennady's room.

"Did you say he has brown hair?" said Komodo.

"That is what my friend said."

"Dark brown, light brown, curly, straight?"

"He said light brown and straight."

"And light eyes? Were they gray eyes, almost without color?"

"Yes. Do you have an idea?"

"No. Not an idea. I know who he is. He was my babysitter twice. The bastard would not let me take a trophy. He is Sergei Pavlenko. He killed the best babysitter I ever had, Maximovich, just last year in San Antonio. He joined that western team, Charlemagne, with some guy who thinks he knows how to use a knife. It will be a pleasure to kill Pavlenko. It will be a pleasure to kill all of them."

Simultaneous to this news, Mara pulled the plug on the modem shared by the two computers, and Justin announced, "We're blown." The Komodo conversation had been in Russian, so he did not know he was telling them what they already knew, but he had an instant education in urgency.

EIGHTEEN

Jay might not speak Russian, but he understood names, he had
been in San Antonio last year, and he knew most of the names the
team used. The names he heard on that tape meant imminent
danger and urgent action. He watched as Frank helped Skosh dress
the team with wires and body armor, then tactical vests and belts
over black tee shirts and trousers. Alex and Theresa fished clothing
and equipment out of lockers. Alex had done this a time or two,
thought Jay, or some form of it. When their demands became arrogant and peremptory, she gave back the same attitude without losing
time in arguments. The specialists were always the first to break
away from her glare. Except Mack. Alex never glared at Mack.

"Justin," said Mara, "find the two lists, yours and mine, that we
made of shopping centers. Check if any is within, say, half a kilometer of this or Bertram's house."

Justin had been unconsciously busy gazing at her legs, until
Sergei shoved him up against a wall, using a fistful of his collar to
cut off his breathing. Frank brokered a peace deal by convincing
Sergei to stop wasting time. Justin regained his breath and did as
Mara asked.

"Do we have a map of this area?" he asked the room at large.
Unfortunately for Justin, the question brought him back to Sergei's
attention. Maps were in the stupid FUT.

The preparatory adrenaline rush was just beginning, but the
delinquents in particular displayed more than their fair share of aggression, and Justin was an easy target. Skosh bravely tried to stand
in their way, but it was Mack who finally called them off.

"Hör auf!"

It was as if he'd flipped a switch. They released Justin without
serious damage and gave him the requested map. Within five min-

utes he had the location and was able to give directions. The mad-men of just a few minutes before were suddenly all business.

"Which direction does the front of the building face?"

"How large is the parking lot?"

"What is behind the building?"

Jay asked for street names that would make up a corridor be-tween the shopping center and the safehouse, including a generous perimeter. He ran to the secure phone in the kitchen to relay orders for a quiet evacuation and sealing of the area.

When everyone was dressed, all weapons had a round cham-bered, all FBI and babysitters armed, and even Alex was made to wear a badly fitting Kevlar vest and a holster with her SIG Sauer ful-ly loaded inside it, Skosh asked, "How long do you think it will take them to get here?"

Mack wrinkled his forehead. "We go to them. If we cannot stop them before they come here, they will burn you out. Listen to the radio. We will warn you if they break through so you can try to evacuate. If we have not warned you, do not open the door, but keep watch—and think."

The last two words held a scornful note.

NINETEEN

David Bertram stared at the navy blue water of the Santa Rosa Sound, which he could see through the sliding glass doors at the back of his safehouse. Today was the day. Today he would avenge his father, his poor, stupid father.

He sipped his coffee with satisfaction, gazing southward on a world of sand and water and peace, and so was not prepared for the boom of pounding fists on the front door behind him. It made him jump. He ignored the spilled, scalding coffee staining the tee shirt against his chest as he checked outside and then opened the door.

Nick, Linda, and the GRU guy—what was his name?—Gennady—poured into the safehouse.

"You're early."

"Shit, David, there are developments," said Nick, who went straight to the coffee machine in the kitchen. Gennady followed him.

"Good morning, dear." His mother kissed his cheek. "Is Sally here? She didn't answer her door at the hotel. We thought she might have come here, but I don't think she knows about this place."

"No, Mom, she's not here. What about the boy? We may need him."

"That's just it. She must have taken him with her."

David felt a burn in his throat with this news, like rising bile, as Nick and Gennady came back holding tall mugs. Aside from the coffee, there were no efforts by any of them to become more comfortable even by the simple expedient of sitting down. They stood by the door, sipping, shuffling, grimacing. Linda wore her pursed lip disapproval face that David knew so well from childhood.

He was about to ask about the new developments he knew would raise more bile in his throat, when Gennady volunteered one of them.

"I have moved the teams." Before David could voice an objection, he held up a hand. "It was necessary. There was a fire in that hangar on the base. The fire department came, and the military police. They discovered them. Our men fought their way out. Well, two fought. The rest were too drunk, but not too drunk to remember wire cutters. They slipped through the fence. The two who tried to shoot their way free were killed. I found an abandoned place not far from here. Komodo is with them now. We can still move against Charlemagne at our planned time."

"Charlemagne!" David was new to the game but he knew that name.

"Yes," said Gennady with a smug smile. "Not the Italians. Charlemagne killed your father. Last year, Sergei Pavlenko joined them in San Antonio. Sally's ex-husband was already a member. He is the brown-haired man you shot, Nick. But it seems he walked away."

"But it was a young blond man who came for Richard," insisted Linda. "I remember him. He was not much older than David."

It was this collection of words, each crowding the next into and through his brain, that made David remember the man next to him on the airplane—and again at the baggage carousel. He pictured the dead man. His missing briefcase. But it was found. Everything was as it should be. He had watched the man walk out without it.

He looked at the case on the coffee table, picked it up like it was an alien thing, opened it, inspected it. He took it to the window.

"What is it, David?" asked Nick.

In the morning light, he thought maybe … was the seam glued down? He opened his knife and sliced the lining, viciously, furiously, as they all watched the thin one-inch wafer flutter to the floor.

Even as Gennady broke the intruding tap in half, they were unaware that four more were installed in that house alone, and several in their hotel rooms. But the issue was moot. Though the reels recorded all their deliberations, no one was listening. The babysitters had gathered everybody into the front bedroom upstairs, while Charlemagne systematically destroyed the remnants of David's hopes.

Gennady felt a momentary pang for the young man. He had been a promising prospect but was not likely to live through this. Moscow had been clear. Only Sally was to be preserved. He set off at a trot to find Komodo. Whatever orders the beast could not manage to execute he would leave to the legendary efficiency and competence of Charlemagne. He congratulated himself on a job neatly done.

Ten minutes later, two of Charlemagne's remaining three targets straggled to the address David had determined was the source of an eerily familiar intelligence behind a computer, or maybe two computers sharing a modem. He wasn't sure. He set off at a trot, his Makarov tucked into an inside holster at his back. Linda grabbed an AK-47 from Nick's car and followed more slowly. Nick settled into the driver's seat, said something about bringing the car around, but opened a magazine instead—to take his mind off things while he waited for Charlemagne to do the work required to rid him of that vicious woman. Too bad about David, but there was no help for it.

...

David was surprised when Theresa came out to talk to him. He thought she had more sense. No matter. He would shoot her and the little brown-haired woman trying to talk sense into her. Not as satisfying as he had hoped, but Theresa would still be dead.

As he drew his Makarov from behind him, he noticed a familiar face in the front window. A non-entity he had known at MIT. That must have been the computer intelligence he recognized. David reserved a third bullet for him. As he brought his sights onto Theresa, he saw the silly little brown-haired woman sight her gun on him. He smiled and then heard his mother's voice coming through the window in front of him, confessing that she had arranged his father's death.

David never heard his mother shout "You bitch!" He predeceased her by less than a second.

TWENTY

Michael felt useless and stupid. He was not sure about his brother-in-law, Sergei. Standing here, in the back of the building, waiting, he heard the sounds of a brief battle as automatic fire came to him in a rapid tattoo from inside. He was only lightly armored and lightly armed because Sergei said this and Sergei said that, and bloody Sergei put a hickey on his sister's neck, damn him, and God knows where else.

Sergei said Komodo would run out the back and circle to his target.

A door opened, framing a heavily tattooed man lightly clad and with only an AK-47 slung on his shoulder. He ran for a small pine wood behind the building, staying low until he reached the trees, then began picking his way in a westward arc. Michael followed, staying far enough back so that any sound he might make on sand and pine needles would be masked by the big man crashing his way to murder.

He no longer felt stupid. He felt only the intense concentration that would win the day if that should be his fate. All his training and all his instincts were engaged. He watched the man move as he followed him, measured his stride, and felt the weight of him in the crushed undergrowth around the trees. It was a short stride for a man of such size and bulk. The way he moved suggested total reliance on brute force, ponderous, without finesse, and not very agile for a renowned knife fighter.

Michael had shed his MP5 to make this pursuit, but he retained his Glock. Three times he sighted it on his opponent's back, but the trees, brush, and uneven terrain interfered with a clean shot. It had to be clean, or he could lose him. It was hard enough to keep up with him and the terrain grew no easier. He could not stop to get a decent shot, so as the distance widened, he elected to shoot at the run, clean or not, before he should lose him entirely.

The shot struck his opponent in the upper right side of his back. Komodo spun with a bellow, firing the AK wildly, emptying a magazine into the forest and at Michael, hitting him with two rounds, both squarely stopped by his body armor, but the impacts knocked the wind out of him and spun him against a tree. The Glock went flying into the brush.

Michael put his hand on his knife in time to meet Komodo coming in low and pointing up, the hardest approach to counter. He used a leg to block the attack, feeling a slice along his calf as Komodo brought him down with a sweep against the cut leg. He landed and rolled away just as the Yakut knife plunged into the sand beside him. He grabbed the wrist that held it.

His enemy was now bleeding profusely from the gunshot wound and breathing heavily but his strength remained gargantuan. Evidently, brute strength made up a lot for a lack of agility. They did not wrestle. Michael held that wrist and by twisting, jumping, dropping, and rolling, avoided the giant's arms and legs as Komodo telegraphed each attempt to hit him, landing one ineffectual glancing fist on Michael's right kidney and then a more serious body blow to the diaphragm.

As he struggled to breathe again, Michael kept hold of the wrist and remembered the training he had practiced the night before. His breath came back with a gasp, and he braced one foot against a tree trunk to gain purchase, then used Komodo's furious thrashing as leverage to bring himself to a stand.

The dragon stabbed the air within millimeters of his neck as Michael stepped behind him, bringing the man's arm with him. He exposed the underside of the wrist behind his back, brought his knife across it, and watched as his enemy's knife dropped into the pine needles.

Michael finished him more mercifully than Komodo had ever done to a victim. He found his Glock, retrieved the MP5, and limped to the safehouse.

TWENTY-ONE

Misha ran point. It was not the necessity of what he was doing that irked him most, though it did. It always did. He was in a more or less permanent state of irk much of the time and wondered what Alex would think of the observation or his use of the English word. It irked him more than usual this time because she was not safe at home. She was in harm's way. No matter what he did, no matter what he said, the bloody woman insisted on worrying about the future. Damn it. *You do not have a future if you do not stay alive now.* He tried to tell her. He argued. The more they fought, the more he wanted her.

He shifted his thoughts in a long-practiced direction. The back of the target sentry loomed before him. The man did not hear him, would never hear him, would never hear anything again, and the others in the building would never hear him die. All of it irked Misha.

He gave the signal to the team behind him. Steve handed him an MP5 submachine gun as he passed into the building. Sergei nodded to him. Mara followed Steve. The gunfire began immediately. They had only four fighters left to defeat, now that the sentry was dead, then five more important targets. The knife fighter was Michael's. Nick was Steve's, and Mara had been assigned to the GRU man. Misha would take out David as he had Sally. She had done her damage by causing the operation and endangering the child. She could not be considered an innocent. Poor, silly, dangerous woman.

Sergei was assigned to take care of Linda because he had recruited her when he was KGB. Misha found that thought more tolerable than the thought of him touching his daughter. The damage these asshole bureaucrats can do, thought Misha. Like Sally, they are too often oblivious to consequences. Sergei had been one of them, in fact had been part of the operation to kill Misha's childhood friend Vasily. Now he did all his damage with a gun. This, at least, Misha understood. Guns were not as insidious. When you kill with a gun, you know you are guilty of something heinous. No such awareness accompanies a pen.

Mara inhabited a special category in Misha's worldview. Sergei had better remember that.

He helped the others clear the building, saw the GRU babysitter exit through a side door, and saw Mara run after her quarry. He knew Michael and Mara were more than adequate for the task ahead of them, but this son-in-law of his? A former babysitter like Steve, but for the other side. Sometimes too much like Steve.

There were no signs of the other three targets, so where were they?

He stood at the building entrance with Sergei. The flies had become thick on the sentry's body, buzzing a grizzly din in the decaying space. He watched his son-in-law shiver at the sight. Good, he thought, let him remember this should he ever think to hurt Mara.

Misha turned on his heel and headed for the safehouse, leaving Sergei to follow. He did not like this silence. He hated not knowing what was going on at the house. Was the bloody woman obeying him for once and staying inside? Was she wearing her SIG? Was she still alive? His pace quickened with this thought, even before the call in their ears from Skosh. At that call, he broke into a run.

TWENTY-TWO

It took Mara and the others less than two minutes to clear the building and account for all four fighters, most of them half naked in the sweltering heat and still hungover. Komodo ran out the back. There was no sign of any of the other four main targets until Misha caught a glimpse of a closing side door leading to the outside. He signaled to Sergei who was closest and who opened it carefully to see the retreating back of Gennady, the GRU babysitter.

"I will …," he began.

"No," said Mara. "We have a plan." She was already running when she reached the door.

Gennady was not headed to Charlemagne's safehouse. His direction meant his destination must be David's safehouse. Mara acted quickly on intuition. A car driven by one of Jay's watchers was parked at the end of the block. She switched her radio out of network and into main.

"Jay," she said. There was an agonizing pause before Skosh answered. "Get Jay," she said. She came level with the car. The driver stared straight ahead watching the retreating back of a man in a suit, but did nothing. Mara knew Gennady did not fit any of the descriptions that had been given out and appeared unarmed. Plus, he was leaving, not trying to get into the area. The car windows were open. It was already eighty-three degrees Fahrenheit under the trees and humid, hotter in the car. Mara reached in, unlocked the passenger door, and sat down, pointing her Glock at the unlucky watcher.

"Hands on the wheel," she said. "Drive."

"What…?

"Straight ahead."

"Jay here," said a voice in her ear.

"I need you to call your guy." She looked at her driver. "What's your name?"

He seemed to have no answer, so she put a round past his nose and out his window.

"Connolly," he said.

"Connolly," she told Jay. "Call him and tell him to do as I say."

"I need to be sure."

"Yes, it's her," came through the radio, blasted by both Sergei and Steve, the latter with an epithet.

Jay called Connelly on another channel, provided authentication, and ordered compliance. Connolly followed Mara's instructions to the letter. Gennady had parked a nondescript rental car on the street a few yards before the driveway leading to David's safehouse. As he pulled away from the curb, Mara told Connolly to follow him.

"Are you local to this area? Do you live here?" she asked after a few minutes.

"Yes."

"Where do you think he is going? It is not the way to his hotel."

"Um. Maybe the beach. On the island."

"Island?"

"Okaloosa Island. There's a popular beach there. Yes, I'd say he's headed for the bridge."

"Is it populated? Are there many people?"

"Yes. Especially with this heat."

Mara laid her Škorpion machine pistol and Glock on the floor and took off her vest, her t-shirt, then her armor, belt, boots, trousers, and socks.

"What are you doing?" asked Connolly.

She had to take the wire out of her ear. She would be on her own. She debated whether to give it to Connolly to monitor but decided if this took longer than a minute and he answered her radio, it could cost him his life, not by the enemy, but by her team. Neither her husband nor her brother would wait for explanations. Mercy prevailed and she dropped the earpiece and wire into a pocket of the vest on the floor. She fished out the black t-shirt and put it back on, then rummaged for her Glock and a suppressor, checked again that the magazine was full and a round chambered, fitted the suppressor, and shook out her blonde hair saying, "There is his car. Park near it."

As soon as he had parked, she demanded he give her his shirt, covered the Glock with it, and stepped out barefoot onto the hot pavement. "Wait here," she said through the open window.

She looked like any other young woman at the beach. A particularly attractive young woman. She heard wolf whistles.

It took her a full three minutes to locate her quarry and position herself ahead of him on the crowded beach. Gennady had shed his coat and tie, shoes and socks, and had opened his shirt to the Gulf breeze as he walked along the wet sand. She approached, smiling.

He smiled back.

She said hi as she walked up to him. He said hi back, too busy looking at her to remark on the shirt she had pressed to his chest. He fell face forward into the water. Mara acted shocked and ran through the crowd screaming "Help him!" She made her exit to the parking lot as the crowd surged toward the dead man.

Even as Connolly wondered if he should call Jay—it had been almost four minutes—she slid into the seat next to him and told him to drive to the safehouse, our safehouse she clarified, the one where Turner was.

Everyone was outside when she arrived, and Sergei was on the ground. So was her mother. Sergei was bleeding and swearing while Steve applied a tourniquet to his leg. Her mother lay on her back, very still. Theresa held her wrist and pulled up an eyelid.

Mara did not notice the burning heat of the pavement on the soles of her feet as she ran to Misha.

TWENTY-THREE

S teve Donovan's target was a no-show. Michael and Mara had fol- lowed theirs and Sergei knew where to find his, but Nick never came near the teams or the remnants of teams Charlemagne had just taken care of. Who would behave like that? Steve asked himself. He knew the answer immediately because he had been one, briefly, un- successfully, but he knew a babysitter by smell if nothing else. The GRU guy was a babysitter for the tattoo guy. So who was Nick sup- posed to be babysitting? Not the collection of drunken louts they had just massacred. Who then? David. Nick was grooming a computer nerd to become a specialist. Steve couldn't help snorting. Then he remembered Mara was a computer nerd and also a highly effective specialist.

Back to the business at hand, he told himself. Because he's a babysitter, Nick will wait it out somewhere. Where? At David's safe- house. All of this thinking took no more than a few seconds. He eased his MP5 off the sorest part of his shoulder and set off at an easy jog. Sally had exhausted Misha's patience, finally. He didn't know how he felt about it. Relief mixed with pain mixed with, he had to admit, some joy. He had his son again. He remembered him- self at eleven and shuddered. Misha was right. Sally had to go. How many deaths was she responsible for now? He couldn't count them. He could only count the ones so far on this trip, the ones he had tak- en care of, the one he was about to, all of them bad guys, but they would not have crossed paths this time out but for Sally's big mouth. And that didn't include any additional information she may have blabbed that could lead these bozos home to Vasily's Carpet.

Shit. Eleven years old.

Steve waited for what looked like one of Jay's watchers to pull away from the curb down from the entrance to David's safehouse, then crept around a high bordering hedge. Two cars were parked side by side in front of the door. One had an occupant in the driver's seat.

He walked up, in full armor, tactical vest festooned with magazines, radio, knife, and holster. The holster was empty because his Beretta was in his hand. He looked at the man reading a Russian magazine. It looked from the side like pictures of Nick he had seen, but he had to be sure. Misha was not keen on mistakes. Steve was not keen on Misha's reactions to mistakes. He tapped on the window.

"Hey, tovarishch," he said.

Nick Beridze turned and saw the muzzle of the suppressor, but had no time to react.

Steve walked back to the team's safehouse and found a disaster underway in front of it.

TWENTY-FOUR

Sergei cleared a nest of two vory in one room, still groggy, barely dressed, and meters from their weapons. He let them get a step closer to their guns before he let them have it. Misha would not approve. Misha did not approve of much. He certainly did not approve of Sergei, though he was more restrained in his disapproval than Mikhail, that is, Michael. He must get used to these Western names.

The root cause of all this disapproval was, of course, Mara. They pictured her as an innocent maiden. Sergei knew her to be all woman, young, yes, innocent in some ways perhaps, but not the blushing bride they thought she was. He smiled to himself as he trudged through the countless rooms in this decayed palace of capitalism. He had been her first, and as long as he had any say in it, would remain her only. But she never blushed.

Sergei cleared room after room, quickly, and efficiently, and met up again with his father-in-law back at the entrance, where Misha's earlier fly-covered work lay staring at the ceiling in a surprisingly large pool of coagulating blood. Sergei could not help a grimace. Misha's ice blue stare seemed like a challenge, as in, *say something so that I may answer you.* Sergei had no desire for one of Misha's answers. The man was always gentler to him than he was to Steve, if anything about Misha could be described as gentle, but that was purely for Mara's sake. Sergei knew better than to take it as a sign of approval.

"They are not here," he said.

Misha raised an eyebrow at this statement of the obvious.

"Where could they be?" Sergei asked.

His father-in-law did not answer but began walking back toward the safehouse. Sergei understood instinctively, because of how he felt about Mara, that Misha had to check on Alex. He wished he could convey this understanding, this empathy, to the iceberg that was Mara's biological father, but they still were not beyond bare tolerance in the relationship. He followed.

They had walked halfway to the house when Skosh's voice broke into the network and their ears.

"There is a problem."

They both began running. As they neared the house, Misha sent Sergei to the left with a hand signal and veered off to the right. They approached using what cover they could find on either side of the property. Sergei stopped behind a large juniper bush planted in front of the neighboring house.

Theresa was outside talking to David. They were about twenty-five feet apart. Who the hell let her out? What the fuck was Skosh thinking? Sergei was going to have a piece of his hide when this was over. Shit. Alex was behind Theresa, but also outside, trying to get her to come back in. Double shit. He did not dare look at Misha's expression. Some things just hold more horror than is necessary in an already overexciting life.

Then he saw Linda. She was walking up with studied nonchalance from behind a car parked on the street, approaching the little scene taking place in front of the safehouse. He knew he had a fresh magazine in his MP5. He silently put his Makarov away and took the MP5 off his shoulder pointing it in her direction. The hand that was toward him was empty, but he could not see the other hand and that bothered him. He watched her attitude. It seemed relaxed, almost friendly. Then he saw just the barest triangle of the bottom corner of an AK-47 stock.

In the next fraction of a second, two people died and three were wounded, one of them critically.

Sergei fired.

Linda screamed, "You bitch!" and at the same instant, brought up her AK to add punctuation.

Alex screamed, "No!" and moved slightly in front of Theresa, her arm stretched out and the sights of her SIG on David.

Theresa stood frozen as she watched David's arm come up, a semi-automatic pistol in his hand, on its way to aim at her head.

Misha fired and killed David.

Sergei's burst from the MP5 interrupted Linda's, but as she died, three rounds escaped the aborted fire from the AK. The first hit Alex and she went down. The second hit Justin in the window where he had placed a speaker and played the tape of Linda confessing to the plan to kill her husband. It was the last thing David heard. The third bullet hit Sergei, causing a lot of bleeding from his thigh and bringing him down. He told himself it was not spurting and therefore not the artery, but he did not like the way it gushed.

He may have lost consciousness. He wasn't sure. The next thing he knew, Steve was applying a tourniquet and Theresa was gently slapping Alex's cheek. And the look on Misha's face was just too terrible to stay conscious of. Sergei allowed himself to pass out again.

TWENTY-FIVE

Skosh and the other babysitters—let's face it, he thought, even Jay understands he is essentially babysitting a gaggle of killers, so he can get off his lawman high horse even if he won't admit it out loud. Jay's shadow, young and over-educated Justin, didn't have the foggiest idea why he was there or what he was doing, but that didn't mean he wasn't babysitting. Once these thoughts had settled in Skosh's brain and he felt justified in calling the FBI guys fellow babysitters—even though he knew Frank would balk at that, being strictly old school—but once that was settled, he turned his attention to their common problems, namely Theresa and Alex. Two of the most powerful men he knew, two men whose word was absolute among their subordinates, Mack and Frank, could not fully control these women. And now he and the others were responsible for their safety.

Skosh put himself in charge. Frank had more experience but was retired and worried about his daughter. Jay was active and experienced but busy with the army of watchers he controlled. Also, Jay was the best shot, though Skosh suspected he and Frank could compete. He wasn't sure about Alex. The only thing he knew about Alex was that she was their most precious charge, despite Theresa being family, because nobody would want to face Mack if anything happened to her.

Everybody climbed to the front bedroom at his insistence to await news. Skosh brought the radio receiver from the conference room, even though they were all wired. He would have been happy with just having a lookout up here, but he did not want the two women unsupervised for even a moment.

The six of them had been up there for almost half an hour when Jay answered a call from Mara. They spent another ten minutes taking turns peering through the blinds to the front yard when they heard a voice outside.

"It's Bertram," said Jay.

They heard him shouting through the glass.

"Theresa! Theresa, I know you're there. I just want to talk to you. I think I have a right to some answers. I won't hurt you. I would never hurt you. See? I'm not armed."

"His hands are clear," said Jay.

"I should talk to him," said Theresa.

"No!" Skosh was gratified that even Alex joined this chorus.

"Wait a minute," said Justin, checking outside. "I know that guy. We were in a couple of classes together at MIT. He's an asshole. Worst kind of mama's boy. A mean coward."

"No shit?" said Skosh through clenched teeth. "Tell us more— some other time!"

"I can't see behind him," said Jay on the other side of the window. "Just because his hands are clear doesn't mean he's not armed. Also, there could be others out there. Too many bushes on both sides. Who set up this safehouse anyway?" He gave an accusing glance at Justin, who shrugged back at him.

"Well, I need the bathroom," said Theresa. "I'll be right back."

Alex seemed uneasy. "I'll just stay with her." She left the room and, in another moment, she was shouting from the stairs.

Justin would have followed them all down the stairs, but Skosh told him to cover David from the window.

"Fire if he shows a weapon," said Skosh. "Don't wait."

"I can't," shouted Justin before Skosh was halfway down. "She's in the way." He knew he was not a good enough shot with Theresa blocking the path of any rounds he might throw at David. Rather than stay upstairs pointlessly, he ran down the steps after Skosh with an idea. Remembering Alex had told him to cue the tape of Linda saying she planned the death of her husband, he pressed play in the conference room and grabbed the speaker, unspooling the wire as he ran to the front room window and opened it.

Frank screamed at his daughter to get back inside. Jay ran back upstairs in a futile quest to find any angle of sight on David that was not blocked by Theresa and now by Alex. Skosh broke into the team frequency and with all the urgency he could put into his voice and the greatest understatement he could find words for, he said, "Skosh here. We have a problem."

Maybe the tape made David pause just long enough for Sergei and Mack to reach the house. Skosh slid down the stairs and into a horror scene. The front door was open. Theresa stood, tall, majestic, and frozen, her great mane of dark auburn hair hanging in waves around her shoulders. Linda's voice came from a speaker held by Justin at the open window. David held a Makarov pointed at Theresa's head from no more than fifteen feet away. Alex stood in a side stance, her right arm extended and her finger on the trigger of her SIG Sauer.

Into this tense scene, Linda came out of nowhere brandishing an AK-47 and screaming, "You bitch!" Though which woman she was referring to, Skosh couldn't say. At the same moment, Justin flew backward into the living room wall, Linda fell amid a burst of automatic fire coming out of a juniper bush, David's head exploded and he fell, and Alex crumpled to the ground.

Theresa turned to her immediately and searched for a pulse. Mack ran up and looked down at the two women, his own SIG still in his hand at his side. David and Linda were dead.

Frank ran to Theresa carrying a bag of medical supplies. "What else do you need?"

"I need her to live," said Theresa through tears. "Come on Alex. Her breathing is not right. Get the damned vest off her. Quick! I need to see."

It was Mack who holstered his gun and knelt to take the armor off his wife. At first, they could not see the bullet hole. Then as Theresa gently compressed the chest, blood and air seeped and hissed from a small hole in Alex's side. There was surprisingly little blood, but Alex lay unconscious.

Theresa checked her pupils. There was no response. "Come on, please, Alex. I'm so sorry. I'm such a fool. Please forgive me. I'll marry him. I will. Just live, Alex, just live for me. I'll need you!"

She checked again. "The pulse is good," she said with a sigh "But I think the lung has collapsed and I'm sure there's a head wound. We have to get her to a hospital."

Alex shuddered through a hissing breath but did not regain consciousness.

"No," said Mack, standing up.

She stared, incredulous.

"Papa," said Charlie, "Steve and I will take care of the other matter and meet you at the airplane."

Mack nodded. Theresa stared at Charlie now. He was drenched in blood and had some active seepage coming from one leg.

"Frank," said Charlie, "load the car when Steve gets here with it. Jay, some of your people can help, but only the locked trunks. Frank, you check every trunk and watch their hands. Jay, when will the ambulances be here?"

"In about half a minute. I called them from the kitchen. Goodwin was hit, but the vest stopped it. He can help."

"She will die without proper attention!" said Theresa, tears streaming down her face.

"Then you will give her that attention," said Mack.

"I can't do it alone and without equipment and my best helper is the patient. Where is Sergei?"

"He needs you as well."

Mara ran up to Mack and buried her head on his chest, sobbing. Mack had no idea what to do. Mara had always treated him as the not-exactly evil but certainly suspect stepfather, though he was her biological father as well. He carefully patted her back, whispered something to her, and she turned to Theresa.

"You must save her. Please save her."

"As I just tried to explain to your father ..." Theresa began her litany of impossibilities, but neither Mack nor Mara was listening. For the first time, Mara did not correct the word father to stepfather. The significance was not lost on either of them.

"Listen to me, Theresa," said Mack. "These men will help you." He pointed to several EMTs walking up from two discreet ambulances. "You will get her ready to fly. Also Sergei," he turned to Jay. "Goodwin?"

"Last priority."

Theresa sobbed.

"Because he's not that badly hurt, Theresa," said Jay. "Concentrate on Alex. Here comes Donovan with the car."

A black Mercedes pulled into the driveway and Frank began supervising as the watchers loaded the trunk, then he and Skosh carried in the open bags. Charlie climbed into the passenger seat. Skosh handed him a wet rag to wipe his face and the car pulled out.

She did not know how she did it, but Theresa managed to check everything on both patients as they were loaded into the ambulances. Mara and Frank rode with Sergei. Mack joined Theresa in the ambulance with the unconscious Alex.

"I don't understand why you refuse to take her to a hospital," she said. "She's unconscious too long and I don't know why, and there's a chest wound. She needs …"

"She would be in more danger there. We are, all of us, in danger. Your father will explain more fully later. We must leave now. There is no succor for us in this country. It is a country of laws, but also very open and very armed. All three things are dangerous. The law is powerful and can be used against us by those who manipulate it. We cannot always hide in such openness, and all weapons are easily available to our enemies without remark. They would not miss such an opportunity. No bullet is reversed by law."

"But if you're leaving, how can I help her?"

"The airplane is equipped. You will have everything you need. And Mara will help. She is also an accomplished nurse." He looked at her with his brow furrowed. "Did you not understand you are coming with us?"

TWENTY-SIX

There was one happy person on the airplane. Danny could not believe the luxury of being in a large private jet, and he reveled in the squalor of unshaven men, filthy and stinking and exhausted. There were a couple of women, he noted, but everybody else was a guy like him, not a bunch of girls, and no Linda. These guys weren't evil in his book, no matter what Mom said. He knew they had rescued him, but he wasn't sure it would be okay to say so. Maybe they wouldn't believe him, either. He had made a plan to escape, but this was better. After all, he was just a kid. He hadn't even worked out where he would go.

All in all, he couldn't be happier.

Steve could not help glancing at his son. He wanted to stare but knew it would make the kid uncomfortable. The last time he had seen him, Danny was a toddler. There had been no pictures, no word, though he knew Misha kept a close eye on the boy and his mother to keep her from jeopardizing his safety. He could not believe Danny was sitting across from him now, firing off questions about airplanes. Sally had not told him that his dad had been a fighter pilot. She did tell him that his dad and his friends were evil men.

Danny's next questions were about the guns everybody wore. David took him shooting once, he said, but his mom had forbidden him to do that again. He asked shyly if Steve would take him out to the range sometime. It was this question that brought home to Steve the magnitude of the change he was making in his son's life. It made him pause, not with a bunch of philosophical considerations, for he was never a philosophical man. He paused with the practical implications. He questioned his ability to guide the boy through this change without damage. Steve's vocation, such as it was, had been

forced on him. He wasn't sorry about what he was and flattered
himself that he was grounded in his own grim reality, but he wanted
any such decision to be Danny's alone, not forced by circumstance.

"Listen, Danny," he said, "I'm super, super tired and I'll probably
fall asleep the minute we're out of US airspace, so I need to make
sure you know a few things. You see that man over there?" He pointed at Frank.

"You mean the one who looks kinda like a frog?"

"The very one. If you need anything or have any questions, you
ask him, okay? If he's asleep you can wake him up, but under no
circumstances should you wake up anybody else. Even me. It'll
probably get boring because it's a long flight. It might be a good idea
to get some sleep yourself. But whatever you do, don't wake up anybody except him. His name is Frank."

Steve worried until they were half a nautical mile out of US airspace, when he fell into an instant deep sleep.

Frank had no concerns about what airspace they were in and so
had been asleep since takeoff. It was a troubled sleep, with nightmares about Theresa being wed to a monster who never turned into
a handsome prince. He felt cheated of a fairy tale ending to her story
every time she repeated 'I do.'

Sergei was in considerable pain. Theresa had disinfected, sutured, bandaged, and medicated for infection but could not do anything about the pain yet. Mara helped her with both him and Alex,
who was still unconscious. He envied her that sweet oblivion. Not
long before he was due to get the blessed shot, Theresa and Misha
got into it and the repercussions fell upon him. As junior man on the
team, it was to be expected, and Misha did practically carry him into
the main cabin himself and then authorized the morphine fifteen
minutes early, but… Sergei was asleep before he could finish the
thought.

Michael wondered what it would be like to have a wife. As he
watched his father unravel, he wondered if he wanted one. Misha
had not grieved like this over Michael's mother, over his sister's
death, yes, but even that was different from this, and Alex was still
alive right now. Did he want to care that much? He once thought he
was in love but the woman betrayed him and tried to kill him. That
eradicated any grief he might have felt for her. Given his circumstances, did he need such an additional level of anxiety as his father

was showing? Alex seemed to think so, which is why she had come and why she now appeared to be on the brink of death. He wanted Theresa, but did he want her that badly? She still had not answered him. What if she said no? With that thought, when he answered this question truthfully, he reached a first true understanding of the devastation his father was facing.

Mara helped Theresa examine and treat the damage to her mother's poor chest and back. The bullet had gone in under her arm and through the side gap in her soft body armor as she held her SIG with a single straight arm, sighting it on David's head. It had ripped through the lung, exited, and embedded itself on the inside of the vest at the back. It was not a hollow point, for some strange reason, which gave them hope.

Sergei also owed his life to this detail. The damage to his thigh was painful, but the bullet had traveled straight through, missing the artery, saving him the agony of surgical removal and not creating massive damage on the way out.

Now that they were out of the airspace, all Mara wanted to do was sleep. She was the one who suggested they move Sergei so Misha could sleep in the cot next to Alex, thus ending a conflict of egos between surgeon and specialist that was becoming increasingly heated. Misha demanded more and more detailed explanations from an exasperated and imperious Theresa. Sergei complained about moving, loudly and unreasonably, but he was in pain after all, and she would make it up to him when he was well enough.

Theresa was delighted with the cramped but well-equipped medical room on the airplane. She had everything she needed except a modern way to investigate the interior of a body without cutting it open. In this case, that did not matter as much with the bullet wounds. She would have to cut, trace, and repair tissues in the path the bullet had taken through Alex's ribcage anyway. Alex was still unconscious.

She found Mara every bit as skilled a helper as Alex had been with Steve's injury.

The continued unconsciousness was her main concern. There was a hefty hematoma at the rear of the occipital on the right side that Theresa checked carefully for signs of fracture, but without an x-ray, she could not be sure it was completely clear, and anyway, there was almost certainly a severe concussion. She worried about internal bleeding, but the signs indicated it was as well as could be expected.

All, except for the large, intrusive, frantic irritation that was Alex's husband. Did he think he could cure her by sheer force of will and minute, critical supervision of the attending surgeon? He was in the way. When he was not in the way, he was in the process of putting himself in the way.

Between directing Mara and tending to her patient, Theresa anticipated his movements and headed him off strategically so that their interaction became a constant bumbling dance of two incompatible bodies intent upon occupying the same cramped space in an airplane at altitude.

Mara's suggestion that Sergei move out of the surgery and into the cabin so that Misha could lie down seemed the perfect solution. Even so, Theresa had to put her foot down and even shout at him to stay in his cot. She offered him a sedative. He glowered at her.

"Please, Mama," said Mara, well within his hearing, "wake up before he drives us all mad."

He glowered at her, too.

Misha had been quiet for half an hour when Frank came back to check on his daughter and urge her to get some sleep.

"I'll sit here with Alex and come get you if anything changes. Go. Sleep."

Theresa went to the main cabin where she found Michael still awake. She sat down next to him and he put his arm around her. She fell asleep on his shoulder.

TWENTY-SEVEN

Having evicted his daughter to the main cabin, Frank took her seat at the side of the gurney where Alex lay as if asleep, unconscious but breathing. A machine on the other side of the bed automatically monitored and displayed her vital signs. To Frank's left, a drop-down cot held Mack, his arm shielding his eyes. Frank doubted he was asleep. He knew he wouldn't be if it were Maryann lying here. But it didn't matter. He had to have his say.

"Alex," He took and held her limp hand. "Frank here. I know—we all know—you came out because of Theresa. I suspect your reason was Charlie. I suppose I should start calling him Michael." He paused at this unwelcome thought, swallowed the acid it caused, and continued. "Because they don't know you, the others—I'm talking about the non-team members—don't understand why it was so important. I want you to know that I know why."

He took a deep breath and hung his head for a moment. Too many uses of the word 'know,' but it was unavoidable. "I know why and I approve. I will do my best to be happy for them."

He choked a bit.

"If Theresa can do half for Char… Michael what you've done for Mack, she will have lived a worthy life. I can't stand in the way of that. You are also not finished with Mack, by the way, so you can't chalk it all up to one good deed. They still need you and now Theresa needs you, so I'm begging you to come around. I'm praying you can hear me and are fighting to come to the surface."

Frank's breath caught. "Can you do that again or did I imagine it?" A pause, and then a whisper. "I did feel it. You heard me."

They grappled briefly in the narrow space between the bed and the cot as Mack pulled Frank from the chair and shoved him toward the door.

It took a few minutes for Frank to wake Theresa without waking the filthy, bloody specialist with his arm around her. Son-in-law, he practiced saying to himself. He went back to the medical room with her, though she insisted it wasn't necessary. He was very glad he did.

Alex was awake, groggy, smiling, and drifting off again. Her hand rested on the blond head of her husband. He sat in the chair next to her, sound asleep with his head on the gurney, an arm stretched across her stomach, the other around her head.

As Theresa raised her hand to wake Mack, Frank whispered "No," and Alex shook her head.

"But he looks so uncomfortable," she said.

"I'll explain later," said Frank. "I'll explain a lot of things."

…

They landed after midnight. Theresa had an impression of a huge house, a mansion, really, and then a cavernous lower-level hallway, gorgeously carpeted down its long length, with doors on either side. It was here that she found her mother and held her for what seemed like her whole life but lasted no more than a few seconds. Her mother was equally unwilling to let go, but the bustle of the returning team, their gear, the stretcher bearing Alex, and the boy watching with sleepy wide eyes as lockers and weapons made their way through various doorways brought them to an awareness of their separate responsibilities.

It took another two hours of jumping at noises, disinfecting cuts and scrapes, suturing Michael's leg, and arguing with Misha about how to care for Alex before Theresa was allowed to collapse on a bed in a room she only dimly perceived. She woke before dawn and turned on a bedside lamp to investigate the weight in the bed next to her. Michael lay there, profoundly asleep. He was clean—ish, she decided. As she gazed at him half in and half out of the covers, she realized it was the first time she had ever seen him without a gun within easy reach.

On her way back from the toilet, she noticed his Glock and holster lying on an ornamental table against one wall. She stepped toward it and was about to reach her hand out curiously.

"Don't." In the dim light and silence, the single word held a suggestion of menace that brought the realities of the last three days to the forefront of her memory.

"Come back to bed."

"Are you ordering me?"

"I am strongly suggesting."

"Why?"

"It seems your father has not told you what you need to know to stay safe with us. Therefore, I must do so. Come here."

The last strong suggestion was an order, she decided, and she was tempted to ignore it until the word 'safe' triggered a mental image of her father stopping her hand from touching a sleeping Misha in the airplane and promising to explain later. It was followed by an intense feeling of shame that she had allowed herself to be so thoroughly hoodwinked into leaving the safehouse to talk to David despite all the evidence she had of the danger. Really, she thought, I was no better than Sally in that moment.

After an interlude that revealed the real reason for his order and reminded her why she had accepted him, they exchanged some home truths. His dealt with the dangers of behaving surreptitiously around him and the others, hers with the inadvisability of ordering her around.

It was not yet dawn when he slipped out to his room, taking the holster and its contents with him, and citing servants as the reason. She suspected that their fathers were the more likely cause.

Michael's instruction paid off in the next fifteen minutes when Theresa walked into Alex's room, where a hospital bed had been thrown up at the foot of a large four-poster. She wanted to check on her but found Misha asleep in the same bed as the patient so crept out and closed the door behind her.

"You'd be better off making a bit of noise," said a loud voice on her right. "And keep it cheerful. Never be furtive. It's like an alarm call."

"Dad!"

The door behind her opened. Misha stood scowling at them.

"We are not specimens in a zoo, Frank."

"Nonetheless, I see your SIG is in your hand."

Theresa looked at the hand down at Misha's side. It was, indeed, holding his pistol. She moved to step away but was blocked by his other arm.

"What did you want?"

"I came to check on Alex."

Misha stepped to one side, opened the door wide, and beckoned her into the room with a lift of his chin.

"Frank," he said as her father began to walk away, "ask Maryann to please come here. I must speak with her."

TWENTY-EIGHT

T he patient smiled. The irritating appendage that was her husband did not. Father-in-law, Theresa reminded herself. He reholstered his weapon and laid both back down on a nearby dresser. Would she ever get used to this? She concentrated on the patient, starting with vital signs, when her mother knocked and was admitted.

Apart from last night's brief hug, they had not seen each other in a year but managed to keep to only another quick embrace before the disheveled, unshaven, scowling man wearing an exquisite brocade dressing gown cleared his throat pointedly and spoke to her mother.

"I apologize for seeing you when not properly dressed. Will you sit down, please?" He indicated a chair next to a Chippendale table. He spoke English, though Maryann's German was more than competent.

"You know that we have brought Steve's son Danny back with us. After breakfast, Steve and I will meet with him in my study. I must speak with Steve before then but do not want to leave the boy alone. Will you sit with him for fifteen minutes and then bring him to us in my office upstairs?"

"Yes, of course," said Maryann, mystified.

He did not continue. He had become very still, triggering in all three women the memory of danger, until they realized he chose his next words carefully and with hesitation but without a hint of threat. They relaxed.

"If he is normal," said Misha, "Danny will be upset after we have spoken with him. Will you be willing to wait for him upstairs? You might take him then to the kitchen for some biscuits. Encourage him to speak of his mother. Allow him to cry. He will need to cry but will be unwilling to do so in our presence."

Alex closed her eyes and frowned. Theresa opened hers wide. Maryann stared into Misha's.

"Are you saying Sally is dead?"

"Yes. But you must allow us to tell him."

"Did Steve kill her?"

"No."

"That means you did. Did you gut her like a fish?"

Alex winced.

A long, dangerous pause full of electricity stretched out, dominating the room before he replied in a soft menacing purr, "She received more mercy than she deserved. Now, I must dress. Please tell August I require coffee in my dressing room. Immediately."

He took his gun with him and closed the dressing room door softly behind him, no doubt in deference to Alex.

...

Steve gave his son a perfunctory introduction before leaving Maryann to her brief task of watching over the boy. She suggested they sit down in the sitting room of Steve's new three-room suite. The place was comfortable but bare of mementos or decoration. The utilitarian furniture lacked character though a few beautiful antique cabinets, a nice carpet, and well-stuffed chairs covered in soft leather provided sufficient comfort. Nonetheless, to Maryann, the place felt cold and unfriendly.

"How do you like your room, Danny?"

The boy shrugged. "It's good. It's really big."

He has his father's eyes, thought Maryann. And his mother's beauty. As the mother of four sons, she was aware that being a pretty child was not always a good thing for a small boy. She searched for a way to open a conversation, but he started one before she could speak.

"My mom signed papers so I can live with my dad. His boss told me so. He had the papers in his coat at the hotel. I didn't bring any clothes. Dad said that's okay, my stuff will be sent here. I had a bath, but these clothes are dirty and I'm going to a meeting. I should have better clothes, don't you think? My dad wore a suit today. Do you think I can get a suit?"

"Eventually, yes of course," said Maryann.

"But I'm going to a meeting this morning." He gave her a worried, almost pleading look.

"Your hair is combed and you don't smell," Maryann said, remembering when her boys were this age.

"That's what my dad said." He nodded with approval at this and looked around the room as if seeing it for the first time. "The men on the airplane all smelled bad. And they all had guns. My mom hates guns, even though her friends all have guns, even Linda. I hate Linda."

"Why?"

"She pretends she likes Mom, but really she hates her. I see how she looks at her sometimes. She hates me, too. The guys all like Mom, but they don't like me either. I bet nobody tells my dad he has eyes like a girl's."

"I bet they don't," said Maryann, truthfully.

"My mom won't let me learn how to fight, like with karate or something. She says it's good to be pretty." He sighed. "It's good for her maybe, but not for me. I hope my dad will let me take karate lessons."

"Is it really bad at your school?" asked Maryann. "I mean the bullies?"

The boy nodded and looked away. "I love my mom," he said after a pause, "but I'm really glad my dad rescued me."

"Rescued you?"

"Yeah. My mom doesn't believe it, but her friends want to kill me. They know I don't like them."

"That doesn't necessarily mean they want to kill you."

He looked her in the eye with a solemnity well beyond his age. "I heard one of them tell her I'm a liability. That was the word he used. I looked it up. He was saying he thinks I'm dangerous."

"What did your mom say?"

"She laughed and called him a tease. He wasn't teasing. I know the difference. He has a gun, too."

Maryann would have to tell Misha. She would have to admit to herself, at least, that he may, just may, have had a reason to kill Sally. He reads minds, she thought with a grimace. He'll know I see the problem. It's dim to me, but I see it.

She swallowed this limited portion of crow with all the grace she could muster as she led her charge upstairs to Misha's office.

TWENTY-NINE

"You're going to send him to Colorado? I just got him and he's going to leave?" Steve's words did not hide the note of belligerence he tried so hard to conceal.

"I did not say that," said Misha. He lifted a silver pot from a tray atop a small, ornamented table and poured coffee into two bone china cups with saucers. "I said we must give him a choice." He handed one cup to Steve.

Steve took the cup and stared at the empty fireplace before them. It was summer and thus no fire, but he wanted one. He wanted dancing flames and warmth and safety. He saw only cold stone and sinking disappointment.

"If we tell him, he will choose his grandparents."

Misha took a long sip of his coffee before answering.

"I think he will stay. He was not happy with his mother."

"How do you know that? And there's a big difference between being unhappy with mom and knowing dad... does what he does." Steve mumbled the last few words into his coffee cup.

"You mean to say he will not want to live in the house of the man who killed his mother."

Damned mind reader.

"Steve, he must not begin adolescence without knowing the truth."

"He never has to know. Can't we arrange a story?"

"No fiction will hold indefinitely. He is at the best age now to learn the truth without additional damage. He must know both the facts and the reasons before he makes his decision. Any later and he will feel betrayed. And he will have access to you. Think, Steve, what it would do to him if someday he took vengeance on the father who lied to him?"

The ultimate argument. If you love him, be willing to give him up. Steve's heart sank to his socks. He stared at his cooling coffee. "But why does he have to make a decision? He'll go to Colorado."

"I think not. He does not know his grandparents and is sufficiently intelligent to understand he will be as badly bullied in any school he attends there."

Steve's head came up with a jerk. He stared at Misha. "Bullied? Why do you say that?"

"Because he looks like you, except he is even more beautiful. His mother was not likely to understand, let alone take action. I think his life in North Carolina was difficult at best. He will not want to repeat that experience in Colorado."

Steve had never told Misha about his childhood. He sighed. "How do I tell him?"

"I will tell him. I will explain that you did not kill her."

Steve snorted and said in English, "Near as makes no difference."

Misha took a moment to process this adage and replied, "He will be interested only in who pulled the trigger. You may, and should, answer any subsequent questions about your agreement when, and if, they are posed. Boys are very literal."

They both had been boys once upon a time and bowed to the truth of this. A soft knock at the door interrupted them. It opened to admit Danny while Maryann indicated she wished to speak to Misha.

Danny was sipping a soda when Misha took his seat and introduced himself properly.

"Tell me about the man who said you are a liability," he said.

Steve's eyes widened involuntarily. He turned his head hoping his son had not seen his surprise.

Danny launched into a description of all his mother's friends. The liability man, as he called him, came at night when he was supposed to be asleep, but unlike Nick, he didn't come to kiss his mom. He came to lecture her about code books and stuff like he was James Bond or something, but he was too tall and scrawny with a beaky nose.

"How many times were you awake when he came?" asked Misha.

"Every time." In answer to Misha's skeptical look, Danny said, "I kept records. It's all written down. That's how I know he works with Arkady, not for him. He said that a lot."

"Arkady? From the embassy?"

Danny nodded.

"And your records? Where are they?"

Danny gave a detailed description of his hiding place, then described his mother's less secure hiding place for the code books she received from Nick, Arkady, and Liability Man. She never used them. Each man had to go over procedures again with her at least once a month.

Misha rang a service bell and summoned Frank.

"Call Skosh," he said when Frank arrived upstairs, then asked Danny to describe the hiding places once more. When he had gone, Misha turned again to Danny and began the difficult conversation, while Steve held his breath.

"You shot her?" said the boy, with a slight tremor in his voice.

"Yes," said Misha.

"Why?" He was fighting back tears.

"Because she refused to stop putting my team in danger. She also put you in danger."

"I just now told you that," said Danny.

"Yes, but there are others who want to hurt you besides the people you told us about now. You know my friend took a bullet saving your life when you were very young."

Danny nodded. "Dad told me. I'm sorry Louis died last year. I wish I could say thank you."

He looked at Misha with a furrowed brow. "What team is in danger? Do you guys play basketball or something?" Both Misha and his dad seemed very tall to him, and he knew nothing about sports. His mom never allowed him to play anything or even watch it on TV.

"Before I answer you," said Misha, "I must have your answer. Do you intend to stay, or do you prefer to live with your grandparents?"

The boy looked at him frankly. "If I stay, will you promise not to shoot me, too?"

"If you promise not to put anyone in this house in what I decide is a danger."

"If I lived here, then I would be in danger, too, right?"

"Yes."

"And so would The Spare?"

"The Spare?" Misha's brow furrowed.

"Yeah. He wants to be my friend. He's kinda young, but he seems pretty cool. I'm a child of the team, he said, so even though it's not polite to point that out to any of the other kids in the schoolroom upstairs, since we're both children of the team, we should be friends." He paused and said, in a smaller voice, "I've never had a real friend before."

"Other kids? Do you mean children of the staff?"

"Yeah. The Spare explained that."

"Can you describe this 'Spare'?"

"Blond, like you, and he has blue eyes. And he's not Spare. He's 'The Spare'. He told me that's important."

Misha glared at Steve who shook his head. He was sure Danny had not left their rooms.

Turning back to Danny Misha said, "When did you speak to him?"

"This morning. He came to my room." Danny turned to Steve. "You were in the shower. He didn't stay long. But he said I should stay. I don't want to go to Colorado, Dad. I wish Mom wasn't dead, but even if she wasn't, I'd want her to live someplace safe, but I wouldn't go back there. Can I stay with you?"

He turned back to Misha. "I promise not to put anybody in danger."

"Then I promise not to shoot you. Now let us discuss the team and how we do not talk about it."

...

Mack looked perturbed when he handed Danny over to Maryann in the outer office. As she led her charge out through the doorway, she heard him tell his secretary to send for Master Matthias immediately. She wondered briefly what he wanted with the eight-year-old child of a staff member but had no time to think about it further. Danny was so obviously bursting with excitement about his meeting with two of the most dangerous men Maryann had ever had the misfortune to meet, that she found it difficult to bring their conversation around to Sally. They sat on tall stools at an enormous farmhouse table in the kitchen where Cook had laid a plate of cookies and a glass of milk before discreetly leaving them alone.

The boy eventually burst into tears, throwing his arms around her neck, soaking a kitchen towel, and wailing with some vehemence before subsiding into shuddering sniffles. When he said he was ready, she took him upstairs to the schoolroom and left him in the charge of the mathematics tutor.

"What are you doing?" she asked the back of her husband's head when she returned to their room. It was obvious what he was doing. His small suitcase was open on the bed and he was throwing a few clothes in its general direction. She picked up a shirt from the floor and folded it.

"Are we leaving?" she asked, hoping a rift had occurred between Theresa and Michael and the wedding was off. That young man was off the charts dangerous in her books, but she reluctantly reminded herself to trust her daughter's judgment about her future.

"No," said Frank. He threw his shaving bag in the case. Maryann arranged it on one side away from the neatly folded shirt.

"I'm meeting Skosh in North Carolina," he said, "and coming straight back. I should be gone less than two days."

"Are you taking a commercial flight?" She wanted to ask where he would get one. She still had no idea exactly where they were.

He looked at her, his eyes bulging, brows up, and lips suppressing a smile.

"I'm taking the small jet."

"There's a small jet? A second jet?"

"Evidently."

They stared at each other in wonder, then burst out laughing, sharing the memory of decades ago when they invested in a second car, a jalopy that had to be push-started. Frank slammed the case shut, with a corner of the shirt sticking out at one side. She opened it, fixed the shirt, and locked it.

She told him about Danny and as an afterthought mentioned the odd summons to an eight-year-old named Matthias, The Spare for short. Leo stared at her when she described the child but said nothing until it was time to leave.

"Whatever you do, Maryann, never mention The Spare to another soul."

After a quick hug, he was gone, without explanation, leaving her to wonder what on earth could be so secret about an eight-year-old boy.

THIRTY

Frank walked into breakfast on the morning of his daughter's wedding. The household had been informed fifteen minutes before he arrived that the date had changed. He knew about the change before he landed because he brought the reason for it. They were going out again—immediately.

Maryann and Theresa did not know, judging by their smiles. Alex suspected. She gave her husband a narrow gaze, which he was busy ignoring. It delighted Frank to see her up and about. She knew the signs of an impending operation, no doubt, but in this case, the panicking servants should have alerted even his wife and daughter that something was up.

They were as cheerful as Mack and Charlie were silent and still. Steve, Sergei, and Mara weren't even there. Packing their gear and cleaning weapons again, no doubt. The bastards were making him break the news.

"Um, Maryann...."

"Hello, Leo. How was your flight?" Her plate was empty. He had come at the end of the meal.

"Fine. Listen, Maryann...."

"We ordered the most beautiful dresses for the wedding, Leo."

A servant put a plateful of eggs and sausages on the table before him. He had lost his appetite. "Are they here already? The dresses, I mean?"

"No, of course not, Dad," said Theresa. "We only ordered them late yesterday."

He looked up at the two blond fucking cowards. They avoided eye contact.

"Maryann listen!" he said with some heat. "You might want to get ready. The wedding's in an hour."

The car took them straight from the chapel to the larger airplane immediately after the ceremony. Alex kissed Misha before solemnly waving goodbye. Maryann handed Frank a freshly packed suitcase. Theresa cried angry tears but kissed her groom passionately.

They spent the flight going over Danny's intelligence contained in the stash Frank brought back from North Carolina.

"We see from Danny's description," said Misha, "that LM is not among those we killed in Florida."

"LM?" asked Frank.

"Liability Man," said Steve. "Danny says he never heard his name."

"Do we know his nationality? Did he have an accent?" asked Mara.

Steve answered again. "He spoke English that sounded normal to Danny, so probably American."

Sergei placed two of Sally's cipher books on the small conference table they were gathered around.

"These are both GRU. Did Danny say who gave them to her?"

"Nick and Arkady, from the embassy," said Steve.

Sergei wrinkled his brow. "Arkady is SVR. I know him. I do not know why he would use a GRU book. But the third book is more interesting. It is not GRU or SVR. It is not even Russian." He passed the book to Misha, who leafed through it and reached behind him to throw it into Frank's lap.

"Stop trying to hide, Frank," Misha said. "We know you are here."

"I don't know why I'm here, and I've never thought it a healthy thing to attend one of your meetings."

"You are here because Skosh needs your instruction when we arrive."

"I'm retired."

"Skosh will benefit from your vast experience. Turner is good but will not be on future operations that take place outside your country."

"And he does not understand the importance of a good car," said Sergei. "Or food."

"In his defense," said Steve, "the Florida safehouse had three working toilets and a decent coffee maker."

There was a general silence in appreciation of the coffee maker.

"And this operation?" asked Frank. "At the risk of making my-self conspicuous at one of your meetings, what is the purpose of this little outing?"

Mack's cold glare lasted a moment longer than was comfortable before he answered. "We must find LM. He has threatened Danny. We must know why, who he is, and for whom he is working. There is too much here that we do not know. Ignorance is more deadly than a bullet. Do you not agree?"

"Sometimes knowledge is even more dangerous," he replied, avoiding Mack's considering gaze. He preferred not to meet those eyes, certain the man would read all about The Spare in his own.

Mack allowed a drop of quiet to permeate the cabin, drowning out even the engines. "Then the remedy in such cases," he said, "is silence."

Frank was unsure whether he meant the word as a noun or a verb.

THIRTY-ONE

S kosh stood on the tarmac next to the Mercedes as the airplane taxied in. He had hoped he'd be allowed more than a week to recover from the Florida op. A lifetime would be optimal, but anything over a week would have been appreciated.

They came down from the airplane looking considerably better than they had climbed aboard a week before. For one thing, they had washed. Pavlenko still limped but he had combed his hair and shaved, though the wind was undoing any good work the comb had done.

The co-pilot stopped the ground crew from opening the hold. Team members themselves always loaded their gear into the trunk of the Mercedes. There was not as much of it as last time. Skosh crossed his fingers. Maybe they did not expect to stay long.

Frank shook his hand. "Where's Jay?"

"At the safehouse. I managed to get some extra funding, so we got a place where a Mercedes won't stand out. Also, it has a big garage."

"The house is not too big, is it? Big places are a bitch to secure."

Skosh squinted one eye. "Smallest place on the block. That's why it was for rent. Also, I arranged the catering."

"And the coffee?"

"I left that to Jay. Never mess with perfection, I always say. How is Theresa?"

"Married."

"So soon?"

Frank nodded. "This morning."

They walked to the FBO lounge in silence. "They must be worried," said Skosh quietly.

Frank nodded again.

...

For the first time in Frank's memory, there were no complaints.

"You should have picked Skosh over me in the first place," said Steve, referring to his short stint working for Frank.

Sergei stared at the pendant light hanging above him from the two-story vaulted entranceway ceiling. "Now this is capitalism," he said.

Having been a guest in their house, Frank was not surprised that Mara, Mack, and Charlie were unimpressed with this cheap imitation of opulence. They were more interested in the radios, telephones, alarm system, and two computers arranged conveniently in the usual place—the dining room.

Everybody, Frank included, was interested in dinner. It arrived at the same time as Justin Goodwin, looking wary and carrying his usual toothbrush-sized backpack and a larger case of computer parts. Jay had flown him in from Florida.

Jay came out of the kitchen and directed the caterers as soon as the team was out of sight. The food was too delicious for much conversation, leaving a wide opening for Justin to put his foot in it as usual.

"So Frank, how is Theresa?"

Chewing ceased. Even Mack sat back in his chair, knife and fork still poised over his plate, and regarded the young man with a bemused expression.

Charlie's reaction was more pointed. He became very still, which Justin seemed to notice and remember vaguely as not a good thing. Frank had to credit his courage but deplored the foolhardy defiant glare.

"Do you mean my wife?" Charlie said softly in a voice of steel. "She is very well, thank you."

But the young idiot couldn't leave it alone, despite the obvious shut-up stare coming to him from his boss, Jay.

"Oh, congratulations! What is her married name so I can send best wishes to the bride?"

In thirty years, Frank had never heard a name. As far as anybody in his business knew, Mack never had any name. Charlie had used the legend Taylor once, and it was pretty well established that both of them were named some form of Michael, but there had never been the least hint of a last name.

Frank now knew the last name. He learned it that morning in the estate chapel at his daughter's wedding. The name was all over the memorials on the walls and engraved on the slate slabs on the floor. As an intelligence officer and history enthusiast, he had the biggest revelation of his life and could do nothing with it, let alone impart it to the eager young special agent whose less than subtle attempt got him no more than two very cold blue-eyed stares.

Mack turned to Skosh. "We will need you and Jay to follow us to the sovereign house here. We must meet with several people."

"Do you want us to watch the Mercedes again?" asked Jay.

"No. You will come in with us."

"What? No! We'll be blown."

"You are a highly placed FBI official. You are already blown. I need Skosh to look for familiar Russians and for you to recognize any criminals. They have invaded our world." He shook his head at this travesty.

"If I may make a suggestion," said Skosh, carefully avoiding mention of the intersection between crime and intelligence work. "Frank is more suited to this task. Though I would be blown, he is retired. He also knows every Russian ever born in this business, while this side of the world is still very new to me."

Mack nodded slightly and took his time answering. "That was well-spoken and a very plausible argument. I commend you. Frank will stay here and use your attempt as an illustration to teach Mr. Goodwin how to ask questions that will not get him killed. Mara will set up our computer, assuming one of these is ours." He gestured toward the table along one wall. Mara glared at him.

"Nein," he said, addressing the glare.

Frank felt relieved. Tradition ran high in this corner of the special ops world, and testosterone even higher. The wannabe tough guys at the bar would not be a match for her and her entourage, but the babysitters did not need the headaches a dust-up would cause during what he hoped would be a limited operation. Mara could cause a dust-up anytime, anywhere.

Mara's answering protest was brief and shot down with the lift of an eyebrow, but Sergei's stare at Goodwin, who also would be staying behind, took longer and was more disconcerting. It relieved Frank's mind to see Justin look away, both from the stare and from Mara.

THIRTY-TWO

Charlemagne parked their armored flash car outside the Fayette Nam Bar and Grill and walked in expensively dressed and obviously packing.

Jay and Skosh parked a small grey government car two blocks down and slunk into the bar looking like government employees drawing per diem. The place was crowded with other government employees, the kind who wear uniforms.

"Special Forces?" asked Skosh.

Jay nodded. "According to Frank, we're a stone's throw—well, maybe a rocket launch—from Smoke Bomb Hill."

Which meant nothing to Skosh, but he did not seek enlightenment.

"What crazy enemy intelligence agent is going to brave this crowd?" he asked.

Jay shrugged. "The kind who wants a beer. I don't know, do I? All that spy v. spy stuff is in your bailiwick tonight. I'm here for the gangstas."

And he saw plenty of those, mostly Cosa Nostra, but a few vory, with their tattooed fingers and dead eyes. There was an occasional interaction between the two groups, a coming and going that suggested a negotiation in progress. Jay was a fan of negotiations that prevented or halted gang wars. Treaties that set up collaboration schemes were not so welcome.

The kinds of collaboration favored by rival gangs involved theft at best, but more often mayhem, extortion, and the maiming and death of innocents. Instinct told him this was not a peace treaty in progress. Representatives from too many disparate gangs without histories of conflict were participating in these talks. They were discussing an alliance. This conclusion did not make him happy.

Skosh found his own reasons for pessimism. The eastern side of the barroom contained an unhealthy number of GRU operatives he recognized from pictures in the files he studied every night in a continuing effort to learn his unwanted promotion. He had never believed in the end of the Cold War. To him, it seemed no more than a continuation on new terms. One of those new terms appeared to be the freedom of foreign military intelligence operatives to enjoy convivial evenings with their American counterparts in a bar outside the southern gate of an army special forces base. Sovereign house or not, he didn't like it.

The two agents stood side by side, conspicuously, at the point where the entrance opened into a large room filled with tables. The name 'bar and grill' was not entirely accurate unless packets of peanuts and potato chips might be considered grill. It was a drinking establishment, nothing more.

They spied their charges at a back table on the left.

"You think they're shielding Mara by not letting her come here?" asked Skosh, surveying the room. Even the wait staff were men.

"Donovan has an expression for your question," said Jay. "Ya think? Of course, they are protecting her. Wouldn't you?"

There was a time when Skosh might have agreed, but he had helped with the beach cleanup of Gennady, the GRU babysitter's body. The ballistics were clear about whose gun it had been. He shivered at the memory.

Jay looked at him sideways. "Yes. I know," he said. "My watcher told me how she went after Gennady. It makes me shudder, too. She appears so soft but is as hard as her brother. Still, I helped rescue her last year, and I would do it again in a flash minute."

Skosh nodded. "Let's go see what they want from us."

Evidently nothing. Misha ordered drinks, to be nursed through an evening of watching and listening, to the room at large and the occasional visits at their table by a wide selection of characters, some sycophants, others carrying a nameless grudge. Skosh recognized a man visiting a table of Cosa Nostra and was sure he was doing his best impression of the inscrutable Asian until Mack said, "That one, then. Tell us at the safehouse."

An older man with gnarled fingers and a sparse comb-over came to their table. His visit proved more interesting—or terrifying—depending on point of view.

Mack initiated the conversation. "Who, on Tuesday nights?"

The man was cautious, which meant he knew the man who had asked the question. "Um. Tuesdays? Um." He closed his eyes to improve his memory. "That would be... that was...." Skosh figured he was deciding if he could safely lie. "Um...Johnny, my son-in-law." He had decided on truth. Then hurriedly, "He probably didn't understand."

"Are you telling me you are responsible, Oscar?" The stillness of that purring question required no answer, so Mack posed another. "And Friday nights as well?"

The answer was written in a wide-eyed look of alarm.

"Is your daughter at home now?"

"No. She works...."

"Are there children?"

The man gazed at his hands and shook his head.

...

Jay had the unenviable pleasure of riding back to the safehouse squashed in the back of the Mercedes between the delinquents, as Skosh called them. Skosh was meeting the police chief at the little house with a wide front porch where a young man tragically fell down the narrow stairs and broke his neck. By order of Mack, who took a betrayal of trust more seriously than most, the deceased's father-in-law discovered the accident and reported the death. By now, Skosh was able to recognize Steve's work in the death, and Charlie's in the bruising.

THIRTY-THREE

"I don't see how I can find this guy," Justin said as Skosh walked through the dining room door. "Computer searches don't produce anything when there's no name, no place, and no description besides tall and thin."

Everybody was already at the table with full mugs of coffee. Justin told truth to power in his usual reckless way and received the expected menacing glares.

"About that...." Skosh stood in the doorway and felt the heat of unwanted attention shift to him. "It may be nothing, but the police chief told me a story tonight that makes that description interesting."

"First, the man you recognized at the bar," said Mack. "Was he one of the Asian men at the front of the room?"

Skosh nodded. "They were boryokudan—what is called yakuza in the West. Gangsters. He's an enforcer, a muscle guy, named Murakami. Whoever else was at that table, must have been important."

Mack nodded. "Now tell us what the chief told you."

All eyes, among them the four icy blues, were upon him so he took the seat next to Jay and began.

"I told the chief something along the lines of, 'It's a pretty straightforward accident,' meaning the son-in-law. He looked at me and said, 'The fact that you're here makes it anything but straightforward, and I already had one of those iffy kinds this week, so my quota is getting full up.'

"Then he told me about a woman who died in a car wreck three months ago." Skosh waited for snorts and eye rolls, but there were none, making him wonder if he was finally respected or if Mack already knew about this and was patiently waiting for his monologue to end. He pressed on.

"She owned a small newspaper in the next county. The woman had been to Poynter and was a serious journalist. Her paper made a reasonable profit, concentrating on local crime, business, and politics. She had begun running a series of articles about the relationship between one of the small-town city councils and a business looking to move into the area. After the second article, her car went off the road and wrapped around a light pole and she died."

Skosh was becoming more than moderately concerned that he had their rapt attention. He resumed. "The woman's husband, Keith, vowed to carry on the business in her memory and managed to bring out another pair of articles about the new business when he received a threat of sorts. This was according to one of the adult children who told the chief about it, but his searchers couldn't find any sign of it and the daughter had not paid close attention to what the father mentioned almost in passing.

"Then last week, Keith shot himself. The chief lives out that way so he responded to help out because the sheriff's office is short-staffed. He did all the initial interviews and told me three things concerning the case that bothered him. First, the missing threat letter. Second, everybody was adamant that Keith did not own a gun. The gun used in the suicide was unregistered. If he was concerned about the threat, which the chief thought plausible, why go to the trouble of finding something unregistered when he could easily walk into his local gun shop?"

Skosh took a deep breath. "The chief's third concern is the reason I am bringing this up. Two days before the suicide, a neighbor saw Keith in a heated argument with a man outside the front door. The man was tall and thin. The neighbor told the chief she thought the man had limited use of one arm because of the way he opened his car door. She didn't get a plate number but thought the car was grey or silver.

"The newspaper folded before the funeral, without finishing the article series."

"Danny said Liability Man was tall with a long face and a sore arm," said Steve. "I didn't see anybody like that tonight. I did see too many obvious gangsters. Since when do they enjoy the privileges of a sovereign house?"

Charlie took off his already loosened tie and sat back in his chair. "Oscar's son-in-law, Johnny, told us the man used the name Earnest, but he did not know if it was his first or last name. His right arm did not move correctly. He paid Johnny handsomely to take those nights off."

Mack looked at the two sitting by the computers and raised an eyebrow. Mara and Justin grinned at each other, turned, and clicked their keyboards like they were in a race. Sergei scowled.

In five minutes, the race became a collaboration with the two of them putting their heads together in deep consultation. Sergei's scowl deepened. Skosh tried to get Jay's attention, but he was busy asking Frank a stupid question. He did not relish the role of hero, but there was no help for it. A fraction of a second before Sergei launched himself at the younger FBI agent, Skosh put himself in the way and paid for it in the coin of pain. He used his skill in karate to minimize some of the damage, but Sergei was a dirty fighter and in a blind rage.

Charlie and Steve pulled him off in a desultory fashion, and Skosh used the table to haul himself to his feet. He realized as he caught Mara's eye that she was concerned, not about him and his bleeding nose, but about the rising jealousy in Sergei. The man was fucking insane. Well, they were all fucking insane. And they were all too very capable of doing real damage in their insanity. As he brought his head down after staunching the flow from his nose, he saw thoughtful looks all around, all except for Justin, happily tapping his keyboard in total oblivion to the danger he had been in or the debt he owed his reluctant guardian angel. Skosh resolved to enlighten him later.

In five minutes Mara produced a name, John Earnest, an address in Fayetteville, and a company name, Brighton Associates. He was chief financial officer of the company. She turned back to her keyboard to find more information.

It was Justin who caused a profound silence.

"Um. Jay?"

"What is it?"

Justin stared at the screen on the FBI computer. "I can't get in," he said quietly. "It's protected."

"What's protected? Him or the company?"

"Both."

"By...?"

"By us. Or more precisely, by the Investigation Division."

"Protected?" said Jay. "Or blocked?"

"Protected."

"What does that mean, Jay?" asked Skosh on behalf of everyone in the room.

"John Earnest must be one of ours."

THIRTY-FOUR

Skosh did not think someone as dark as Jay could visibly pale, but the man took on an ashy hue. His face lost all color and animation.

"Was Sally working for the FBI?" asked Frank. "Could the boy have made a mistake?"

Mack glowered at him. "There was no mistake."

Jay shook his head. "I've never heard of him. Where did he come from?"

"I don't know," said Justin. "I can't find him anywhere in the system. Even if the operation were blocked, he should be in the system, unless the name is a legend or codename."

"Of course, it's a legend," said Jay. "But I don't even recognize the description. Tall, thin, and with an arm injury. Nobody. I do not know him."

Into an unbroken silence dropped a soft, accented voice.

"I know him," said Sergei. "He is on Semianov's list."

"I know every name on that list," said Jay hotly. "There is no Earnest."

"He is Paul Crutchfield on the list. I have met him."

"Crutchfield died in a house fire last winter. He...."

"He is very good with languages," said Sergei. "Though he is a murderer, we put his talent to good use. His real name is Victor Borodinov. Crutchfield and Earnest are two of his game names. He must not see me."

Frank asked, "So he's an illegal?"

Sergei nodded.

"And SVR, not GRU?"

Sergei nodded again. "Also he is a vor, but not a killer. He went to prison because he killed a man he thought was fucking his girlfriend, but he is not a killer. He is well educated and has achieved rank."

"And Arkady from the embassy?"

"Also SVR now and was in my directorate. He is a killer."

The quiet purr from the head of the table was directed at Sergei. "We have made it known we are here," said Misha, tilting his head to one side. "Why must Borodinov not see you?"

It took Sergei time to formulate his reply with just the right words. "He killed the wrong man."

He squirmed under Mara's glare.

...

"Army guy," said Steve.

The two words halted an hour-long argument in full swing. It had taken him a while to bring it to the front of his memory after Skosh's succinct list, taken from Danny's copious notes, of the men making it a regular habit to call on his dim, pretty ex-wife Sally. The GRU guy, the killer SVR guy, the non-killer SVR guy aka Liability Man aka Earnest/Crutchfield/Borodinov, the vor Nick. Danny had mentioned another, Steve knew, because he asked. He and Sally had been divorced for almost a decade and it still pissed him off. He wracked his brain for the memory of his son's words.

"Danny said something about an Army guy. He insisted it was somebody in uniform."

Much of the discussion began to center around the question of why. Why were so many interested in Sally? Why, again, did they all want to eliminate Danny? Why did Borodinov's mission feel more dangerous than the others? And now, who was Army Guy?

Justin came up with another precocious question. "Why protect Borodinov and his business? We know they're not part of the Bureau. If our people are working on this, the information should be blocked, not just protected."

Sergei inadvertently hit upon part of the answer. "You are asking us to distinguish between two English words. It is unfair."

"You have nailed it, Pavlenko," said Jay. "The people who placed the protection did not know the difference. They are not Bureau."

"And they are in your computer, Sir," said Mara.

Jay lost again the little color he had regained and so failed to recognize the mark of respect Mara had given him. Specialists were rarely polite to their minders, let alone respectful.

"They will know how you live," said Mara, "your family, the results of your last polygraph, your financial records."

"They cannot know all of that," Jay insisted.

"If I can, they can." Mara's quiet ambiguity and the stillness with which she delivered the statement would have made even Steve shiver if he were not so used to it in her father and brother.

"Call your family," said Mack. "Send them to your escape hatch. Then I must use the secure line."

...

The watches began at midnight with perimeter checks, squabbles over rooms, and grumbling. Skosh knew having plenty of everything would never stop the sniping and complaining. These were as essential to any operation as coffee.

"Listen, Justin," he said as they each staked out space in one room. "You might want to be more careful about how you act with Mara. Especially around her husband."

"Husband?" Justin seemed genuinely puzzled.

"Yeah. Husband. The unhinged killer with the colorless eyes is her husband. How did you not know that?"

"I knew they had something going, but I didn't think they were married."

"You knew they were a couple and you still got as close as you could?"

"All's fair, as they say. I didn't see a ring." Justin smiled. "But if they're married, I guess I'm out."

Skosh blinked. "You know," he formed his next words as slowly and precisely as he could, "even though we're in a nice house with a Mercedes in the garage and good food and coffee, this is not Kansas anymore, don't you?"

"Why would it be Kansas? It's North Carolina."

Skosh used his thumb and forefinger to press his eyes closed. "I mean, Justin, that the world you and I know as normal—though frankly, my family had a lot of that illusion dispelled during the war—that world, the one with police and grocery stores and streetlights and Thanksgiving Day—that world is not this world. This world is guns and knives and no sleep and bad coffee and people who want to kill you and know how to do it. Our jobs, yours and mine, require us to keep this world at bay so that other people can live in that world thinking all is well. We deal in chaos to keep it away from civilization."

Justin looked puzzled.

Skosh tried emphasis. "Chaos—bad. Civilization—good. This place is chaos. Fair does not exist in chaos. So any rules of civilization you think there are concerning things women—and other luxuries—do not apply here, whether they're married or not. Don't even look at one of their women. Don't even look at a woman you suspect they are looking at. You will get hurt. I got hurt for you today. I'll not get in the way of that again. I promise you."

"So that's why you guys are so careful around them?" asked Justin. "You know, early on I decided against ribbing Steve about his eyelashes. I guess I got too familiar with all the joking and tediously detailed intelligence." His eyes opened wide. "Sergei was coming after me today, is that what you're saying? Thanks. I mean it, but let me take my licks."

Skosh shook his head. "I'd be glad to, but I didn't do it for you. I did it for the computer. You're going to help us find Army Guy tomorrow. You need to be alive to do that."

THIRTY-FIVE

Everybody—specialist, babysitter, and agent alike—wished the food could always be this good but knew better.

"How did you manage to find these caterers for me, Jay?" asked Skosh through a mouthful of home potatoes.

Mack curled his upper lip when potato bits escaped Skosh's fork.

Jay tilted his head and smiled. "Southern cooking, pal."

"Yeah, well, Florida's in the south...."

This was the closest anyone got to a peaceful non-operational conversation that morning.

Justin and Mara sat side by side at the end of the table where they could turn their seats easily to the computers. They chatted over toast and bacon until Sergei and Steve came in from their generous three hours of sleep.

Sergei pulled Justin out of his chair and to the floor, sweeping his plate after and on top of him. Despite what Skosh considered to have been a successful explanation and warning the night before, Justin took the bait. He came up swinging.

Jay shouted, "Goodwin!" but there was no simultaneous admonition from Mack, who took a sip of his coffee and watched.

"Your subordinate requires instruction," he said to Jay.

"And you are content to let Pavlenko provide it?"

Because that was what he was doing, blow after blow. Jay knew better than to interfere and possibly make it worse.

"I am," said Mack. And he took another sip.

But Mara was not so content. She placed a dainty hand on Sergei's arm as it was poised to drive again into Justin's belly.

I imagine, thought Skosh, she delayed so long because, like Jay, she knows her intervention can make it harder for Goodwin. He looked at Mack. Maybe that was his reason as well. No, it wasn't. He was savoring his coffee. He just didn't care.

Skosh sighed and made himself unhealthily noticeable by picking the young agent up off the floor and dragging him to the downstairs bathroom for first aid. Jay met them there.

"What the fuck, Goodwin?"

The f-word from Jay? Things had to be serious.

Goodwin could not answer. Swollen lips, flowing nosebleed, and bruised ribs prevented speech. He did glare daggers at his boss, probably feeling innocent, which was true in the moment before the attack, but only in that moment.

"I think we should separate the computers," said Skosh. "Opposite sides of the table."

Or planet.

Justin managed a painful squeak. "We share a modem."

"We'll get longer cables," said Jay. "And you won't speak to her, smile at her, or look at her. Is that clear?"

More daggers, but Justin nodded.

A meeting was in progress when they returned. The detritus of breakfast, dirty plates, platters, crusts of bread, butter wrappers, butter smears, and spilled coffee littered the table. Sergei smirked as Skosh and Jay cleared the mess and Justin sat painfully in his chair, carefully not looking in Mara's direction.

"Alex spoke to Danny about Army Guy," said Mack. "The boy saw him only one time, as he watched from the upstairs landing while the man spoke to Sally just inside the front door. He wore a camouflage uniform and was wide. That is the word Danny used, not fat. Also, he was not much taller than Sally, with closely cut grey hair and no hat. Danny watched again from the front bedroom window while the man climbed into the passenger side of a dark sedan at the curb."

"Senior officer," said Steve. "Because of the grey hair and he must have a car and driver. Did Danny say anything else?"

"They kissed."

"Peck on the cheek? Deep French kiss? What?"

"Alex was his interrogator. She would not ask such a thing. I think an older man visiting Sally would not be content with a peck on the cheek. Her father is still in Colorado."

Was Mack being humorous, or at least sarcastic? Skosh studied the impassive face until the blue eyes turned to him. There was the suggestion of a hint of a shadow of a twinkle. Skosh marveled, then remembered Mack had just spoken to Alex. This could be considered a good mood.

"Sounds like an O-6 or higher," said Jay. He turned to Justin. "Look at all commanders at Fort Bragg who are full colonels or general officers. Also, check Pope Air Force Base. Under six feet, stocky build, grey hair, probably Army but Air Force also sometimes wear BDUs."

...

By the end of the meeting, with all currently attainable information in place, including Skosh's earlier recognition of the Asian gangster, the true tedium began, with multiple surveillance assignments targeting senior commanders, to be followed after dark by a pub crawl and a burglary. Skosh would help with the nighttime burglary of Brighton Associates. Justin would accompany the delinquents on the pub crawl. When Skosh mentioned his concern about this to Frank and Jay, he was told in no uncertain terms to bring it up with Mack himself if he was all that worried; they certainly would not. Skosh decided he was not all that worried.

THIRTY-SIX

Special Agent Justin Goodwin nursed his third beer of the evening, standing in the smoky recesses of their third bar of the evening, watching his companions become increasingly touchy and hyper-vigilant.

"What are we looking for again?" asked Steve for the hundredth time, though Justin knew damn well the man had the description of their quarry burned into his brain.

"Middle-aged, stocky build, grey hair, buzz cut, eye for the ladies." Justin recited it like a litany and noticed Sergei silently mouthing the words with him. "Three finalists from today's stake-outs, two Army, one Air Force. We're looking for the one...."

Steve interrupted him. "The one who wanted to, and probably did, fuck my ex-wife. Yeah, yeah, yeah I know. Shit, everybody wanted to do that. Hell, I wanted to."

And more in that vein. Justin gathered it was a sore subject.

"Speaking of the ladies," Steve said as he stepped into the path of an attractive young woman. "Hi. What's your name?"

As pickup lines go, it was lame in the extreme. Justin might have said so but was interrupted in the thought by a large man who stepped up close and personal into Steve's face.

"What's it to you, pretty boy?" said the man. "You must be Air Force to have such girly eyelashes."

Sergei muttered, "Shit."

"You must be a grunt to have such a sloped forehead," said Steve.

Of course, the big man had no chance. Though Justin had been on the receiving end of some of Steve's skills, he could not believe the speed with which he brought the man down.

In the parking lot, amid a plethora of expletives, Sergei lamented the hopelessness of their task. "It is impossible. How many bars are there in an Army town?" He shoved Steve into the back seat and climbed in front.

Justin started the car but hunched over his hands, side by side at the top of the wheel. "I think we're on the wrong track."

"Ya think?" said Steve. "We were the oldest guys in there. Most of them weren't even twenty-five."

Justin wanted to tell him to speak for himself but had learned wisdom in the last few hours. He remembered his dad after the divorce, his desperate loneliness, the drinking, and the DUI charge. He'd been arrested coming home from a hotel bar. Nothing fancy, just a haunt of the mid-level business traveler, the fading beauty, and the occasional whore. He headed for one of those hotels lining the highway, three in a row.

They scored at the first hotel lounge. The quarry was there and so was Mack. He sighed as they pulled up chairs and sat down at the little round table that held his beer. "You were unsuccessful."

"And you were not," said Sergei. He received a raised eyebrow in warning.

"Did you fight?"

"Of course," said Steve. There was some reluctance in the admission.

"How many did you vanquish?"

"One."

"Justin pulled us out before others could join," said Sergei.

More raised eyebrows, but these seemed to indicate respect, though Justin might have been mistaken.

Mack sipped his beer. "Which of you thought to look here?"

Justin felt himself blush as Steve tilted his head toward him. Mack's regard was disturbing even when not negative.

"This is my first beer," he said. "The target is on his third whiskey—neat—since I arrived."

"Target?" said Justin.

The blue eyes—no, it was the stillness of the stare not the color—made Justin regret the question.

"He is at an end," said Mack. "If Borodinov does not kill him, I will. He knows this and his remedy is whiskey."

"He knows about you?"

"He knows there is always retribution for betrayal."

"He betrayed Borodinov?"

"He is about to. Our enemy has been too slow. If he knows we are here, he thinks we are searching in noisy bars where young soldiers look for pretty women. You, I mean the three of you—why English has no distinct plural in the second person familiar is a mystery—you helped to reinforce this impression. Borodinov does not know what we have in the young Special Agent Goodwin."

He received three blank stares and continued. "First, Goodwin limited the necessary public display so that a major bar brawl did not make us as slow as Borodinov. Then, he thought of something other than pretty women for just enough time to know where to find a disappointed middle-aged man. And now, he will use his credential to convince the colonel to accompany him quietly."

Mack rose. "I have parked the Mercedes on the west side of the building, Agent Goodwin. We will meet you there.

THIRTY-SEVEN

"I don't understand why I'm going with you instead of one of the FBI agents who could stop an arrest with the flash of a badge," said Skosh. "I don't carry a credential. Company policy."

"They are all about law and order," said Mara. "You are about lawlessness and disorder, at least in other countries."

Skosh watched the blonde head next to him shine on and off under the flash of passing streetlights until he caught himself nearly running a red light and slammed down on the brakes. He wondered how anybody so adorably cute could be so fucking deadly.

"All we need is for you to drive, Nakamura," said the icicle in the back seat. More like a vast expanse of treeless tundra back there.

"Charlie, please be civil," said Mara.

"There's nothing civil in what we do, Mara."

"But we can treat each other in a civil manner."

"I dispute that Skosh qualifies as part of 'each other.' Your husband does not think any of these people qualify, judging by the way he pounds his fist into them, especially Goodwin. Does he interest you?"

"I don't want to discuss it," said Mara.

"Every private thought belongs to the team. Do not forget that. We will discuss it." Then, after a lengthy pause, "But not here."

While Skosh waited for Charlie and Mara to finish breaking and entering, he allowed his mind to wander over the revelation that there were no private thoughts on the team. How did such a rule come about? How was it enforced? Why was it necessary? As an intelligence officer, Skosh was aware that his mores often resembled those of the slightly thoughtful criminals he had met and sometimes had the misfortune to work with. His official enemies in the game came equipped with a moral compass similar to his own. Sure, there were arrests, accidents, betrayals, even the occasional murder, but what kind of survival imperative would outlaw private thoughts?

Speaking of survival imperatives, Mara and Charlie had been gone too long. Skosh's dislike of the blue metal building five hundred feet away on a downward slope from where he was parked burgeoned into loathing.

A small white door had been set in one corner. No windows. Who ever heard of an 'Associates' headquartered in a metal barn with no windows? Associates belonged in offices, with secretaries, nursery-provided potted plants, a parking lot with lines painted on it, and above all, windows.

He got out of the car quietly, closed and locked it, then stepped to the edge of the trees sheltering him and the car. He was about to step out and begin a quiet walk toward the looming metal box of a building before him when a female voice to his right whispered, "Get back to the car."

"Where is Charlie?"

"He is inside, listening, but cannot get out. Use the car phone to call Frank. Tell him we dare not use our transmitters. They have extensive security and a scanner. It is a meeting. About fifteen people. At least five are fighters, but all are armed. Tell him to reach the rest of the team. You will have to meet them and bring them here. There is not much cover."

"Come with me."

"No. Do as I say, damn it. I have the authority here and will make your life a misery if you do not follow my orders. I need the team here now. This minute. Go, and be fucking quiet about it."

...

Skosh revised his definition of adorably cute as he waited for the Mercedes to pull up next to him at a gas station half a mile from Brighton Associates. While he waited, he noticed a shop front across the street with a for sale sign and 'News Courier Times' painted on the window.

THIRTY-EIGHT

When Michael heard the scanner, he stopped in mid-sentence. "Go get...." Their system was shielded but the scanner would pick up an unidentified signal and spark a need to investigate.

"Help," said Mara.

He had to depend on her ability to interpret his sudden stop. That she answered correctly with just one word finishing his thought, then cut her mic heartened him. He had been about to cut the throat of the mammoth looming in front of him but thought better of it. With Mara gone, no ability to communicate, and the team not yet here, he could not risk discovery of an inexplicable bloodless corpse. A search would not be good for him right now.

He slipped behind the sentry and up a supporting pillar studded with narrow footholds leading into the metal support structure of the roof. It was an ordinary metal building, painted navy blue on the outside, but left raw on the inside, with a cement floor and no niceties like air conditioning or even windows in the late summer heat of North Carolina. Roll-up garage doors at the north and south ends of the building had been left open ten inches, presumably to provide airflow, but the measure failed to give relief to anyone but the mosquitoes who feasted on the sweltering bodies inside. At least the tangos could swat at them, setting up a continuous slap-slap tattoo. Michael could do nothing but contribute blood to the nutritional needs of the species. Occasionally, he passed a slow hand under his nose or chin to stop the sweat from dripping onto the man standing below him.

The space inside echoed with voices and scraping chairs as ten men sat around three long folding tables pushed together to make a conference table. A large safe stood against the wall near a corner with two tall filing cabinets and a small table holding a coffee maker.

The meeting resembled every business gathering Michael ever had attended, methodical, tedious, and tense. That it was populated by representatives of various criminal entities made no difference in the dynamic resemblance to an intelligence planning group. Borodinov steered the discussion almost as well as Misha would. When he left them, citing another engagement, Michael hoped someone was still outside to track him. He was about to risk a word to Mara, but the gathering devolved into professional sniping among the criminals as they closed briefcases rich with information, pushed their chairs back, and prepared to leave.

At the same time, his earbud came alive, suddenly and briefly. Four brief sound bursts as of someone tapping a transmitter. He recognized it. Papa had made them memorize Morse Code as children, against their many objections. It was so old-fashioned. Four dots: H. Mara was here, back with the team. He did not hear the signal come through on the scanner below. It was too brief to pick up and the breakup of the meeting was too noisy.

Michael considered carefully how to communicate what he knew they needed as unambiguously as possible. He tapped a dot and two dashes on the transmitter at his belt. W. He was on the west side of the building. He waited fifteen seconds before sending the next. D for *Dach* in German then waited two beats and followed with R for roof in English. Five beats, S, *sofort*, then N for now. He repeated S, then heard, in the clear, Sergei giving the channel for detonation and his father giving the order, "*Sofort.*"

Then, the center of the roof and the roll-up doors at each end exploded.

…

Mara was not pleased by their excessive protectiveness. They conspired to deny her an equal role, coming up with lame excuses or far-fetched scenarios, trying to make her assigned task seem more important than it was. Her stepfather was the worst, but her husband came in a close second. Michael and Steve were more hard-nosed and modern in their approach, but they did nothing to support her. This time, Steve went so far as to say out loud, "Shut the fuck up, Mara."

She seethed as she set the charge in the center of the roof and ran back to her position in the southeast corner next to Misha. He handed her the gauntlets she would use to slide down the rope to the floor of the building thirty feet below. Then he donned his own.

She set the receiver frequency of the detonator on hearing a single word from Sergei, who spoke it aloud in everybody's ear after Michael's first S code became clear and imperative. Sergei had put the packages together, calculating the blast requirements for the partially open roll-ups and the steel-supported roof.

They were not separate blasts. They were a single blast, cubed. Sergei was that precise. Misha gave the order and dropped through the hole, even while the debris was still airborne. Mara measured the distance behind him and followed him into a gun battle, arriving almost on top of him. Why hadn't he rolled? He was firing long bursts from his MP5, covering her, but he did not stand.

Mara took two rounds in her armored vest, they made her spin and stole some of her breath, but she responded instinctively. She stood, giving herself the slightest advantage over Misha's position on the floor. Their mutual target, the one pinning Misha and coming ever closer to hitting her somewhere lethal, was to their left. Because she was standing, Mara could see the top of his head beyond the large safe. Bad angle, maybe two square inches of target, but plenty for her. It was this guy's bad luck that Louis had been her teacher. Mara's was the last shot fired.

...

Misha watched the colonel's body roll into a ditch. The man would not appreciate his pity, so he had been careful to conceal it. Steve proved himself once again as a master interrogator. The colonel told them everything without violence.

All Steve said to him was, "So Colonel, how's it feel to be a traitor?" The forest they stood in under dripping leaves became the man's confessional. They were his three priests. Misha's SIG administered penance and the man took it as absolution.

Half an hour later, most of that time spent barreling down country roads after Skosh's urgent call, they stood under more dripping trees while he dressed Mara in the tactical gear they had brought with them. Misha was pleased to see Sergei bend himself to the task before him after giving Skosh an initial evil eye. The man knew explosives. It was good to have this capability again after the loss of Vasily. A loss aided by Sergei. The thought made Misha's jaw clench.

As he watched Sergei work, he appreciated his son-in-law's ability to quell the demons in his own private hell surrounding Mara. He knew that hell. He and Louis had nearly killed each other in the one surrounding Alex. Steve was careful, never looking at either Mara or Alex, but Misha knew it was Alex who interested him the most and always had since the day he met her in Chicago after Vasily's death. He was younger than she was, but not by enough to make Misha comfortable.

Michael was settled with Theresa, thanks to Alex, though she did not know why he had approved her project. It was very good for the team and must now be extended to Steve, but Misha had no earthly idea how to go about it. He dared not ask his wife. It would call her attention to the man who did his best to remain invisible to her. He appreciated Steve's discretion. Of course, Misha would probably kill him otherwise, so he had incentive not to let his glance linger too long. For now, the only practical solution was for Alex not to become a widow again until she was too old to interest anyone.

For the first time in his life, Misha felt required to live.

But he also required his daughter to live, which was why he peremptorily quashed her bid to be the first down the rope into the midst of a firestorm. She was unhappy. So was he. This was more than an operation; it was a situation. Every junction was murky, every decision a choice between evils, every step precarious. And now his mortality had become another enemy.

As he slid down the rope, he could think of only one word when he felt the impact on his left hip. It was Steve's word.

Fuck.

...

Justin sat in Skosh's rental car parked under the trees with the other three government men staring down at the building below. The sky had begun to brighten in preparation for dawn, but there was no cheer in the light. A miserable soaking drizzle had set in, making the windshield wipers necessary. It leaked through windows they had cracked open in an effort to breathe. The mosquitoes followed the rain so that within the car the silence was broken by random slapping sounds from all four occupants.

From outside the car, after the initial explosions, came the sounds of popping gunfire, in steady single shots and short bursts. It had been going on for two minutes. Too long, according to Frank.

The firing stopped and a form streaked toward them running at full speed from the building. With one mind, they all climbed out and stood in the rain, their hands on their weapons, loosened in their holsters but not drawn. The figure was fast, very fast, but small. And blonde, without the Kevlar hood.

She managed to say, "Ambulance," when within earshot, gasping as she closed the remaining distance.

"We have them standing by," said Skosh. "How many?"

"One."

Her face streamed with water. It was difficult to tell in the murky light, but Justin was sure she was crying. The clue was in the way she gasped for air.

"Who and how bad?" said Frank.

"Misha. It's bad."

"The tangos?"

"All dead. Except one. We will explain the intelligence we found later. This is not over. Borodinov is missing."

...

Skosh faced off with the new leader of Charlemagne straight away.

"The man is in agony, for God's sake!" He knew he was shouting. He knew how dangerous was the man he shouted at, and how dangerous was the man in agony on the gurney between them. He did not care. Mack's breathing was a series of gasps produced to take the place of screams.

The FBI's emergency surgeon stood at the head of the gurney, holding a walloping dose of morphine drawn up in a syringe and ready to go. Skosh shouted again, echoes bouncing off the walls of the hangar. "I don't give a fuck about your fucking policies, Charlie. Stop being such a fucking hard ass and let him have some relief. Be human for a change. He's your father, damn it!"

There was an audience of... everybody. They stood around in a solemn clot of filthy, tired, dispirited people, too exhausted even to shuffle their feet. Charlie answered without shouting and it was worse, not just because of the underlying venom, but because of his hyper-rationality at a time when anybody else would be, should be, raving.

"I owe you no explanation, Skosh. At your insistence, I allowed the X-ray to delay us. Each moment you shout at me delays us. You, not I, have added to his agony." Charlie paused, visibly leashing his temper. "He will receive the morphine after I have had a chance to speak with him privately. He needs relief; I require his mind; Charlemagne's exigency elevates my requirement over his need. It is my call. I have made it. Get out of our way or I will shoot you here. Now."

The words were scary enough. The ice-cold low tone took that adjective off the charts. The threat did not make Skosh step aside, though he knew it looked that way. It was the glimpse into Charlie's calculated thinking, the revelation that the team had the ultimate claim. Their lives were hell. He was glad they were going home, finished or not. He needed a break from their Gehenna.

Then he was told to board the airplane.

EPILOGUE

J ay had never flown first class before. Charlemagne let them off at
Reykjavik and insisted on giving them first-class tickets home.
Charlie's threat briefing during the flight also had been first class.

For too many reasons, the first thing Jay would do in Chicago
would be to arrange Goodwin's transfer to his office. The computer
skills would be handy of course, but more important was what Jay
had discovered at Reykjavik.

Frank did not get off the airplane. More than that, he had been
asked, in Jay's hearing, if he had any messages for Maryann and
Theresa. They were radioing ahead. To their lair. And to Maryann.
Even after this present gargantuan threat was eliminated, Frank and
his wife would be irreparably tainted by what Jay referred to as
TMK, too much knowledge.

Almost as bad, because the young agent knew too much without actually understanding Frank's situation, Goodwin had a mild
case of the same. Jay had it, too, of course, but enjoyed enough in-
sight and experience to bury it deep. Goodwin, on the other hand,
did not even know he was infected. Jay would keep him under his
thumb for as long as it took to enlighten him.

Meanwhile, his own family would have to stay in the escape
hatch. In a month's time, only luck and the skills of Charlemagne
would determine if they could come home.

...

Justin asked for a martini, shaken, not stirred. He got an iced concoc-
tion of vermouth and vodka in a squat glass. So much for first class.
He drank it too fast, making his head spin and the salted nuts important in keeping his stomach down.

Chicago. He had been there once, as a boy. His dad had put the
boat on Lake Michigan and taken him along the shoreline. The place
was huge, the price of gas for the engine astronomical, and the wind
incessant. He'd had a bad sunburn. But it became one of the happiest

memories of his childhood. Maybe they could go fishing next summer if Dad was up to it.

Winter would be a bitch, though.

...

The good news was Skosh was finally going home and would have a decent plate of sushi in about a month. Mack might live, and they had hauled in a shit-ton of intelligence as briefed by Charlie.

The bad news was he would not be eating his sushi on the Ginza. Even if he lived, Mack was unlikely to be sufficiently mobile to be active by then, meaning his scary-as-fuck son, the one he had just pissed off in the hangar, would be in charge of the op. And now, Skosh had only a month to coordinate with everybody from the officials of Okinawa Prefecture to the behemoth that was the U.S. Department of Defense.

Before any of that could be addressed, once he landed in North Carolina, he still had several American authorities to placate and an enormous day-old mess to clean up. Just as Skosh was leaving Charlemagne's airplane, Steve put a cherry on top of this cake of horrors by telling him about a colonel lying in a ditch along a country road with one of Mack's bullets in his head.

"He didn't cut the guy's throat?"

Steve shrugged. Skosh waited.

"Maybe he felt sorry for the guy," said Steve.

Skosh had never known pity to be part of a specialist's emotional repertoire.

Steve gave an exasperated snort. "The guy bonked my wife. Okay?"

"Ex. For almost ten years."

"Yeah, well I have a long memory. You might want to consider that, Nakamura."

"So all that great intelligence the colonel provided is going to be visible on the body, probably courtesy of you, and because I didn't know about it until now, already in the local press?"

"No. Not in the press. Brighton shut that down, didn't they? As killers go, they're almost as effective as we are."

"But not quite."

"Let's hope not."

...

Theresa made use of the time it would take the team to fly home by getting acquainted with the surgical room at Vasily's Carpet. She acquired new supplies, threw away obsolete and questionable items, and disinfected and arranged everything in a modern, rational manner. The surgeon who came from Vienna to lead her seemed to approve. It was hard to tell. Was it nationality that made him as dour and stern as Misha, or just a natural consequence of long-unassailed supremacy in his field? The butler had it, too, but he was French, so maybe it was not nationality.

The FBI surgeon on call had managed to slide the gurney under a portable X-ray in a hangar before putting Misha on the airplane, and the FBI radiologist had described in detail the mess he saw. These reports came to Theresa by fax. Her request that Mara and Sergei be rested and alert on landing was sent to the airplane by radio. They would be rested but filthy. Cleanliness would have to be imposed once they walked through the door. Theresa would give them twenty minutes max.

Alex thought she would be helping. Theresa knew better and would leave it up to Michael to handle that. They were not sure Misha would live, let alone regain any kind of mobility. Alex was likely to be a liability.

As the gurney rolled through the door with its heavily sedated occupant, Alex predictably lost her shit. Maryann, obeying a signal from Michael, led her away sobbing. Steve watched her go.

In that instant, Theresa had a vision of life at Vasily's Carpet without that frightening man on the gurney, understood a tenth of the stakes, and began playing her part in the preservation of all their lives by trying to save one.

The End

If you enjoyed this volume of the last three books in The Charlemagne Files Collection, please consider leaving a short review at your favorite bookstore.

Join the Charlemagne Files newsletter for more stories and information about the series, its world of covert operations, and the lives of the characters on the team. Sign up at charlemagnefiles.com/contact.

CHARLEMAGNE AND THE SECTION

The fictional world of The Section follows a few conventions. It may help the first-time reader of The Charlemagne Files to know some of these.

Who/what/ where is The Section?

The Section is a department of an intelligence agency of the United States. Its employees are civil servants. It includes support staff members who provide identity documents, financial controls, and physical and document security. The offices are near the East Coast, maybe Virginia.

The operational agents are called babysitters. They arrange on-site logistical support for freelance specialists during operations. Most operations are not conducted within the United States, with some exceptions.

Babysitters themselves do not carry identity documents in their names during an operation and never carry any official identification from their organization. Their purpose is to allow the organization to deny any association with them or their mission.

Nicknames

Babysitters in The Section receive nicknames from their coworkers when they join the office. These names are often undesirable and used mercilessly among the members of the office. It is part of the team-building process in a stressful occupation.

Coins

Challenge coins are traditionally stamped with symbols or mottos that designate the intelligence unit of their owners. The tradition is that when members of the unit are present at the bar and one produces his coin, all must produce theirs. Anyone failing to show their coin is responsible for the bar tab. If all produce their coins, then the challenger who first produced his or her coin is responsible for the tab.

File designations

The highest classification of information is Top Secret. Beyond Top Secret, more sensitive information is strictly controlled in a number of ways including designation as Sensitive Compartmented Information (SCI). This requires an additional clearance and often a named clearance based on Need-To-Know.

In The Section, files on specialists or specialist teams receive a one-word code name, printed across the file and restricted to very few people. When a solo or specialist team is employed on an operation, another designator word will refer to the operation and will be used for funding, reports, etc.

The Section's file name for Charlemagne is WEDGE. Thus CETUS WEDGE (second book of the Charlemagne Files) means an operation dubbed CETUS using the team called WEDGE.

Specialist

A team or solo operative used by Western governments for black operations conducted without fingerprints in high-risk situations expected to involve death.

GLOSSARY OF GAME NAMES

<u>Charlemagne</u>

Original Team

Mack: so dubbed by Western babysitters because he uses a knife at times; Austrian leader and decision maker of Charlemagne; called Misha by other members of his team; probable real name is Michael; last name is unknown.

The Frenchman: deceased marksman and technical expert of Charlemagne; real name is Louis; last name is unknown.

Vasily Sobieski: deceased explosives expert and martial artist whose father was a noted solo specialist; no aliases.

Later Team

Charlie Taylor: marksman; son of Mack; probable real name is Michael; last name unknown.

Steve Donovan: martial artist; former fighter pilot; abandoned real name was Daniel Martin Kessler.

Mara Sobieski Pavlenko: technical expert and marksman; daughter of Vasily Sobieski and biological daughter of Mack; wife of Sergei Pavlenko.

Sergei Pavlenko: explosives expert; former KGB babysitter; husband of Mara Sobieski.

<u>Babysitters</u>

Frank Cardova: long-time babysitter of Charlemagne; later, head of The Section; real name is Leo Vilseck; Section nickname is Buddy.

Justin Goodwin: FBI special agent and IT specialist; no aliases.

John Nakamura: official game name; real name unknown; usually called by his Section nickname, Skosh.

Jay Turner: FBI counterintelligence agent with a private agenda; no aliases.

Family members

Alexandra Sobieski: widow of Vasily Sobieski and daughter of former Charlemagne babysitter and head of Section Fred Dolnikov; no aliases. Now married to Mack.

Maryann and Theresa Vilseck: wife and daughter of Leo Vilseck, aka Frank Cardova.

Sally and Danny Kessler: ex-wife of and son of Steve Donovan.

GLOSSARY OF TERMS

AK-47 - developed by Mikhail Kalashnikov in 1947, one of the most ubiquitous firearms worldwide. It is reliable, uses standard 7.62 x 39mm ammunition, is inexpensive and fully automatic. Pretty much standard issue for insurgents and terrorists everywhere.

Babysitter - a government officer or agent responsible for the care, feeding, and security of a specialist under contract to that government, as well as for the fulfillment of the contract.

Beretta - an Italian-made weapon by the oldest continuous firearms manufacturer in the world.

BDU - battle dress uniform, loose fitting and designed for terrain camouflage and free range of motion.

Dangle - slang for an otherwise uninvolved person used as bait in an operation to trap a target.

Glock - semi-automatic pistol manufactured by an Austrian company.

HK - Heckler & Koch, a German manufacturer of popular automatic weapons, especially submachine guns and assault rifles.

M-16 - 5.56 mm American military assault rifle.

Running point - a term used in military and business applications to designate the lead in an operation. In a specialist operation, the position requires stealth and silence in removing especially dangerous obstacles such as watchers and snipers.

SAS - Special Air Service, the special forces unit of the British Army founded in 1941.

SCIF - Sensitive Compartmented Information Facility, a secure facility used by American and British military, security, and intelligence service to process sensitive compartmented information.